WARPED REMAINS
David Jemal & Kara Leigh Miller

WARPED REMAINS by David Jemal and Kara Leigh Miller

ANAIAH EPIC
An imprint of ANAIAH PRESS, LLC.
7780 49th ST N. #129
Pinellas Park, FL 33781

First Anaiah Epic eBook edition October 2019

Edited by Anaiah Press
Book Design by Anaiah Press
Cover Design by Eden Plantz

DEDICATION

(DAVID): To my wife, who believed in the impossible. And to my parents, this is for you.

(KARA): For all the teens looking for something different—this one's for you!

ACKNOWLEDGEMENTS

(DAVID): I have to first start by thanking my awesome wife, Sarina. Without her insights, thoughts, and suggestions, I would never have been able to call this "a book"—thanks for allowing me to dream! And to my family, thanks for always pushing and supporting me to write a book—took a little longer than expected!

Big thanks to NYT Bestselling Author, Johnathan Stone, who took the time to read *Warped Remains* and offered his helpful guidance. And to Ric Medrow, who was a big inspiration in my life.

To Kara, thanks for being the most amazing co-author! Without you, the words in my mind would never have made the page. I am indebted to you.

Thanks to everyone on the Anaiah Press publishing team. Without your constant, daily support, we would still be in the infant stages of the editing and cover design.

(KARA): First and foremost, thank you to my husband, who puts up with my constant need to be on my laptop as I write and edit and just generally get lost in the world of publishing. None of this would be possible without your constant support.

As always, thank you to my writing tribe—Rosie Somers, Kat Daemon, Scarlett Holloway, and Jennifer Pierce—y'all keep me going when I'm ready to quit.

And I can't forget Courtney Lynn Rose, who helped with edits early on and gave us some valuable feedback.

Thank you to the best editor on the planet—Eden Plantz! Your feedback is insightful, and your comments always make me laugh. And, of course, to the rest of the Anaiah Press staff: thanks for all your help making this book shine.

To my co-author, David, thanks for having the guts all those years ago to "break the rules" and strike up a conversation with me. If you hadn't, we probably wouldn't be here right now. You've got great ideas, so keep 'em coming!

Last but certainly never least, thank You, God, for blessing me with the talent, patience, and persistence to pursue this dream. Through You, all things are possible.

CHAPTER 1

Emily Sheffield

THEY HATE ME. AND WHY wouldn't they? I'm a screwup. A troublemaker. At least, that's how my family feels. Even now, standing in the airport on my way out of their lives, they're looking at me like I'm an embarrassment. The black sheep.

And I hate them for that. Those thoughts make my breath catch. Tears burn the back of my throat, but I refuse to give in to the emotions raging inside of me. I won't give my parents the satisfaction of knowing how much they've hurt me. But they have. It's like a knife has been plunged into my chest, the serrated edge tearing me apart. I lift my chin and harden my expression.

"Emily." My father looks at me with sad eyes. "I know this is hard for you, but we love you very much."

My mother nods in agreement. "We just feel this is a necessary step in becoming a mature young lady. It's really best for everyone."

"Everyone but me, you mean." None of them will admit it, but I know they think they'll be better off without me. Maybe they will. What do I know? I cross my arms over my chest, refusing to look at any of them a moment longer.

"Honey, please don't be upset with us. You really didn't leave us any choice." Mom pats my shoulder, and I jerk away from her touch.

"Shipping me off to the middle of nowhere to live with two people who are older than dirt is not your only choice. It's just the easiest and least messy." I turn away from them and stare out the large window that overlooks the massive parking structure.

"Calm down, young lady." My father's stern face is reflected in the window, but I ignore him. "And stop being so dramatic. You're going to Alaska, not the middle of nowhere. There are people who spend their entire lives wishing they could go there and never do."

I roll my eyes. Like I care about people I don't know. Why should I? No one ever cares about me, not even my parents.

"Besides, you love your grandparents," Dad says. "Just think of this is an extended vacation."

Scowling, I shift on my feet and avert my gaze once more.

"Em, don't be like this." My brother, Erik, stands beside me and gently nudges me with his shoulder. "It's only going to be for a few weeks. Then you'll come back home, and everything will be fine."

"Whatever."

Nothing will be fine ever again. I'm leaving my home, my friends, my school, my boyfriend. My heart shatters when I think of Matt and how he so carelessly dumped me the second he found out my parents were sending me away. Tears sting my eyes. My best frenemy, Ashley, is probably throwing herself at him again. She's always wanted him, and now, thanks to my stupid parents, she's going to get her shot.

"You'd better get going. You don't want to be late for your flight." Dad smiles tightly and shoves his hands into his pockets.

"Yeah, getting through security will take some time," Mom adds as if I've never been through this process before.

Sighing, I sling my carry-on bag over my shoulder. I checked my bag when we arrived, so I don't have to wrestle with trying to jam a suitcase into an overhead compartment. My mother pulls me into a hug. I keep my arms at my sides, and I'm positive I hear her sob. For a second, I think she actually cares. She really should've been an actress. "I love you, Emily, please don't forget that."

She releases me, and then my dad hugs me. I give him the same stiff response. "Be safe, and call us as soon as you land, okay?"

I give him a dirty look. They'd threatened to take my phone away—I think they were worried I'd convince one of my friends to help me run away. The thought did cross my mind.

Dad sighs heavily. "Grandma and Grandpa Sheffield will be waiting at the airport to pick you up. Make sure you call us."

"Whatever."

When Erik steps up to hug me, I stand ramrod straight with my arms at my sides, and I don't hug him back. While I know none of this is his fault, that he's a victim of his upbringing, too, I hate the world and everyone in it. Living in Erik's shadow is dark and lonely.

"Show those Alaskans how to do things, Emmy," Erik whispers, and I can't stop from smiling. He's the only person in the world who can get away with calling me Emmy. Reluctantly, I soften and wrap my arms around him briefly.

"I will." I give him a squeeze before releasing him and walking toward security.

I don't bother to look back; my family is probably already gone anyway. I cannot believe they are shipping me off to Alaska like this. They know how much I hate it. Last time we visited, I got so sick, I missed two whole weeks of school. At the time, I was convinced I'd contracted some weird, deadly, as-of-yet-undiscovered disease that had been lying dormant in the snow and decided to make itself known by taking over my body. But it turned out to be just the normal old flu.

I step into the security line behind some guy who is slightly taller than me and who smells really good. He moves forward in line and begins the process of emptying the electronics from his bag and taking off his shoes. I watch in fascination at how confident and at ease he appears. It's like he's oblivious to everything and everyone around him. I don't know if that's good or bad. One of the first rules of being in New York: always watch your surroundings. He must not be from around here.

The security officer waves me forward. *Here we go.* I despise airport security. It takes forever, and taking my shoes off is such a pain. There's something gross about walking barefoot on a floor that sees as much action as an airport. I shudder at the thought and put my shoes up on the conveyor belt.

Even with socks on, the floor is cold and sticky. "Gross," I mumble.

"Excuse me?" The guy ahead of me turns around and stares at me.

He has piercing blue eyes, which momentarily shocks me. I swallow and lick my lips. "Uh, nothing, I was just…" I shake my head. "Nothing. Sorry."

He tilts his head to the side, smiles, and then turns away. He steps through the metal detector, and I lose sight of him as he gathers his stuff and is swallowed up by the crowd on the other side.

If only I could be swallowed up like that and disappear.

After making it through security, I head toward the SunDun terminal—all the way on the other side of the airport. By the time I get there, most of the seats are occupied. *Great.* It's almost two hours before my flight is scheduled to leave, and I am not going to stand the whole time. I find a single empty seat near the windows, and I claim it before someone can steal the chair. I accidentally elbow the person next to me.

He looks at me and smiles.

It's the same guy from the security line. Heat creeps up my neck and erupts on my face. "Uh, sorry. I didn't mean to hit you."

"It's okay." His voice is soft but deep. "These seats really aren't made for strangers, are they?"

I laugh. "No, they're really not. The seats on the plane are worse though."

"Oh, I know. The flight here I was squished between a very large man who had to have the tray down so he could be on his laptop, and a pregnant woman who apparently had horrible morning sickness. It wasn't fun." He laughs, and I smile in response. He's got a great laugh, and it helps brighten my mood a little. "I'm Aiden, by the way."

"Emily."

Before either of us can say anything else, his cell phone rings. He rolls his eyes and gives me an apologetic shrug. "Sorry." He stands, says hello, and walks away.

I sigh and slouch in my seat. Hopefully, he won't be gone too long. Time crawls by, and I'm getting more bored by the second. Finally, I hear the familiar announcement. "SunDun Flight three-seven-two-two from New York to Seattle may now begin boarding."

That's another thing about this trip—a three hour and fifty-two-minute layover in Seattle, Washington, before boarding a much smaller plane to Anchorage. At least my parents gave me money for food, but I still hate them for making me go in the first place. I stand, adjust the strap of my carry-on bag, and walk toward the woman who's checking boarding passes.

She scans mine and hands it back to me with a smile. "Enjoy your flight."

I nod and head off to board the plane.

CHAPTER 2

Aiden Cohen

ALMOST SIX AND A HALF hours later, I'm off the plane and standing at baggage claim in the Sea-Tac International Airport. My legs and back ache from being stuck in the seat for so long, and I twist my body around in all different angles, trying to ease the tension as I watch the baggage carousel move in a slow circle. It feels like I've been standing there for a good hour, even though I know it's only been several moments.

Seriously, where is my suitcase? I walk around the carousel to see if I possibly missed it. Nope. No sign of my bag. Or any bag, for that matter. What if the airline lost my luggage? My heart races, and I walk faster, as if that would somehow magically make my suitcase appear.

"Aiden?"

"Emily?" A tiny bit of relief fills my veins, and I take a deep breath. She'd been in the back of the plane, and I'd been near the front, so we didn't have a chance to talk during the flight, but seeing her friendly face calms my racing heart.

She smiles broadly, her perfect white teeth flashing like a beacon during a storm. Then she takes a moment to study me before tilting her head. "Waiting for your bags, huh?" There's a teasing lilt to her tone, which lowers my anxiety another notch.

"Yeah." I sigh. "I really hope they're not lost." I scrunch up my face at the thought.

"How many do you have?"

"Just one. It's black and gray camouflage."

She adjusts the strap of the oversize purse draped across the front of her body. "So, do you have to catch another plane?"

I nod. "Yeah. But not for another four hours."

She laughs, then covers it behind a badly faked cough.

"What?" I ask.

"You do know that if you're waiting on a connecting flight, they just transfer your bag from one plane to the next, right?" Her eyes sparkle with humor.

"Seriously?"

She nods, fighting to hide her smile.

In all the times I've flown in the past, I've had a direct flight, so this whole layover thing is new to me. But do I feel like a complete idiot now. I sigh. "No, I didn't know that." My shoulders sag. "Well, at least I don't have to worry about lost luggage, huh?"

"Exactly." She punctuates her reply with a firm nod. "I have a long layover, too. Want to grab something to eat?"

My eyebrows lift, and my eyes widen. Did she just ask me to hang out with her? "Uh, yeah, sure."

She smiles again, and my chest tightens. I've never seen such a pretty smile. "Great." She begins to walk toward the food court.

I fall into step beside her, unable to wrap my mind around how lucky I am to have someone to hang out with, especially someone so beautiful. God really does work in mysterious ways. "Where do you want to eat?" I survey our choices—which aren't a lot.

She shrugs, looking around. "How about there?" She points to a full-service restaurant. "Looks like there's plenty of room to sit."

"Sounds good."

A hostess seats us at a two-person booth against the wall. "Your waitress will be with you shortly." She plops two menus down on the table.

I grab mine and flip it open. My stomach grumbles loudly, and Emily looks at me over the rim of her menu. "Someone sounds hungry."

I laugh. "I really should've eaten breakfast this morning knowing I was going to be flying all day. Those snacks they give you on the plane are a joke."

She nods. "They're gross, too."

I return my gaze to the menu and browse the burger selection. "So, where are you headed, anyway?" There aren't many places

8

she can go from Seattle. I mean, there are, but then she'll be flying back the way we just came, and that seems silly.

"Alaska." She makes a sour face. "To my grandparents."

"No way," I say, disbelief filling my voice.

She lowers her menu and stares at me as if I'm lying to her.

"What?" I ask self-consciously.

"Where are you going?" She narrows her eyes.

"Alaska," I say.

"Shut up." Her tone is all playful attitude, as if she thinks I'm trying to be cute or something.

"I'm serious." I don't know what else to say to get her to believe me. I'm not even sure why it matters. She'll know the truth when we both board the same plane.

"Why are you going to Alaska?"

"I live there."

She snorts. "Seriously? You *live* there? Why?"

Before I can respond, the waitress arrives. "Good afternoon. How're you two doing today?"

"Fine, thank you." I smile.

"Can I start you off with something to drink?" she asks, her gaze moving between me and Emily.

"Go ahead," I say to Emily. My father taught me a lot of things, but the one he will never let me forget are proper manners. His lessons are permanently ingrained in who I am.

"Oh, uh, I'll have a strawberry lemonade, please."

"That sounds good. I'll have one, too."

The waitress nods and jots down our drinks on her notepad. Then we place our orders.

Emily gets a bacon barbecue cheeseburger with French fries, and I get a chicken tender sandwich with mozzarella sticks. When the waitress leaves, I fold my arms on the table, eager to talk to her more, to learn more about her. "So, why do you seem so surprised by the fact that I live in Alaska?"

She shrugs again. "I don't know. You just don't look like that's where you're from."

I raise a brow. Most people I meet are intrigued by the fact I live in Alaska, but no one has ever told me I don't look Alaskan—

9

whatever an Alaskan is supposed to look like. "And where do I look like I'm from?"

The corner of her mouth lifts in an almost smile, but it vanishes as quickly as it starts, almost like she's suddenly shy, or afraid to relax and have fun. "The country." She laughs. "I can see you in living on a farm somewhere in like Kentucky or something." Her hazel eyes spark with mischief. "All you're missing is the southern drawl."

Is she implying I look like a redneck farm boy? I'm not sure how I feel about that. "Well, sorry to disappoint you, but I've never even been to Kentucky."

"Hmm." She drums her fingernails on the table. "Okay, so be honest with me. I visited Alaska once before, years ago, and I hated it. How do you live there?"

This time, I shrug. "I've lived there my whole life. I don't know anything else. How do you live in the city? Isn't it noisy and crowded and unsafe?"

She straightens, and all laughter leaves her face. "How do you know I live in the city?"

"I don't. But considering you were leaving from New York and said you were going to your grandparents... I just assumed. Am I wrong?" I know I'm not. I wasn't in New York that long, but I was there long enough to know how people there are different than people in Alaska. And I hated it there.

"No," she says slowly, drawing out the word. "You're not wrong." She studies me intently. A little too intently.

I shift in my chair. Thankfully, the waitress arrives with our drinks, and I focus on opening my straw and taking a sip. I clear my throat. "How long are you going to be in Alaska?"

She turns her head and stares in the opposite direction, suddenly unwilling to look at me. "I don't know."

Okay, that's weird. "Looks like we'll be on the same flight again," I say, hoping to cheer her up.

I usually don't have any issues talking to girls, but there's something about Emily that I find intimidating. Maybe it's because she's from a big city and can handle herself. Or maybe it's because I know all the girls in my hometown, so it's easy to talk to them.

Emily, though, she's guarded, and as badly as I want to pry, I don't. That wouldn't be polite.

Our food arrives. I hesitate, waiting to see if Emily will say a blessing. She doesn't, so I quickly lower my head and say a silent prayer of thanks. We eat in silence for a while. I keep stealing glances at Emily, hoping she'll say something, but she doesn't.

"Want a cheese stick?" I ask, holding one out to her.

"Thanks." She takes it, then inches her plate closer to me. "Want some fries? There's no way I'm going to be able to eat all of these." She takes one and tosses it in her mouth, catching it effortlessly.

"Impressive." I lean back, eyes wide with awe.

"It's a gift. I can catch any food thrown at me. I have a one hundred percent accuracy rate." She grins proudly.

"Really?" I wipe my fingers on my napkin.

"Yup." She nods. "You should try it." She picks up a fry and throws it at my face. I attempt to snatch it out of the air but fail miserably. The fry smacks my cheek, then falls to the floor. She giggles. Then she does it again. And I miss. Again.

Next thing I know, there are six fries flying at my face. There's no way I can catch all of them, so I snatch two of them out of the air and the others hit my nose and forehead. "That's not fair."

Emily giggles uncontrollably, and her face turns crimson. My breath catches at the sight of her like that. Her eyes are vibrant and wild.

"Think you can do better?" I challenge.

"I know I can."

"Okay." I grab a handful of fries from her plate and toss them at her one at a time, and she catches every single one of them.

My jaw drops. She hadn't been lying, and now all I want to know is how she learned to do that. "Okay, that's the coolest talent ever."

"Right?" She takes a deep breath, then reaches for another cheese stick at the same moment I do, and my hand lands on hers.

"Sorry." I jerk my hand back, but my palm tingles with how soft her skin is and how small her hand is beneath mine. What will it feel like to hold her hand for real? I swallow and then take a drink.

"No, I'm sorry. I should've asked first," she says.

"It's okay. You can have anything you want." I freeze momentarily, realizing what I said and how it must sound. But then she blushes, and my heart clenches. The only thought racing through my mind is that she's going to be in Anchorage. With me. *Thank you, God.*

CHAPTER 3

Emily

BOARDING THE PLANE TAKES FOREVER, and all I want to do is sit down. But a large, elderly man is blocking the aisle as he tries to heft a too-large suitcase into the overhead compartment, and I'm stuck behind him.

I wait a few seconds, hoping he'll get his luggage stored and move out of the way. But after several moments, he's still struggling. If my hands weren't already full, I'd help him. "Excuse me," I say.

The man doesn't move, doesn't even acknowledge that I said anything. Annoyance flares inside of me. I sigh loudly, hoping he'll hear that and move out of my way. But he doesn't. So, I try again. Only this time, a handsome, knowing smile catches my attention. It's Aiden. He's in the window seat, watching me try and fail to get past the old man. He smiles and then winks. Heat creeps up my neck and face, and I'm sure my cheeks are beet red. I look away quickly, and he chuckles.

We spent the last four hours together, eating, talking, laughing, exploring the airport. He's hot and funny and smart. And so nice. He's a lot nicer than Matt's ever been to me. Maybe getting forced to go to Alaska isn't going to suck as much as I thought. I wanted to ask him all about his high school and what it was like, but I really have no idea how long I'll be in Alaska, and I don't want to get his hopes up. Or mine. Just because we spent a few hours together doesn't mean it will be anything more.

I take a deep breath. Finally, the guy ahead of me moves down the aisle, and I follow, eager to get to my seat, but I can't stop myself from glancing back at Aiden, who's still watching me. I arrive at my seat, which is smack dab between two old people. The man in the aisle seat happens to be the same man who was blocking my way a moment ago.

"Excuse me," I say. The man doesn't move. "Excuse me," I say louder.

Eventually, the old guy guarding my seat looks up. "Oh, sorry." He wobbles to his feet, and I move past him to sit, noticing the massive hearing aid hanging from his right ear. Apparently, he really can't hear me.

I drop my carry-on bag to the floor and kick it under the seat. Plugging my headphones into my phone, I close my eyes and rest my head on the back of the seat. Sleep is a lost cause, but at least with my eyes closed, I can pretend I'm somewhere else. And I can think about Aiden and his vibrant blue eyes. His dark, wavy hair. His goofy smile. Our hands touched briefly while eating, but he didn't try to hold my hand or touch me in anyway after that. Too bad, because I would've let him.

There's a tap on my shoulder. A pretty flight attendant smiles down at me. Splotches of red lipstick color her otherwise white teeth. "I'm sorry, miss, but I'm going to have to ask you to put away all electronic devices until the captain announces they're allowed to be used."

I take my earbuds out, sigh, and turn to look out the window only to realize the woman sitting next to it has the shade pulled down. This is going to be the longest flight ever. Seriously, why can't I be stuck in the seat next to Aiden?

"Hello, and good afternoon. My name is Christopher Lakin, and I'll be your pilot during this flight. Captain Brandon Franks is co-piloting with me. We should have clear skies and a safe arrival in around four hours. Thank you again for flying SunDun Airlines."

As soon as the pilot stops talking, the pretty blonde flight attendant who told me to shut off my music stands in front of my section and begins the obligatory safety demonstration. I yawn. *Boring.*

Finally, after a few more minutes, the flight attendants make their way over to the back to buckle in, checking to be sure everyone's seats are in the upright position and tray tables are up and locked. I don't understand why we can't just get on the plane, buckle our seat belts, and go. All this extra stuff is such a waste of time. The plane makes its way onto the runaway, and with a throttle, the plane tilts its nose in the air, and we begin take off. I hate this part.

As soon as the plane is in the air and the fasten seat belts sign goes off, I breathe a sigh of relief and relax a little. But just as quickly, my heart is in my throat. I'm going to stupid Alaska. To stay with my grandparents. I bet Alaska doesn't even have WiFi or cable. Do they even have cell phone reception?

How can my parents expect me to go from fashionable city girl socialite to backwoods nobody who has to wear a parka? No one looks good in a parka. I don't mind the snow we get during a New York winter, but I hate the cold, and Alaska is cold all the time. I bet my neighbors will be real-life Eskimos.

All of this because I went to a party I shouldn't have. I'm not the one who threw a beer bottle at the cop. Nor am I the one who got into a fight and killed a kid. Yet, I'm the one getting banished to a no-name town in Alaska. Because I'm not lucky enough to be in Anchorage. Oh, no. I'm in a tiny town south of there. It's like the armpit of Anchorage.

"The captain has turned off the fasten seat belts sign, so you're free to move about the cabin. We'll be starting our complimentary beverage service in a moment," the flight attendant says.

It's only then I notice how dry my throat is, and thankfully, it doesn't take them long to reach my seat. I get a soda and a tiny bag of cookies. I really should've bought more snacks to bring with me, ones that don't taste like cardboard. I open the soda and take a sip. Flying always gives me a headache, so I close my eyes and try to rest, but it's not helping all that much.

I have no idea how much time has passed, but the hum of the PA system jolts me awake. I rub my eyes and yawn. My tray is still down, and my half-eaten bag of cookies sits next to my cup of now flat soda.

"Attention, folks." The pilot's voice fills the cabin. "There's some congestion on the runway, so we're going to circle around a few times to allow ground crews to get things cleared up. Please be patient, and we'll land as soon as possible."

Whoa. I really slept the entire flight? That never happens. I stretch my arms over my head and arch my back, trying to work out the kinks. I yawn again. "Are we in Anchorage already?" I ask the elderly man seated beside me.

He nods. "There's a herd of moose on the runway."

"Seriously?" I laugh. Only in Alaska. I settle back in my seat, hoping it won't take too long to land. I need to get on solid land again, and a small thrill of excitement shoots up my spine at the thought of seeing grandma and grandpa. Without Erik around, I'll be the one they spoil. Not to mention, I really want to talk to Aiden again.

Thirty minutes pass, and then an hour, and we're still circling the airport. My stomach rumbles, and I swallow hard. My throat is dry and scratchy, and my temples throb with an impending headache. I really need to get off this stupid plane. I take a drink, and the warm liquid turns my stomach.

What I really want to do is go back to sleep, but that's not going to happen, so I turn on the small television and flip through the channels. I settle on a bad 80s high school drama. The acting is horrible, and the special effects are even worse. I settle into my seat, the ache in my head getting worse.

The plane shakes, and the captain's voice comes over the intercom again. "We've run into a bit of turbulence, folks. Nothing to worry about. We're going to make a larger loop back around, and hopefully, we'll have clearance to land by then. Thanks for your patience and for flying with SunDun Airlines."

I groan inwardly. We're never going to get off this plane at this rate. I close my eyes for only a second, and then the small TV screen goes totally black. What's going on? I look over the seats in front of me and see their screens are blank, too.

A tall man with black hair, wearing a suit, rushes up the aisle, and from the corner of my eye, I see a flash of silver. A badge. The air marshall? He disappears into the cock pit. What on earth is going on?

A second later, the flight attendant's calm voice surrounds me. "It appears as though the pocket of turbulence we're experiencing is larger than we originally anticipated. The fasten seat belts sign is back on, and we ask that everyone remain seated with the seats upright and the trays closed. Please stay calm, and we'll be out of this in no time."

No sooner does she quit talking than the plane dips sharply, rises, and then shakes violently. My cup tips, spilling soda all over the tray and onto my lap. I yelp with surprise. Another rumble shakes the plane. I grip the arm rests and squeeze my eyes shut. A frantic woman in the back screams, and then other passengers begin to scream, too. There's so much crying and shouting.

"Are we going to... to die?"

"Shut up. It's just a little turbulence."

"I just want land. I'm getting very nauseous."

"Oh, God! We're all going to die! Lord save us."

My temples feel like they're ready to implode, and my stomach lurches. I grab the first thing my hand touches — the old man in the seat beside me.

He raises his eyebrow and pats my hand. "It's going to be all right. We're in the best of hands. Just relax." He smiles. "My name is Theodore. And you are?"

"Emily." I return his smile. The plane shakes again, and I whimper. This type of turbulence doesn't qualify as fun in my mind. I take several deep breaths. It'll be okay. The likelihood of this plane crashing is slim. Besides, we're flying around the airport. We're so close to landing. It's perfectly safe, and I'm fine. It'll all be fine.

"Maybe I can be of some help. I do have some—too many—years of experience and knowledge. I'm willing to listen if you're willing to talk. You'll be surprised by how much better you'll feel."

It's nice knowing there's someone willing to lend an ear in a time of need. Talking to Theodore does help, and for a few moments, I forget about the turbulence and the rocking plane. What can it hurt to talk to him? But before I can open my mouth, the teenager with a blue Mohawk sitting in front of me shouts, "She's dead!"

I turn to see what he's pointing at. A woman in her mid-thirties is lying in the aisle on her back. Unmoving. I squeeze Theodore's arm. Each breath is like swallowing razor blades—sharp and excruciating.

What is going on? Did she... Is she... dead? How is that even possible? Wasn't she wearing her seat belt? I tighten my own.

The pilot's voice fills the cabin again, still as calm as ever. "Looks like this turbulence is going to hang with us until we can safely land. Please remain calm and seated with your seat belts fastened. We're working to get this under control."

His words offer me no comfort.

"Captain, we've just lost all ground communications and control of engine one." The PA systems suddenly goes dead.

This is it.

I'm going to die.

I close my eyes.

CHAPTER 4

Aiden

THE CO-PILOT'S WORDS SWIRL IN my mind. *Captain, we've just lost all ground communications and control of engine one.* I begin to hyperventilate. They've lost control of an engine. What does that mean? Are we going to die?

I really don't want to die. *Please, God, don't let me die.*

The speakers hum to life, and then the pilot's voice silences the cabin. "At this point, our situation is dire, and our best hope is to try to land, so please buckle in and prepare for a bumpy landing. Since we've lost both engines and contact with the ground, we are on our own. I promise to do everything possible to get us all back on solid ground safely. Please remain calm, and Godspeed."

The line clicks dead.

What? The runway isn't clear for us to land, and there are no safe places to land that aren't in the middle of a town. Bile rises up my throat, and I force it back down, gagging.

The plane roars and shakes with another blast of turbulence. Then we whip around as if we're on a merry-go-round. The spinning becomes faster, and I can't see the seat in front of me. I squeeze my eyes shut and grit my teeth as I breathe slowly. Inhale through my nose. Exhale through my mouth. And repeat. There's another large bump, and my eyes pop open. The oxygen mask falls from above my head and dangles in my face.

And then... Darkness.

Someone screams.

My heart stops.

The cabin is pitch black, not even the emergency lights are on. The plane seesaws and shakes vigorously. It reminds me of those natural disaster simulators, the ones that shake and blow and recreate the worst situations. This is a million times worse. I can't see anyone or anything around me.

Someone yells, "Help me! Someone help me! I can't find my seat belt. Where is my seat belt? I'm going to die—"

The scream of shattering glass pierces the cabin. Something scrapes across the floor, followed by a loud boom. More screams. I put my hands over my ears, but it does nothing to block out the horrible noise around me.

"Ouch! What the… is that my luggage?" a deep, male voice bellows.

Then, as if on cue, all the luggage bursts free from the overhead compartments, the rumble equivalent to that of an earthquake. I instinctively throw my hands over my head for protection.

"My baby! Help!" a woman wails. "Someone grab my baby! I can't see him. Please! Help! Someone help me! Help me. Please!"

"I can't find my inhaler." There's wheezing right next to my ear, and I assume it's the woman seated beside me. "I'm going to die without it."

"Forgive us, God! For we are all sinners, and this is our only way for redemption back into Your good graces. Hallelujah! Praise the Lord, we are coming home."

Maybe that guy is right. Maybe this is the start of the reckoning. I close my eyes and force all thoughts from my mind. *Mom, Dad, I'm so sorry I didn't listen to you. I'm sorry I had to find my birth mom. You were right about her. I'm so sorry. And God, if You are listening, please show us mercy and protect us. Amen.*

I'd hoped the pilot would get us through this, but now, I'm not so sure. I hold my breath. Which would be a less painful way to die? Suffocation or a plane crash? I'm pretty sure both options are unpleasant. *Please let it be over quickly.*

"Attention, please. This is Tom Davis, United States Air Marshall. Captain Lakin hasn't been able to regain our ground communications, and we've encountered a strong tail wind that has pushed us off course. By our calculations, we're somewhere over the Aleutian Islands. The pilot is doing everything in his power to land us on the closest island as quickly and safely as possible. Please stay seated, and remain calm."

The nose of the plane dips, and my seat belt tightens, cutting off circulation in my waist. I brace my feet on the floor and push back in an effort to alleviate the pressure of the seat belt, but we're going so fast. The plane sways from side to side. There's so much screaming. I wish everyone would just shut up.

In an instant, the plane picks up speed and descends. Hard. Fast. Out of control. All my hope for a safe landing vanishes. I put my hands on the back of the seat in front of me so I don't end up falling forward any more than I already am. All around me, people continue to scream. Everything is still in total darkness, but I can hear just fine. I can hear people crying. Kids whimpering and calling out for their parents. The thuds and thumps of people being ejected from their seats, smashing into the hard, unforgiving overhead compartments, nearby seats, and other passengers.

Please make it stop. Just make it all stop.

The loudspeaker hisses to life. "Prepare for impact."

Seconds feel like decades, and an eerie calm settles over the cabin. It's like everyone holds their breath, waiting for impact. The nose of the plane jerks upward, and I'm slammed back into my seat. And then there's a deafening boom followed by a blast of hot air. My seat belt snaps, and I'm thrown out of my seat. A stab of pain shoots through my head and down my spine. I groan, and my eyelids flutter close.

CHAPTER 5

Aiden

OPEN.
CLOSE.
OPEN.
CLOSE.
I blink slowly. My head throbs, and my whole body aches. Groaning, I manage to get my eyes open, but a blinding light makes me squint and drape my arm over my face. What the…? I roll onto my side and sit up. My eyes widen despite the harsh light, and my heart sinks. The front half of the plane is lodged between two massive trees and is on fire, the flames extending high into the sky, the heat stifling. Pieces of the middle section and the wings are scattered across the ground. And the back end of the plane is in the ocean, half submerged and half sticking in the sand.

People remain in their seats, several of them frantically trying to get out while others are passed out or… dead. Moans and groans of pain seep into my foggy brain. People are shouting for help, but the ringing in my ears deafens me to their cries. I get to my knees and double over in pain, clutching my stomach. The stench of burning flesh and aluminum fills the air and makes me gag.

"Ow… someone, please, help…" A faint, female voice to my left draws my attention. The woman who'd been sitting next to me during the flight is an arm's length away, her right leg twisted at a ninety-degree angle.

I cringe at the sight and struggle to my feet. All of my limbs appear to be in working order. I take a cautious step and wince. My knee is sore, and my legs are stiff, but I'm alive. I could be one of those poor souls burning to death in the front of the plane. I close my eyes, take a deep breath, and say a quick prayer for the dead and dying before making my way over to the woman with the broken leg.

I kneel beside her. "You okay?"

She groans. "My leg."

"Yeah, I know. Is anything else hurt?"

"I don't think so."

I nod. "I'm going to have to move you out of the way of"—I gesture around me—"everything." I have no idea how I'm going to do this, or even if I can, but I have to try. It's going to be painful for her, and I'm already cringing thinking about how loud she'll scream.

"My wife! Someone help my wife!"

I look up and see an older gentleman pointing at me.

"Hey, kid. Yeah, you. Come help me. My wife is trapped under this row of chairs, and I can't lift it by myself."

"But... I..." I glance down at the woman in front of me.

She smiles weakly. "Go on. I'll be okay here another minute or two."

I swallow hard and get to my feet. I keep my gaze trained on the old man so I don't have to see all the death around me. The stench is unbearable, filling my nostrils with its atrocious odor.

"Hurry up," he screams, waving frantically.

Breaking into a run, I reach him and try to assess the situation. His wife is deathly pale, and I fear the worst, but this guy thinks she's alive and will stay that way. I don't say anything to the contrary, but she really doesn't look good.

"You lift this side, and I'll do that side. Okay?" he says.

I nod.

"Good. On the count of three, we lift and move it over there." He motions toward what used to be the window seat section of the plane. "Ready? One... two... three... lift!"

Using all my strength, I lift my side, and together, we manage to lift it away and flip it over so his wife can get to safety. My muscles burn with the effort, and I bite my tongue to stop from crying out in pain. The man kneels before his wife, wrapping his frail arms around her. His wife forces a smile. Her left arm is smashed to the point where it'll never heal.

I slowly back away and step on something that crunches beneath my foot. I look down and see I'm standing on a severed hand. "Oh, God!" I cup my hand over my mouth and jump back, horrified. There are dead bodies all around me. Twisting in unnatural ways, a pile of limbs taunts me with my horrific reality. My stomach heaves and rolls, threatening to bring up the chicken sandwich and mozzarella sticks I'd eaten hours ago. I shiver. This can't be happening. Maybe this is all some nightmare, and when I wake up, I'll be home.

But this is real. The plane did crash. People are dying by the second. And somehow, I'm alive. I don't know if I should thank God or not. I turn around to assess more of the damage. People are crying and hugging their loved ones who perished in the crash, while others are giving condolences to those who lost their loved ones. Others appear to be trying to organize the survivors and give orders. A few people are running in and out of the tail end of the plane, pulling out remaining survivors. I stand there, watching everything, unable to move despite the fact people are shouting at me to help. I don't know where to begin.

My gaze settles on the woman with the broken leg. I rush back over to her and drop to my knees, wincing at the sharp jolt of pain that shoots up my thigh. I gently touch her shoulder. "Hey." I lick my lips. "Do you want me to move you now?" She doesn't respond, and at first I think she doesn't hear me. I lean closer. "I'm back. How about we get you out of the way now?" There's still no response. Hesitantly, I put my shaky hand in front of her nose and mouth.

Nothing.

No… *Please, God, no.* I press my fingers to her neck. No pulse.

I gag and crawl away from her. Then I throw up. I can't believe she's dead. If I hadn't left her, would she be alive now? Is her death on my hands? I wretch again, so violently my shoulders heave with the effort, tears prickling the corners of my eyes. I inhale deeply, trying to get as much air into my lungs as possible, which only causes me to gag more. Forcing myself to move, I get to my feet and turn around. Twenty yards ahead of me is Emily. My heart sinks at the possibility she might be dead. I make my way over to her.

She's face down, inches from the plane. Dried blood is matted in her hair and covers one side of her shirt. I suck in a deep breath through my mouth and gently flip her over onto her back. I brush the hair away from her face, and I'm struck by how beautiful she is. Her skin is creamy and soft, a stark contrast to her bloodied hair and torn flesh. That gash on her forehead makes me wince in pain; I can't imagine how badly it hurts her. Her eyes are closed, and she's unmoving. My heart's racing as I lean down. *Dear God, please let her be alive. Please let her be alive.* I place my ear to her chest and pray for a heartbeat.

CHAPTER 6

Aiden

I HEAR A FAINT *THUMP* *thump*, but I don't know if it's hers or mine. I hope it's hers, but as loud as my heart is pounding and with the chaos around me, I can't be sure. I put my trembling hand in front of her mouth and nose, and I feel something, but it could be the breeze.

"Emily?" I gently nudge her shoulder. No response. I try again. "Emily? Can you hear me?" Still no answer. I suck at this. What am I supposed to say? It's not like I took a course in how to wake up an unconscious person. And even if I did get her to wake up, what if she's injured? I won't be able to help her.

"Emily, it's me, Aiden. We met at the airport. Can you hear me?" I roll my eyes at how stupid I sound. "Please wake up." I sit back and stare at her, watching for the slightest movement, and that's when I see her chest rise slightly. I freeze, afraid if I move, she'll somehow stop breathing.

Her arm twitches, and hope swells in my chest. I kneel closer to her. "Emily?" After a long couple of seconds, her eyes pop open, and she gasps for breath. I fall back onto my butt and hang my head, expelling a bent up breath. Relief washes over me in waves.

"What happened? Where am I?" She props herself up on her elbows and looks around. Her eyes widen, and I can see the horror on her face.

"Our plane crashed." The steadiness of my voice surprises me.

She sits up abruptly and winces. "We crashed?" She twists around, taking in more of her surroundings, and her jaw drops. "We crashed," she repeats, bringing her knees to her chest and hugging them. "This isn't real. This isn't real."

"Hey, it's going to be okay." I put my hand on her shoulder, which is stiff and cold.

Emily rocks back and forth, muttering "we crashed" over and over until I start repeating those same words in my mind, too. And then she begins to shiver uncontrollably. I move closer and wrap my arms around her. She's trembling so violently, it causes my body to shake.

"Hey, it's okay. We survived. It's going to be okay." If only I believed what I'm saying.

She buries her face against my shoulder and clings to me. Her tears soak through my shirt, but all I can do is hold her and stroke her back. Is she in shock?

"Theodore," she gasps and jerks away from me.

"Who's Theodore?" I ask.

"The old man who was sitting next to me. Where is he?"

I stare at her for a moment, unsure if she's genuinely concerned or if she has some sort of head injury. Or if she's trying to focus on something other than the carnage around us. Finally, I shrug. "I don't know. I'm sorry."

She narrows her eyes and wipes away her tears. "I have to find him."

My stomach drops. Even if she does find him in this chaos, chances are he didn't make it. But I don't say that because I don't want to upset her any more. "Okay," I say slowly. "I'll help you find him, but let's make sure you're okay first." I get to my feet and wipe the dirt off my pants. "Is anything hurt?"

She stares up at me like I'm crazy. "How are you so calm right now?" Her voice cracks, and a fresh round of tears trickle down her cheeks.

"I'm not." I rub my shaking hands on my jeans and blow out a breath. "I'm just good at faking it."

That earns me a faint smile. Emily slowly gets to her knees and cries out, her face contorting with pain. "Ouch! Oh, that hurts!" She flops back down and clutches her left leg.

I crouch beside her. "What hurts?"

"My leg." She bites down on her lower lip.

I nod. "Okay, lay down."

"Why?"

"Because you're hurt, probably hit your head, and I don't see anyone else running over here to your rescue."

She glares at me, and her bottom lip trembles slightly. "You don't have to be mean about it."

I sigh and rub my forehead. "Sorry. I didn't mean to snap at you."

"No." She shakes her head. "I'm sorry. Thank you for helping me." She lays down, wincing in pain with each movement she makes.

I put my hands on her knee and work my way down her leg. I have no idea what I'm looking for, but I don't feel any bones sticking out, and there isn't any blood. When I get to her ankle, she shouts at me to stop and jerks her leg away.

"That hurts," she says.

"Can you walk on it?" I stand and offer her my hand. She takes it, and I help her up. At first, she puts all her weight on her right foot, and then slowly puts some on her left foot, her hands on my shoulders for support.

"Ow." She furrows her brow. "I think maybe it's just twisted. It hurts, but I can walk on it."

"Good." I force a smile.

She doesn't make any move to let go of me, and I don't mind. Concentrating on her hands on me is better than acknowledging what's happening around us. I've seen enough, and I don't want to see anymore. Although, at some point, I'll have to face the situation.

"How's your head?" I ask.

"Huh?" She looks at me like I've lost my mind.

"Your head." I point to her forehead. "You're bleeding. Does it hurt?" I roll my eyes; of course it hurts.

She reaches up and gingerly touches her head. When she pulls her hand away, her fingertips are coated in blood. "I honestly can't feel anything up there. It doesn't hurt…" She glances around. "I don't think it's my blood." Her face pales.

"We'll get it cleaned off, okay?" I nod as I speak, hoping my words and actions help calm her because focusing on her keeps my mind off everything else right now.

"Where are we?" Emily looks up into my eyes. The severity of things is finally settling over her, and I wish I could take it away.

"I don't know." To my right is an open area, pitch black. To my left, water. "The air marshall said we were landing somewhere in the Aleutian Islands, but I don't know which one."

Nodding, she asks, "Do you know what time it is?"

"I have no idea. It's almost dark, though." Nothing like stating the obvious. As horrible as it is, at least the flames consuming the front of plane gives off enough light to see.

"What're we supposed to do now?" She shivers and wraps her arms around herself.

It's only then I notice how chilly it is, despite the fire. A strong wind whips around us, blowing Emily's hair into her face. She pushes it back, smearing the blood further into her hairline, and shivers again. I suppress a shudder and glance over my shoulder. There's a group of survivors converging a few hundred feet away from the wreckage. "I guess we go join them."

"Yeah, okay. I want to find Theodore first," she says.

I have a gut feeling he probably didn't make it. Not a lot of people did, but knowing he was sitting right beside Emily, there is some hope. "He might actually be over there with the group. We should check there first." I offer the suggestion selfishly, not wanting to walk through the wreckage and step on human remains again.

"That's a good idea." She gives me a grateful smile.

I put my arm around her waist and turn her toward the group of survivors, keeping most of her weight on me and off her bad foot. I keep my gaze straight ahead, refusing to look at the dead bodies littering the ground.

CHAPTER 7

Emily

The pain in my ankle shoots up my leg, slicing at my nerve endings. Tears burn my eyes, and my heart pounds erratically. I put more of my weight on Aiden and struggle to stay on my feet as we make our way toward the group of survivors. As hard as I try not to, I can't stop from looking around. Fire, blood, death, screaming. My ears ring, and bile fills the back of my throat. I stumble.

Aiden catches me. "You okay? Want to sit?"

"No." I swallow back the urge to throw up. "I'm okay." But I'm not. All I want to do is get away from all this death and suffering. With each step I take, another memory of the crash sweeps through my mind. "This is really happening, isn't it?" I mumble, not expecting an answer.

He nods. "Unfortunately, yes."

I momentarily close my eyes, trying to block out everything around me, but its short lived.

"Hey, here's two more."

I force my eyes open to see a black-haired guy pointing at us.

"Come on. We're doing a head count, and we need everyone present. Is there anyone else with you?"

"No." I scan the group for any sign of Theodore. I'm not sure why I care so much about a strange old man. Probably because he tried to keep me calm when the plane was going down. I owe it to him to make sure he's okay.

A man in a tattered, navy blue suit stands at the front of the group. "Is this the last of them, Tom?"

"Yeah, afraid so, Jason. Our final check for survivors didn't reveal anyone else."

Considering the size of the plane, the group of survivors isn't that large. I would guess there are maybe twenty or twenty-five of us total. When I think about how packed the plane was, my stomach lurches. All those people... I shiver. Aiden tightens his arm around my waist and pulls me closer. His body is warm and comforting.

"Okay, everybody, please, quiet down." Jason claps his hands. "I know you're all scared, and a majority of you have injuries, but if we're going to make it through this, we need to calm down and work together."

His voice is soothing, and I step forward to get a look at him. Aiden is still by my side. I glance at him, grateful for his presence. Even though we only met hours prior, he's gone out of his way to find me and make sure I'm okay. One way or another, I'll repay him for that.

When the group quiets, Jason continues, "You all probably have a million questions, as do I, but I'm afraid I don't have the answers. I suggest we—"

"Who are you?" someone off to my left shouts.

"Yeah, and who put you in charge?" someone else yells.

Jason raises his hands to calm them. "I'm Pastor Jason Thompson, former Wisconsin state congressman. There's a lot of death and suffering going on right now, and I know you're all scared and confused. I am, too. But God will get us through this."

The crowd murmurs, but no one else challenges him. I huff and shake my head.

"I take it you don't believe in God?" Aiden says.

"Nope." That's a conversation I'm not having with him or anyone else for that matter. I continue to scan the group for Theodore—all to no avail. Between the dark and the way people are huddling together, it's impossible to see anyone clearly.

"We'll find him," Aiden whispers.

Sighing, I nod. I just hope when we do, it's not too late.

"I have no idea where we are, but the air marshall indicated we were attempting to land near the Aleutian Islands, which is good for us because it will make rescue easier." Jason nods at the guy standing on the outskirts of the group. "Tom?"

Hope inflates in my chest. Of course we'll be rescued. With today's technology, there are black boxes and GPS. Someone will find us, and we'll all be okay. I hold that thought close, letting it wrap around my heart.

A man steps forward, and I squint against the darkness to see him. "Tom Davis, Air Marshall." He holds his badge above his head and turns around slowly so we can all see it.

"So, help is on the way?" the woman next to me asks.

I glance over at her. She's short and chubby, her dark hair is frizzy and sticking up all over the place, and she's twisting her hands nervously. I have a sudden urge to comfort her, but what can I say?

"That is the hope," Jason says. "However, I doubt we'll see any help tonight, so I suggest we hunker down and wait for the sun to rise."

"Slow down for a second." Tom steps up to stand beside Jason. "We don't have any idea where we are, and neither does anyone else. We lost communication with ground almost thirty minutes before we went down, and the tail winds pushed us several hundred miles off course."

A scream builds inside of me, and I fight to keep it contained. No one knows where we are? How is that possible?

"But we can agree we're near the Aleutian Islands, correct?" Jason gives Tom a knowing look, as if to say *please agree with me*.

"Yes, but we don't know which one we're on, and if we crashed on one that's owned by Russia, then we've got bigger problems than the weather." Tom crosses his arms.

I don't know if his bluntness is refreshing or terrifying. I've always hated liars, so for that reason, I'm glad he's being brutally honest, but right now, I need to know things are going to be okay.

Murmurs and not so hushed frantic whispers spread through the group.

"Okay, settle down. Please." Tom holds his hands up in a show of surrender. "I'm not saying this to frighten anyone, or to dash anyone's hopes, but we do need to be prepared, and the only way for that to happen is for everyone to have all the information."

"What information do we need to have?" Jason asks, his voice just as soothing as before. Why isn't he panicking, too?

"I'm not sure." Tom rubs the back of his neck.

"What do you mean you're not sure?" an elderly man to my left asks.

"I mean, I don't have all the information yet, so I can't share it with you. I need to do a little investigating, but in the meantime, Jason is right. We should all just hunker down for the night and regroup in the morning."

The group erupts in more shouts, but everyone is trying to talk louder than the next person, making it impossible to understand what anyone is saying.

"Wait." I clear my throat and raise my hand, which seems to get everyone's attention. "You want us to sleep out here? Shouldn't we try to find help instead? These islands are inhabited, right?" I ask, hoping no one else hears the panic in my voice.

"We don't really have much of a choice." Jason sighs. "Look, I know this isn't ideal, but all we have to do is get through the night. Then we can regroup in the morning. Does anyone have a working cell phone?"

Instinctively, I reach in my pocket only to come up empty-handed. I have no idea what happened to my phone. Beside me, Aiden pulls out a cell phone, but the screen is smashed so badly, he can't swipe his finger across it. I look over my shoulder. Several people have cell phones in their hands, holding them in the air.

"My battery is dead," Tom says.

"I don't have a signal," says the older woman standing beside me.

"Me either," says someone else.

One by one, everyone with a phone agrees. No service. My shoulders slump, and I hang my head. We can't even make a call for help. I take several short breaths, which makes me dizzy. My eyelids are heavy with exhaustion, and I rub my face in an effort to stay awake.

"Tom," I call out to him. "Doesn't the plane have a radio or something we could use to call for help?"

"The front of the plane is destroyed." He points toward the ocean. "Even if we could retrieve a radio, it probably wouldn't work."

Oh, no. All those people in the front of the plane… I squeeze my eyes shut against the barrage of horrific images flashing through my mind.

The crowd is getting louder by the moment. Jason hushes them. "Okay, calm down. Anchorage knew we were there. The pilot did have communication with them for a while, right?" He turns to Tom, who nods. "See?" Jason turns back to the crowd. "When they realize we've disappeared, they'll send out a search party. Just because we can't make a call doesn't mean we can't help them find us." He emphasizes his words by pointing at us. "So, I suggest we go down to the water's edge and start to build a signal fire. We'll break into groups. One to build the fire, another to scavenge whatever they can from the plane. Seats, blankets, pillows, food, water. We'll gather all the luggage, too, and get whatever we can from them."

"You're making it sound like we're going to be here a while," says a man from the back of the group.

"God spared us for a reason, and He won't let us down now. But that doesn't mean we can't be prepared for the worst."

I roll my eyes. God isn't going to save us, and the sooner Jason realizes that the better.

"We need to build a shelter," Aiden says, and for some reason, his voice startles me.

I put my hand over my chest, but my heart won't slow.

"The weather around here is unpredictable at best, and if it doesn't snow, it will rain. If it pours, the fire will go out. There's not much we can do about that, but we have to get ourselves out of the elements as best we can," Aiden says.

I stare at him in awe. He sounds so grown up and mature.

"That's a good idea, son. What's your name?" Jason asks.

"Aiden. I'm from Alaska, and I've studied these islands in my classes. I know the climate well, and I can help."

He's cute *and* smart? That's a wonderful combo, and one that would, under normal circumstances, put him out of my league. But these aren't normal circumstances, and right now, we only have each other.

"Great. Okay, so we'll need to find whatever we can to build a temporary shelter."

A full body shiver shakes me from the inside out. Why do I get the feeling the shelter isn't going to be temporary? I swallow hard and turn to Aiden, who looks just as skeptical as I feel. "Now what?" I whisper.

He shrugs. "I guess we pick a group and help out."

"All right." Tom steps forward and clears his throat. "The stronger, uninjured men should gather wood from those trees over there. The women can search what remains of the plane. And the injured"—he glances behind him—"you can sit off over here to the side, out of the way. Do we have any doctors or nurses in the group?"

A loud murmur ripples through the group, everyone looking at everyone else, shaking their heads.

"No?" Tom's gaze scours the crowd. "Does anyone have any medical training?"

A tall, thin woman steps forward. "I'm certified in CPR, and I took a couple semesters of college classes for nursing, but I didn't finish."

Tom frowns.

Jason smiles. "It'll do. What's your name?"

"Amy."

"Okay, Amy, why don't you see what you can do to help the injured." He holds out his arm as if to welcome her to some super-secret club or something. Once she is by his side, he says, "All right, let's get to work. But please, be careful. And remember, God is watching over each and every one of you."

I blow out a breath and turn to Aiden. "Guess I'm searching the plane." I really wish I could search for firewood with him, though. I have no idea what we'll find inside the plane, but the nagging thought of dead bodies shoves its way to the forefront of my mind. It's enough to make me want to vomit.

He nods and shoves his hands in his pockets. "Yeah, okay. So… I'll meet you down by the fire in a little while?"

"Yes." My throat is dry and scratchy. What I wouldn't give for a drink of water right now. If I got lucky, I'd find some in the plane. I stand there for a moment longer, watching Aiden walk away with a small group of guys. The blood on my forehead is starting to dry, and I scratch at it. Flakes of red fall in front of face, and I force back the urge to gag. There's no cut, so I know it's not my blood. I shudder to think whose it might be.

"Do you really think we'll be rescued?" There's an older woman with ghost-white hair standing next to me.

Where did she come from? I stare at her, unable to comprehend her question. "What?"

"Do you think we'll be rescued?" she repeats.

"Yes," I say immediately, but deep down, I'm not so sure. I really want a shower.

"I'm Marjorie."

"Emily." I smile.

"Well." She takes hold of my arm. "Let's go see what we can find in that plane, huh?"

I look down at where she's touching me, welcoming the comfort of the contact. "Yeah, let's go."

When we get down to the tail end of the plane, there's already a dozen people searching through it. I'm not sure I'll be much help, but I need to do something to keep myself occupied, so I make my way down what's left of the aisle and join the handful of people that are there. I find several suitcases and duffle bags, which I pile up on some seats, when I see a tuft of hair sticking out from beneath a couple of seats that had been ripped from the plane.

I try to shove them away but can't move them on my own. "Hey, I think someone's trapped over here. I need some help."

A young woman rushes over and helps me move the chairs. That's when I see him. "Theodore?" My eyes widen as I take in the sight of him.

He's white as a ghost, and there's dried blood on his nose and the corner of his mouth. His head is twisted at an uncomfortable angle. Oh no. Please not Theodore. I don't need to check his pulse to know he's dead. I drop to my knees and gasp, squeezing my eyes shut. *Please let me wake up. Please let me wake up.* But when I reopen my eyes, I'm still in the busted plane, and Theodore's lifeless face is still staring at me.

"Is he family?" asks the girl who helped me move the seats.

I shake my head and cup my hand over my mouth, nausea getting the better of me. I get to my feet and force my way out of the plane. I run toward the beach where the guys are making a huge pile of branches and firewood. I don't see Aiden, but then again, I'm not really looking for him. I separate from the rest of the survivors, double over, and dry heave until my throat is raw and burning.

CHAPTER 8

Aiden

BY THE TIME WE GET the fire going, the sky is pitch black. There are no stars, and the moon is hidden. It's all so bizarre. If there are people on this island, wouldn't they have heard the crash? Or wouldn't they see the flames from the fire?

"Hey, Aiden!"

I stop at the sound of my voice and turn to find Tom walking toward me.

"How familiar are you with these islands?" he asks.

I shrug. "I've done extensive research on them and have written several papers. Why?"

He takes hold of my arm and moves me away from the fire and the survivors who're converging around it. "I have my suspicions about where we are, but I need someone who knows the area to confirm what I'm thinking." He glances around as if he's worried someone might be eavesdropping.

"And what're you thinking?" A knot forms in my stomach. Alaska is known as The Last Frontier, and these islands… the conditions are often much worse.

Tom straightens and crosses his arms. He's got massive biceps, and his bushy brown eyebrows lift slightly. "Would you be up for exploring with me tomorrow?"

"Uh, yeah, I guess."

He nods. "Good, we'll leave before everyone else gets up. And don't tell anyone." He turns to walk away.

I stare at him for a moment. That's weird. I probably shouldn't have agreed to wander around the island with him—alone—but he is an air marshall. He's probably the safest person to be around, and I'm sure Emily will... My eyes widen. I can't leave Emily here alone tomorrow.

"Tom! Wait!" I jog up to him. "There's this girl—Emily—we're traveling together, and I won't leave her. So if she can't come, then I'm not going."

His gaze is deadly, and the muscle in his jaw ticks. I swallow hard. Issuing an ultimatum isn't the smartest thing I could've done, but I'm not leaving Emily to fend for herself.

Finally, after what feels like forever, Tom gives a curt nod. "Fine, but it's just the three of us. Got it?"

"Got it." I smile. When he walks away, I blow out a breath. Now all I have to do is find Emily and tell her. The group who'd been searching the plane begins to trek down with their arms full of supplies. I stand and watch, looking for Emily, but I don't see her anywhere. My stomach drops. Is she hurt? *Please, God, don't let her be hurt.* I'll never forgive myself if something happens and I'm not around to help her.

I take off on a run toward the wreckage, intent on finding her, when I notice a figure several feet down the beach, sitting with knees tucked to their chest. From here, I have no idea if the person is male or female, but I hope it might be Emily. Even if it's not her, no one should be alone right now. Not after all we've been through.

"Uh, excuse me, I don't think you should be sitting—"

"Aiden?" She turns to look at me.

"Emily." I exhale with relief and sit beside her. "What're you doing down here all by yourself?"

She rests her head on her knees and looks over at me with tears in her eyes. The blood is gone from her forehead, and her hairline is wet. "Theodore's dead. I found him in..." She takes a deep breath and turns away from me.

"Oh." I frown. "I'm so sorry." I don't know who Theodore is to her, whether he was family or just a friend she'd made on the plane, but my heart goes out to her. It's hard enough to wrap your mind around the fact we survived a plane crash, but to lose someone she knows? And then to be the one to find his body? I can't even imagine how she's feeling right now.

I don't know what to do or say to make her feel better. Should I put my arm around her and try to comfort her? Or just sit here and listen should she decide to talk about it? I pick up a handful of sand and let it slip through my fingers. She didn't push me away earlier when I'd put my arms around her. In fact, she'd returned my embrace. I wipe my hand on my jeans and put my arm around her, pulling her close.

She rests her head on my shoulder and sighs. As horrible as our circumstances are, I like the feel of Emily close to me. Because even though I won't say it out loud, I'm scared, too, and I need her just as much as she needs me.

"It's awful. Seeing him like that." She straightens and shakes her head. "That could've been me," she whispers so quietly I almost don't hear her.

"But it wasn't. You can't think that way."

Without another word, she stands and wipes the sand from her jeans. "I see the fire is going."

I stand, too. "Yeah, once we got it started, it didn't take long for it to really take off." I laugh nervously.

"Looks like they're having another meeting." She nods over my shoulder.

I turn to look, and sure enough, the group is converging again with Jason and Tom at the helm. "Before we go see what it's all about, there's something I have to tell you."

"Okay," she says slowly, cautiously.

"Tom approached me right before I came over here. He said he thinks he knows where we are but wants me to go exploring with him tomorrow because I'm familiar with the area."

"That's kinda weird."

"Right? That's what I thought, too, but then I got thinking… He's the air marshall. I would feel safer with him than with anyone else."

She nods. "I agree. There's something about Jason that gives me the creeps."

"Jason?" I tilt my head with confusion. "What's wrong with Jason?"

41

"I don't know. Anyone who talks about God that much weirds me out."

I stare at her, dumbfounded. She mentioned earlier she didn't believe in God, but this Is a whole other level. And not something I cAN get into with her right now. "Anyway, I told Tom I'd go with him, but only if you could go, too." I quickly avert my gaze, worried she might think I'm crazy.

"You did?" Disbelief drips from her words.

"Yeah. I didn't want to leave you behind. I mean, you're really the only person I know and I don't—"

"Thank you." She cuts me off by flinging her arms around my neck, and I stumble back a step before I realize she's hugging me.

I wrap my arms around her and bury my face into her hair, inhaling deeply. She smells of sweat and the ocean. "You're welcome. He said he wants to leave in the morning, before anyone else wakes up, so don't say anything, okay?"

"I won't." She releases me and shoves her hands into her pockets.

"We should head over to the group," I say.

"Yeah." She keeps her head down as we walk back toward the other survivors. I notice she's no longer limping or favoring her bad foot.

Emily stops and stands off to the side, close enough to hear what's going on but not close enough to be a part of the group. I stand beside her.

"I was able to locate the passenger manifest," Tom says. "And the total number of passengers on this flight was a little over four hundred, including the crew. As we can all see, there are just over twenty of us left."

Someone lets out an audible sob.

"We have a lot of lost souls," Jason adds, his tone solemn. "Let us pray for them." Jason bows his head, and slowly, everyone around me does the same.

I lower my head, too, and listen to Jason's comforting words. When he's finished, I add my own amen. When I look up, Emily is staring at me with an expression I can't decipher.

"Should we do something with them?" a tall, blonde girl asks. She can't be much older than I am, and standing next to her is her mirror image. Twins. "The dead people, I mean."

"What?" Emily nearly shouts, which makes me jump. "You can't be serious." The entire group turns to stare at her. "We've barely been here an hour, and you want to do something with the dead bodies?" Her tone is incredulous. "Help is going to come, and when it does, they can deal with the dead."

"Yeah, I agree." I nod.

She turns and gives me a grateful smile. I smile back, and she slips her hand into mine, giving it a firm squeeze. Why is her hand so cold? I lace our fingers and then cover both our hands with my free one in an attempt to warm hers.

"The young lady is right," Tom says. "We leave them be for now. Our priority is getting through the night."

"I agree," Jason says with a nod. "We need to focus on our immediate situation. We don't know where we are. Look around." Jason waves his arms in a semi-circle to make his point. "Dense woods surrounds us on one side. We don't know what kinds of animals are in there. And we don't know what lies beyond those woods."

My stomach drops at the thought of wild animals attacking us while we sleep. Or attempting to eat all those dead people. I close my eyes and will the thought from my mind. Right now, I need to focus on getting through the night. We all do.

"Jason's right. We should probably have people take turns sitting up and keeping watch. Just in case," Tom says.

I nod again. That's actually a really good idea, and I know it will help me sleep tonight. Maybe. I give Emily's hand a squeeze, and she leans closer to me.

"I can take the first watch." A bald man with beefy arms steps forward.

"Thank you. What's your name?" Tom asks.

"Bob."

"Okay, Bob. You and I will take the first watch." Tom nods, then looks out at the crowd.

43

One by one, people step forward to volunteer. I consider doing so, but Emily has a death grip on my hand, and I'm guessing she doesn't want me to. Still, I'm capable of helping, and I feel like I should. I lick my lips, intent to speak up when Tom beats me to it.

"Looks as though we have plenty of help. This should get us through until the sun rises." Tom nods again, and I momentarily envision him as one of those bobblehead dolls. I have to swallow an inappropriate laugh.

"All right, folks." Jason claps. "Let's try to get as much rest as we can. I'm going to hold a prayer service over there by the tree line if anyone wants to join."

The group splits apart. "Want to go to the prayer thing?" I ask Emily.

"No." She disentangles her hand from mine and crosses her arms.

"Okay then." As much as I want the comfort I know Jason's words will bring, I also really want to try to sleep so I can wake up tomorrow, be rescued, and put this whole nightmare behind me. "So, now what?"

She shrugs, then yawns. "I'd really like to try and sleep." Her words are monotone, and her expression is flat. She's not the same girl I'd met at the airport. She's a lot more subdued and quiet. Not that I can blame her.

"Okay," I finally say. "Let's go find a spot near the fire."

We walk around the fire until we find an empty spot. Someone had managed to bring down some seats from the plane, and there's one unoccupied seat left. I nudge Emily toward it. She doesn't argue.

"I'm going to see if I can find a couple of blankets." I hook my thumb over my shoulder in the direction of the heap of supplies. She nods and tucks her knees to her chest.

Surprisingly, I'm able to find two blankets. I grab them and make my way back to Emily, who is curled up in the seat, eyes closed. I gently drape the blanket over her, and then wrap the other blanket around my shoulders like a cape before sitting on the ground next to her chair. The sand is cold, and I shiver. It's going to be a long night.

CHAPTER 9

Emily

I FIDGET WITH THE SEAM *of my jeans.* "Can I please go to the hospital and see Matt?"

Mom makes a noise that sounds an awful lot like a grunt. "You can't be serious. You really think we're going to let you see any of your friends right now?"

"He's in the hospital. I just want to know he's okay."

"Then you can call him when we get home." Mom turns to stare out the passenger's window.

"Dad?" I turn toward him, my gaze pleading. "Please? Ten minutes. I just want to make sure he's okay. And to say goodbye." My breath catches, and my throat burns with unshed tears. I'd given up fighting them about going to Alaska because I know that's a fight I can't win, but they have to let me say goodbye to my friends. I won't stop until they do.

"You have ten minutes. Not a second longer. Understand?" He's using his no-nonsense tone again, and I take the small victory.

"Thank you." I remain silent for the remainder of the drive. Mom won't even look at me, let alone speak. And Dad is hyper-focused on the road, but I don't miss the way his temple throbs with how hard he's clenching his jaw.

Dad pulls into the hospital parking lot. "Ten minutes, Em. You don't want to make me come in after you." His icy tone sends chills down my spine.

"I won't." I'm stunned he's letting me go in alone. I thought for sure they'd go with me, but I don't question him. I hop out of the truck and rush inside. Finding Matt's room is easy, and I walk *in, fully expecting to see his parents and baby sister there. But they aren't there. What I do see, though, stops me cold.*

Ashley is sitting on the edge of the bed, holding Matt's hand. Holding his hand like he always holds mine—fingers interlocked like a boyfriend is supposed to hold his girlfriend's hand. Rage ignites inside of me, and I ball my hands into fists. I always had a sinking feeling Ashley wanted Matt. I no longer have any doubts.

"Emily." Shock clouds Matt's tone, and he jerks his hand from Ashley's. "You're okay."

"Yeah, I'm fine. Looks like you are, too." I glare at Ashley then at him.

Ashley doesn't move off his bed. She flips her hair over her shoulder and gives me a fake, sweet smile. "We were worried about you, Em."

My eyes widen, and my fingernails dig into my palms. "Oh, were you?" I take another step into the room.

An inferno of heat flames inside of me, and I take several deep breaths to calm myself. But the urge to lunge at Ashley is all-consuming, and I force myself to look away from her before I give into my urges and rearrange her face.

Matt looks at me with sad eyes. "Are you okay?"

I unclench my hands and walk closer to him. "I'm fine. I was questioned by the police, though, and I'm sure they'll want to talk to you two as well."

Ashley jumps off the bed, her eyes wild. "What? You gave them our names? Why would you do that?"

"They already had your names. And if you tell them the truth, you won't get into trouble. They're only trying to verify the witness statements they've gotten."

"My parents are going to kill me." Ashley paces at the foot of the bed.

"Do you mind?" I ask, nodding toward Matt. "Could you leave us alone? I don't have a lot of time."

Ashley glares at me with so much vehemence, I actually take a small step back. I've never known anyone who can give a look like she can. Eventually, she leaves with a huff, slamming the door behind her. A snotty retort is on the tip of my tongue, but I don't say it. I came here to see Matt, and I'm running out of time.

I look at Matt and smile before leaning down to kiss him. He turns his head, and my lips land on his cheek. I pull back, my mouth open in shock. My heart sinks. I don't need to ask any questions. The truth is written all over his face.

I awake with a jolt, my heart in my throat. I fight to draw in a deep breath, and it's then I realize my face is wet. Reaching up, I wipe away my tears. I sit up and stretch; my neck is sore, and my limbs are stiff. The memory of last night floods me, and I try to sink further into the small, uncomfortable seat, pulling the blanket tighter around me. That's when I notice Aiden. He's still beside me, huddled up on the sand, shivering. I frown, feeling bad that he slept on the ground all night.

"Aiden," I whisper and lean over to nudge him. "Hey, Aiden."

He shifts but doesn't answer me. Could he really be sound asleep? Every noise kept me awake last night, making it impossible to close my eyes for more than an hour at a time. "Aiden," I try again.

This time, he opens his eyes. "Huh?"

"You're shivering."

"I'm cold," he says in such a matter of fact way I can't help but let out a quick bark of laughter.

I scoot over in the chair and lift the blanket off my body, motioning for him to sit with me. He does, and I drape the blanket back over the both of us. He put his over us, too, but the warmth of two covers and our body heat does nothing to stop his shivers. I snuggle closer to him and rest my head on his shoulder. He doesn't seem to mind. In fact, he puts his arm around me. My stomach flutters with excitement, which is a weird feeling to have in this situation. It feels somehow… wrong.

His body continues to shake, and so I climb onto his lap. He wastes no time wrapping his arms around my waist and squeezing me tight to him. Matt would never let me sit on his lap. But Aiden? He's holding me so close, it's like he enjoys having me close. The thought he might sends a thrill up my spine.

"Getting warm?" I whisper against his neck.

He nods and runs his hands up my back. "Thank you." He makes no move to release me, though, and I don't complain. Being wrapped in his embrace makes it easy to forget where I am and how much trouble we're all in—unlike what happened with Matt after that fateful party.

We sit like that for a while, neither of us speaking. I turn my head enough to stare out at the ocean, waiting for a boat to appear on the horizon or to hear a plane overhead, but other than the sound of the fire crackling and the waves crashing, everything is silent. Does anyone even know we've crashed? Surely, they must.

"How did you end up here?" I ask, unable to handle the silence any longer.

"My plane crashed," he says around a yawn.

I playfully nudge him. "I know that. But why were you on the plane in the first place?"

He sighs heavily, and I worry maybe I crossed the line. Maybe he doesn't want to talk about it. Or maybe it was just rude of me to ask. "I was visiting someone."

"Oh." I chew on my lip. "Your girlfriend?" I mentally smack myself. What is wrong with me? Why can't I just shut up and stop asking so many questions? Then again, this was need-to-know information, especially when I'm currently sitting on his lap and snuggling. I wasn't a cheater like my supposed friend Ashley.

"No, not my girlfriend." I think I feel him pull me closer, but I'm not positive. "I don't have one of those," he says softly. "What about you? Why are you here?"

"Plane crash," I retort without thinking.

Aiden laughs, the motion shakes me lightly, and I smile again. Then, I turn my face back toward him and rest my head on his shoulder. I tell myself it's for the shared body heat, but I know better. I know how my insides are tingling and warm and fluttery, and I can't deny I like Aiden. A lot. It's strange considering I barely know him, but he makes me feel safe, and right now, that's really important.

"The real reason?" he asks.

"I got into trouble with some friends. Went to a party that got out of control. My parents were sending me to Alaska to stay with my grandparents for a while, work on their farm, learn some responsibility." I roll my eyes. "The whole thing is so stupid." I sit up but don't move off his lap. And I don't give him all the details, either, because I'm embarrassed, and I don't want him to think less of me.

"Do you do that a lot? Partying, I mean."

I shrug. "Yeah, I guess. Why?"

He scrunches up his face with an emotion I don't understand.

"What's that look for?" I ask.

"Nothing," he says quickly. "It's just… well, the only parties I go to are hosted by my youth group. I'm guessing that's not the kind of party you go to."

"Oh." I chew on my bottom lip. So, he's religious. I didn't expect that, but it makes sense considering his question about God last night. I hope he's not one of those people who constantly preaches to others. He seems so perfect in every other way; if he turns out to be a Bible thumper, that will suck.

Aiden pulls me back so my head is on his shoulder, and our bodies are once again pressed together. I don't argue. We fall into another comfortable silence, and my mind races with questions. Where are we? How long will it take for someone to find us? Will anyone ever find us? What if they don't? What is beyond all the trees? Does anyone live here? If we are found, will my parents still make me go to Alaska? Or will they be so relieved I'm alive they'll let me come home?

"Hey," I say suddenly. "Weren't we supposed to go explore the island with Tom this morning?"

"Shoot." Aiden's eyes widen. "Yeah, he said he wanted to leave before everyone woke up, but…" He glances around.

A commotion to my left draws my attention. Jason and the other survivors are waking and congregating in the same place they had last night. "Guess it's too late for that now, huh?" I sigh, not wanting to move but knowing we have to. There's always been something about pastors that makes me uncomfortable, but part of me is glad we have a leader who can keep everyone calm, while Tom keeps everyone in line.

"We should probably go join them," Aiden says.

"Yeah, probably," I grumble. "But it's so warm right here. I don't want to get up."

He chuckles, the sound deep and raspy. "I don't want to get up, either, but we need to do something to help get us rescued."

"I know." Flinging the blanket off me, I stand, and a shiver wracks my body. It wasn't this cold when we'd crashed, and I hope the temperatures won't continue to drop. It will make being out here even more unbearable than it already is. I hold my hand out to Aiden. He takes it, and I drag him to his feet.

Yawning, he stretches his arms over his head, causing his shirt to lift slightly, and I see a strip of tanned flesh. His stomach is flat and smooth. I quickly look away so he doesn't catch me staring, and so he doesn't see the blush on my cheeks.

"Sadly, this was not the worst night's sleep I've ever had." He laughs.

"It was for me."

I glance at him. It sucks we met under these circumstances. Under different ones, I could see him as serious boyfriend material. Although, under other circumstances, I probably wouldn't have given him a second look with how wrapped up I was with Matt. I miss him, but I have serious doubts he feels the same. He didn't seem too upset over the fact we broke up. Maybe I should just forget all about him—he's more than likely forgotten about me— and move on.

"You two, c'mon, come join us," Jason shouts at us and waves us over to the group.

CHAPTER 10

Emily

"GOOD MORNING, EVERYONE," JASON SAYS as soon as we come to a stop at the back of the group. "As you're all aware, rescue hasn't arrived yet, but it will." He smiles in a way that makes me narrow my eyes. Who is he trying to convince? All of us or himself?

"According to my calculations, we've been here a little over twelve hours now. The supplies we managed to salvage will last us until help arrives, and I have complete faith that will happen today."

"And what if it doesn't?" someone near the front of the crowd shouts.

Instantly, Jason's smile falters. "Then we should come up with a contingency plan."

I look around at the crowd of survivors. It seems smaller to me than it did last night. To my left, I see two blonde girls. They appear to be about my age. My heart rate quickens. As soon as Jason is done rambling, I'm going to go talk to them. I mean, having Aiden by my side is great, but other than us and those two girls, everyone else is old. My inherent need for socializing is gnawing away at me, and if I can make a couple more friends, why not? Strength in numbers and all that.

"What do you suggest we do?" A heavyset man with a baseball cap on his head steps away from the group and addresses all of us. "Look around. We have water, and we have woods. How are we supposed to survive out here?"

"All right, settle down." Tom steps in, clearly eager to calm everyone before things get out of hand. "No one is suggesting we need to plan to live here permanently, but it's not a bad idea to figure out what we're working with."

The man in the baseball cap gives a curt nod, then rejoins the group.

"We're going to split up in groups and search our surroundings. I suggest maybe four to six people in each group. If we keep 'em small and send everyone in different directions, we can cover more ground," Tom continues. Jason stands beside him, smiling and nodding his agreement. They do work well together. "We're looking for any sort of supplies and food. For all we know, there could be a town close by or people who live here. But the only way to find out is to actually go out there and look. Does anyone have any objections?"

"Yeah, what happens if we're all out hunting for supplies and rescue arrives? Then what?" one of the blonde twins asks.

"We'll leave a group here on the beach," Jason offers. "Those who are injured can stay here, and I'll wait with them. If help arrives, we'll let them know there are more of us. We'll make sure they wait for everyone to return so we can all go home safely."

I nudge Aiden's shoulder and give him a look that says, "Why does Jason get to stay when he's not hurt?"

I have no idea if Aiden gets my non-verbal communication, but he shrugs in response. I roll my eyes and shake my head. I wonder if Jason will tell rescuers there are more of us or if he'll save himself and forget about the rest of us. I would hope a man of God wouldn't do that, but stranger things have happened.

"All right." Tom claps his hands. "Let's break up into groups." He points to me, Aiden, and four other survivors standing nearby. "You six head north."

I'm about to speak up and tell him he has no right to tell me what to do and that I don't want to go anywhere, but then an image of my dad's stern face flashes in my mind, and I keep my mouth shut. I zone out as he splits up the rest of the groups. I don't really need to know who's going with whom and where and how many. I just need to know my group. By the end, Jason is staying behind with three injured survivors, proclaiming he'll pray for us. Aiden takes my hand and leads me toward the others. There's an older man with graying hair who smiles when we approach.

"I'm Larry," he says. "And you guys are?"

"I'm Emily. This is Aiden."

"I'm Sierra, and this is my twin sister, Sienna."

I stare at the twins. There isn't a single difference between the two of them, and I have no idea how anyone can tell them apart. As if that isn't bad enough, they are tall, blonde, and beautiful. They remind me way too much of Ashley, and I rethink my idea about befriending them. The last thing I need is another frenemy who will lie to my face and steal my boyfriend. They're staring at Aiden. He doesn't seem to notice, though, which is a slight comfort.

But Larry notices the twin bombshells. If he doesn't close his mouth soon, he'll end up with a mouthful of bugs. *Ugh.* Could he be any more obvious? Talk about creepy.

Just then, Tom walks over and joins our group. "I'm sure you all know me."

I stare at him, confused. Tom didn't put himself in our group, did he? It's possible I missed it when I zoned out.

"Okay, well, nice to meet everyone," Larry says.

"Can I have everyone's attention again, please?" Jason's booming voice quiets the groups. I have to give him a little credit—he knows how to handle a lot of people and how to keep them from freaking out. "First and foremost, be safe and stick together. We have no idea what's out there. Second, let's plan to all meet back here around noon so we can share what we found. Finally, and most importantly, remember that God is watching over you."

Everyone nods. Everyone except me. I roll my eyes at the whole God part. If God really cares about any of us, we wouldn't be stuck on this island. Still, Tom's plan is decent, and I'm glad I don't have to just sit on the beach all day and wait for help to arrive. I hate sitting still and being bored. At least exploring wherever we are gives me something to do. It'll keep my mind occupied, and it will be nice to spend some more time with Aiden, providing the twins don't try to weasel their way into his face. But I don't trust them one bit.

"I suppose that's our cue to get moving." Larry turns and heads north.

The twins fall into step behind him, with Tom following, and Aiden and I bring up the rear.

CHAPTER 11

Aiden

IT FEELS LIKE WE'VE BEEN walking for days. My feet ache, and the uneven terrain doesn't help. Not to mention we haven't seen a single thing this entire time. Nothing except grass and dirt and trees and ponds of water. Everything looks exactly the same, and if I didn't know better, I'd think we were walking in circles. I haven't even seen so much as a squirrel, which is really disturbing. And now that I'm aware of it, I don't hear any birds, either.

How much further are we going to go before we realize there's nothing out here? I glance around at the rest of my group. Larry is trudging forward, seemingly oblivious to everything around him. Tom's head is on a swivel, like he's trying to see everything at once. Emily is in step beside me, acting like she's actually looking for something useful. Should I speak up and say something, suggest we head back? I don't think any of them will get mad, but Tom gave us explicit instructions. And I bet Jason will be disappointed if we come back with nothing.

When Larry and the twins are far enough ahead of us, I tap Tom on the shoulder. "What happened this morning?" I whisper.

He glances forward then back at me. "I snuck off last night, after everyone was settled. I didn't want to wait."

"Oh." I step over a fallen log and motion to it so Emily doesn't trip. "Did you find anything? Do you know where we are?"

He looks over his shoulder then to his right. *Paranoid much?* "I found a lot, actually. But not here. I'll find you later." And then he picks up his pace, leaving me staring after him. I shake my head, wondering if my initial impression of Tom is right.

Emily sighs. "Any idea what time it is?"

I snap out of my thoughts. "No, but it feels like we've been out here forever."

She chuckles. "I know, right? I'm starving, and my mouth is dry."

I haven't really thought about food or water until she just said something, and now it's dominating my thoughts. My stomach growls. I lick my lips and suppress a groan at the knowledge we'll have to turn around and hike all the way back, too.

"So, what was that about with Tom?" She inclines her head in his direction. "Why'd he ditch us this morning?"

I shrug. "Said he didn't want to wait so he hiked out last night. Alone."

Her eyebrows shoot up, and she clutches my arm. "Are you serious?"

"Yeah. He said he'll catch up with me later." I kick at a stone on the ground. "I mean, I don't know him, but he's acting crazy paranoid."

"Can you blame him?" She holds her arms out then drops them to her sides. "Look around. This place isn't exactly happy."

"I know." We fall silent, both of us looking for something— anything—that will give us a clue as to where we are.

"This silence is killing me," Emily mumbles after several moments.

"So, let's talk." I smile.

"Okay, how old are you?"

I raise an eyebrow and grin. "We're going to play twenty questions?" Not exactly what I had in mind, but if it passes the time, I'm game. And besides, I want to get to know her better.

She playfully shoves me. "No, we're going to play Q and A until we get back to the beach."

"Fair enough. I'm seventeen. You?"

"Seventeen. I know you were born and raised in Alaska." She gives me a sideways glance that I can't quite interpret, but it's fun and a little flirty, so I don't worry about it too much. We slow our pace as the rest of our group moves ahead. "I know you don't have a girlfriend." She laughs. "I assume you're a senior in high school?"

"Yup." I nod. "Would you like to know my SAT scores? They're pretty good, and I'm very proud of them."

She gives me a dirty look. "I didn't take the SATs."

I almost trip over a large rock but catch myself before I do. "You didn't? Why not? Don't you want to go to college?"

Emily shrugs and shoves her hands in her pockets. "College really wasn't that high on my priority list. I was too involved with other things to really care, but now…"

We walk a few steps in silence, and when she doesn't continue, I prod. "Now what?"

"I think I'd like to go to college. God knows I can't keep going on like I have been. My parents will never let me come home."

I frown, remembering what she'd told me about the party and getting into trouble, her parents sending her to stay with her grandparents. If anyone can relate, it's me. I know what it feels like to have parents bail on you, not want you, think you're nothing but a mistake and a problem. I hate that she knows how that feels. I don't wish it on anyone, least of all her.

"Well," I sigh, "it's never too late to change. You can always take the SATs when we get home and apply to colleges."

"Yeah, that's true." She's thoughtful for a moment then says, "Okay, tell me your favorites."

"Favorite what?"

"Everything. Colors. Movies. Food. TV shows. Music. Books."

"Okay, okay." I laugh, interrupting her rambling list of items. "My favorite color is green. I'd eat pizza every night if I could get away with it." As if on cue, my stomach growls again. Man, I hope we get out of here soon. "I like reality shows, *Living in the Wild*, *Rat Race*, *The—*"

"*Search for Love*?" Her eyes widen, and she giggles, pointing at me. "Admit it, you watch *The Search for Love*."

I stick my tongue out at her. "No! I was going to say *The College Life*."

"Uh-huh," she says with disbelief.

I roll my eyes but can't stop from smiling as I try to remember what else was on her list… "Movies. Action. If they don't have a lot of action, I get really bored. I like all sorts of music." I laugh. "Punk rock, alternative, country, even love songs. They get me every time."

"Yet you don't watch *The Search for Love*."

I glance over at her, shaking my head. "What is with you and that show?"

"Nothing." But there's a distinct twinkle in her eye that says otherwise. "So, do you have any hobbies?"

"Wouldn't you like to know?" I wink, fighting back another smile. "I like to crochet hats and booties for newborn babies."

Emily stops abruptly and stares at me, her mouth agape. I can't help myself. I fling my head back and laugh. She scowls and then smacks me.

"Sorry." But I'm really not. "Seriously, though, I like to play soccer. I'm not on a team or anything, but I'll get together with some of the guys and we'll play. Oh, and I've been volunteering at an old age home since I turned fifteen. I help with repairs and lawn maintenance and will sometimes read to the residents. And, of course, there's youth group. I do a lot of stuff with them— camping, hiking, community service. Y'know, the normal stuff. So, what're your favorites?"

She doesn't speak for several moments, and I open my mouth to ask what's wrong but don't get the chance. "Wow. You're like the perfect child or something. You go to church and volunteer and don't party." There's a harshness in her tone that I don't like. "Are you sure you want to be associating with a screw up like me?"

Whoa. Where did all this come from? Does it really bother her that I go to church? "You made a mistake." I grab her arm to turn her to me. "That doesn't make you a screw up."

She grunts and pushes my arm away. "Yeah, right. If you only knew."

"So, enlighten me." I gently bump her shoulder with mine, hating how she's suddenly so upset. Our situation is far from ideal, but that doesn't mean we can't make it bearable, and the best way to do so is to keep things as lighthearted and fun as possible. And I'm going to do whatever it takes to make that happen.

Taking a deep breath, she shakes her head. "Trust me, if you knew, you wouldn't want anything to do with me."

"Try me."

"Don't say I didn't warn you." She keeps her gaze everywhere but on me as she begins to speak. "I'm the type of girl who likes to have fun. Partying, drinking, doing drugs. If others were doing it and it looked fun, I had to do it, too. The last party I went to got really out of hand, but that's a long story for another day." She twists her hands in front of her, clearly very nervous. "Last year, I was literally flunking school because the parties and my friends were the most important thing to me. I got kicked off the cheerleading squad, almost got expelled from school." She kicks at a rock and glances up at the rest of our group, which is several feet ahead of us now. "My parents threatened to send me to Alaska then, too, but I pulled myself together, and I was doing good for a while. But then… Well, I'm here, so I guess that's all you need to know."

I let her words sink in for a few moments before responding. The whole party scene wasn't ever my thing, but I have friends who are a lot like Emily. And I pray for them every day. I'm going to start doing the same for her. I don't know her very well, but she strikes me as smart and compassionate, and I know she can do a lot with her life if only she'd give herself the chance.

"Told ya it was bad," she mutters.

"It could be worse," I say, hoping to cheer her up a bit. "You still have to give me your favorites."

She laughs and shakes her head in disbelief.

"What?" I ask self-consciously.

"I just told you I'm into some really crazy stuff, and all you can think about is knowing my favorites. Most people who know me or hear my story run in the other direction. I'm trouble with a capital T."

"Nah, I don't buy it."

"Then maybe you're not as smart as you think." The corner of her mouth lifts in an almost grin, and I know she's teasing. "Seriously, Aiden, I'm not a good person, and you'll be a lot better off if I'm not in your life."

Wow. She really believes that! I don't know which is sadder—
that she thinks of herself so poorly, or that she believes others think
that way of her. "Well, I'm probably a lot smarter than I think I
am, and I know I'm capable of making my own decisions about
people. And like it or not, you're not getting rid of me so easily."

Finally, she glances at me and smiles gratefully. "Thank you."

I shrug. "No reason to thank me."

"Okay, so my favorites... Music is E-D-M all the way."

"What on earth is E-D-M?"

"Electronic dance music."

"Oh." I'd never heard it called that before, and now I feel a
little stupid for asking.

"I have a weakness for pasta and French fries, but not
together." She makes a disgusted face. "Eww. That would be
gross." She laughs. "Um, I don't really watch a lot of TV, but when
I go to movies, I like romantic comedies. And I'm embarrassed to
admit I don't read all that much and never anything that doesn't
come with CheatSheets."

I chuckle. "I hate CheatSheets."

Emily jerks her head around to glare at me. "How can you
possibly hate CheatSheets? They're the greatest thing since...well,
nothing. There's nothing better than CheatSheets."

"If you say so." I wink again.

We catch up to the rest of the group only to find they've all
stopped. Larry is crouched on the ground, head tilted to the side.
"I think I found something," he says.

It's about time! I seriously didn't think we'd ever find
anything. "What is it?" I ask, trying to get closer.

"A shoe." Larry pulls it from the mud and it's faded, crusted
with dirt.

Tom's gaze darts around nervously. "Could it be from
someone on the plane?"

"Could be. We landed really hard," says one of the twins.

"Yeah, maybe someone was thrown from the plane," says the
other twin. "Maybe we should look for the owner."

Emily rolls her eyes and mumbles something under her breath
that I can't quite make out, but she's probably thinking the same

60

thing I am—the twins, unfortunately, live up to the dumb blonde stereotype.

"I highly doubt that," I say, nodding at the shoe. "It looks really old, as if it's been left here for years. If it was from the plane, we'd see some burn marks or something, right? And it certainly wouldn't have gotten buried and covered with that much dirt overnight."

"Aiden's right," Emily says. "That shoe's been here a long time."

Larry stands. "I agree. All right, let's search this area a bit more, see if we can find anything else, then we'll head back to the beach."

We split up into pairs and search the surrounding area, careful to stay within sight of everyone else. A shoe left in the middle of nowhere like this is really creepy because it only means one thing: someone was here. But who? When? And more importantly, what happened to him or her that a single shoe would be the only evidence left of their time here?

"Tell me you're not a little freaked out," Emily whispers to me.

"Will you be mad if I lie?"

She frowns.

"I'm kidding," I say. "Of course I'm a little freaked out. Who wouldn't be?"

"Hey, guys." Tom taps his watch. "It's getting close to noon. I think we should head back. Has anyone found anything else?" Everyone takes a turn saying no. Tom nods. "All right. Larry, mark the spot where we found the shoe just in case we decide to come back for any reason."

"You got it," Larry says.

I stifle a groan at the thought of trekking all the way back out here again anytime soon. But if rescue doesn't show up... I shake my head. No, that won't happen. We will be rescued today. We have to be.

"All done," Larry announces and wipes his hands on his jeans.

Tom waves his hand to indicate we should follow him, and we all do. Without question. I really hope we have the chance to talk once we get back to the beach, because I have a lot of questions for Air Marshall Tom Davis.

CHAPTER 12

Emily

AS WE MAKE OUR WAY back to the beach, the other groups are converging, too. Jason is waiting for all of us, the injured survivors sitting around him like he's their one-way ticket to meeting God. People approach him and hand over the items they found, including Tom.

After a moment of studying the items, Jason looks up, the smile gone from his face. "Okay, so, we have a shoe, a bucket, a small length of rope, and seeds. That can only mean one thing: there are people living here. Or, there used to be. The only question now is, where are they?"

For once, I totally agree with Jason. The only way those items got here is because there are other people here. And if there are other people here then there must be houses. Food. Water. Cars. Phones. All we have to do now is find these mystery people and get them to help us.

"So now what? Do we send out a search party?" Larry asks.

"We could, yes." Jason nods. "Or we could stay put."

"You can't be serious." Tom raises his voice, startling me. "What good will it do to stay here and do nothing?" He makes his way to the front of the group and stands beside Jason. "Obviously there are people on this island. We need to find them."

A majority of the group nods in agreement, me included.

"Yeah, we've got to do something. For all we know, everyone back home thinks we're dead. What if no one is looking for us?" Larry asks.

My eyes widen, and a pang of fear stabs my gut. I clutch my stomach and double over. I don't know why that thought hasn't crossed my mind before, but Larry could be right. How often do people survive a plane crash? Sweat drips down my back, and I swallow against the dryness in my throat. If the world thinks we're dead, we're on our own.

"You okay?" Aiden gently places his hand on my back.

I nod and straighten. The group is speaking in harsh whispers and accusatory tones. The full reality of our situation is sinking in, and if a decision isn't made soon, things are going to degrade into anarchy. I'm tempted to suggest to Aiden that we break away from the group and fend for ourselves. I don't want to be here when things get out of control. When it becomes life or death, even Jason won't be able to keep everyone in line.

"It's been over seven hours since sunrise," Marjorie says.

I glance at her, surprised to find her standing so close. She'd been nice to me last night when we searched the plane. I'm glad she's okay.

"Nobody has heard or seen a plane flying around. There are no boats on the horizon." Marjorie points toward the ocean. "I hate to be the one to state the obvious, but the longer we're stuck here, the lower the odds become of us being found."

Jason gives a sympathetic smile, and a ball of dread lands in my gut. Tom remains silent. I rub my hands up and down my arms but that does nothing to rid my bones of the chill settling deep within.

"I know you're all scared. So am I. But on the bright side, we've managed to gather enough supplies to last us a couple of days. I suggest we keep the fire burning hot so any planes flying overhead will see it, and we can build an SOS in the sand," Jason says.

"You're right," Tom says.

My jaw drops. Tom—the man who, so far, has been honest and direct and in-charge—now wants to just sit around and wait for help? I can't believe what I'm hearing.

"We should do that, but we also need to be doing more." Tom's voice is firm. "I suggest a small group pack some supplies and hike across the island. I'll lead them."

My breath catches. During our hike, Tom told Aiden he'd found something. What does he know, and why isn't he telling the whole group? I don't know what he's hiding, but I'm going to find out. And if Tom still does need Aiden's help, I'm hopeful I'll be included, too.

"And what if you get lost?" Jason crosses his arms over his chest. "What if rescue arrives while you're gone and we can't find you? What about wild animals?"

I narrow my eyes and tilt my head. Why does it seem like he's trying to stop us from exploring the island? We might find food or shelter or help. Isn't that what we all want?

"I don't know about anyone else, but I'm willing to take my chances if it means we can find help." Tom mimic's Jason's stance, and the two of them have a silent stare-off that quickly becomes uncomfortable.

Unease spreads through my body, and my skin feels like it's on fire. Nothing about this is right. I shift on my feet, and Aiden moves closer. His hand finds mine, and our fingers lock. His hand is warm and comforting in mine, and the tension in my shoulders eases a bit.

"I'm with Tom on this one." Larry gives Jason an apologetic shrug. "I think a group of people should hike the island while the rest of us stay here and keep searching for supplies from the plane. We should be able to find enough stuff to build a raft or…" Larry pauses then smiles brightly. "The life vests under the seats. We can use those with some other things to build a raft sturdy enough to send out a group to look for boats or land." He's way too excited about this idea, and I shift my weight uncomfortably.

"By my calculations, we're somewhere in the Pacific Ocean. Or possibly the Bearing Sea depending on which side of the Aleutian Islands we're on. If we manage to build a raft, how will we guarantee it will hold up? It could get popped and sink, or you could be attacked by a shark. And then what? You're stranded in the ocean." Jason shakes his head, defeated. "I'm sorry, but I think it's too risky."

As much as I want to rally behind Larry's idea, I can't. I wouldn't want to be on a homemade raft. Getting eaten by a shark is a real fear. So is drowning.

"It was just an idea." Larry sighs. "Then I volunteer to join Tom and hike across the island."

Jason hangs his head momentarily, as if he were hoping the plan would change, then looks out at the group. "Does anyone else volunteer to go with them?"

Without hesitation, I raise the hand Aiden is holding, bringing his into the air with mine. He gives me a sideways glance and a curt nod. Marjorie raises her hand, too, and so do two other men whose names I don't know. Aiden and I join them off to the side, away from the main group.

"Anyone else?" Jason asks.

I look around the group, waiting for a few more hands to go in the air, but none do. That's fine with me. Although, the more people who volunteer, the safer it might be. There's always strength in numbers. But knowing Aiden will be with me eases some of my fears.

"Are you absolutely sure about this, Tom?" Jason's tone is pleading. "You have no idea what you'll encounter out there."

"I know." Tom nods. "But we have to do *something*. These supplies won't last more than a couple days…" He glances at the mass of hungry, scared faces, his gaze landing squarely on me for a long moment. I want to look away, but I can't. He gives me a faint smile, then returns his attention to Jason. "We're going to be fine."

"Okay." Jason pats Tom on the shoulder in what I guess is meant to be a comforting show of camaraderie. "The rest of us will stay here and wait for rescue. In the meantime, we're going to ration what food and water we have so that we can—"

"Rations? I have a two-year-old boy. How will I feed him?" another woman asks as a frightened toddler clings to her leg.

"I'm diabetic. I need to eat to keep my blood sugar up." A frail, older gentleman takes a step forward and stumbles. Larry steadies the man.

Jason sticks his hand in the air, demanding silence. "You all have valid concerns, which is why I'd like to make another suggestion." He directs his attention to the those of us who volunteered to explore the island. "Stay here with us tonight and help us gather more supplies and food. Then, first thing tomorrow, you can head out. This way, if help arrives tonight, you'll all be here, and if it doesn't, then we can rest knowing we have a plan in place."

Tom looks to us for an answer. I really don't want to sit on the beach for another night, but Jason makes some valid points.

"Yes," I say, and eventually, the rest of the group agrees, too.

"All right, we'll stay for the night, but we're leaving as soon as the sun's up tomorrow," Tom says.

Where have I heard that before? A knot forms in my stomach. What if he takes off and leaves without us like he did last night? My heart races, and I shift nervously on my feet. I don't want to be left behind again.

"Fantastic." Jason claps his hands and beams a vibrant smile. "We managed to collect a lot of stuff last night, but it was dark, and I know we didn't get everything. A lot of seats and blankets were thrown out of the plane when it crashed. We can start by gathering those and building a sleeping area over by the fire." He points to the massive pile of wood burning several yards away from the wreckage. "I assume I don't need to say that the elderly, women, and children all get the seats first?"

No one objects, and a strange sense of pride washes through me at the realization this group of strangers is working together so well, that despite not knowing each other and being scared, everyone is willing to help one another.

"Does anyone here have any survival training or know anything about edible plants? There has to be some berries or fruit or something we can eat," Jason says.

No one speaks up, and a little bit of the hope I have slips away. Things are so much worse than I thought. I'm eager to get away from everyone. It's becoming harder and harder to breathe. I pull my hand from Aiden's and flex my fingers. He tries to catch my gaze, but I refuse to meet his eyes.

"Okay, keep a look out as you're searching for stuff. Hopefully, we can find some sort of fruit tree. While the groups were out searching this morning, we did find several large pots that we can use to boil water from the ocean. Mark is an engineer, and he's going to build what we need to make the water drinkable." Jason nods to a tall, lanky man in his late thirties. Mark waves to the group.

"Are there any other questions or concerns?" Jason asks and is met with silence. "All right then. Let's get to it. May God protect you."

The group disperses. I've never been the type of person who likes to be told what to do, and having a complete stranger dictate my every move isn't settling well. My entire body itches, and I can't get rid of the constant nausea rumbling in my stomach.

"Hey, guys," Tom whispers and motions for his small group to gather round. "I don't know about the rest of you, but I don't have a good feeling about this island."

"Neither do I," Aiden says.

"Wait. What?" I jerk my head toward Aiden. "What do you mean?"

Tom and Aiden share a look that unsettles me. "I don't want to make assumptions until I know more, but has anyone else noticed the severe lack of wildlife around here? Not so much as a mosquito."

I swallow the sudden lump in my throat. I hadn't noticed—until now. But he's right. There haven't been birds or bugs of any kind. Not even pesky flies. "So what does this mean?"

"I'm not sure." Tom glances around as if, once again, he's worried someone might be eavesdropping. "But we have to explore this island. We need to know where we are."

Larry nods his agreement. So does Aiden.

"Okay, so what should we do now?" I ask, knowing I won't be able to sit around and do nothing. Not now.

"I suggest we gather our supplies now, so we can easily get to them tomorrow morning."

"That's a good idea," I say. "I noticed a large, hallowed log when we were out walking this morning. We could hide everything there for safekeeping."

"Perfect." Tom glances over his shoulder, and I follow his gaze. Mark, the engineer, is staring at us, and a shiver wiggles up my spine. "Okay, we'll meet up later." Tom turns on his heel and walks away.

I inhale sharply, the pain in my chest like razor blades. "Tom! Wait up!" I jog after him.

When he stops, there's a mix of compassion and annoyance etched across his face.

I ignore it. He's not going to get away without giving me some answers. "You're not going to ditch us again, are you?" I cross my arms.

Shock crosses his expression, but it's gone as quickly as it appears. "I didn't ditch you. I was investigating a hunch."

Clearly, he doesn't know what it means to ditch someone. "And what did you find?"

He sighs and rubs his forehead. "I told Aiden I would talk to him later, and I will. But now's not the time. We have an audience." He nods over my shoulder.

I turn to find Mark staring at us. Again. What is up with that guy? Does he want to be part of our group? If so, why didn't he volunteer? And when I turn back, Tom is gone. Frustration bubbles up inside of me, and I head toward the water, needing a moment to myself.

"Emily!" Aiden calls after me.

I ignore him. The salty, cool air and the monotonous splash of the waves calms me. My breaths come easier, and the pain in my chest eases. I tilt my head back and bask in the sun's rays. Closing my eyes, I clear my mind.

Everything's going to be okay. We're going to get rescued, and then I'm going home. *Everything's going to be okay.* I repeat the phrase over and over, hoping I'll start to believe it.

CHAPTER 13

Aiden

BY THE TIME EVERYONE FINISHES collecting supplies, the sun is almost down. Jason has set up camp around the fire and is handing out rations of food and water to the survivors. Emily is sitting on a plane seat near Tom, Larry, and the twins. She's barely spoken to me since we got back from our hike this morning. Is she mad because I held her hand during Jason's assembly? I don't know why she would be. Then again, I know very little about girls. I've only ever had one serious girlfriend, and that relationship only lasted six months.

My entire body aches, and it takes all of my energy just to put one foot in front of the other. I trudge over to Jason, take a ration—which is a sandwich, a tiny bag of pretzels, and an apple all wrapped up in an aluminum tray—and then make my way toward Emily. She looks up and smiles.

I nod to the spot next to her. "Is that seat taken?"

She scoots over. "It is now."

I smile and sit beside her. I peel the foil back and open the pretzels. What's here is a snack, not a meal. My stomach growls, and I know this won't fill me. Hopefully, it will ease the hunger pains. Emily turns her head away from me and speaks to the twins. I finish my food quickly and then sip at the bottle of water. I overhear snippets of their conversation and learn the twins have decided to join our exploration group.

"Did I do something to upset you?" I ask her.

She jerks her head to look at me, her eyes wide. "What? No. Why?"

I shrug. "You haven't spoken to me at all today, and you seem to be avoiding me." I fidget with the cap of my water bottle.

"I have a lot on my mind. That's all."

"Oh. Okay." I nod. I have a lot on my mind, too, but that's only more reason I want to spend time with her. Being with her, talking with her—it keeps my mind off everything else.

She nudges me with her shoulder. "Do you want to take a walk?"

"Yes," I say much too quickly, and she smiles. I stand, toss my trash onto the fire, and then fall in step beside Emily. We're quiet for a while, and the further away we get from the camp, the darker it gets. The hairs on my arms stand on edge, and a shiver works through me. The temperature is dropping rapidly.

"Did you find your suitcase?" she asks me.

"No. Did you?"

She nods. "Yeah. While we were gone this morning, Jason and the others retrieved all the luggage they could find and piled it up. You should go through it, see if you can find your stuff. That's how I found this." She holds out her arms to show off the sweater she's wearing.

"I'll do that when we get back. Thanks for the tip."

"Sure." She shoves her hands in her pockets and stares at the ground as we walk.

I wonder what she's thinking but am too afraid to ask. I want to hold her hand or put my arm around her. Something to feel closer to her. But after the way she's been acting today, I don't want to do anything else that might push her away.

"Do you think rescue is coming?" She looks at me with big, sad eyes. "And don't lie to me."

I take a deep breath. "I think it's weird that rescue hasn't shown up yet."

"You didn't answer my question."

My stomach knots. I don't want to answer her question because I know she really doesn't want the truth. And I don't want to say it aloud, either, because then it all becomes real. Hope is the only thing we have left right now, and if I destroy that, what happens?

"Aiden?" Her soft, hesitant voice tugs at my heart.

I sigh and shake my head. "No, I don't think rescue is coming."

She lets out a small gasp.

"But I don't think we're stuck here. I think we're going to find a way off this island." I try to keep my voice steady and firm, but I'm not sure she believes me. "And I think Tom knows more than he's saying. If we stick with him, we'll be okay."

She nods but doesn't say anything.

I'm such an idiot. I should've just lied to her. Frowning, I kick at the sand and refrain from groaning. My father is always telling me I'm too honest at times. I've never realized that could be a bad thing—until now. Lying goes against everything I believe, though, everything I've been taught in church. But is it wrong to lie if you're doing it for the right reasons, like giving someone hope in an otherwise hopeless situation?

"We'll go with Tom and the others tomorrow. I'm sure we'll find something," I say.

"Yeah, maybe." She stops and turns to stare at the ocean.

I stop beside her and cross my arms over my chest so I won't reach for her hand, even though I want to.

"Do you believe we were sent here for a reason? Like, the whole ordeal with the party to my parents sending me to my grandparents to the plane crash to this unknown land to meeting you. Do you think that was all planned? Or do you believe we just have terrible luck?"

"I don't really believe in luck," I say cautiously. "I think He"—I point to the sky to indicate I'm talking about a higher power—"knows exactly what He's doing and where we're supposed to be. So, yes, I think it was all planned. God put us here for a reason."

"And what reason is that, huh? So we can all die here?" she snaps.

I tilt my head, unsure how to answer. "Maybe." I shrug. "I don't know, but I do know that we're going to be okay."

"How can you know that?" Frustration drips from her words. "How can you so blindly believe in something—someone—you've never even seen?"

I sigh. Is she really interested in learning more about God, or is she just lashing out because she's scared? I'm guessing it's the latter. "Are you all right, Emily?" She's been acting so strange all day. Granted, being here isn't easy, but she acts like she's stuck in her head and can't get out.

"Being stuck here gives you a lot of time to think. That's why I want to go on the hike tomorrow. I need to get away from this beach," she says. Then, she hangs her head. "Matt and I used to go to the beach together a lot."

I frown. "I'm sorry." I want to pry and find out more about this Matt guy, but I don't think she really wants to talk about him. And honestly, I'm not sure I want to hear about the guy who she still so obviously cares for. How deep do those feelings go?

"So? Are you going to answer my question?"

I offer a faint smile. "I'm not sure I can answer it. I mean, how do you explain something that you just believe in with your whole heart?" I take a deep breath, hoping I can say what I want to without tripping over my words. "I've always believed that everything happens for a reason. Including meeting you and the crash. Although, I can't even begin to fathom why God chose this situation for all of us."

"That is the big question, isn't it? Why? Why a plane crash? Why us? Why did we survive and so many others didn't?"

"I don't know." I sigh. "Maybe He's just not done with us yet. Maybe we still have a purpose. Lessons to learn."

"I wish I was as confident as you are." She finally looks at me.

The sight of her smile makes my breath catch, and I move closer. "You're stronger than you know."

"I suppose—" Before she can finish, a deafening boom sounds behind us. The ground shakes, and the sky lights up with a vibrant burst of flames. A wave of heat blasts past us. Emily covers her ears and drops to her knees, head down. She screams.

I instinctively cover her body with mine and glance over my shoulder. "Oh, my gosh!"

74

"What?" She bucks me off her and stands.

"The plane." I point to what is left of the rear part of the plane. "It's on fire. I think it exploded." Survivors run around, screaming and grabbing at the supplies, moving them out of the way of the fire.

Her eyes widen. "What happened?"

"I don't know." I take off on a dead run toward camp, and she follows.

"Aiden!" She grabs my arm. "Those people there are bodies in that part of the plane."

I stop short, and my heart races. Bile rises up my throat, and I turn away, not wanting to throw up in front of her. I put my head between my legs and pull in several long, deep breaths. After a moment, the nausea passes, and I straighten.

"Okay?" she asks.

I nod, and we take off again toward camp. The screaming and shouting and cries echo through the night, making the entire scene even more horrific. The stench of burning flesh fills the air.

"Grab whatever you can and get it out of the way," Tom shouts as soon as we're in earshot.

"What happened?" I shout over all the noise.

He shrugs. "I don't know. We were just sitting there, and then it went up in flames. Three people were injured. C'mon, grab something and help." He waves at us to follow.

"No! My husband's in there!" A woman runs at the flames. One of the other survivors grabs her around the waist, but she breaks free and rushes into the burning plane. Then she lets out a high pitched scream.

I glance at Emily. Her hands are shaking, and tears pool in her eyes. Her lips tremble as she stares at the woman, but she's not looking away.

"Emily." I take hold of her shoulders and look into her eyes. "Go back to where we just were on the beach. You don't have to help."

She shakes her head. "No, I want to help."

"Okay, but—" A crack of thunder cuts through the sky, followed by a torrential downpour. I'm soaked within seconds, and so is Emily.

She buries her face in her hands, and her shoulders shake uncontrollably. "I want to go home," she wails.

I wrap my arms around her and pull her to my chest. She doesn't make any effort to move away, and I stand there holding her in the rain, watching as our only source of heat and light is doused to nothingness. I send up a desperate prayer, begging God to help us out of this situation.

CHAPTER 14

Emily

IT TAKES ALMOST AN HOUR for the rain to stop, and when it does, I'm soaked and frozen to my core. I can't stop shivering, and my teeth chatter so violently they ache. Standing near the now extinguished fire, I wrap my arms around myself in a feeble attempt to regain some warmth and look around. Everyone is as wet as I am, and they all look just as miserable, too.

Tom stops near me, a sympathetic expression tugging at his features. "Emily?"

His voice pulls me from the trance I've been in. Blinking, I focus my gaze on him. "Yeah?"

"Where's Aiden?"

I shrug. "I don't know. He said he was going to help…"

Tom nods. "Are you okay?"

I laugh. It's a wholly inappropriate reaction, I know that, but I can't seem to stop myself. Am I okay? No. I'm not. I don't think I'll ever be okay again, at least not as long as I'm stuck on this horrible island.

With a sigh, Tom takes off his waterproof jacket and drapes it around my shoulders. His hands rest on my upper arms. "Sit." He guides me down until I'm sitting in one of the plane seats, then he kneels in front of me. "You're going to be okay, Emily. We all are."

I nod like my head is on autopilot.

"Stay here. I'll find Aiden to come sit with you." He stands.

"Thank you," I mumble, but he's already gone. Why is he being so nice to me? What did I do to deserve such kindness? My parents aren't even this nice to me.

A moment later, Aiden is crouched in front of me. I don't give him the chance to say anything before I fling my arms around him. He hugs me back, and it's exactly what I need right now. The weight of everything crashes down on me, and I'm powerless to stop the onslaught of tears.

Everyone who can helps us probably thinks we're dead.

Rescue isn't coming.

I'll never see my parents again. Or my brother. Or my friends.

"Shh, it's okay," Aiden whispers.

I wish I believed him. I wish I had his faith so I could blindly believe God will protect me. But I don't. And He won't. If He was real, if He truly cared, we wouldn't be stuck here, suffering.

"Can we have everyone's attention, please?" Tom's booming voice cuts my pity-party short.

I pull away from Aiden and wipe the tears from my face, sniffling. Aiden cups my cheek with his large, warm palm. "Emily." His tone is as pained as the look in his eyes.

"C'mon." I stand. "We better go see what Tom wants." I step around Aiden and shuffle through the wet sand toward the converging group. Guilt stabs at me for not offering Aiden the same comfort he just gave me, but I'm emotionally spent.

Aiden steps up beside me, and silently, he slips his hand into mine. Lips trembling, I give him a small smile and squeeze his hand. Somehow, I'll pay him back for everything he's done for me.

"Did anyone see what happened?" Tom asks.

A chorus of no's and simultaneous head shakes ripple through the group.

He rubs the back of his neck. The stress of the past couple days is displayed on his face like a neon sign. My heart aches for him. For all of us.

"Okay, well, we need to clean up the damage," Tom says.

My eyebrows shoot up to my hairline. The "damage" is nothing more than twisted metal and… charred bodies. I gag. He can't seriously be suggesting what I think he is. Is he?

"You're not saying we have to…" Larry falters, then clears his throat. "Move the bodies?"

"That's exactly what I'm saying." Tom's tone isn't quite as commanding as it was a second ago. "As unpleasant as it is, we can't just leave them scattered on the ground."

Jason steps up and places a hand on Tom's shoulder. "Tom's right. These poor souls need to be laid to rest."

"You want to bury them?" My voice sounds oddly detached from my body.

"What? No. No way," says the man standing right next to me.

"What do you suggest, then?" Marjorie asks, arms crossed. "Would you rather burn them some more?"

The group erupts in shouts and protests. Some people start shoving each other, some punches are thrown. I yank on Aiden's hand, and we move out of the way. "This is crazy," I mutter.

"Okay, people, let's settle down," Jason says, but no one is listening to him.

"I'm not burying anyone," a man hollers.

"Burning them is sadistic," someone else shouts. "How dare you even suggest that!"

"Well, we have to do something," Marjorie argues.

"Yeah," Larry jumps in. "If we leave them, we're asking for wild animals to attack."

"If an animal was going to attack, they would have already," the man from earlier says. "Stop being stupid."

"I'm stupid?" Larry points at himself. "Let me show you how stupid I am." He balls his hands into fists and raises them, preparing to fight.

Marjorie plants herself between Larry and the other man. "You want to talk about being stupid. What do you think will happen if we just leave all these dead bodies lying around? They're going to start to smell. Is that what you want?"

I watch in utter horror as our once considerate group of survivors turns on each other.

"Enough!" Tom's voice echoes around us. Everyone stops, but the tension is still thick enough to choke on. "Burning a body is illegal. If we do anything, we bury them, and we keep a record of who is buried where so when rescue does arrive, we can properly report the deceased to the authorities." There's so much passion and vehemence in his tone, I wonder if he lost someone in this crash.

"Look," Jason says, ignoring Tom's statement. "I know many of you have lost loved ones, and they mean a great deal to you, but Marjorie is right. The bodies will begin to smell, worse than they already do, and for our own safety, we don't want to invite wild animals into this camp." He pauses, and his expression softens. "I vote for a proper burial." He raises his hand as if taking a vote.

The very last thing I want to do is dig holes and bury dead bodies, but I also don't want to walk around them every time I move. But I'm only seventeen. I shouldn't have to make these decisions. The threat of fresh tears burns my throat.

"Exactly how are we supposed to dig graves without any shovels?" Mark asks.

Silence descends as people consider his question.

"We don't," Tom says.

"Tom," Jason says, confusion and hurt dripping from his tone.

"We move them out of the way, and *when* help arrives, they can decide what to do with the dead."

"Move them where?" Jason asks.

"Over there." Tom points to where the remnants of the rear of the plane sit. "We can pile them under that section of the tail. It will provide some cover."

"But it won't help with the smell," Marjorie says.

I glare at her, wishing she'd just shut up already. Despite having valid arguments, I don't want to hear them. I don't want to even think about them.

"We can build makeshift walls around them, and then we'll cut up the life rafts and use them as a tarp," Mark suggests. "It's far from perfect, but it can work until help arrives."

The group is once again silent, but no one voices any objections.

"Okay then," Tom says. "Mark, you can lead a team to build the structure. Marjorie, can you get a group together and get that fire going again?"

Marjorie nods.

"Everyone else who is physically capable, let's get these bodies moved," Tom says.

"When the task is done, we'll pray for these lost souls," Jason says solemnly. "They're in God's hands now."

As soon as the work begins, so does the rain—again. It's going to be a long night.

81

CHAPTER 15

Aiden

A SHRILL SCREAM PIERCES THROUGH the rain. I bolt upright, my heart in my throat. Emily is thrashing in her seat, and that's when I realize she's the one screaming. "Emily." I shake her. At least, I hope I do, but my hands are trembling so badly, I don't know if it's her or me shaking. "Emily, wake up. You're having a nightmare."

Before I know it, Tom is by my side, crouching in front of Emily. "Hey, kiddo, wake up."

Finally, Emily's eyes snap open, and she stands abruptly, her movements jerky and frantic. "What? Where I am?" She claws at her neck. "It burns. I can't breathe. I can't breathe."

"Easy, Emily." Tom is on his feet, his hands on her shoulders. "You're okay. Hey, look at me."

Her eyes focus on him, then dart toward me. There's so much fear in her gaze it makes my chest seize. "What…?" She blinks rapidly. "I-I'm sorry. I was dreaming."

"You were screaming," I say. My voice cracks. "Are you okay?"

She nods. "Yeah." She smooths the hair back from her face, and that's when I notice the tears streaming down her face.

Tom slips his hands from her shoulders. "If you need me, I'll be right over there, okay?" He points to where he'd been sleeping.

"Thanks."

He gives me a knowing look and then heads back to his makeshift bed. Emily returns to her seat, her blanket wrapped around her tightly. Not that it does any good. Everything is soaked from the nonstop rain. I sit beside her. "Are you sure you're okay?"

But even as I ask that question, I know the answer. She's not. She's terrified and shaking. I put my arm around her, and she rests her head on my shoulder, tucking her feet under her and curling into my side. "Do you want to talk about it?" I ask quietly.

She's silent for so long I think she might have fallen back asleep, but then she speaks. Her voice is low and weak. "I was dreaming about the party. A kid died there. But not any kid. Johnny Foster. He was my first boyfriend."

I pull her closer. "Emily, I'm so sorry." I know firsthand how it feels to lose someone close to you, and it's the worst thing in the world.

"I didn't actually see it happen, but I heard it. I was in the other room, drunk and high. The police showed up soon after and tossed gas bombs into the house. It burned like nothing I've ever felt before. I couldn't see. I couldn't breathe." Her words hitch on a sob.

Now it makes sense why she was screaming about not being able to breathe.

"And Matt, he left me there."

"He left you?" Anger burns in my gut, and I grit my teeth.

The only answer I get is the rise and fall of her shoulders. She's crying. I momentarily close my eyes and take a deep, calming breath. I cannot fathom how or why her boyfriend could leave her like that. Although, I'm not in any position to judge, because hadn't I done the same thing to my cousin, Ed?

"Aiden?" She says my name so softly, like a prayer, that I almost don't hear her.

"Yeah?"

"Thank you for being here with me."

I rest my cheek on top of her head. "I can't imagine being anywhere else."

"I can."

I can't help but laugh. "Well, yeah, but even if we were somewhere better than here, it wouldn't be better because you wouldn't be there."

She drapes her arm across my stomach and gives me a squeeze. "That's a really nice thing to say."

"Tell me about the party," I urge. My mother always taught me that it helps ease the burden if you talk about it, and I'm hoping it will help Emily.

She takes a deep breath. "It was supposed to be like every other party. Matt picked me up, and we drove to Lynn's house. The party was in full force when we got there, and the first thing I did was go for the beer. After a couple drinks, Matt convinced me to smoke some pot."

I cringe at how she talks so casually about drinking and doing drugs. Was she addicted? Is she going through withdrawals being stuck here? I pray that's not the case.

"We—me, Matt, and all of my friends—were dancing and singing along to the music. I was so drunk and high. I didn't care about anything but having fun." She snorts. "Someone decided to play with water balloons, which quickly turned into people shaking up beer and spraying it around. At first, it was great. Lynn didn't think so, but I did."

I listen intently, afraid to move or speak for fear she might stop talking.

Emily sighs. "It was shortly after that when I heard shouts from the other room. There were a couple of guys screaming and shoving at each other. People were chanting at them to fight, and I joined in." She curls tighter against me, almost as if she's trying to make herself smaller.

"And they started to fight," she continues, her tone hollow. "Bottles were being smashed. Furniture was tipped over. Matt and I were attempting to leave when someone screamed that the guy was dead." Her voice cracks on that last word. "That's when the police showed up."

I close my eyes, unable to imagine willingly being in that type of situation.

"So, yeah, that's how I ended up on that stupid plane." She pulls the blanket up to her face. "Now you know why I'm such a rotten person. I knew things were out of control, and I didn't do anything to stop it."

"Hey." I put my finger under her chin and tilt her head up so she's looking at me. "You made a mistake. We've all made mistakes, but it's how we choose to act afterward that matters."

She shakes her head and buries her face against my shoulder. "You don't understand. You've never done anything like that, something that gives you nightmares and makes you question who you are."

"You're wrong," I say emphatically, and I know I have to share my story, too. I think hearing it will help Emily more than me simply listening to her story. She needs to know I'm not perfect, that I've made mistakes, too.

"I do know," I continue. "When I was younger, I had this cousin. Edward. Everyone called him Eddie." Just saying his name makes my heart hurt. I lick my lips and force myself to continue. "We were the same age, and we were always together. We were practically brothers, only we didn't fight like siblings." I sigh. "But we were polar opposites."

"You keep talking about him in past tense. What happened?" Emily asks.

I gulp. Other than the therapist my mother made me see, I've never told this story to anyone else. "There was this kid, Chad, and he's also our age. We all went to the same school."

Emily doesn't say anything, but I know she's listening, so I continue.

"Chad's your typical jock: good-looking, played almost every sport, liked to party and have a good time. One night, Eddie and I went to this party. I don't know why we even went. It wasn't what we normally liked to do." If I could go back in time, I never would've gone to that party. "When we got there, the music was blaring, and there was alcohol everywhere. Eddie loved it. Me, not so much, but we're there together, and so I stuck it out for his sake. He starts dancing, trying to have a good time—and we did for a couple of hours. I wasn't drinking, but Eddie was."

A wave of nausea hits me, and I swallow it back. Emily had the courage to share her story, now it's my turn.

"Then Chad came along. He asked what Eddie was doing there when nobody but me liked him, and that he wasn't wanted there. Chad told him to get lost. Eddie, having had one too many drinks, shoved Chad. Eddie was only five foot two and scrawny. Chad was twice his size in height and weight."

"What was Chad's problem with Eddie? I mean, there are plenty of people I don't like, but a party is a party, y'know? If I don't like someone, I usually just ignore them."

"Chad and Eddie had never liked each other. But it got worse when Chad stole Eddie's girlfriend." I frown. Eddie had loved that girl something fierce, and she'd left him without a second thought. I'll never forget how heartbroken he was, how he refused to leave his room for weeks after the break-up. Pushing those thoughts away, I continue.

"Eddie starts screaming about how Chad stole the only good thing that has ever happened to him. Chad got up, smiled, walked over to Eddie's ex-girlfriend and kissed her. I don't think I'll ever forget the look on Eddie's face. But that's not even the worst of it. Chad, being the jerk he is, announces to the party that the only reason Amanda was with Eddie was because she felt sorry for him and that he was nothing but a charity case."

I swallow hard, knowing I can't stop now but wanting to do just that. "Eddie charged at Chad so fast, I couldn't stop him. And, of course, all of Chad's buddies were there. They gang up on Eddie and beat the snot out of him." I close my eyes against the image of Eddie lying there, beaten and bloody.

"Oh my gosh," Emily whispers. "They killed him?"

"No." A very large, selfish part of me wishes they had because then maybe I wouldn't feel so guilty all the time. "I just stood there, Emily. I didn't intervene. I didn't do anything to help him."

She sits up and looks at me. "There wasn't anything you could have done. You were outnumbered."

"Yeah." Logically, I know that, but it doesn't make it any better. It doesn't erase my betrayal.

"So, what happened?"

"Someone—not me, because I was still shocked and too scared to interfere—took Eddie home. I don't even know who. I was going to follow, but I was too embarrassed to show my face, to look him in the eye and apologize for being a coward, for not being there for him when he needed me the most. I wanted to tell him I was there for him, but I knew that was a lie. If I couldn't stand up for him against someone like Chad, how could I ever have his back any other time?"

Tears burn my eyes, and I blink them back. What will Emily think of me after I tell her this? Will she still look at me the same? Or will she be scared and want nothing to do with me? Will she trust me? I swallow my fear and keep going.

"The next day, Eddie wasn't in school. I thought he was just recuperating and, in no time, he'd be up and running again. But I waited by his locker the day after, and he wasn't there. Three days passed, and no sign of him in school. He hadn't called me, and he wasn't returning any of my calls, either. I started to get really worried. So, I went to his house."

My heart is pounding, and I'm sweating. I feel dizzy, like my world is about to twirl over and collapse with me in it. I want to rip out my hair, strand by strand.

"It's okay." Emily moves her hand up to my chest, her palm resting over my heart. Can she feel how hard it's racing? "Keep going."

"When his mother answered the door, I knew something was horribly wrong. She's never home during the day because of her job. Her face was red and puffy, and she was full-on sobbing. She kept asking me if I knew, and I had no idea what she was talking about. And then she said four words that I will never forget: 'Aiden, Eddie killed himself.'"

"No," Emily gasped.

All I can do is nod.

She puts her arms around my neck and hugs me. "I'm so sorry, Aiden."

"It was my fault," I whisper.

"No." She takes my face into her hands. "It is not your fault. You didn't know he was going to kill himself."

I stare into her eyes for a long moment. "The guilt consumes me twenty-four seven. I can never get away from it, but I made a promise to Eddie. I promised him that I would never mess up like that again, that I will always defend and protect those I love and care about. It will never bring him back, but I feel like he's looking down on me and seeing how hard I'm trying to be better, to learn from what I'd done."

"I think he'd be proud of you." She smiles.

Without thinking, I lean forward and press a quick kiss to her lips.

CHAPTER 16

Emily

THE RAYS OF THE BRIGHT morning sun shine across my face and jolt me from my sleep. Thank God the rain finally stopped. I yawn and stretch my arms over my head. "Ouch." My neck is stiff, and my back is sore. Slowly, I stand and stretch a bit more, then I glance around. "Aiden?" His spot next to me is empty and so is the ground around our chair. "Aiden?" I spin around and look for him.

My gaze darts back and forth across the camp. Where is everyone? How come no one is still sleeping? Did they leave without me? There's no way Aiden would leave without me, right? *Oh, God. Please tell me I'm right.*

Wait. I pinch my arm to make sure I'm not dreaming again. "Ow." I rub my arm and look around again, panic clutching my chest. Then I remember that a group of us are supposed to head out at sunrise to hike the island. I tilt my head up. The sun is high in the sky. My stomach rolls. Did I oversleep and miss them leaving? Why didn't anyone wake me?

"Emily. I was just coming to see if you were awake yet." Aiden jogs out of the tree line, a smile on his face. How can he smile after what happened last night? But I can't deny I'm happy to see him. If it hadn't been for him, I would've been awake all night, unable to fall asleep again.

"I thought everyone left me." I phrase it as a joke, but deep down, it's not. I stare at his handsome face, and my cheeks flush at the memory of his much too short kiss last night. Will he try again? I want him to.

"Most of the group is meeting with Jason. I was with Tom and the others. He thinks one of the survivors set the plane on fire last night."

"What?" I shout then lower my voice. "Why would anyone do that?"

Aiden shrugs.

I cup my hand over my mouth and shake my head. "You don't believe that, do you?"

"I don't know."

"So, what's going on now? Are we still hiking the island?" I fold the blanket I slept with—although I don't know why when it's still damp—and set it neatly on my chair.

Aiden reaches around me to grab the blanket, and he shoves it into one of the backpacks we salvaged. "You're going to want to bring this with you. Tom says to pack as much as we can carry."

I nod. "Okay," I say, drawing out the word. "Why? Aren't we coming back?"

"I think so, but it might not be for a couple of days."

Dread coils in my chest. "A couple of days?"

He nods. "It'll be fine. I promise I won't leave your side, okay?"

"Okay."

"Good." He smiles. "Then let's get packed. Tom wants us to hear what Jason has to say before we head out."

I shove clothes, socks, an extra pair of shoes, and my hairbrush into my bag. "What about food and water?"

"Tom's got that all packed and ready to go. We'll take turns carrying the extra bags."

Wow. Tom's thought of everything. No wonder he's such a strong leader.

I sling the backpack over my shoulder. "Okay, I think I'm ready."

"Let's go then."

"Aiden, wait. Before we go." I clear my throat and step up to him. "Thank you for last night. For waking me up and listening to me and telling me your story." I take his hand and give a gentle squeeze. "And for sitting with me all night." I look away, embarrassed.

He turns my face back to his and smiles warmly. "You don't have to thank me for that. In fact, if I'm being honest, I really liked having you fall asleep in my arms."

My face heats, and I want to look away again, but I can't. His gaze holds me mesmerized. "I liked that, too," I whisper.

With a wink, he laces his fingers through mine and leads the way down the beach to where Jason stands in the center of the survivors. We come to a stop at the back of the group.

"I was sure rescue would arrive last night, but alas, it did not. Which can only mean one thing. God isn't ready for us to go home yet," Jason says.

I roll my eyes. God has nothing to do with this. If He did, we wouldn't be here in the first place. Why can't anyone but me see that? And I really wish Jason would stop preaching and start focusing on the situation at hand. We need plans and action. Not speculation and faith.

"I know we're all still hoping for rescue, and we should. We need to take that hope we all have and harness it. Make it something tangible you can hold onto because right now, that's all we have. Hope. And faith." He pauses to look out at us.

"Hope and faith isn't going to get us off this island," one of the twins shouts.

My jaw drops. Finally, someone says what I've been thinking. I just can't believe it's one of them who had the guts to do so.

Jason scowls, then quickly forces a smile. "Well, lucky for us, we do have a plan." He angles his body toward Tom. "I assume you're still making this ridiculous hike across the island."

Whoa. Why does Jason suddenly seem so combative toward Tom? Did something happen between the two of them?

"Ridiculous hike?" Tom laughs bitterly. "It's the only logical plan we have. And yes, we're leaving as soon as you're done talking."

Jason ignores Tom's jab and keeps speaking. "We were able to collect quite a bit of food and water, but even if we ration like we did last night, we only have enough for a few days. Our situation is becoming more dire by the hour."

"All the more reason to explore and find food," Tom mumbles.

I cover my laugh with a cough, and Aiden nudges me, smiling.

"But," Jason says. "Hope is not lost." He holds up his hand, which is closed into a fist. "One of the groups found seeds yesterday. And seeds mean we can grow our own food."

"Growing food can take weeks or months. What will we do in the meantime?" Marjorie asks.

He makes it sound like we're going to be here forever, that we should create a whole life here. Planting food. Building shelters. What a joke.

"We search the island," Tom says. Several people in the group nod with agreement. "Are you about done? We're wasting daylight." He crosses his arms over his chest.

I hold my breath and wait for Jason to say something else that will cause a disagreement. But he doesn't. Still, the tension between those two makes me uneasy. If they continue to butt heads like this, there will be chaos. And I have no idea how any of us will survive that.

The group disperses. Aiden and I join Tom and the others. Tom's face is red, and the muscle in his jaw ticks. He drags his hand through his hair and blows out a breath. I don't blame him for being angry. There's no reason for how Jason spoke to him just now.

"Okay, all the supplies are at the hollowed log Emily mentioned. We each have our own packs, and then there are four extras filled with water and food. Hopefully, we'll find a source of fresh water as we're hiking, but we've packed for the worst case scenario," Tom says in a hushed tone.

"Excuse me." Jason walks over with an air of authority. "May I have a moment of your time?"

"Make it quick," Tom snaps.

I take a step back, putting myself closer to Aiden. He reaches down and takes my hand. The feel of his fingers curling around mine calms me, and my heart doesn't race as fast as it did a moment ago. I give his hand a squeeze and smile. He returns the gesture.

"I really wish you wouldn't take off. There's not many of us to begin with, and losing eight of you for God knows how long will only hinder us. Especially when four of our strongest men are leaving." Jason's gaze is pleading as he looks at each of the guys in turn.

Aiden shifts his weight and moves even closer. His body heat wraps around me like a safety blanket, and I sigh.

"Why are you so dead set on making us stay here?" a guy name Bob speaks up before Tom can. "Don't you want to find food and water and help?"

"Of course I do." Jason actually sounds offended. "But your odds of finding trouble are much greater than finding help."

I narrow my eyes. "How do you know that?"

He averts his gaze. "I don't know anything for certain, but you're marching into the unknown. Wild animals live in the jungle. How will you defend yourselves?"

"I'm sure we can manage," Aiden says.

"I'm an air marshall," Tom says. "I'm armed. We'll be fine."

My blood runs cold at Tom's words. I've never been a fan of guns, and now I'm planning to hike across an island with an armed man I barely know? What am I thinking?

"I've been praying about this ever since the idea came up, and I don't have a good feeling," Jason says with a shake of his head. "Won't you please reconsider?"

His pleas wiggle into my mind, and for half a second, I consider doing exactly as he asks. But one look at our "camp" and the way everyone is shuffling around, defeated and weary, I know I have to do this. I *want* to do this.

"We don't have a choice." Tom pushes through the group and stands face-to-face with Jason. "If we don't do this, if we don't find more food, people are going to starve."

Tom's words strike icy fear in my veins. I glance helplessly at Aiden, hoping he can say something to make this better, but I know he can't, and it's unfair to put that pressure on him.

Jason takes a step back, and his eyes widen with surprise. But then, slowly, he lowers his head with a subtle nod. "I'll pray for all of you." And then he walks away.

Tom stares after Jason for a moment before turning back to us. "Okay, are we ready?" He turns and marches toward the jungle, and we follow.

I take Aiden's hand and tug him to the back of the group. "That was… weird," I whisper and scrunch up my face.

"No kidding. What's up with Jason today?"

I shrug. "I don't know."

"Neither do I."

We fall silent, and I stare at Tom's back. I have a feeling he's not as innocent as he wants everyone to believe, either. But what's his secret? I shake my head… Our current conditions are not ideal, and everyone is stressed to the max. I'm just being paranoid. Tom isn't harboring some deep, dark secret. He's fine. Everything is fine.

The silence stretches. What's left to discuss? Until we have more information about where we are, making guesses and assumptions is a waste of time. And with the water supply running low, I'm not going to talk unless I absolutely have to.

The sun continues to rise, and with it, so does the temperature. Sweat beads on my brow, and my steps become heavier as a wave of homesickness hits me. I miss the things I always took for granted—food and water for starters. But I also miss my bed, my pillow, the stuffed penguin Matt gave me on our first date, air conditioning, my blow dryer… The ability to shower and wash my hair with shampoo and conditioner. I groan.

Most of all, I miss my parents and my brother. My chest constricts, and my breath catches. If I had known this was going to happen, I would've been nicer to them before I left. I take a deep breath and momentarily close my eyes—long enough to trip on a large rock. I stumble forward and put my hands out to catch myself. Instead, Aiden's arms wrap around me, and he catches me before I face plant on the ground.

"You okay?" He releases me but doesn't pull his hands away completely, like he's waiting to make sure I won't topple over.

"Yeah, thanks. I wasn't paying attention." I laugh nervously.

"You should. The trees are getting thicker." He nods ahead of us to indicate the massive trees and dense foliage.

Embarrassment heats my face. "I will." I wipe my sweaty palms on my hips and move forward, each step maximizing the heartache seizing my chest.

CHAPTER 17

Aiden

WE'VE BEEN WALKING FOR OVER three hours, and we haven't found a thing. Emily's stumbled and almost fell four times. I don't know if she's tired, scared, or so lost in her thoughts she's not paying attention. Either way, I don't allow myself to get farther than an arm's length from her, afraid if I do, she'll end up seriously hurting herself.

"Okay," Tom announces and stops. "Let's take a quick break."

"Finally," Emily mumbles.

I drop my backpack to the ground and use it as a seat.

Emily copies me. "My feet are killing me," she complains.

I glance down at her shoes. She's wearing a pair of those cheap canvas sneakers that don't have any support. "Don't you have actual sneakers?"

She nods. "But I've only worn them once. I was afraid they'd be worse than these." She sticks her foot out to show off her shoe.

I frown. "I think you should put the sneakers on."

"Maybe you're right." She busies herself with getting her sneakers out of her backpack and changing her shoes.

"Here." Tom hands me two bottles of water—one for me and one for Emily.

"Thanks." I take them, and when Emily sits back down, I hand her one.

I twist off the top and take a long drink. It's warm, but at least it's wet, and it soothes my scratchy throat. I take a moment to look around. Everything looks exactly the same as it did when we left the beach. Trees. Grass. Rocks. Maybe Jason is right and we are wasting our time. Maybe we should've followed the shoreline around the island. At least that way we would've eventually found our way back to the others.

"We'll take fifteen minutes and then keep moving," Tom announces. "We need to find a good spot to make camp before dark."

"Wait, you mean we're not going back to the beach tonight?" one of the twins—Sierra—asks. The only reason I know it's her is because she's wearing a T-shirt with her name painted across the front.

Tom gives her an incredulous look. "What's the point? So we can hike back out here in the morning to turn around and go back again tomorrow night?" He shakes his head. "No. We keep going until we find something."

"And what if we don't find anything?" asks the other twin, Sienna.

"We will," he assures with so much confidence, it gives me pause. He's been out here once before. Did he find something then? What? What does he know that the rest of us don't?

Tom and the twins carry on their conversation, and I tune them out, focusing on Emily instead. Her complexion is pale, yet her cheeks are red. Sweat makes her hair stick to her forehead, and her shoulders rise and fall heavily with each breath.

"Someone needs to turn off that sun." Emily uses her hand to shield her eyes. Her tone is snotty and tired, even a little bored.

She's clearly struggling with the elements and this hike, so I decide to do what I can to help take her mind off things. "If you could be anywhere in the world right now, where would you want to be? And you can't say home."

She gives me an odd look. "What?"

"C'mon, just play along." I smile.

"Okay. Hmm." She looks off into the distance, lost in thought. After a moment, she turns back to me. "Does it count if I say right here?" A sly grin spreads across her face.

"You know what I mean." I tilt my head, giving it a small shake. "I'm just trying to help take our minds off this awful situation."

"Fine." She sighs. "Since I was twelve, I've always wanted to go to Australia."

"Why Australia?"

She shrugs. "I don't know. I find the whole place to be beautiful."

"Care to elaborate?" I fake a bad British accent, and she laughs.

"Well, for starters, I've heard that Lake Hillier has pink water, and that is something I've never seen before."

"Pink water?" I smirk and try not to laugh.

She narrows her eyes. "Do you want to hear my answer or not?"

This time, I do laugh. "Okay, sorry. Go on."

"Then there's the Great Ocean Road, which is one of the world's most scenic coastal drives. I really want to see the Twelve Apostles rock formations, which are these limestone stacks on the road of The Great Ocean Road. I mean, I want to stand next to them and touch them, not just stare at them on my laptop screen." She laughs. "Oh, and the Katherine Gorge in the Northern Territory. It's this amazing national park where you can see these thirteen stunning gorges, canoe, boat, or even go in a helicopter." Her eyes are alight with excitement, and I can't stop from smiling.

"You're right. It does sound beautiful."

She puts her elbow on her knee and props her cheek in her hand. "What about you? If you could be anywhere right now, where would you want to be?"

"With you." I wink.

Her face flushes, and she quickly turns her head. Did I go too far? I'm almost positive she's into me like I'm into her, but maybe I'm wrong.

I gently nudge her. "Hey, sorry if I—"

"No, you didn't." She smiles warmly. "So, it's your turn to answer the question."

"I've always wanted to go to Israel. I feel like there is so much to learn about the culture. There are so many natural places to go there—Ein Gedi, Masada, the Kinerat, Tel Aviv, The Western Wall. If you think about it, it really is beautiful. And the religious history…" I stop before I go on too long about something I know she doesn't really care about. "Of course, I'm just basing everything I've said off of what I heard and seen." I laugh.

"Someday we'll get to go on these vacations. Maybe together," she says so softly I have to strain to hear her.

My heart pounds loudly in my chest, and I have to stop myself from putting my arm around her and pulling her closer. "Definitely," I say. I can see the shift in her demeanor—the slump of her shoulders, the way her eyes dull. She's getting bored. Or sad. And all I want to do is make her laugh again. "Tell me, Emily, what do you want to be when you grow up?" I do a horrible impression of a stuffy therapist.

She laughs loudly, which earns us dirty looks from the twins, but I don't care. Hearing Emily's laugh is a bright spot in this otherwise dark situation.

"I've always loved fashion and make-up, so I think I would've done something in that field, but honestly, I'm undecided. I really don't know what I want to do for the rest of my life. Is that weird?"

"Not at all. Most people don't know what they want in life until they go to college for a year or so. Me personally, I want to pursue a career in education."

"You want to be a teacher?"

"Yeah, or a college professor. I like studying, and I like helping others. So if I could apply both, why not?" I take a sip of water, feeling like a nerd for telling her that. She's a self-admitted party girl, and I'm sitting here talking about studying. I'm an idiot.

"When we get rescued, maybe you can help me get my grades up."

She wants to willingly spend time with me? I smile at the thought. "Yeah, def—"

"How are you two doing?" Tom interrupts. "You both seemed to have a rough night last night. You doing okay?" He looks back and forth between us.

"Yeah, I'm okay," I say with a nod.

"About last night," Emily says, fidgeting with the cap of her water bottle. "I haven't had a chance to thank you, Tom, for waking me up and being there."

Just like she'd done with me earlier, she doesn't look Tom in the eye. Is she embarrassed about thanking him? Is it hard for her to say those words?

"It's not a problem." Tom rubs the back of his neck. "You remind me an awful lot of my daughter, and she used to suffer from night terrors." He blows out a breath then turns away. "All right, break is over. Let's gather our stuff and get moving. We need to cover as much ground as we can before night fall." He's already walking away, leaving us to catch up.

We walk for another few hours. No one speaks, and everyone's steps are becoming smaller and more labored. It has to be close to lunchtime, and I hope Tom will agree to stop again soon. I keep my gaze on the ground, watching where I'm going and also hoping to find something—anything—that will help. So far, all I've managed to do is memorize every type of rock that is situated in this soil. Small metallic black rocks, red oval shaped rocks, white with some flakes of red rocks, and some mud balls. Other than those rocks, everything looks exactly the same—generic.

But still, we keep walking. Sweat drips out of every pore in my body. The sun is the hottest it's been since we crashed. Fatigue and nausea are on the verge of surfacing, and I quickly swallow it back down. I can't look weak. Not in front of the group, and definitely not in front of Emily.

I glance over at her. She still looks very tired, but there's a new determination in her eyes. I admire her for that. While I still don't know all the details, I know enough to understand that where she came from—the city girl, party lifestyle—she's so out of her element here. Despite that, she's strong. Anyone else would probably have caved to the heat and given in to defeat. Kind of like the twins. I'm trying hard to tune them out, but their incessant complaining is slowly chipping away at my resolve. More than once I've had to bite back the urge to scream at them to shut up. And based on the way Tom keeps distancing himself from the group, I bet he feels the same way.

"Eww!" Bob stops and covers his nose with his arm. "What is that God awful smell?"

The rest of us stop, too. I tilt my head and take a big whiff. A rancid smell assaults my senses, and I bend over, gripping my knees with my hands. I breath in and out through my mouth in an effort to rid my nose of that smell.

"It smells like…" Emily makes a disgusted face. "Poop."

"Like animal poop?" Marjorie asks, her eyes lighting with hope. Animals means food.

Bob nods. "Yeah, but I'm not sure I want to know what kind of animal takes that kind of dump."

"Everyone search the ground," Tom says.

"I am not looking for piles of poop." Sienna crosses her arms and glares at him.

Tom steps up to her, their faces inches apart. I hold my breath, unable to look away. Emily moves to stand beside me, and she takes hold of my arm. I straighten and prepare to step between them if necessary.

"Sienna, is it?" he asks with a subtle tilt of his head.

She nods.

"If you're not going to help, then feel free to march back to the beach." Tom spins around to face the rest of the group. "Anyone else refuse to help?"

No one says anything, but there are several head shakes to indicate there won't be any further dissension.

"Good, then get looking," he snaps.

"Fine." Sienna balls her hands into fists. "Sierra and I are going back to the beach then. Y'all are crazy!" She storms away with her sister close behind.

I take a deep breath, relieved that Tom didn't do anything stupid. I return my gaze to the ground and begin to look for piles of poop. I can't believe this is what my life has become. Emily sticks close, and we search the same area. Tom either doesn't notice or doesn't care. A second later, a high-pitched scream pierces the otherwise quiet jungle.

"Sienna!" Sierra screams. "Someone! Help!"

CHAPTER 18

Emily

WITHOUT THINKING, I RUN TOWARD the sounds of Sierra's screams.

"Emily!" Aiden shouts and then runs after me.

Soon, the rest of the group is following. I come to a dead stop when I see Sierra. She's standing over a hole filled with a blackish liquid, tears streaming down her face and still screaming for her sister.

"Sierra," I gasp, out of breath. "What's wrong? What happened?"

"My sister." She sobs and points to the large, black hole. The smell here is a hundred times worse than it was back where we just were. I gag and fight the reflex to throw up. Sierra's still crying too hard to say anything else.

Just then, a hand reaches out of the hole and grabs my leg hard enough to cause me to fall backward. And then I'm being yanked toward the hole. I scream and kick at the hand holding my ankle, but it's not working. I grasp and claw at the ground, hoping to find something I can hold onto. Panic squeezes the breath from my lungs. This is it—I'm going to die. "No!" I scream. "Help! Sierra, help me!"

"Emily!"

In the next moment, Aiden's hands are under my arms, and he's trying to jerk me away from the hole. Tom and Larry are on their hands and knees, reaching for the hand wrapped around my ankle. They grab her hand and yank and pull, but Sienna's fingers slip through theirs. Sierra drops to her knees and lets out a gut-wrenching wail.

I yank my knees to my chest and then bury my face against Aiden's shoulder. He wraps his arms around me, and I sob.

"Shh. It's okay. I've got you," Aiden whispers in my ear and strokes my hair.

I can't stop shaking. I cup my hand over my mouth, push Aiden away, lean to the side, and throw up.

Aiden rubs my back. "Are you okay?"

I nod and wipe my mouth with the back of my hand.

Sierra lunges toward the hole, and Tom grabs her before she gets too close. "Let me go!" She twists around and tries to jerk out of his hold. "I have to get her out of there."

"It's too late." Tom has her in a bear hug, making it impossible for her to get away but that doesn't stop her from trying. "She's gone. And if you go in after her, you will be, too."

My racing heart makes my nausea worse. Sweat beads on my brow, and I shiver. Aiden wraps his arms around me again, holding me close. His body heat helps the chill working through me. When I don't feel like I'm going to throw up anymore, I release him and take a small step back.

"Here." Aiden hands me a bottle of water. "Take small sips."

I nod and take the bottle. My hand trembles, and I spill a little down my chin.

"She's not dead!" Sierra is thrashing against Tom's hold again. This time, he releases her. She collapses on the ground and buries her face in her hands.

Tears burn my eyes, and I blink to keep them at bay. I can't begin to imagine what Sierra must be feeling right now. She and her sister have been inseparable, and now Sienna is dead. My mind wanders back to that morning in the airport, to when my brother hugged me and called me Emmy. Tears slip down my cheeks, and I hastily wipe them away. What would I do if Erik died? The thought is too much, and I force it out of my mind.

"What happened?" Tom asks, his hands on his hips as he looks to me for answers.

"I don't know." I shake my head. "I heard Sierra scream, just like everyone else did. When I got to her, she was standing there crying. Then Sienna grabbed my ankle."

"Ugh, that smell." Marjorie covers her nose and mouth with her hand. Her eyes are wet, but I'm not sure if that's because she's crying or because the stench is making her eyes water.

"What is that?" Bob leans cautiously toward the black hole. "Is that animal feces?"

"Uh, yeah, what kind of animal digs a hole to poop in?" Larry asks.

"No animal I know of," Aiden says. He's still by my side, hovering as if he's afraid of what will happen if he leaves me alone.

"Because an animal didn't do this. Humans did." Tom frowns and looks over his shoulder as if he expects someone to be there.

A chill works through my veins, and I suppress a shudder. Instinctively, I look around, too, suddenly much more aware of my surroundings. Aiden steps closer and puts his arm around my waist. I lean into him.

"Then that means... She sank like she was in quicksand." I take a deep breath, my thoughts disturbing and morbid. "That is big enough to swallow a whole person. Whoever did this has been here a long time. A hole that size and that full doesn't happen overnight."

"No, it doesn't." Tom drags his hand through his hair, and I notice the worry lines etched around his eyes. Have those always been there?

Sierra rocks back and forth on the ground. "I want to go home," she repeats.

"I'll take her back to the beach," Bob offers. He kneels beside her. "Do you want that, Sierra? Do you want to go back to the beach?" She nods, and Bob helps her to her feet.

Tom clutches Bob's arm. "Do not tell anyone what happened."

"Why?" I ask before Bob can. "Don't they deserve to know? I mean, what if they want to come with us next time? Or they take off on their own? For all we know, there could be more holes like this."

"Until we know what's going on and who's responsible for this, we keep it a secret," Tom says so firmly, no one dares argue with him. He returns his attention to Bob and Sierra. "If they ask, tell them Sierra is ill and you're bringing her back."

"And what happens when you guys return and Sienna isn't with you?" Bob narrows his eyes.

"By then, we'll have some answers." Tom scoops his backpack off the ground and puts it on. "Until then, keep your mouth shut." He turns to head back the way we came. "C'mon, let's go."

I glance at Aiden. Is this really happening? How can Tom be so cold and uncaring? Sierra just lost her sister. A girl died! And he's acting like it's nothing more than an inconvenience. He's the polar opposite of how he was last night with me. I don't get it.

"It'll be okay," Aiden whispers, but I'm not sure he believes that. I don't.

One by one, the group falls in line behind Tom. Once again, Aiden and I bring up the rear, which is fine with me because I don't want to be around any of them right now. We walk in silence for what feels like an eternity. Each step I take becomes harder and heavier. My left leg itches horribly, and I use my right foot to scratch it. I freeze mid-step and look down.

"Oh my gosh." I stop and stare at my ankle. "Oh my gosh." I frantically fumble around in my backpack until I find my bottle of water. I pour the lukewarm liquid on my ankle and scrub at it.

"Emily." Aiden turns back to me. "What're you doing?"

"It's on me." I scrub harder and faster. "Where she grabbed me. It's on me." Tears cloud my vision, and I rub at my ankle so hard, I cry out in pain. "It's on me."

"Okay, easy." He swings his bag around to the front of his body and pulls out a tattered T-shirt. "Here, use this to wipe it off."

I snatch the shirt from him, douse it in water, and resume scrubbing at my leg. Even when it's all off, I keep rubbing at the same spot. "She's dead," I mumble. "And we just left her there."

"There wasn't anything we could do for her," he says softly.

His words do nothing to calm me, though. "That could have been me. She was pulling me in there with her." I look up at him through teary eyes.

He brushes a strand of hair from my face, his hand lingering on my cheek. "She was trying to get out, Emily. Nothing else."

My lips quiver, and I nod.

"Hey, what's the hold up? She hurt?" Tom calls back to us.

"She's fine." Aiden's reply is curt and stern. "Do you want to keep going? Or do you want to go back to the beach?"

"No, I want to keep going." If I go back to the beach, I'll have to see Sierra, and I can't face her knowing I hadn't done anything to help her sister.

"Then let's get moving!" Tom hollers.

Aiden helps me up. I adjust my backpack, and we catch up with the rest of the group. Aiden nudges me to go ahead of him, and he follows closely behind, which I'm pretty sure he's doing because he's worried I'm going to freak out again. I wish I could say I'm not going to, but I'm not sure of that fact.

I keep my head down and my pace steady. The once lush, green foliage is turning browner the further we get inland. There's a funky smell, too. Not like the poop from before, but something stale and moldy. Acidic. I scrunch up my nose then sneeze.

"God bless you," Aiden says.

My stomach growls, and I open my mouth to ask Tom if we can stop to eat, but then I snap my jaw shut. Knowing we've already lost time with Sierra and Sienna, and then I had to stop, he will probably bite my head off for simply asking.

An hour passes. And then another.

"Does anyone else think it's weird we haven't seen a single animal yet? Not so much as a squirrel. Or a bird," Larry says.

"I was thinking the same thing," Marjorie says. "What do you think that means?"

I glance at Aiden, brow raised, and we share a knowing look. Something is definitely off about this island.

Larry shrugs. "That there's no food on this island to sustain wildlife. What other explanation could there be?"

"That someone has hunted all the animals and now there's none left," I offer.

"Yeah, but all the birds, too? I haven't even seen a spider or a flower. And no one hunts bugs for food." Marjorie waves her arms around to emphasize her point. "And we just saw a huge hole of human feces. Where *are* we?"

That is the million-dollar question. Hopefully, by the end of the day, we'll have some answers. Not knowing is the worst, but combine that with the bone-seeping fear I feel, it's unmanageable. I want to curl up into a ball and sleep for days, and when I wake up, I want all of this to be nothing more than a horrific nightmare.

Tom stops and holds up his hand for the rest of us to do the same. Then he points to something ahead of him. "Do you guys see that?"

I move to the front of the group to get a better look, and there, a few feet away, is a purplish-white flower, around two feet high, swaying ever so slightly in the light breeze.

"Is that a flower?" Marjorie shoves past me. She laughs.

I smile at her apparent glee. Aiden slips his hand into mine and gives it a reassuring squeeze. It's refreshing to know something so beautiful could live in such a deserted and ugly place. An intense spark of hope ignites in my chest, and I blow out a pent up breath. Maybe we really will be okay after all.

We're all so mesmerized by the sight of that beautiful flower—of which no one know its origins or name—that no words are spoken. We seem to do that a lot, be silent. Oddly, it's not awkward or uncomfortable. In fact, I prefer the silence over the constant bickering and snotty tones.

"Do you guys feel that?" I ask, tilting my head up to the sun. "The air. It's different. Cleaner."

"I noticed." Tom smiles. "You know what that is?" He points to the flower. "That's a good sign. If a flower like that can grow here, then that means other things can grow, too. Things like fruit trees and crops." He waves his arm to indicate we should move forward. "Come on. I have a feeling we're close to something."

To my surprise, Larry and Marjorie clap. Maybe it's the way Tom delivered his speech. Maybe it's the hope that has everyone excited. Or maybe it's really something in the air. Either way, the unity and comradery passing through the group in this moment is refreshing. In light of everything we've been through, harmony and teamwork is the only thing we have right now.

I grin from ear to ear. "This is amazing, isn't it?" I ask as I gently graze my fingers over the flower's petals. They feel like velvet and remind me of the purple, crushed velvet pillow I have on my bed. Man, I miss my bed. I miss my blankets and my air conditioning.

"It's amazing how it's alive and thriving in this climate," Aiden says. "It's very strange. It doesn't look like it belongs here, so where did it come from?"

I give him a dirty look over my shoulder. "Who cares about how or where it came from? Just look at how its petals are swaying. Like it has no care in the world. Like it can forget about the heat and lack of rain. If only we could all be so lucky."

"That's looking on the bright side of things," he says with a smile. "I must be rubbing off on you."

"I can't say I dislike it." My arm brushes against his, causing a chill to shoot down my spine.

He winks, and I quickly turn my head, not wanting him to see the blush I know is on my face.

"I'm feeling really good about this, guys." Tom's steps are getting bigger by the moment, until he's practically running. "We can't be too far away from food, water, or even people! We're going to keep going straight, all right?"

As we continue to walk, the rocks became less frequent, and the air becomes richer, making breathing easier. Something is definitely changing. The entire atmosphere is somehow brighter, more electric. How is that possible?

Twenty minutes later, the scenery completely changes. Clear blue skies. A clean, refreshing breeze. Chirping birds. Green grass. Dandelions!

"I'm not sure I agree with Tom," Aiden whispers.

"What? Why?"

He shrugs. "I don't know. Something about this whole thing just doesn't feel right. It's like we crossed some invisible barrier between a dying island and a beach resort. How can one half be so miserable and the other half be so alive?"

I shrug and contemplate his question. He's right, but I don't have an answer, and I'm not sure I want one. I don't want to analyze this situation. I just want to take it for what it is—a good sign. Why can't he do the same? "Maybe your God is finally coming through for us," I say.

He laughs.

Tom stops at the edge of a small cliff. He drops his bag to the ground, raises his hands above his head, and whoops with excitement. The rest of us stand beside him and look down at the valley below. It's completely flat and grassy. Not a single patch of dirt or rocks anywhere in sight.

"Are those...?" Marjorie's voice cracks.

"Buildings," Tom says proudly. "Those are buildings."

CHAPTER 19

Aiden

I HAVE NEVER SEEN ANYTHING like this before in my life. Two large buildings, equidistant from each other, sit below us like a mirage. I'm terrified maybe that's all this is. Each building is made of red brick with a green, Spanish-tiled roof. They look like something straight out of a magazine. In front of each is a garden with a multitude of flowers in a rainbow of colors—white, red, orange, purple, blue, and yellow.

The gardens appear to be too well-kept. Everything about this feels wrong, and Emily is wrong, too. This isn't God's handiwork. This is evil. I suppress a shudder.

"Do you think people live here?" Emily asks.

"If we're lucky, yes," Larry says.

Tom turns to face us. "That"—he points behind him to the buildings—"is exactly what we've been hoping to find. And I know we're all excited and curious, but we have to tread carefully because we have no idea who lives down there."

"You honestly don't think whoever's down there is dangerous, do you?" Marjorie crosses her arms.

"I don't know, but I don't think we need to take any chances. The quicker we can get down there and assess the situation, the better. Which is why I suggest we divide and conquer the exploring duties."

"Wouldn't staying together be safer?" Emily asks.

"Ideally, yes, but it's already mid-afternoon, and we need to cover as much ground as we can before the sun sets. It's the only way we're going to cover everything. While that down there is our salvation, to whomever lives there, we're probably going to appear as crazy people looking for food and shelter."

Emily laughs, and I can't help but smile.

"I mean, look at us." Tom waves his arms down the length of his body then nods to each of us. "We're plane crash survivors. We haven't showered in a couple of days. Our clothes are dirty and ripped. We're covered in sweat and dirt. I'm sure we're going to look terrifying to them."

"But if we approach cautiously and tell them what happened, they'll help us, right?" I ask. They have to help us, because if they don't, who will?

"Hopefully," Marjorie answers.

"All right, so there are two buildings and five of us. Larry, you take Aiden and Emily into that first building. Marjorie and I will take the other. Knock three times then wait a full minute before knocking again four times."

I adjust my backpack and shift on my feet. My stomach is in a knot, and my eyes burn from lack of sleep and the glaring sun. I press the heels of my hands against my eyes and rub the exhaustion from them. Or rather, I try. It doesn't really work, and I end up yawning much too loudly.

"We'll each do three cycles of knocks. After the third time, I think we can safely assume no one is home. That or they're deliberately hiding from us, but I'm guessing it's the former. At that point, feel free to enter the building and look around. Leave the door open," Tom says emphatically. "And if you encounter anyone, scream."

"I don't like this." Larry crosses his arms and shakes his head. "We have no idea who or what is down there, and we don't have any way of protecting ourselves. What if they have weapons?"

The mention of weapons has my heart racing. It's something I hadn't considered, but it makes perfect sense. Living out here, in the middle of an island, of course the owners of those buildings would have weapons—probably guns.

"After what we've seen and what happened to Sienna, we're not alone out here," Larry says.

"We're not exactly unprotected, either, remember?" Tom rubs the back of his neck. Then he holds up his right leg and lifts the hem of his pants. Strapped to his ankle is a gun. "Federal air marshalls are armed."

Emily's eyes widen, and she takes a big step back. I don't know why she seems so shocked by this information—Tom told us this before we left the beach.

I move to stand beside Emily. "It's okay," I whisper. Doesn't she realize this is a good thing? We're protected.

"Then that solves it. You're the only one with a gun, so we're sticking together. You can clear the buildings first, and then we can search them," Larry says.

Tom is silent for several moments, but then he finally nods. "All right, fine. We'll approach the first building together, as a group. Once we know it's empty, I'll clear the second one before Marjorie and I search. Everyone okay with that?"

I nod. So does Emily and everyone else.

"Good. Our priority right now is food, water, and medicine. Grab as much as you can. When you're done, bring the supplies outside and wait for us." Tom pulls the gun from his ankle.

I follow as the group descends upon the buildings, but I don't get too far before a hand touches my shoulder. I turn slowly to find Emily staring at me with a frown. "What's wrong?" I ask.

"Are you sure we should be doing this?" she whispers.

"It's kinda late to turn back now." I put my arm around her shoulders and pull her closer. "Don't worry. If we stick together, we'll be fine."

She gives me a small smile, but I'm not sure she believes me. I'm not sure I believe me. None of us have ever been in a situation like this before, so none of us can say with any certainty what will happen. But I have God on my side, and I say a prayer for our safety.

The embankment down to the valley is steeper than it looks, and we have to tread cautiously. Tom reaches the bottom first, and he extends his hand to help Emily and Marjorie down. Once I hit the ground, I help Larry.

"Thanks, man," he says.

"No problem." I glance at Emily, who's staring at me with a strange look. As best I can tell, it's a mix between pride and confusion.

"Let's go." Tom motions for us to follow.

"Wait," I say, and everyone freezes. I point to the roof of the buildings. "Do you guys see that?"

"Solar panels," Marjorie says, her tone full of disbelief.

"Does that mean...?" Emily looks at me.

"Electricity." I grin.

Tom resumes leading the way, and I'm more eager than ever to get inside. The closer we get, the more I realize how similar the buildings are. They're each two stories with no porch, just three cement steps leading to the front door. There are two windows on either side of the door, and a small, brick chimney juts out from the roof.

Tom climbs the steps while the rest of us wait at the bottom. He knocks loudly three times and then stares at his watch, counting one minute. I hold my breath. The seconds tick by so slow, it seems like the minute will never end. Finally, Tom knocks again, and I blow out the breath I've been holding. Another minute passes, and no one answers the door. After the third round of knocking, Tom opens the door and steps inside, gun raised.

The rest of us remain outside, waiting. I glance around. Despite the cool breeze, everything is so still. Not so much as a blade of grass moves with the wind. A few birds circle in the sky, but I still don't see any other animals.

"It's so peaceful here," Marjorie says.

More like eerie, but I don't say that.

"Who do you think lives here?" Emily asks.

I shrug. Even though we're keeping our voices low, every spoken word sounds amplified, like they're being broadcast through a bull horn.

"This building is clear," Tom says as he steps outside. His face is pale and sweaty.

"C'mon, let's get this over with," I say. Standing out in the open like this makes me nervous. My skin tingles, and my palms itch. I need to get inside.

116

Tom nods. "Be safe, and stay together. We'll be right next door."

I take Emily's hand and lead her inside. Larry follows. The minute I cross the threshold, I'm hit with an odor strong enough to knock the breath from my lungs. Mold, dust, and something else I can't name hangs heavy in the air. I gag and cover my mouth with my arm.

"Ugh, gross." Emily covers her nose, too.

The front door opens to the living room, which is sparsely furnished. A fireplace sits in one corner. There are no pictures on the mantle or on the walls, and everything is covered in a thick layer of dust. A small couch and a single recliner are the only pieces of furniture in the room. No coffee table or end tables or lamps. I look up at the ceiling to find a single overhead light.

"It doesn't look like anyone's lived here for months," Emily says.

"More like years," Larry says.

I trail my finger across the mantle, and it comes away black. I wipe my finger on my shorts and find the only light switch in the room. "Think it works?"

"Only one way to find out." She grins.

I flick the switch, and the room fills with light. "They have electricity!" I can barely contain my excitement. Power means working appliances. We can cook food. Maybe even take a shower.

"I don't think I've ever been so happy to see a working light." She laughs.

"Hallelujah!" Larry says much too loudly, and I wince. If there is someone hiding inside, they know we're here now. "I'm going to check upstairs." He points to the stairs a few feet away. "You two stay together." And then he disappears from my view before I can remind him that Tom told all three of us to stay together.

"Come on, let's go see what else we can find." We leave the living room and head into the kitchen. It's much the same in here, too. No décor, just a long table with six chairs and the standard appliances—all covered in the same dust. The smell in this room is much stronger.

117

Cabinets line the far wall. Emily opens them, one by one. "They have food."

The shelves are full of canned goods, boxed cereal, crackers, chips. My mouth waters at the sight, and then my stomach growls. I walk to the fridge and open the door. "Oh, gross." I slam the door just as quickly as I'd opened it and force back a gag. Instantly, my stomach recoils, and I'm no longer hungry.

"What is that?" Emily asks.

"Everything in there is spoiled. The milk, eggs, all the food. Covered in mold. And I'm pretty sure I saw maggots, too."

She gags. "That explains the smell."

I nod. "C'mon." There's a door off to the right. I push it open to reveal a bathroom that looks like something straight out of dorm room—multiple stalls, stand-up showers with discolored, moldy curtains, and a wall of sinks. It's as dirty as everything else. I turn on the sink faucet. "Running water."

"Thank God." Emily sighs. She turns around as if she's looking for something else. "There have to be bedrooms somewhere, right?"

I raise a brow. "Uh, yeah, I would think so." Why is she so concerned about finding the bedroom?

Her face turns red, and her eyes widen. "I didn't. I was just…" She turns her face away and clears her throat. "We should grab the food from the cabinets and wait outside for everyone else."

"Good idea." We return to the kitchen, and I take my bag off my back. "We'll put all the clothes in your bag, and we can fill mine with food."

"Okay. I wonder if there's a box or something around here we can fill up and carry back." She heads toward the living room.

"Emily! Don't wander off alone." I chase after her.

"Why? I doubt anyone's coming back anytime soon."

"Still, I don't think we should split up." I follow her through the building, searching for something to use to carry food back to the beach.

She pushes open a door, and the hinges squeak. I cringe at the sound, hoping no one else hears it—which is ridiculous

118

considering the only people in this building are me and her and Larry.

"Found a bedroom," she says, smirking at me over her shoulder.

I shake my head and step into the room behind her.

"All that's upstairs are bedrooms and a bathroom," Larry says. "Everything's covered in dust, just like down here."

His voice startles me, and I jump a little. I scowl at him, hoping he realizes how much of a jerk he is for sneaking up on me like that. "How many?" I ask.

"Five."

Six chairs at the table six bedrooms… Either there's a large family living here, or it's some sort of communal living situation. Either way, that's a lot of people who could possibly return at any moment. "We should hurry up," I say.

Emily picks up a rectangular laundry basket and holds it up proudly. "This will work, right?"

"Work for what?" Larry looks back and for the between us.

"Carrying food," I say to him. Then, to Emily, "Yeah, that will work really well." I take it from her and head back to the kitchen. "Is it just me or is the smell getting worse?"

"It's definitely getting worse. Let's do this fast and get out of here."

We work quickly and silently to fill the laundry basket and my backpack with all the food we can fit. I put my backpack on again and lift the now full basket. The weight is much more than I expect, and I end up dropping the basket. The cans and boxes scatter across the floor.

I mutter a curse before I can stop myself, then silently apologize to God and ask for forgiveness.

"Okay, here." She takes off her pack and hands it to me. "You take this one. It's lighter so you can still carry the basket. Then I'll take your pack with the food."

"Are you sure?"

She nods. "Hand it over and let's get out of this stink hole."

"Deal."

"Come on, you two." Larry stands at the door, holding it open for us.

CHAPTER 20

Emily

WE WALK OUT THE FRONT door with our arms full and head back to where Tom is standing with Marjorie

"Nice job, you two." Tom smiles.

"What did you two find?" Aiden asks.

"Not much. That building looks like some sort of research lab. There wasn't any food, but I did find some antibiotics," Marjorie says.

"And I collected anything we could use as a weapon." Tom opens his bag, and I glance inside to find scalpels and knives.

"Well, it's more than we had when we left the beach, but there's not enough to feed twenty-three—now twenty-two—of us for God knows how long," Larry says.

He's right. I frown. "No one's been here for a long time. Where do you think all the people went?"

"Maybe this is just some sort of vacation spot or something," Aiden suggests.

"But why would everyone leave so abruptly? I mean, whoever lived here literally left everything. Why would they do that?" I look to Tom for an answer, but he doesn't respond. None of this makes any sense.

"And who vacations near a research lab?" Marjorie asks. "That building gave me the creeps." She shudders.

"All right, let's calm down." Tom clears his throat. "I know this situation seems weird, but if you think about it, this is the best thing to have happened to us since we crashed."

"How so?" I cross my arms over my chest and glare at him.

"I'll be honest. I don't know what is going on. I don't know why there's a research lab with all the modern scientific equipment. For Pete's sake, we're in the middle of nowhere, right? Has anyone been able to find a map or anything of the sort while they were investigating? A phone or CB radio? A laptop?"

I tilt my head and slice a look at Aiden. Now that I think about it, there are no electronics whatsoever. Not even a television. One by one, everyone says no or shakes their head. It isn't lost on me that Tom hasn't answered my question.

"All right then." Tom sighs. "I'd hoped we'd find some sort of confirmation as to our whereabouts, but it seems we're all still clueless as to where we are." He bends down and grabs a can of food. He studies it for a moment before holding it out in front of us. "Does anyone find it strange that some of the food is months to a year old? The expiration date on this is in a few months."

An expression of dread fills Marjorie's face, and her eyes widen. "We can still eat it, though, right?"

Tom nods. "Yes, and I'm sure we'll exhaust this—"

Before he can finish, Larry's body arches forward in an awkward way, and then he falls face-first to the ground. An arrow sticks out of the side of his neck. Blood gushes from the wound so fast, there's a puddle around his head within seconds. My eyes widen, and a scream builds in my throat. There's no way he can still be alive.

Tom kneels beside him and puts his hand on Larry's back. "He's not breathing." Then, Tom glances up and shakes his head.

"Run!" Aiden shouts and shoves me back toward the building we just left. Tom and Marjorie are right behind us. My heart is lodged in my throat, and I can't breathe as I rush through the doorway. Tom's the last one inside, and he slams the door then locks it.

"Are there any other doors in this building?" He looks between me and Aiden as he checks the ammunition in his gun.

I don't realize tears are spilling down my cheeks until I feel them drip off my chin. I try to wipe my face, but my hands are shaking too badly.

122

"Hey!" Tom snaps his fingers in my face. "Are there any other doors in this building?"

"No," Aiden says curtly and steps in front of me, putting himself between me and Tom.

"Make sure all the windows are shut and locked," Tom orders. "Marjorie, double check for any other ways in or out of this building." He turns to look out the front window without speaking to me again. He probably thinks I'm useless right now. I can't argue.

A moment later, Marjorie returns. "There's another door in the kitchen. It was partially hidden by the fridge, so I had Aiden help me move it to block the door."

I don't remember seeing a door in the kitchen. "Did you open it?" I don't know why that's the question I choose to ask when I finally get my mouth to cooperate, but a thought wiggles its way into my brain, and I can't shake it.

Marjorie stares at me like I'm insane. Then, she shakes her head. "No, why?"

"Maybe it goes down to a basement or something," I say. "Maybe there is another way out so we don't have to use the front door. Or maybe there's more food down there."

"All windows are shut and locked. I closed all the blinds, too," Aiden says, returning to the living room and interrupting my rambling. It's not like Marjorie or Tom are listening anyway.

"Is Larry dead?" I whisper. No one answers. No one has to. We all know what we saw out there. "Where did that arrow come from?"

"I don't know." Tom doesn't pull his gaze from the window. We all fall silent until he finally turns around. "I don't see anyone moving around out there. The tree line is quiet, too."

"We shouldn't be here." I pace the living room. My hands begin to shake even more, and I have to tuck them in my armpits to stop the trembling. "That's why they shot Larry. We're in their home and stealing their food."

"Emily, calm down." Aiden takes hold of my shoulders and turns me to face him. "We're safe inside here."

I nod, but my eyes fill with tears, and I can't see him clearly.

"Aiden's right." Tom tucks his gun into the back of his jeans. "This is the safest place right now, and this is where we're going to say until the sun rises."

"What?" I shout. "We're going to stay here? What if the owners come back? What if whoever killed Larry decides to attack us?"

"I have a gun. We'll be safe." But Tom's voice isn't as assured as it was when we arrived.

"We left all the food outside," Marjorie says.

Tom grumbles and drags a hand through his hair.

"Not all of it." Aiden nods to his backpack. "There's plenty in there to get us through the night."

Marjorie sighs with relief. "What if they're still out there come morning?"

"We'll slip out before sunrise and make our way back into the jungle before anyone sees us." Annoyance flares in Tom's voice. "Right now, we should be thankful we have a roof over our heads and food to eat. We'll have to take turns keeping watch throughout the night, though. I'll take the first watch. In the meantime, we should all eat something and get ourselves cleaned up."

"All the lights work, and there's running water," Aiden says. "There's a bathroom off the kitchen and another one upstairs."

"Good. And you're sure no one can get in or out that door in the kitchen?" Tom sets his gaze on Marjorie, who nods emphatically.

I scoop Aiden's bag off the floor. "I'll make something for us to eat." I'm not a very good cook, but I'm sure I can heat some soup from a can. Hopefully, the task will help calm me and take my mind off what's happening, but all I can see is Larry falling to the ground. *We didn't even try to help him.* Setting the bag on the kitchen table, I grip the edge, hang my head, and close my eyes. *We just left him there, just like we left Sienna.* We're going to be okay. Tom is an air marshal. He's trained for bad situations, and he has a gun. He'll protect us.

Then why don't I feel safe?

"Hey, you all right?" Aiden's voice is soft at my ear.

"Yeah, I think so." I straighten and unzip the bag.

"Here, let me help." He takes the food out and sets it on the table. "Can you look for a can opener?"

I rummage through the cabinets and drawers until I find a handheld can opener. Like everything else, it's caked in dust. I rinse it off in the sink, then hand it to Aiden. I repeat the process with a large pot. Then I search for bowls and spoons and cups.

Being in the kitchen like this feels too normal for our current situation. It also reminds me so much of home, of the evenings I spent helping Mom prepare dinner. Back when we still got along, when she actually wanted me around and I wasn't the family pariah. I'd give anything to hear her voice right now, even if she was scolding me, or to feel her arms around me.

I freeze, and my heart runs rampant, leaving me gasping for breath. I set the bowl I'm holding back onto the counter, setting it down harder than necessary. Tears pool in my eyes, and I try to blink them away.

"Emily?"

Aiden's voice is faint, but it snaps me back to the present. He places his hand on my shoulder, and I turn into him, burying my face against his chest. And then my tears fall hard and fast.

"Hey, easy." He rubs my back. "It's okay."

"I didn't hug them," I sob.

"What? Who?"

"My parents. When they dropped me off at the airport, I didn't hug them. I didn't tell them I loved them." I pull back and wipe my face.

"So, when you get home—and you will get home—hug them extra hard and tell them how much you love them. But I'm sure they know that already."

I shrug and glance around for a tissue box or roll of paper towels, but I don't find any. I return to the sink and splash cool water on my face. Aiden's wrong. My parents have no idea how I really feel about them. My actions sure didn't show it, and I'd screamed that I hated them. There's no way they can know the truth, and that terrifies me almost as much as being stuck on this stupid island. Aiden comes up behind me and wraps his arms around my stomach, his chin resting on my shoulder. I don't know what I would do without him here, constantly comforting me.

"Everything is quiet out there," Tom says as he walks into the kitchen. Marjorie is on his heels. "I have no idea where that arrow came from or who shot it." He frowns.

I break away from Aiden's embrace. Dwelling on the things I didn't do and say won't help anything, so I push the thoughts and emotions away and focus on the current situation. "I suppose it's good no one is out there, right? That means we're probably safe."

Tom nods. "For the time being, yes. But we can't let our guard down. We'll take shifts keeping watch. Do any of you know how to shoot a gun?"

I shake my head. So does Aiden.

"I do." Marjorie raises her hand. "I own a gun shop and shooting range."

Tom smiles broadly. "Good. Then you and I will take turns tonight. I don't want to leave anyone in charge of our safety if they don't know how to shoot." He glances at me and Aiden with what can only be described as disappointment.

"Wait," Aiden says. "Just because we can't use a gun doesn't mean we can't help."

"He's right," Marjorie interjects before things escalate between the guys. "You and Emily can take care of other things, like cooking and bringing us coffee and making sure we stay awake. We should take shifts in pairs. Me and Aiden, and Tom and Emily."

"Perfect," Tom says.

"Don't we get a say in this?" I say before I can stop myself. I want to help and take my turn keeping watch, but I don't want to do it with Tom. He seems nice enough, but I don't know him well. I don't know any of these people that well, and the thought of sitting up in the middle of the night with a strange, older man doesn't sit well with me.

Tom raises a brow. "Excuse me?"

I don't mean to be snotty, but his gaze is intense and fiery. I cower and clear my throat. "I mean, why can't I sit watch with Marjorie?"

126

He narrows his eyes. "This isn't some sleepover party, Emily. This is real life, and our lives could very well be in danger. Pairing one man and one woman is the easiest, safest, and most effective way to handle this situation."

Sexist much? But I have the good sense not to say that. Instead, I nod. "Fine, whatever."

"The food is ready," Aiden says, interrupting the tense exchange.

I take over the task and serve everyone a bowl of food. Marjorie and Tom sit at the table while Aiden and I stand at the counter. After eating cold airplane meals for the past two days, the hot soup tastes like heaven, and I devour it.

"We should see if there are any extra blankets or pillow around here somewhere. There's only one bed down here, so someone will have to take the couch," Marjorie says.

"Yeah, but there are five bedrooms upstairs," I say.

"Upstairs is off limits. We all stay down here. Together." Tom's voice leaves no room for argument.

"I'm pretty sure I saw a linen closet in the living room." Marjorie stands.

Wait, there's a linen closet? How come we didn't look through it? Or notice it? I stifle a yawn and set my dishes in the sink. "I'll go check." I return to the living room and look around. I don't see a closet door anywhere, and I'm starting to think maybe Marjorie was seeing things.

"Over here," she says as she walks into the room. She points to a door secluded in the corner and obstructed by the couch.

"Oh." I open the door and peer inside. Nothing. "It's empty."

"Bummer." She sighs. "For what it's worth, I'd much rather have you sit watch with me. But don't take offense to Tom. Every law enforcement officer I've ever dealt with is brusque like him. I'm convinced it's a requirement of the job." She laughs.

"Thanks." I give her a grateful smile. Maybe sitting up with Tom won't be so bad after all. I can pick his brain about our situation and his plans for our escape back to the beach tomorrow.

CHAPTER 21

Aiden

I LEAVE THE BATHROOM AFTER having showered and changed, feeling better than I have since I left New York. Emily is sitting at the kitchen table, staring off into space. Tom, after eating and showering, promptly fell asleep on the couch. Marjorie and I are officially starting our watch at ten o'clock while Tom and Emily get some sleep. Then, around one or two in the morning, we'll wake them so Marjorie and I can sleep for a few hours before we head back to the beach.

"Hey." I pull out the chair opposite Emily and sit. "You really should try that shower. It's great."

She smiles. "Will it help me fall asleep?"

I shrug. "Maybe." We fall into a comfortable silence. I can't help but wonder what she's thinking. Our situation is awful, and I'm sure that's weighing on her mind, but since Tom snapped at her, she's been quieter and distant.

"You know," I say, breaking the silence. "I'm a champ at pulling all-nighters. I can sit up with you and Tom if you want."

Shock registers on her face. "You'd do that for me?"

I avert my gaze. "Yeah, why wouldn't I?"

A long sigh cuts through our moment, and I glance up to see Emily smiling at me. The sight warms me from the inside. "Thank you, but you don't have to do that."

I nod and try to hide my disappointment. When I first started dating my ex-girlfriend, we would sit up all night on the phone, talking, getting to know each other, laughing. That's what I miss the most about being in a relationship, and a large part of me had hoped I could have a night like that with Emily. But since crashing, it's been one crazy thing after another.

"What's the purpose or reasoning for all this?" she asks, waving her arms around.

"This building?" I'm not sure what she's asking me, but I don't want her to think I'm dumb, so I don't ask for clarification.

"This building. The plane crash. This island. Sienna and Larry's deaths…"

"I don't know," I say with a frown. Like I was years ago, she's searching for answers. I found mine in church, but I'm not sure she wants to hear that. Still, I can only tell her what I believe. "We're not meant to know God's plans, just that He knows what He's doing. Including this." I motion around to indicate the building.

"That's not answering the question. That's deflecting it with a fake reasoning."

I sigh heavily. "What do you want me to say? I'm trying my hardest to stay positive. You know, the whole fake it until you make it? And please don't call my beliefs fake reasoning. That's not fair."

"I'm sorry." Propping her foot on the edge of the chair, she hugs her knee to her chest. "I'm just scared," she whispers. "I'm scared of what the night or even the next day will bring us. I'm scared about the next hour. None of us have a clue about what's going on, who's out there, who might die next. And that scares the daylights out of me."

"Emily," I say softly. Standing, I pull her to her feet and wrap her up in a hug. She puts her arms around my neck, and her warm breath breezes across my skin. "All of us miss our families, our friends, our lives. And we're all scared on some level, but we will get through this."

"How do you know that?" Her words are mumbled against my shoulder.

"Because I have faith. And because we have Tom on our side, and he's kinda scary with that gun."

She laughs, and my heart soars. I adore that sound.

"Thank you." She pulls back enough to look into my eyes. "I'm sorry we're here, but I'm glad I met you."

"Me, too. In fact, meeting you has been the only thing that's made this situation bearable."

A small smile pulls at her lips, and before I can talk myself out of it, I lean forward and press my lips to hers. And I don't immediately pull away like I did the other night. At first, she's stiff with shock, and I realize I've made a mistake. But before I can break away, she welcomes my kiss. Her lips are softer than anything I've ever felt, and her breath is so warm I'm sure my internal temperature goes up a few degrees.

The want for more radiates from both of us, and the kiss deepens. Emily moves her hands from my neck, over my shoulders, and down my arms until she slips them around my waist. I groan and force myself to break away from the kiss. If we keep going like this, we might never stop. I rest my forehead to hers and try to catch my breath.

"You should probably go sit with Marjorie." Emily steps out of my hold and tucks her hands in her pockets.

My eyes widen, and my heart races more than it already is. Did she not like the kiss? "Are you trying to get rid of me?" I say it jokingly, but the fear of her answer is very real.

"What? No." She shakes her head adamantly. "I just mean well, it's ten, and your shift is starting. And I want to shower." She looks everywhere but at me.

"Right." I breathe a sigh of relief. "Sure. Of course. Do you want me to sit up with you and Tom during your shift?"

"Yes, but I'm not going to let you."

I raise a brow. "You're not?"

"No. I'm afraid we'll spend too much time kissing, and then Tom will get mad. And as you said, he and his gun are scary."

I laugh. "Fair enough."

"And we have a long hike back to the beach tomorrow. You need to get some sleep because I'm not carrying you all that way."

Smiling, I step closer and place a gentle kiss on her lips. "Go enjoy your shower."

She nods then disappears into the bathroom. I head into the living room to find Marjorie sitting in the empty recliner, gun on her lap, staring at the window. Tom's snoring loudly on the couch.

There's not another chair, so I grab one of the kitchen table chairs and set it next to Marjorie.

"It's been quiet," she whispers.

"That's good, right?"

"I don't think so." She goes to the window, pulls the blinds to the side, and peeks out. "It's like having kids. When they're loud and making noise, you know where they are and what they're doing. But when they're quiet…" She lets go of the blinds and returns to her chair. "That's when you have to worry."

I don't allow myself to think about what she's implying. "Do you have kids?"

"A daughter. Brandy. She's in her second year at NYU." Marjorie smiles. "She fell in love with the city and has been begging me to visit so she could show me the sights. I surprised her for her birthday. We spent three days together in the city. I was flying back home."

"That's nice. I'm sure she was thrilled to have you there." I lean forward and rest my elbows on my knees.

"When we get off this island, I'm moving there to be closer to her."

"That's great. Family is so important. I can't wait to get back home to mine." A wave of melancholy settles over me, and I shift in my chair, sitting up straight again. I miss my parents something fierce, and I hate that I left them to go chase down a woman who doesn't want me.

"Brandy is all I have left. Her father, my husband, died several years ago. I stayed in Alaska, though, because of the business. It was Brandy's life, and I couldn't bear to sell it. But now." She shakes her head. "There are more important things."

"Well, I'm sure your daughter will be very happy to have her mom living closer." I smile.

"Do you have any siblings?"

"No. I'm an only child. My parents can't have kids. I was adopted as a baby."

"Oh."

That's the standard response when I tell people I'm adopted. I don't know why. It's not like it's a bad thing. "I was in New York visiting my birth mom. It was the first time I ever met her, and it didn't go so well."

"I'm sorry, Aiden." Marjorie pats my shoulder. "Sometimes, God has plans for us that we don't understand. I'm sure there's a reason you ended up with the family you did."

Yeah, because my biological mother is a rotten, selfish human being. "I'm lucky to have the parents I do. They've never made me feel like I'm not their son. I only wish I would've listened to them and not gone to the city looking for her."

"Hey." She gives me an awkward, one-armed hug. "I'm sure your parents understand. And you'll get the chance to tell them when you get home."

I nod. "Thanks." I glance up to find Emily standing in the doorway, eyes wide and filling with tears.

"Sorry." Emily clears her throat. "I'm just going to go to bed and get some sleep."

Shoot. I stand. "Excuse me," I say to Marjorie and then go into the bedroom. "Emily?"

She stands in the middle of the room, arms crossed. "Why didn't you tell me?"

"What?"

"Our first night here. I asked why you were in New York. Why didn't you tell me?"

"I barely knew you."

"You barely know Marjorie, but you didn't have any problems telling her."

I sigh. "I know. But it's not easy to admit to myself, or anyone else, that the woman who gave birth to me doesn't want me. She kicked me out of her house, Emily. She didn't even care that I was there or how I was doing."

She drops her arms to her sides. "If anyone knows how you feel, it's me." She points to herself. "My parents don't want me around, either, remember? They were shipping me off to my grandparents."

I frown. She's right. I never once considered that, though. To me, it seems like Emily's parents love her enough to take drastic measures to ensure she's safe and cared for. I was dumped on the steps of the local hospital by my parents. That's a completely different scenario.

"I'm sorry I didn't tell you. I guess I was embarrassed," I finally say after several moments of silence.

"I'm sorry I snapped at you about it. Being stuck here without any answers or rescue in sight is really starting to mess with me."

"It's messing with all of us." I close the distance between us and kiss her again. "Try to get some sleep. I'll be in the next room if you need me." I leave her alone, hoping she'll find enough peace to get the rest she needs. I'm positive I won't find any tonight.

CHAPTER 22

Emily

"FIRE!"

MY EYES SNAP OPEN, and I bolt upright out of the bed. I blink, trying to adjust to the dark, and that's when I see Aiden rush into the room.

"Emily! Get up. C'mon, we've got to go!" He's waving his arms frantically.

I fling the covers off and shove my feet into my shoes. "What's going on?"

"The research lab is on fire." He grabs my bag and slings it over his shoulder. He's already got his pack on, too.

"What?" I sniff the air. "I don't smell any smoke."

"This building isn't on fire. Not yet anyway. But it's spreading fast. Now come on. We need to get out of here and into the jungle before someone sees us."

My heart races as I run out of the building behind Aiden. Marjorie is already outside, acting as a lookout. She ushers us away from the building. Tom takes the lead, gun in hand. The research lab building is engulfed in flames, lighting up the sky better than the sun. The heat is like a moving wall, getting closer and closer. This has to be some sort of nightmare. How did it catch on fire? The stink of gasoline hangs in the air. My eyes widen. Someone started the fire!

"Emily!" Aiden grabs my hand and drags me away from the scene.

The four of us make a mad dash toward the trees. I glance around furiously, praying I don't see anyone lurking. But someone is out here. The question is where are they? And why are they attacking us?

Tom stops abruptly, and I run into him hard enough to cause me to fall back. Aiden catches me. Once I'm steady, I move around Tom, but he holds out his arm, stopping me. A few feet in front of him stands a woman. She's tall and thin with long, stringy brown hair. Her clothes are worn and tattered, but her eyes are sharp and focused. She's holding a bow with an arrow pointed at Tom's head.

I gasp.

"Put the gun down," she instructs.

Slowly, Tom lowers his gun to the ground and then puts his hands up in a show of surrender. I can't believe what I'm seeing. Why is he letting go of the only weapon we have? Why doesn't he just shoot her so we can get away from here?

"Who are you?" she asks.

"I'm a U.S. Air Marshal," Tom says calmly. "We're a group of plane crash survivors. We've been scouring the island for help and supplies."

Aiden moves to stand by my side, and she whips the bow in his direction. He puts his hands up immediately to show he's not a threat.

"A plane crash?" She diverts her attention back to Tom.

"Yes. SunDun flight three-seven-two-two. We've been here for almost four days now, and we were hoping to find someone who can help us or have a working phone or something," Tom says.

All this "let's get to know each other" is getting on my last nerve. We're in a dire situation here, and no one seems to care. "Did you kill Larry?"

"Emily!" Tom snaps without removing his gaze from the woman.

"Who?" She gives me a dirty look.

Okay, so apparently she isn't a killer. "Are you one of them?" Interrogating her while she's holding a bow and arrow isn't the smartest thing I've ever done.

"One of who?"

"One of the people chasing us and killing us."

136

"I used to be." She lowers the bow and arrow. I let out a sigh of relief. "If you guys want to live, going into the jungle isn't the answer."

Tom reaches for the gun and tucks it into the back of his jeans. "Those buildings are going up in flames fast. They're no longer safe, either."

"Follow me." She shoves by Tom and marches back toward the building we just vacated. Tom turns to follow her.

"You can't be serious," I say, clutching Tom's elbow. "You're going to trust her?"

"If she wanted to kill us, we'd be dead." He jerks his arm from my grasp. "Look." He lowers his voice so it's more of a hiss. "I don't want to trust her, but what other choice do we have? We either take our chances in the jungle, or we take our chances with her."

"What if this is a trap?" I say, panic lacing my words. "What if she's leading us back there so she can kill us?"

"Emily." Tom puts his hands on my shoulders and bends his knees slightly so he's eye level with me. "If she wanted to kill us, she wouldn't have shown herself. She would've stayed hidden and picked us off one by one."

My bottom lip trembles. I have the urge to grab Aiden's hand and run as far and as fast as we can, away from Tom and Marjorie and this crazy strange woman.

"I'm not asking you to trust her," Tom says, holding my gaze. "I'm asking you to trust me."

"He's right," Aiden says. "We have no choice but to trust her."

I throw my hands up in the air in frustration. "This is ridiculous," I mutter as I reluctantly follow them.

The woman enters the building and heads for the kitchen. She shoves the fridge to the side and opens the door it was blocking. It's pitch black inside, and I keep my hand on the wall so I don't fall or lose my bearings. She leads us down a small flight of stairs and then heaves open a metal door built into the ground. A beam of light shines out.

Tom narrows his eyes. "What is this place?"

"A bunker. It was installed about sixty years ago. Let's go. We don't have a lot of time."

"Sixty years? How long have you been here?" I ask, not hiding the shock and panic in my voice.

"I'll answer all your questions as soon as we're inside."

Marjorie climbs down first, then me, Aiden, Tom, and finally the woman. She slams the door and a massive lock clicks in place, making me jump. I hope this woman is one of the good guys because if not, we just locked ourselves in our graves. My hands tremble, and I flex my fingers.

Without a word, she walks down a long corridor, and we fall in line behind her. After a few feet, we emerge into an open space that's furnished better than the building. In one corner is what looks like a well-stocked science lab. She sets down her bow and arrow and removes her jacket.

"Are you four the only survivors?" she asks.

"No. There are almost twenty more back near the beach where the wreckage is." Tom stands in the same spot as if he's afraid to make any sudden movements. "Are you going to give us your name?"

She steps up to Tom and extends her hand. "Doctor Brenda Hill."

Tom shakes her hand. "I'm Tom Davis. This is Marjorie, Aiden, and Emily."

"What is this place?" Marjorie asks. "And who are the other people out there killing us and setting the building on fire?"

"They're my former colleagues." Brenda bites her lip. "We came here almost thirty years ago as part of a massive government project."

"Okay, I'm confused. That doesn't explain why they're trying to kill us," Aiden says.

"What kind of project?" I ask. My gut clenches, and the contents of my stomach twist, causing me to have to fight the urge to throw up. There's nothing right about this island, and now I'm sure that's because of whatever these scientists are doing here. My mind races with all sorts of crazy scenarios about genetic testing and cloning.

"Biological and nuclear weapons testing," she says bluntly.

"I knew it," Tom says. His face is pale, and his eyes are wide. "We're on Amchitka, aren't we?"

"What?" Aiden shouts, his gaze landing on Tom. "That's been your suspicion this whole time? Why didn't you say anything to me?"

"What's Amchitka?" Marjorie asks, seemingly as confused as I am.

"An island that the US government used for nuclear testing after World War Two. They shut down all testing in 1994, and the island is restricted to government officials only." Aiden recites the facts as if he just read them moments ago. *Impressive.*

"Oh, no." I cup my hand over my mouth and turn away.

Aiden puts his arm around my shoulders and guides me toward the couch. I sit and hang my head between my legs, inhaling deeply and exhaling slowly. When the nausea passes, I lift my head. Aiden's staring at me with concern.

"Feel better now?" he asks.

"A little." My gaze darts back to Tom, who's in deep conversation with Brenda. I stare at them for a moment before turning to Aiden. "I want to go home."

He pulls me into a hug, and I rest my head on his chest. "So do I," he says, stroking my hair. "Maybe this woman is the answer we've been hoping for. She's got to have some way to communicate with the outside world."

"Then why hasn't she used it to get out of here?"

He sighs. "I don't know."

Maybe this woman is crazy, and she doesn't want to get off this island. Maybe she likes it here for some strange reason. Or maybe she's lying to us and plans to kill us. I swallow hard and wipe a sheen of sweat from the back of my neck.

Tom and Marjorie approach us. "Brenda says we can stay here until the fire dies out."

"How generous," I mumble. I don't like this woman one bit. "Did she give you any real answers or explanations?"

"A few." Tom glances over his shoulder at Brenda, who is tinkering at her lab. "As far as I can gather, a group of scientists were sent here to develop and test biological and nuclear weapons, but the solitude got to some of them, so they left and new people were sent in to replace them."

"Still doesn't explain why those other people want us dead," I say. Why doesn't anyone else feel like this is a big deal?

"Brenda seems to think the scientists who wanted to go never made it. She thinks that's who those people are." Tom keeps his voice low.

"That doesn't make any sense," Aiden says, narrowing his eyes.

"I agree." Tom folds his arms over his chest. "I don't like this."

Finally, he's thinking rationally and making sense. "So, what do we do now?" I wish he would've realized this before we followed her down here.

"We wait," he says.

"Wait for what?" Marjorie looks just as dumbfounded as I feel.

"For her to fall asleep. Then we're out of here and headed back to the beach."

I sigh with frustration. "Why'd we even follow her here in the first place then?"

"She had an arrow pointed at my face. I needed to diffuse the situation and make sure no one else died." His words are a harsh whisper, his gaze angry to match.

This needs to stop. Now. I stand and march over to Brenda. "Tell me what is going on. You said those other people are your colleagues. Why are they trying to kill us? Why is there a large hole of crap in the middle of the jungle? What kind of weapons are you testing here?" I fire question after question at her, not really giving her a chance to respond. "Why are you still here? You have to have some kind of phone or radio or computer that we can use to call home for help, don't you?"

"Emily, easy." Aiden places his hand on my shoulder, but I'm too wound up to calm down.

"No." I twist away from his touch. "I need to know what's going on. We all do." I turn to glare at Tom and Marjorie. "And she's the only one who has any answers." I point at Brenda.

"I already told your friend all I know." Brenda juts her chin toward Tom.

"You're lying, and you're hiding something." My voice is much louder than necessary, but my anger is rising by the second, and I'm ready to explode.

"Okay, that's enough." Aiden grips my shoulders firmly and forces me to move away from Brenda. He takes me into the kitchen area, which is partially secluded from the living area. "I know you're scared, so am I, but provoking this woman isn't the answer."

I bite down on my bottom lip to stop the impending tears. "How can everyone be so calm? Why isn't anyone demanding answers?"

"Tom is a trained professional. Let him handle this. He wants to live and get off this island just as badly as the rest of us. He won't do anything to jeopardize that." Aiden gently takes my chin and turns my head to face him. "I promise you. We will get out of this. Alive."

I nod, but I don't believe him. He can't promise something he has no control over, and as long as we're trapped in this bunker with that woman, I don't feel safe. I don't care what assurances Aiden or Tom or anyone else gives me.

I return to the couch, and that's where I stay. I keep my gaze trained on Brenda, who moves about the bunker like all of this is perfectly natural. Marjorie and Aiden are in the kitchen with her. I cross my arms and lean back. This entire thing is so crazy.

"Holding up?" Tom asks as he sits next to me.

"Barely."

He gives me a sympathetic nod. "Nothing about this situation is ideal, but if we stick together, we'll be fine."

I adjust and tuck my legs under me. "Is this island really a nuclear testing site?"

"Yes, but it hasn't been active in well over twenty years."

"But…" I swallow hard, unable to wrap my mind around what I'm about to ask. "Isn't there still radiation in the air? Have we all been exposed?"

"I don't know." He sighs. "And Brenda isn't exactly forthcoming with answers, but after she falls asleep, I'm going to have a look around." He subtly nods toward the science lab area and the file cabinet in the corner. "One way or another, I'll get the information we need."

"Don't you think it's strange she has a lab set up down here when there was a whole research lab up there?" I point up to indicate the building that's now probably nothing more than a pile of ash.

"I do," he confirms. "Which is why I want to look around before we leave."

He's so calm and collected, unlike the curt, take-charge, bossy guy he'd been up to this point. Maybe there's more to him than I thought. Maybe he's not so mean or scary after all. I lick my lips. "You said I remind you of your daughter. What's her name?" I don't know why I choose to ask him that, but if I'm going to literally trust him with my life, I want to know more about him.

"Her name was Lucy." He smiles wistfully.

"Was?" My voice is barely above a whisper.

"She died when she was fifteen."

"Oh." I frown. "I'm so sorry, Tom."

"She was on the plane that crashed into the Twin Towers on nine-eleven." He rests his arms on his knees and hangs his head. "It was her first time flying, and she was scared to death." He looks up at me, and his eyes are red and wet with unshed tears. "I promised her flying was the safest form of travel and that she'd be fine." He laughs bitterly.

"There was no way you could've known," I say. My heart breaks for him. No wonder he's so angry all the time. Losing a child is the worst possible thing any parent can go through.

"No." He clasps his hands together as if in prayer. "But I was supposed to be on that plane with her, and instead, I'd volunteered to work an international flight to Paris. I failed her."

Without thinking, I scoot closer and drape my arm across his back, giving him an awkward hug as if he were my father.

"I swore I would never fail anyone ever again." He straightens, and my arm falls away. "And I'm not about to break that promise. I'll get us out of here, Emily. You have my word." And then he stands and joins everyone in the kitchen.

Right then, I vow not to give Tom any more trouble. I'll do as he says and trust him.

143

CHAPTER 23

Aiden

EMILY EVENTUALLY FALLS ASLEEP ON the couch with her head in my lap, but her sleep is fitful, and she moves around a lot. I can't shake the feeling that she's right—about everything. There's something off about Brenda, and she hasn't bothered to answer any of the questions Emily asked. Why is that?

"Is she all right?" Marjorie crouches next to the couch and nods at Emily.

"She's scared."

Marjorie snorts. "Aren't we all?"

I nod. "What's Tom's plan? How long are we going to just sit here?" Brenda had retired to her room about forty-five minutes ago, and I'm itching to get out of here and back to the beach. Not that I like the thought of hiking through the jungle in the dark.

She shrugs. "I don't know. He hasn't told me anything."

"Brenda has to be sleeping by now, don't you think?" I glance in the direction of the bedroom. There's no lights on. No movement or sounds. "We can slip out now without her knowing."

"I think Tom wants to wait until the sun starts to rise." Marjorie sits with her back against the couch. "Going out in the dark isn't a good idea. We still don't know who's out there."

"What if she wakes up with the dawn?" I ask.

Just then, Tom approaches. He's got a handful of papers. "I've been snooping."

"They teach you that in air marshall school?" I ask sarcastically. I don't know what's come over me or why I'm acting like a brat, but I can't sit here a second longer. My skin is crawling, and I want to climb out of it, leave all this stuff behind.

Marjorie whips around to look at me. It's the same expression my mom always gives me when I get into trouble. I give her an apologetic shrug.

"Aiden," Tom begins. "Just because I fly around the country doesn't mean I'm not fully trained like every other law enforcement officer out there. And the number one lesson I was taught—always stay calm and never act like you don't have complete control of a situation, even if you don't."

I remain silent and wait for him to continue. Emily shifts and rolls over so her face is buried against my stomach. She mutters something incoherent and then goes still again.

"These scientists were sent here to test a new biological weapon." Tom looks at the papers. "As best I can tell, it was a gas that would cause a person's nervous system to essentially freeze, rendering them useless."

"Why would anyone want to do that?" Marjorie asks.

"You paralyze your enemy, you can kill them easier," Tom says. "But there's more. Initial testing was done on the wildlife, which explains why we haven't seen many animals or birds around here."

"Oh, dear God." Marjorie cups her hand over her mouth and stifles her gasp. "That's awful."

"You got all that information from some papers?" I ask with disbelief.

Tom nods. "These are Brenda's field notes. She's been meticulous about documenting every day on this island. All the testing and the results and even the people. She kept a detailed log about everyone and everything, including two people named Tracy and Greg. She actually talks about them a lot."

"This is so creepy," I say.

"Listen to this…" Tom shuffles through some of the papers to find what he's looking for. "I found some torn pages that appear to be from Brenda's personal journal. The date is missing, but listen to this… 'I had another nightmare last night. The same one I've had since I was thirteen. My parents are on vacation, only this time, I'm with them. We're in the lobby of the hotel when Mom says she forgot something in her room, but she doesn't have her key, so Dad

146

has to go back with her. Being an impossible teenager, I refuse to go with them. Dad tells me I can go ahead and wait outside on the bench. But I don't listen. I wander down the sidewalk, and then the hotel blows up. I run back toward the building, hoping I can save them. But I can't. I never can. And then I wake up in a cold sweat. I know I wasn't there when they died in a terrorist attack, but the helplessness is still very real, almost tangible.'" Tom pauses to flip the paper over. Then he continues.

"'I'll be forever grateful to the US government for their quick acting and for eliminating the man who killed my parents. But I can't get past the anger and the need for revenge. That attack took more from me than just my parents. It stole my faith in humanity. It stole my dreams of ever having kids of my own because what sort of messed up person would bring a defenseless child into this horrible world we live in? It's what led me to sign up for this project, to help develop the weapon that will prevent anything like this from happening again. It's my life's mission to develop the perfect weapon, to keep the world safe.'" Tom flips to the next page. "That's where it ends."

"Wow. So, she's like a mad scientist or something?" I ask. My hand resting on Emily's waist stiffens.

"Tracy and Greg?" Marjorie whispers. "Who are they?"

"There's notes on them, too." Tom scans the next couple of pages. "Here it is. 'Tracy and Greg aren't doing well. The solitude of this island and our experiments are weighing heavily on them. They wander around aimlessly and keep talking about going home. This morning, they put in an official request to relinquish their posts and return back home. Permission was granted, and their replacements will arrive within three days' time. I'll be sad to see them leave. Greg's changes to the formula have seen some wonderful results.'"

"Wait," I say. "They weren't just testing? They were tweaking and changing the weapon? Why?"

"I don't know. I haven't been able to find an answer to that, but I'm sure it's in here somewhere. But listen to this…" He shuffles a few more pages. "'Tracy and Greg left to meet the transport yesterday, but so far, we haven't met their replacements.

If they decided not to send any, why weren't we notified?'" Tom flips to the next page. "'Today is supply day. The transport usually arrives around nine a.m., but when I got to the airstrip, the crates of supplies were already there. As we gathered them and headed back to the building, I noticed movement in the trees. I'm positive it was Tracy and Greg, but that can't be. They left days ago. Didn't they?'"

"So, she thinks those two were left here intentionally?" I ask, trying to piece everything together. "If that was the case, why didn't they go back to the building?"

Instead of answering me, Tom continues to read. "'We've been given a new course of study today. Instructions, along with a new biological compound, were sent with our supplies. It's something Greg was working on while here. He and Tracy volunteered to be test subjects and are now in quarantine while the effects are studied closely. We have to do the same here. I'm astounded. It's too soon for any human trials just yet. We don't even know what this is. No one wants to volunteer, so we had to draw sticks. Kevin is now our test subject. We'll expose him to the compound tomorrow morning.

"'Day fourteen. Kevin is unnaturally pale, but his spirits seem to be high. He's moving around his room unassisted, and he's eating more than usual. Day twenty-two. Kevin is exhibiting traits of a wild animal. He's resorted to eating with his hands at all times and is defecating in the corner. He sleeps on the floor. His temper is out of control, and he's stopped communicating,'" Tom reads.

"It all makes sense now," I say, glancing between the two of them. "Greg. Tracy. Kevin. They created something that turned humans into savages."

"Seems that way, but why would they do that? It's not like savages can be controlled or used in combat." He searches through the pages. "I need more time to read through these."

The sound of furniture scraping across the floor silences all of us. I hold my breath, waiting for Brenda to appear from the hallway. After several beats and no sign of her, I say, "I think we're out of time."

"I agree. We need to get out of here," Marjorie says, standing. "For all we know, she lured us down here and plans to use us as her personal guinea pigs."

I glance down at Emily, intent on waking her up, but she's already awake. Tears pool in her eyes, and I know she's heard everything. I give her a sad smile, wishing she didn't have to know what I know. She sits up and rubs her eyes while yawning.

"Okay, grab whatever you can, and let's get out of here. Be extra quiet," Tom says. He shoves the pages into his pack and then goes back to the lab to get more.

Marjorie heads into the kitchen and jams as much food as she can into her bag. I get up to do the same when Emily grabs my hand, pulling me back down onto the couch. "What're the effects of radiation exposure?" she whispers.

I search her face for some indication as to what's going on in her head. There's something different in her gaze, a fearful determination I haven't seen before. "I don't know," I say, knowing that's not the answer she wants. "I really don't think we've been exposed. The effects of nuclear bombs last hundreds of years. If there was still radiation on this island, there wouldn't be any life at all. No trees or grass."

Her shoulders slump, with relief or disappointment, I have no idea.

"Everyone ready?" Tom asks.

"If you leave this bunker, you will die." Brenda stands at the end of the hallway, arms crossed. She's unarmed, but the mere sight of her standing there strikes terror in my veins. Instinctively, I move Emily so she's standing behind me. Then we slowly inch toward Tom and stand behind him. Marjorie does the same.

"We need to get back to the beach," Tom says. "We need to warn the other survivors so they have a fighting chance."

"If they're still alive," she says coolly.

"Why wouldn't they be?" Tom asks.

"When I reported the effects of the last biological compound we'd been testing, I was given very specific instructions that no one is allowed to leave this island. Ever." Brenda's expression unflinching.

"Are you going to try and stop us?" Tom reaches for the gun in the waistband of his jeans.

"Those people out there... they're not human anymore. They're animals. They can smell you, sense your fear. You don't stand a chance in that jungle." Brenda pushes off the wall and saunters into the living area as if we're casually discussing the weather.

"You've managed to survive all this time," Emily says.

"They know my scent and know I'm not a threat. They leave me alone."

I tilt my head, unable to shake the feeling that there's still more she's not telling us. "Why not just leave? Why stay here with them?"

"Because I'm still working. Watching them. Studying them."

"Controlling them?" Tom asks, and Brenda nods. "Then lead us back to the beach. Help us help the others. You're the only one who can. Please."

Behind me, Emily shifts. I can only imagine what she's thinking. Maybe she is right about going out on our own. Maybe we would be better off together, away from everyone else.

"I can't," Brenda says.

"This is useless," Emily mumbles.

I turn to look at her and mouth the word, stop. Her snide comments aren't helping the situation, and I'm pretty sure Tom is getting angry.

"I read your research notes," Tom says, challenging her. "I know about your parents. I know why you're here and what you're trying to do."

I want to smack him upside the head. What is he doing?

Brenda remains silent, but her forehead wrinkles as if she's deep in thought.

Tom continues, "What was in that compound you gave Kevin?"

Brenda's face is a mask of indifference. "A genetic enhancement. It was supposed to sharpen the senses, make it so our troops could hear better, see further, run faster. Make them real-life super soldiers. It was intended to give them an advantage, but the science was wrong, and it had the opposite effect we wanted. It turned them into deadly predators."

"Why weren't the experiments stopped?" Tom asks.

"They were. The government sprayed the island with toxic gas, a gas that's equivalent to what you'd find in a nuke. It was supposed to kill everyone and everything on it. Then they shut down all testing and labeled the island off-limits to the public."

"Clearly, that didn't work," Marjorie says snidely.

"Thought you said you were still working," Emily says, her tone sarcastic. "Which is? Are the experiments still going on or not?"

"No, it didn't work. In fact, it only made them stronger. Whatever was in that compound made them immune," Brenda says to Marjorie. "As for me, I knew it was coming, so I hid out down here until I figured it was safe to come out."

"Why didn't the government pull you out?" Tom asks. "They knew you were here, that you were fine."

"My contact warned me and has been helping me ever since," Brenda says.

"Are you seriously telling us the government—*our government*—did all of this?" Emily's tone is colored with disbelief and disgust.

"That's exactly what I'm telling you."

"This contact of yours," Aiden begins, "how do you contact him?"

Brenda paces in front of us as if she's debating on what else to say. Finally, she speaks again. "There's an airstrip five miles straight behind this building, and there's a dock on the eastern most side of the island. My contact drops supplies once a month. The next supply delivery is scheduled for the day after tomorrow. If you can catch the transport, you can get off this island."

My eyes widen, and my heart races. Emily snatches my hand and squeezes. We're going to be rescued! My prayers have been answered. Hope and excitement swell in my chest, and I can't stand still. I fidget. Now, more than ever, I want to get back to the beach.

"What do you mean *if* we can catch the transport?" Tom asks.

"Because of the natives, they never actually stop. They do a sky drop. And the time is never the same. So, if you're not there when the plane flies over…" She shrugs. "Then you're out of luck."

My heart sinks. There's no way at all to catch an airplane.

"Can't you get in touch with your contact and let him know we're here?" Tom asks.

"No." Brenda's face droops, and she appears tired. I wonder how old she is, how long she's actually been here, if she has any family back home—wherever home is for her. "And don't ask me that again." There's a dangerous edge to her tone.

"What happens if there's an emergency?" Marjorie asks. "You're telling us you're stranded on this island with no way off and no way to talk to the people who put you here?"

Yeah, I'm not buying into that, either.

"Believe me or not, I don't care. You can stay here where it's safe, or you can take your chances out there. But I've helped you enough." Brenda turns on her heel and disappears down the hallway.

"Let's get out of here," Emily says. She leads the way down the corridor and up the steps. She pushes open the door and gasps.

CHAPTER 24

Emily

I CAN'T BELIEVE WHAT I'M seeing. The building is intact. Not so much as a hint of smoke. No fire damage. I rush toward the kitchen window and peer outside. Only the research lab is reduced to a pile of fiery rubble—everything around it is untouched.

"What? What is it?" Aiden asks, shoving his way into the kitchen. "No way."

"My thoughts exactly," I say.

"What is going on around here?" Tom asks as he offers his hand to Marjorie and helps her out of the bunker. "It's like they're toying with us or something."

"All the more reason to get out of here as fast as we can," Marjorie says. "I grabbed more food from down there, but maybe we can snatch that laundry basket and take it back with us."

"I'll grab it," Aiden offers.

"No!" I say too quickly. "It's too dangerous. You'll be out in the open, exposed to those things."

"I'll cover him," Tom says, holding his gun up.

"Cover him against people you can't see? We have no idea what these people look like or where they are. Brenda said all their senses have been heightened." I wave my arms around in an effort to emphasize my point. But I can tell by the looks on their faces that no one agrees with me.

"It'll be fine, Emily." Aiden gives me a reassuring smile. "We need that food for everyone else back at the beach."

"Then I'm going to help you grab it. It's heavy; you'll need help carrying it." I cross my arms over my chest and dare him to argue.

"He carried it out of the building. He can grab it and carry it to the tree line," Marjorie says, putting her hand on my shoulder in a very motherly gesture. "Then we can all take turns carrying it back to the beach."

"We really don't have time to stand here and debate this," Tom says. "I'll go outside first and make sure we're clear. Aiden, you run for the basket while Emily and Marjorie head for the trees. Got it?" He phrases it as a question, but it's clear by his tone that none of us have a choice. We've been given our orders, and we have to follow them.

This is it. My moment of truth. I made a promise to myself that I would trust him and do as he says. But my heart is in my throat. Every person in my life I've trusted has betrayed me in some way. And they are people I loved. Family. Friends. Tom is a stranger. He could turn his back on me and not even blink.

All right, God, if You're real, now's the time to prove it. Please let us make it back to the beach safely. Protect Aiden and Tom and Marjorie. And me. Please don't let me die.

"Emily?" Aiden's hand is on my arm. "We're going to be okay." He nods to emphasize his point.

"Okay." I release a shaky breath and nod. "Okay," I repeat.

Tom steps outside while the rest of us wait inside. I hold my breath, expecting to hear a gunshot or a scream or some sort of noise to indicate there is trouble. But there is only silence. The sound of nothingness calms me a little. He waves his hand for us to come out. As soon as I'm off the last step, Marjorie yanks me toward the tree line, and I have to run at her speed, which is a lot faster than I'm prepared for, and I stumble a couple of times.

As soon as we reach the first tree, I stop and turn around. Aiden and Tom are a few steps away. When they make it to cover of the trees, I breathe a sigh of relief. Aiden sets the basket down and pulls in a lungful of air.

Thank You, God! Maybe all that stuff Jason and Aiden talk about isn't so crazy after all.

"All right, we're going to hike straight through the jungle and back to the beach. It's faster than going around, and the tress will offer us some protection," Tom says. "I'll stay in the lead and make sure the way is clear."

I lift one side of the basket, and Aiden lifts the other, then we fall in line behind Tom. Marjorie brings up the rear. She's holding the bow and arrow that Tom swiped from Brenda. Knowing there are two armed people—one in front and the other behind us—makes this journey seem a lot less scary. No one speaks for a long while. At first, I'm okay with the silence, but it begins to grate on my nerves. How can everyone be so calm? After everything we've seen and heard, why aren't we talking about what happens next?

"What're we going to tell everyone at the beach?" I ask.

"Nothing." Tom doesn't stop or slow his stride. "Until I have a chance to read the rest of Brenda's notes, we tell them nothing."

"They're going to wonder where we found all this food," I point out.

"So, we tell them about the buildings and the food, but that's it. No mention of the scientists or the inhabitants or the weapons testing."

I wish I didn't know about any of that stuff, either. "What about the airstrip and the dock? And the supply transport? You know Jason will question us if we take off again."

"For the love of everything holy, Emily!" Tom spins around and points at me. I ease back, afraid he's going to go off on me. "Is this really the time for twenty questions?"

I drop my side of the basket. "Yes, it is. If we're not all on the same page when we walk back onto that beach, there's going to be trouble. So, excuse me for wanting to know what the plan is."

"You are so much like my Lucy. She had a stubborn streak a mile long." His mouth twitches as if he wants to smile, but he doesn't. "I don't have a plan yet. But rest assured, when I do, you'll be the first to know."

I stay put, staring after him. I don't know what to make of what he said. He appointed himself our leader. It's his job to give us direction and know what to do. Aiden lifts the basket and follows Tom. With a heavy sigh, I catch up to Aiden and take hold of the basket so he doesn't have to bear all that weight alone.

"He'll figure it out," Aiden says.

"I'm sure he will." And I actually believe that.

We walk for another couple of hours. This time, the silence is rife with fear and irritability.

Tom drops his bag to the ground. "Okay, let's take a break." He sits on his pack and opens a bottle of water. "Emily's right. We're going to have to tell everyone else about the airstrip and dock. And if we can't catch the plane, we're going to need the supplies it drops. But I don't want to tell them about everything else. It will only cause undue panic."

"I agree," Marjorie says. She and Tom have gotten really close since we set out on this journey the other day.

"So, we'll tell them about the buildings and the food. Then I will tell them that I found a journal that outlines a delivery schedule. I'll convince Jason that we need to send out a couple small groups to wait for the transport."

"You really think Jason will buy that?" Aiden asks.

"I'll have to make sure he does. The minute any of us mention rescue, I guarantee no one will care what else we have to say." Tom takes another drink then pours some of the water over his head. "But a group of us trying to bombard a plane isn't going to work out. For any of us. So, we have to be smart about this."

Marjorie is nodding with everything Tom says. "If the plane doesn't stop this time, at least the pilot will know there are people here, so one way or another, we're going to get help." She smiles brightly.

"You really think so?" I ask, hopeful.

"Yes," she says emphatically. "God has answered our prayers."

I can't help but smile. Hours ago, I would've rolled my eyes or made a sarcastic remark, but not now. God had answered my simple prayer earlier. I don't need any more proof.

"That's all well and good, but I need you all to give me your word we won't say anything else." Tom looks at each of us in turn.

When his gaze lands on me, I nod. I understand his reasoning, and I do agree. But I don't like lying to everyone. Lying is the biggest reason I don't get along with my parents. I lie, they catch me, and we fight. But this situation is much different than me lying about going to a party. Lack of knowledge has the potential to get these people killed. They need to know what's on this island so they can protect themselves. But I know Tom will disagree, so I keep my mouth shut. I have to trust he knows what he's doing.

"By my calculations, we should be reaching the beach within the next hour or so. When we get there, let me take the lead," Tom says. He finishes his water and then stands. "C'mon, let's get going. I want to get out of this jungle."

"Me too," I say, looking around. I can't shake the feeling that we're being watched. The hair on the back of my neck stands on edge, and goose bumps break out on my arms.

Tom slows his pace until he's walking beside me. "I'm sorry I snapped at you earlier. You have valid concerns. I just didn't have any answers." He forces a chuckle.

"It's okay. I tend to be argumentative. I didn't mean to push," I say.

"Thanks." He takes the lead again.

Ten minutes into the walk, Aiden says, "I'm going to lose my mind with all of this silence."

"So, let's talk." I smile, grateful he said it before I did.

"What do you miss most about home?" he asks.

His question surprises me. Talking about home will only make this whole thing worse, in my opinion. Focusing on right now is better than thinking about all the things and people we don't have here with us. "Um everything?" I laugh. "My friends. I haven't gone this long without talking to them in, well, forever. I'm always on social media with them."

"Who's your best friend?"

"Ashley. Sort of."

"Sort of?" He chuckles. "Okay."

"We're more like frenemies. When we get along, we're inseparable. But when we don't, it's like Bad Girls of New York." I shake my head. "I'm pretty sure she moved in on my boyfriend—ex-boyfriend—before I was even on the plane."

"She sounds like an awesome friend."

I roll my eyes. "It works for us. Nothing else matters."

"Okay, easy. I didn't mean any disrespect."

"No, I'm sorry. I'm just tired and cranky." I readjust my hold on the basket. My palm is sweating like crazy, and I'm worried I'll end up inadvertently dropping it. "What do you miss most about home?"

"Swimming." He laughs.

I jerk my head around to look at him. "Swimming? Seriously?"

He nods. "I was on the swim team for three years. I didn't join this year because I'm focusing on community service, volunteering at the retirement home. But I love the water, and I miss it. I would jump in the pool and do laps until my head was clear."

I find myself smiling as Aiden speaks. He's such a wholesome, good, boy-next-door, and it's clear that the simple things in life are enough for him. If it wasn't for this plane crash, I never would've given him a second look. He's not my usual type, but maybe that's my problem. Getting involved with boys like Matt is what landed me here in the first place. I snap myself from this line of thinking—it's not doing me any good.

"You do realize we're on an island, right? We're literally surrounded by water," I say.

"I know, but we haven't exactly had a chance to relax and do anything that resembles fun. And now that we know what we do…" He frowns.

I open my mouth to respond when Tom turns to glare at us. "Think you two can keep it down? We're trying *not* to draw attention to ourselves."

My patience snaps, and the tips of my ears burn with aggravation. "We're just talking."

"Yeah?" His eyebrows shoot up to his hairline, and then he scowls. "Talking is making noise, and noise draws attention, which we do not need. So, if you must talk, keep it to a whisper." He turns his back to us again and continues to walk.

"Whatever, Dad," I whisper. I stick my tongue out at him, and Aiden snickers. When Tom is a few feet ahead of us, I lean closer to Aiden. "When we get back, we're going swimming. Tom already said he's taking the lead, so we'll let him. We'll find something else to do while he's lying to everyone."

Aiden shakes his head, but I don't miss the smile he's trying to hide. "I think you're a bad influence." He winks.

I falter for a moment. I know he's only teasing, but his jab leaves a bad taste in my mouth. My parents said they wouldn't let me be a bad influence on Erik. I thought they were being dramatic and grasping for some sort of justification for shipping me to Alaska —until now. Are they right? Am I a bad influence? Do I convince people to do things they don't want to do and get them into trouble?

"Hey, I didn't mean—"

"I know." I smile tightly.

CHAPTER 25

Aiden

EMILY HASN'T SPOKEN A WORD to me since I made that joke about her being a bad influence. I'd only been kidding, but clearly, she didn't take it that way.

"We're here," Tom calls over his shoulder. He stops and faces us. "All right, so remember, I'm going to take the lead. Don't answer any direct questions, and don't say a thing about Brenda. Okay?"

I nod. I'm glad Tom's taking the lead and handling everything because I don't want any part of it. All I want to do is get Emily alone, apologize, and then get off this island. If Brenda is telling us the truth, then rescue will be here Friday. That's only two more days. All we have to do is survive the inhabitants, and then we'll be headed home.

"Okay then, let's—"

"Wait," Emily says. "I get why you don't want to cause a panic, but don't you think they have a right to know what's going on? How can they protect themselves if they don't know the real danger they're in?"

I resist the urge to roll my eyes. Why can't she just leave things alone? I mean, I admire how she's concerned with everyone's well-being, but she seems to enjoy pushing Tom's buttons. She's been instigating him since we left the beach yesterday. I don't get it.

Then again… I think of Eddie and how I didn't defend him. My heart sinks. Emily's absolutely right. We need to warn the others and give them a fighting chance. I open my mouth to say just that, but I don't get the chance.

Tom sighs with frustration. "Just let me deal with it, okay?" Without another word, he walks away and emerges from the jungle.

When I step onto the beach, Jason and the other survivors rush toward us. It's a barrage of questions and hugs and handshakes and hands grabbing at the basket of food. I gladly relinquish my hold on it and hand it over.

"We're so glad to have you guys back here with us. I've been praying daily for you." Jason smiles and pats Tom on the back. "Wait, where's Larry?"

My heart races, and I swallow hard, waiting for Tom to answer that question.

"We'll explain everything," Tom says, dodging the question. "First, let's take an inventory of the food we found and eat. I'm starved."

"All right, everyone, gather round." Jason waves his arms until the group crowds around him. "As you can see, Tom and his group managed to find some food, and this"—Jason picks up a can of soup and the can opener and holds it up in the air—"this is what hope looks like!"

The group erupts in cheers.

"This is a turning point for us. We will now have the sustenance we need to refocus our efforts on finding rescue," Jason says. "So, let us eat!"

There's another round of hoots and hollers. I glance over at Emily, who is scowling and clenching her hands into fists. I hope she doesn't say anything to ruin this moment. These people need the hope Jason gives them, even if it is false.

"I will speak with Tom privately, get a full report of their adventure, and then we'll regroup here in two hours." Jason drops the food back into the basket. A burly guy whose name I don't remember picks up the food and carries it away. The people follow him.

"Nice job, you guys." Jason smiles. "Things around here were becoming dire, and hope was quickly slipping away."

"Where's Sierra?" Emily asks.

162

"Oh, she um…" Jason rubs the back of his neck and averts his gaze.

"Jason," Tom says sternly. "Where is Sierra? And Bob?"

I hadn't realized either of them were missing, but now that I take the time to really observe everyone, they're nowhere to be found. My stomach knots, and I have a sinking feeling the lies and half-truths Tom plans to tell aren't going to work.

"Sierra came stumbling out of the jungle very early this morning. It had to be around one a.m. Her hair was disheveled, her clothes torn, her shoes gone. She had a huge gash on her cheek, and she was mumbling about evil people and a sink hole that took Sienna. I think she was in shock because she didn't speak much, and when she did, it wasn't very coherent. Best I could gather, Bob is dead." Jason looks extremely upset by this. "What happened? I thought they were going with you?" Jason hones in on Tom.

I step back and take Emily's hand, intent on letting the two men hash this out.

"We encountered some trouble along the way. A sink hole or quicksand. We're not sure." Tom's gaze sweeps over us, his warning clear. "We lost Sienna. Naturally, Sierra was distraught and wasn't feeling well. Bob offered to bring her back here."

"Well, Bob didn't make it back here. And we found Sierra hanging from a tree this morning," Jason says sadly. "God rest her soul."

Emily gasps and pulls her hand from mine. I reach for her again, but she takes off on a run. I shrug apologetically and then chase after her. "Emily!" But she doesn't stop until her feet hit the water. I come to a stop beside her, panting for breath. Man, this girl could run. "Are you okay?"

She shakes her head, and the glistening of tears on her face catches my attention. I put my arm around her and pull her into a hug. She rests her head against my chest and cries. I know she and the twins weren't friends. They'd barely spoken to each other, so I don't understand why she's so upset. And I'm afraid if I ask, she'll only get mad at me.

"Want to get out of here?" I ask.

She looks up at me. "And go where?"

I shrug. "We'll go for a walk along the beach. If we stick to the shoreline, we should be safe."

She nods. I lace my fingers with hers, and we head down the beach, the water lapping at our ankles. "I don't know what got into me," she says. "In a matter of one night, we lost four people. Any one of us could be next."

I give her hand a squeeze. "Hey, don't think like that."

"It's hard not to."

"I know." I sigh. "Promise me something?"

"What?"

I tug on her hand, and we both stop. "If you're feeling overwhelmed or sad, please talk to me. I'm a great listener." I grin, and I'm rewarded with a smile from her. "You're not alone here, okay?"

She nods again. "Thank you."

We resume walking, mostly in silence this time. If I try hard enough, I can imagine we're on vacation, exploring some tropical oasis. It's a pleasant fantasy, but it's nearly impossible to ignore reality—especially when that reality can get us killed.

Her steps slow. "Maybe we should go back."

"Do you want to?" I ask. I don't, but I'm not going to force her to do something she doesn't want to. But I really want to spend some time alone with her. And I'd really like to kiss her again.

"Don't you?" she asks.

"I think we can go a bit farther. We're just a holler away from every one. We won't go too far away from the group. Promise."

Emily smiles. "Okay. Besides, you're here to protect me, right?"

I laugh. "Absolutely."

"It really is pretty here. Too bad it's crazy land."

"Crazy land is putting it mildly. It's more like a freak show," I say as we continue to walk. The sounds of the group behind us get fainter with each step. We can't go too much farther, but I can't deny I like the low hum of noise. It's easier to deal with everything when there aren't a bunch of hungry, scared people shouting for attention.

"I've always wanted to see a freak show." She says it more to herself than to me, and I don't respond.

A distant sound of rushing water reaches my ears, and I tilt my head to try to figure out where it's coming from. "Do you hear that?"

"No, what?"

"It sounds like water."

"Uh, we are right next to the ocean," she says like I've lost my mind.

"No, it's not the ocean. It sounds like it's coming from the jungle." I gently yank on her hand to get her to follow me, but she digs her feet into the sand and doesn't move.

"We're not going back into the jungle. Not alone and not unarmed." She shakes her head adamantly.

"I just want to go peek. We won't actually go into the jungle." When she still doesn't move, I pretend to pout. "Please?"

"And you say I'm a bad influence." Reluctantly, she agrees, and we slowly walk toward the tree line. "Is this a trail?" she asks.

"I think so." That's exactly what it looks like. There's a defined but slightly overgrown, dirt path weaving through the trees.

"Let me guess, you want to follow it."

I nod.

"You really think that's a good idea?"

"No," I say. "But we've come this far, might as well keep going, right?"

"What if it leads straight to them? What if it's a trap?"

I stop and face her. "You really don't trust anyone or anything, do you?"

She shakes her head. "Trust gives people an open door to hurt you."

Whoa. I wasn't expecting that answer. "I haven't hurt you, have I?"

"No," she says quietly.

"Then trust me not to hurt you now." I lick my lips. "Look, this path has been here a while, and it doesn't look like it's been used in a long time. I doubt it's a trap." I give Emily's hand a squeeze and smile reassuringly. "And I have a good feeling about it. I'm not getting any weird vibes."

"I better not die," she grumbles and follows me down the path.

The dirt is more like fresh mud that nobody has stepped in for the last century or two. So strange. A cold breeze whips by, causing my shirt to cling to me. The mixture of rotting and fresh plants hangs in the air and makes my head spin like a carousel. In the near distance, insects croak while birds chirp in a melodic rhythm. The sounds and smells remind me too much of the valley with the buildings.

We take small steps, observing our surroundings carefully. My heart races, and I half expect someone or something to jump out at us any moment. Part of me wants to turn back and run toward the rest of the survivors, but I don't want to appear weak in front of Emily. The first sign of danger, though, and we're out of here.

"I'm not going to lie," Emily starts. "This is the scariest thing I have ever done in my entire life. No exaggeration."

I half smile. "It's not that bad."

Swish! Swish! Swish!

Emily jumps. "What was that?"

"I don't know." It doesn't sound like the noise I heard earlier, but it's not identifiable, either.

Hand in hand, we baby step our way toward the noise. The sound gets louder with every step we take. After walking several more feet, we come upon the deafening noise—a roaring river of white foamy water, cutting diagonally across the jungle.

"What is a river doing in the middle of the jungle?"

"I have no idea." I let go of her hand and crouch near the riverbank. "But it looks natural. Not man-made."

She shrieks and points at the water. "Look! There are fish in there."

I laugh. "Well, we know where to come get food should we need it."

She scrunches up her face. "Ew. I hate fish."

I stand. "See? Nothing bad happened. It's amazing what we can find together."

Her body relaxes, and a warm smile graces her beautiful face. "I like how you said together."

"Well, two is better than one, right?"

"Not always." She laughs. "Having two girlfriends is never good."

I smirk. "No, it's not. I guess it's lucky for you I don't have two girlfriends." I brush a strand of hair behind her ear.

"More like it's lucky for you," she says. "I don't give cheaters a second of my time."

"Neither do I." I wrap my arms around her, holding her as close as possible. I lean down and press my lips softly to hers, waiting and hoping she'll reciprocate. And she does. Much more enthusiastically than I could have ever imagined. With every pulse and heartbeat, the kiss intensifies. The entire world seems to disappear, and the only thing I can focus on is Emily and the way her mouth aligns perfectly with mine.

There is nothing better than being here with her, our limbs intertwined, our heartbeats in sync. The pulse of the water rages behind us, blocking out our harsh reality. In another world, this would've been the perfect fairytale—boy and girl sharing a kiss in a beautiful outdoor haven, solidifying their feelings for each other.

Unfortunately, that's not the case. When this kiss ends, we will still be here, the forest will still be here, the crash will still have happened, the fight for survival will still be very real, and the mission to find rescue will still be looming over our heads.

We mutually pull away, breaking the magical moment. I take a deep breath and look into her big, gorgeous eyes. She looks as frazzled as I feel. Even though the beach is still in our line of sight, the hairs on the back of my neck stand on edge, and a chill settles over me. "We should head back." I slowly start moving down the path when a hand lashes out and grabs my shoulder.

"Thank you," she says. "You have this way of making me feel so special and beautiful. It's like every bad decision I made in the past doesn't matter, and I can't thank you enough for that."

Heat flushes my cheeks. "I feel—"

"Shh." She puts a finger to my mouth. "Please don't say anything. I just wanted you to know how I felt, and how I probably wouldn't have survived this long without you by my side."

"Yes, you would have," I mumble around her finger. She removes it, and I lick my lips. "You're much stronger than you give yourself credit for, Emily. And don't ever forget that God is always on your side, too." I'm praying I can get her to accept Him, but I don't want to be too pushy about it.

"Thank you." Her bottom lip trembles slightly, and I want to kick myself for making her so emotional. I only meant to compliment her, not make her cry. She takes my hand and squeezes.

"Ready to head back to the beach?" I ask.

"Do you think this path loops around to beach? Or do you think it goes deeper into the jungle?"

I shrug. "I don't know, and I don't think I want to find out." I laugh nervously.

Her happy expression falters, but she quickly masks it with a smile. "Yeah, you're probably right." We walk back the way we came, retracing our steps until we hit the beach. "Are we going to tell the others what we found?"

"I think so. Is there any reason we shouldn't?"

She shakes her head. "Hopefully, it won't matter because we'll catch the transport and get home, but if not…"

"We will," I say firmly. I won't allow her, or myself, to think otherwise.

She nods but doesn't say anything else, and we walk in silence. As we get closer to the wreckage, the sounds of laughter hangs in the air. I smile. Clearly, the food is the morale boost everyone needed. A sense of pride swells in my chest knowing that my actions helped those people, that I'm responsible for their hope. That is something I'd never been able to give Eddie.

"Aiden." Emily's voice is low and icy.

I freeze. "What?"

"Do you see that?" She nods to her right.

There, behind a large part of the wreckage and a few feet from the jungle, is a hand dug cemetery. A quick count shows at least thirty mounds of dirt, each one marked with a small stack of carefully placed rocks. "What the...? You don't think those are the graves for the people who died in the crash, do you?"

"No," she says slowly. "They can't be, can they?" She turns to me. "The structure we built for the dead was still in tact when we walked by it. These can't be the crash victims."

My stomach sinks. "Then whose graves are they?"

"Hey! Aiden! Emily!" Tom jogs toward us, waving his arms to get our attention. "Where have you been? I was ready to organize a search party."

"We took a walk," I say. "Why? What's wrong?"

"Nothing. Jason is getting ready to speak to the group about our plans for rescue."

"Oh. Okay." I shift on my feet. "We just found that." I point to the cemetery.

Tom's eyes widen, and his gaze jerks back to mine. "Are those the dead passengers?"

"I don't think so," Emily says. "But that one on the end looks fresh."

Tom takes several deep breaths and pinches the bridge of his nose. "We have more important things to worry about right now."

I want to argue but don't. It won't do any good. And Tom's right. Our focus needs to be on catching the transport and getting home. Emily and I follow him back to the beach and take a spot near the back of the group.

"Do we have everyone now?" Jason asks.

"Yeah," Tom says.

"Good." Jason clears his throat, and I have a sudden, intense feeling of dread. It hits me hard and fast, and I clutch my chest, rubbing at the sharp pain. This isn't going to be good.

CHAPTER 26

Emily

MY STOMACH GROWLS, BUT THE thought of food has bile rising up my throat. Bob didn't make it back. Sierra killed herself. And all the other dead passengers are piled carelessly in the sand, a heap of limbs covered by nothing more than scrap metal torn from the plane.

"I have been speaking with Tom for the past hour or so," Jason says, his much too calm voice cutting through my thoughts. "He's filled me in on what he and his team found when they hiked across the island. Obviously, they found food. But they also found some buildings. God is truly blessing us with the stuff we so desperately need to survive."

The group erupts in shouted questions and disbelieving looks.

"All right, all right. Settle down." Jason waves his hands in an effort to calm everyone. "The buildings were abandoned but well-stocked with supplies. After some investigating, Tom was able to find out why. Apparently, this island was the site for research. A group of scientists were sent here to explore and study the wildlife."

I start to laugh and quickly cover it with a cough. Aiden shoots me a knowing look, and I smile. Tom said he wasn't going to tell Jason the truth—and he hadn't. But his lie is shrouded in enough truth to be believable.

"While Tom wasn't able to determine if any of the scientists were still on the island, he did find a delivery schedule. Every month, a transport arrives to drop off food and supplies. And the good Lord is on our side, folks, because the next delivery is scheduled for Friday," Jason continues.

The chorus of whoops and cheers has me covering my ears.

"Didn't I tell you all? Hope and faith. We needed to keep our hope high and our faith intact. We did, and now it's paid off. We will be going home!" he proclaims loudly.

"Tell them the rest!" Tom shouts, which instantly silences the group.

My stomach rolls, and I try to mentally prepare myself for what the backlash will be once the group hears the truth about our rescue.

Jason shakes his head with what looks like disappointment, but then plasters his signature smile on his face. "There is an airstrip and one dock on this island. If the delivery schedule Tom found is accurate, then we know the supplies will be air dropped, but we don't know what time. Now, before you all get upset, hear me out," he says before the crowd can cause another disruption. "Tom has suggested, and I agree, that we send a group to stake out the airstrip. Another smaller group will go to the dock, just in case."

I nudge Aiden and whisper, "Why is a group going to the dock?"

Aiden shrugs.

Did Tom find something else in those papers that he's not telling us?

"Tom will lead a group to the airstrip. And I'll head the group to the dock."

Unease swirls in my gut. What is going on? I look to Aiden, who's just as confused as I am. I try to focus on what else Jason's saying, but I can't.

When Jason finally stops talking, I approach Tom. "Hey." I'm careful to keep my voice calm and low so no one will overhear me. "I thought you said the transport wouldn't be at the dock."

"It won't," Tom says, glancing over his shoulder. "Which is exactly why I want Jason leading the group there. I have a plan to get the plane to land, but I can't have any distractions, so I'm only taking a select few people with me."

"Okay. So, where do you want me and Aiden?"

"I want you in Jason's group."

172

I shake my head and open my mouth to protest, but Aiden speaks up before I can. "Yeah, of course." He smiles. "We'll be happy to go with Jason. Just get that plane on the ground so we can go home."

I jerk my head to stare at him, eyes wide. He avoids my gaze, though, and I know he knows I'm not happy. I cross my arms and keep my mouth shut. Nothing I say will matter now anyway. But Aiden is going to get a piece of my mind as soon as Tom leaves.

Tom nods. "Thanks. I'm taking Marjorie with me. And we're taking off in ten minutes."

"What?" I blink, positive I misheard him. "Just the two of you?"

"Yes," he says slowly, as if he's afraid his answer might upset me. "I found some hand-drawn maps of the island that shows the location of the airstrip. There's a small communication tower, and I want to get to that before the plane gets to us."

"Why?" I ask, unable to stay quiet a moment longer. "Why are you sending us to the dock with Jason when you know the transport won't be there? You're not planning to leave us here, are you?" Utter panic laces my words. I can't stay on this island another day. My breaths come hard and sharp.

"Em—"

I hold up my hand to silence Aiden. He snaps his mouth shut and, once again, looks away from me. I hold Tom's gaze, refusing to let him get away without an answer. It's a fair question, and he knows it.

With a heavy sigh, Tom rubs his hands over his face. "Of course I'm not going to leave you here." He actually sounds offended. "I'm not going to leave anyone here."

I want to believe him; I really do, but doubt nags at me.

"The airstrip is miles from the remaining building. The dock is less than a mile. If things go badly, I want you two to be close enough to get to safety. If there is even the slightest hint of danger, you two are to get back to the building and into that bunker." He looks at each of us in turn, his expression hard and stern.

My arms fall to my sides, and I swallow hard. "Why are you giving us special treatment?" But I don't really need him to answer

173

JEMAL & MILLER

that. I know. He's trying to make amends for not being able to save his daughter. A sob builds in my throat.

"You two are still kids. You don't need to be out here in the middle of all this." He waves his arms around.

"Thank you, Tom," Aiden says.

"Uh, yeah, thanks," I say, forcing myself to snap out of my daze. Under any other circumstances, being called a kid would've set me off, but I'm grateful to Tom for his concern. Although, if things go bad, I won't feel right running for safety while everyone else is exposed to the danger.

"You two should grab some food and try to relax before you head out," Tom says. "And be sure to pack whatever belongings you have. We won't be coming back to this beach."

I stare silently after Tom as he walks toward Marjorie. My chest constricts painfully at the thought of heading to the dock without him. I might not always agree with him, or like how he orders people around, but I've grown to admire him in a very short period of time. He reminds me too much of my dad.

"I'm sorry I upset you," Aiden says. He stares at the ground. "I don't like the idea of going with Jason any more than you do, but I trust Tom's judgment."

"Yeah." I sigh. "I trust him, too."

"So, you're not mad at me?" He glances up at me hopefully.

I smile. "No, I'm not mad. But I am hungry."

He laughs and takes my hand. "C'mon, I'll buy you lunch." He winks, and we walk over to Phil and the stockpile of food.

"Hey." Phil smiles and waves when he sees us. "I can't thank you enough for bringing back this food."

I shrug. "It's no big deal, really."

Phil hands each of us a can of soup and a package of crackers to share. "Others are warming the soup over the fire." He nods to the still raging fire down the beach.

"Thanks." I take the food, and my stomach growls. I don't want to eat soup again, but it's not like I have many options. What I wouldn't give for a large, extra cheese pizza right now. My mouth waters.

174

After pouring our soup into a metal pan we salvaged from the wreckage and heating the food, Aiden and I settle on the beach, away from the crowd. We eat without talking. The broth is barely lukewarm, which makes the already bland soup taste even worse. I force down as much as I can then set the rest aside.

"Do you really think it's this easy?" I ask.

"What?"

"Rescue. I mean, we've been here for days now. No one has found us. Who knows if they're even looking anymore. Then we just happen upon buildings and a woman who's a scientist and a supply transport that will conveniently be here soon. I don't know. It just seems all too easy." I hug my knees to my chest and stare out at the ocean.

"Ever heard that saying, don't look a gift horse in the mouth?"

"That's the dumbest thing I've ever heard."

He lazily shrugs one shoulder and spoons more soup into his mouth. "Jason's right. The big guy up there—" He lifts his eyes up to the sky—"really is watching out for us."

"Yeah."

"Hey." He sets his food down and nudges my shoulder with his. "You okay?"

"I don't have a good feeling about this plan." There. I said it aloud.

"Neither do I, but we have no other options. I'm willing to take the risk if it means there's a chance we can go home."

"That's the thing, though. If Tom has an idea how to get the plane to land, why don't all of us just go with him? That way we're all there and ready to leave."

"I don't know, Emily." He sighs, and it's only then I notice how tired he looks. His eyes are dull, and his shoulders slump.

"With the natives running around, it doesn't seem safe to make the plane wait while Tom rounds all of us up, y'know?" The more I think about this, the more upset I get. Despite trusting Tom, this plan is just dumb.

Aiden shrugs. "Maybe we should ask him before he takes off."

I glance over my shoulder, but I don't see him anywhere. Even if we do ask him, I doubt he'll give us an answer. I just need to trust him. And God—He didn't let me down earlier, so I pray He doesn't now, either.

"No, we'll just do as he says." I give him a grateful smile. "Just promise we'll stick together through this."

He drapes his arm around my shoulders and pulls me down so I'm lying on my back. The sand is soft and cool beneath my body. Aiden brings himself to lean over me. He brushes the hair from my forehead and smiles.

"I wouldn't dream of leaving you," he whispers. "Not here and not when we get home."

My heart races, and I nervously lick my lips. I'm positive once we get off this island, my parents will welcome me home. How can Aiden and I have any sort of relationship when he's in Alaska and I'm in New York? Maybe going to stay with grandma and grandpa won't be so terrible after all, because I'm not sure I want to go back to the city. Or my friends. Or Matt. None of them will ever be able to understand what I've been through—not like Aiden does. And he makes me feel safe, something I've never felt with Matt.

I lift my head enough to align my lips with his until our mouths collide, sending a burst of fireworks through my bones. I can't stop my heart from pounding in my chest, and my blood flows rapidly to my cheeks, making my face red with heat. I wrap my arms around his strong, broad shoulders and pull him closer. His body is so warm and strong, and I never want to leave his embrace. The kiss deepens for a much too brief moment before he breaks away.

I rub my fingers over my tingling mouth. "Why did you stop?"

He smiles briefly before leaning back down to kiss me. My entire body is on fire, and Aiden's kisses are only stoking the flames.

"Ahem."

Aiden jerks away, and I tilt my head toward the sound. Jason stands over us, eyes narrowed, arms crossed. Kneeling in front of me, Aiden pulls me up to a sitting position.

"Can we help you?" I snap.

"You two about done?" The corner of Jason's mouth twitches as if he wants to smirk, but his expression remains accusatory.

I awkwardly try to brush the sand from my hair.

"Uh, yeah, um, we were just…" Aiden's cheeks are bright red. He's embarrassed. That's so adorable.

"We're reconvening to go over final plans, and then the groups are heading out. Can you two disentangle yourself long enough to join us?" Jason asks. For a man of God, he's quite snarky. My sarcastic side is rather impressed.

177

CHAPTER 27

Aiden

"THAT WAS EMBARRASSING," I SAY as I stand and help Emily brush the sand from her back.

"So, you're embarrassed to kiss me?" she says, a playful twinkle in her eye.

"No." I laugh. "I'm embarrassed we got caught like that."

"Don't be." She adjusts her ponytail. "Jason shouldn't have been spying on us."

I frown. "He wasn't spying. We're on the beach, out in the open for everyone to see us."

She glares at me. "Why are you suddenly defending Jason?"

"I'm not," I say quickly. "I'm just not big on PDA. I've always believed that intimacy should be private." He shrugs. "And for the record, kissing like that it's not something I do a lot. Or ever, really."

She smirks. "C'mon. We better get over to the group before Jason scolds us again."

I reach for her hand, entwine our fingers, and we walk toward the group. The atmosphere is tense and fearful. The same emotions are warring inside of me, too. I don't want to tell Emily how scared I really am because I don't want to worry her any more than she already is. I'm just glad we'll be together.

"Ah, the young lovebirds have joined us." Jason smiles and holds his arms out to us.

Heat travels up my neck and erupts on my face. I've never met a pastor like him before—he's… odd.

"Now that we're all here… we have a very important mission on our hands. One God has so graciously given to us, a chance for rescue, a do-over, if you will. This is our opportunity to really look inside our ourselves, to cast out our sins and go home as better people." He claps his hands then raises them to the sky. "But, we still have a journey ahead of us, and we must plan accordingly." He nods to Tom, who smiles tightly in return.

Tom steps up beside Jason and clears his throat. "In order to make sure we don't miss the transport, I suggest we head out soon, get as far as we can before the sun sets. Each group should stay on the beach and follow the tree line. *Don't* go into the jungle. We don't want anyone to get lost." His gaze sweeps over me, Emily, and Marjorie, his unspoken warning clear. "And remember, stay together at all times."

"Very smart advice." Jason smiles like a teacher praising a student.

"What about supplies?" Marjorie shouts.

"Everyone should take their personal belongings. Whatever you want to take home with you should go with you. As for supplies and food, I'm going to turn that over to Phil. But before I do that, I want to take a moment to remember all those passengers we lost. They were taken from this world much too soon. If we could all bow our heads in a moment of silent prayer."

I lower my head and remain silent in remembrance. I didn't know many people on the flight, but I think of Larry and Bob and the twins. They'd become my friends, and now they're gone. I pray no one else will die before we're rescued. I pray I can stay strong and keep Emily safe. I pray God will give me the strength I'm going to need to get through this mission.

"Amen," Jason mumbles before lifting his head. "Allow me another moment, if you will, to thank God for watching over us, protecting us, and giving us the strength we've needed to make it this far. Without Him, the world is dark. Okay." He claps his hands and rubs them together. "Back to business." Jason holds his arm out toward Phil, indicating it's his turn to talk.

Phil steps up and frowns. "I'm not very good at this whole public speaking thing. Not like Jason anyway." He laughs nervously. "Thanks to Tom and his group, we have more food than we did this morning, which is good. But the bad news is, it's not enough to last us that long. If for any reason things don't go as we hope… well, let's just say we'll be in a dire position. For that reason, I suggest we start rationing now. Smaller portions less frequently."

"But Tom said we're getting rescued!" shouts a woman off to my right.

"I never said that," Tom says. "I said there was the possibility we'd be rescued."

"All right, calm down everyone," Jason says. "Phil is simply preparing us for the worst case scenario, so please, settle down and let him finish."

Phil nods. "Sorry to have scared everyone. We're going to divide the remaining food equally among the groups. I suggest eating twice a day. A late breakfast and a late dinner. That way, you'll have enough food to last you the entire day. Obviously, you'll have water."

"What if we're not rescued?" asks the same woman. "Is there more food where they found this?"

"No, this is all of it," Tom says, shooting me a warning glare.

I give a subtle nod to indicate I understand, but I don't. There's a lot more food in that buildings, and more is delivered every month. Why's he trying to hide that information? Unless he's trying to protect everyone from wandering into the jungle and getting killed by the natives, which is a strong possibility.

"Then if rescue doesn't happen and we're here—" Phil's words stop abruptly as he makes a gurgling sound. He falls to his knees, eyes wide. Blood trickles from the corner of his mouth and a dark, red circle forms on his chest. He crumples to the ground with a sickening thud. An arrow sticks out of his back.

My jaw drops. Beside me, Emily screams. The loud, piercing noise makes me flinch. And then, chaos erupts.

"What is happening?"

"Did he just get shot with an arrow?"

"Who would shoot him with an arrow?"

"Who has the bow and arrow?"

People are whipping their bodies around, looking for any sign of who shot the arrow. But the situation is identical to what happened with Larry. There's no one in sight. The only difference is I know who's out there, and I know what they want. I move closer to Emily, and she clutches my hand so hard I'm afraid she'll break my fingers.

A big bulky guy with a ponytail holds up his hands in surrender. "I don't want to die. Whoever is out there, I'll do whatever you want." Another arrow whizzes through the air and punctures the guy's chest. He falls face down, dead in an instant.

"RUN!" Jason yells.

Everyone begins running in a million different directions. I can't keep track of who is where, so I yank on Emily's hand and drag her away from the scene. Dozens more arrows slice through the air, and people drop hard and fast around us. Blood stains the sand, and the smell of iron is thick. There's so much screaming and yelling it's impossible to form a clear thought. Emily jerks her hand from mine, covers her ears, and screams again.

"Don't look," I say. "Keep your head down, and I'll guide you." The last thing I need is for her to lose it. Right now, we need to get off the beach and to some semblance of safety. Although, I'm not sure anywhere is safe. I grab her hand again, and she doesn't fight me.

Each step becomes harder, my feet heavier. Sweat drips down my temples, and my shirt sticks uncomfortably to my body. My heart races, and it hurts to breathe, but I can't stop. I need to get Emily some place safe. Just then, a body falls in front of me, an arrow piercing the girl's head. My steps falter, and then I stop all together. I look around, everywhere but in front of me. So much death. So much blood. So much fear. *God help us.*

"Get to the dock!" Tom shouts as he runs by me, snapping me out of my stupor.

I'm still frozen in place, unable to process what's happening around me. How is this possible?

Emily grabs my arm, shaking me. "Aiden! Let's go. C'mon. We have to go." Her voice is frantic.

I nod but am still unable to form any words.

"Which way is the dock? Where are we supposed to go?" Her tone rises with each word, her fear palpable.

I glance around. Everyone who isn't dead is scattering into the jungle. Into the one place where they'll likely die. I want to shout at them not to go in there, but I know, even if they can hear me, they won't listen. They're too scared and looking for anything that will protect them.

Tom said we should go to the dock, because from the dock we can get to the building and the safety of the bunker, but running down the beach, in the wide open, will make us targets. "C'mon, this way," I say, leading Emily toward the tree line.

"What? No." She shakes her head. "We can't go in there."

"I think we'll be the safest by the river. The one we found in the jungle. There should be enough of a cover there. We'll be able to hide out until things settle down."

After a moment, she agrees. We run as fast as we can and find the path. We hustle over broken branches and fallen logs. The sounds of the beach massacre fade, and the only real noise is our heaving breathing. More like panting. A few minutes later, we arrive at the river. It's still roaring and cutting through the jungle, completely out of place. The memory of earlier when Emily and I kissed flashes in my mind. I momentarily close my eyes and try to catch my breath.

There are two giant rocks right next to each other a little to left of the river. Why didn't I notice those before? "We need to hide," I say, nodding toward the rocks.

Slowly and carefully, we creep over to them in fear of snapping a stick that would signal our location. I sit with my back against the rock. Emily does the same. We're deathly silent as we catch our breath.

Emily hugs her knees to her chest. "What was that?" Her voice trembles.

I twist to peer around the rocks. "I don't know, but it has to be the natives, right? There's no one else on the island." At least, I hope that's the case. Brenda didn't mention anyone else, but then again, we know almost nothing about her. Maybe she's one of them and she set us up.

"They killed everyone within minutes." Tears streak Emily's face, and she clenches a handful of her hair. "Do you think we're next?"

"Absolutely not," I say.

"How can you be so sure?" She turns to look at me, and her gaze is stricken with fear. I want to take all of that away, to wrap her up in my arms and keep her safe.

"Because I won't let anything happen to you. That's why." I survey our surroundings again and settle back against the rock, momentarily satisfied that we're alone. "And because God is watching over us." I clutch her hands in mine and delve into a prayer. When I finish, she looks at me with so much gratitude it steals my breath.

"Why are they trying to kill us?" she whispers.

I shrug. "Brenda said they're not human. Not fully anyway."

"She also said there weren't many of them, but all those arrows… they were coming from everywhere."

"Maybe they're not the only natives on the island." As soon as the words leave my mouth, I regret them. *Way to inspire confidence, Aiden.* I shake my head. "I remember one of my history teachers, Mr. Schwartz, talking about this. He once told us that there are still islands that have their own tribes, who still use old fashioned weapons and live without any technology."

"So, do you think that's what Brenda and her—"

I slap my hand over Emily's mouth, silencing her. She swats my hand away, and I hold my finger to my lips, motioning for her to be silent. I tilt my head and strain to listen. I hear footsteps.

"What?" Emily whispers.

"I think someone is coming."

She whips around and glances furtively at our surroundings. The only sound is the rush of the river. There are no birds. No crickets. Nothing. Just silence. My heart races, and my body hums with anticipation. Adrenaline pools in my veins, preparing me to fight or run. To do whatever it takes to survive.

A twig snaps. Faint footsteps echo in the distance. I take Emily's hand, squeezing it as I move to a crouching position. Part of me wants to know what these natives look like, but a bigger part of me just wants to run.

The footsteps get closer. I swallow hard. Another twig snaps, closer to us than the last one. I'm ready to jump out of my skin. Fear paralyzes me.

"Psst, who's there?" The voice is distant but vaguely familiar despite being muffled. "Psst. Hello?"

Emily looks at me, eyes wide. "Is that…?"

"I don't know."

We wait, which is stupid. We should be running. Finding a new place to hide. All the noise stops. The silence is terrifying. I hold my breath. The footsteps stop right in front of the rocks. Emily shuts her eyes tightly and bites down on her bottom lip. I can tell she's trying not to cry out. We're trapped. If we move, the person will see us. But staying put makes us easy targets. Without warning, the person jumps right in front of us, arrow in his hand, wielding it like a knife.

Emily screams and folds herself into me as if she's trying to escape. Instinctively, I pull her closer and then nudge her behind me as I stand.

"Aiden?" Jason lowers the arrow and sighs.

"Jason?" I snatch the arrow from him. "What're you doing with this? You could've killed us."

"I figured it would be helpful to have some form of protection." He crosses his arms, but not before I notice his hands are shaking. Jason collapses onto the ground, taking shelter behind the rocks. "Thank God it's you two."

I clench my hand around the arrow. "What are you doing here? How did you find us?"

Jason wipes the sweat off his face. "Tom shoved me in this direction, told me to get to the dock. I saw the path and thought I might be able to find a place to hide."

"Is Tom still alive?" Emily asks.

"Yes. He and Marjorie took off down the beach. There's not many of us left. We were massacred out there." His face pales as the words leave his mouth.

"Dear God," Emily groans. "All those people…"

My temples throb with a budding headache. I drop the arrow, rub my eyes, and blow out a long breath. "Okay, Tom's right. We need to get to the dock. Before we're next." But not because we will find rescue, but because the building is close to that dock, and the building means protection.

"I agree." Jason stands, and his normal in-control façade is back in place. "I don't know who's shooting at us, but I overhead them speaking in some strange language I don't recognize. Clearly, they're skilled hunters, and I assume they can track us as well. We need to be extra careful."

Our situation is much worse than he realizes. I wonder if I should tell him everything I know. I open my mouth to do just that when Emily stands beside me. Her entire body is shaking, but her face is stone cold. I've never seen her look like that before. Goose bumps spread out on my arms, and I'm horrified by what comes out of her mouth.

CHAPTER 28

Emily

"WHERE DID YOU GET THE arrow, Jason?" My voice is steady and accusatory. Nothing he's said so far makes any sense. "And how did you get close enough to hear these people talk?"

Aiden gives me a surprised look, his eyes wide and jaw open. I don't pay him much attention, though, because I'm too focused on Jason. I'm a master liar, and I can tell when someone is lying to me. And Jason is definitely lying.

"I found the arrow on the ground," Jason says, his gaze darting around nervously. "So, I picked it up."

I narrow my eyes, but before I can say anything more, Aiden speaks up. "There were a lot of arrows flying through the air, and not a single one missed its intended target."

My thoughts exactly.

"Fine. I yanked it out of a body. Is that really want you want to hear?" he snaps.

I bend over and pick up the arrow. "There's no blood on this."

Jason throws his hands up in the air. "Why does it feel like I'm the one on trial here? I was on that beach with everyone else. I was a victim of that attack just like you two were. Maybe I should be asking you two how you got away so easily?"

"All right." I cross my arms over my chest. "Then answer my other question. How did you hear them talking?"

Jason takes a deep breath. "It was chaos on that beach. I was trying to get to safety just like everyone else. I tried to maneuver my way around the forest and stay close to the water like Tom suggested. But the beach isn't safe, so like I said, I saw this path and followed it. A few feet in, I heard two people speaking. I slowly approached because I didn't know if they also spoke English. They never saw me, and I kept it that way. I tiptoed away and that's when I happened upon you two."

"Wait." I hold my hand up. "How do you know they didn't see you or follow you? For all we know, they could be watching us right now!" That thought sends my heart racing, and I swallow hard. My throat burns, and all I want to do is curl up and go to sleep.

"If they were, we'd be dead already," Jason says. "And you both know that."

"All right, let's just calm down," Aiden says. "Obviously, these people are close if you saw them on the path, which means we need to get out of here. Now."

"I agree." Jason nods. "We need to get to the dock. It's our only hope."

My stomach lurches at the idea of wandering through the jungle or going back to the beach where we have no protection. Aiden turns to me and gently takes hold of my shoulders. He looks into my eyes, and for a fleeting moment, the fear isn't so debilitating.

"Are you ready for this?" he asks.

I nod, even though I don't really want to go, but there is no other choice.

"Good." Jason claps his hands, then cringes at how the noise echoes. "Okay, then I suggest we follow this path. This way, if we get lost, we can find our way back. Plus, it offers some protection should we need it."

With a curt nod, Jason scoops up the arrow, takes the lead, and starts down the path. I keep a safe distance, and Aiden stays by my side. "I don't like this one bit," I whisper.

"Me either," he says.

"He's lying to us about something." I stare holes into Jason's back.

"I agree."

"You know, I can hear you two," Jason says without turning around to look at us. "If you're that distrusting of me, feel free to go it on your own."

"Maybe we will." My foot catches on a rock, and I stumble. Aiden steadies me before I fall.

"Easy, Em," he whispers before releasing me.

"For what it's worth, I'm not the enemy here." Jason stops and turns to face us. "There's safety in numbers, so like it or not, keeping me around is the best thing you can do right now. Not to mention, I have this arrow that could be used for self-defense. What do you two have?"

"Brains," I mutter.

Jason sighs with exasperation and rolls his eyes.

"Or maybe with more people, we'll only be noisier and, therefore, attract them to where we are," Aiden says, distracting Jason from responding to what I said.

"That's not going to happen," Jason says. "One extra pair of feet won't make that much of a difference."

Both Aiden and I stare at him. He's right. One extra person probably won't make much of a difference.

"Fine." Jason extends the arrow to Aiden. "Take it. If it will make you feel better, you can hold it."

Aiden takes the arrow and shoots me a look that says, "Is this guy for real?" I shrug.

Jason begins to walk away again, grumbling under his breath. "I never wanted this, you know. I didn't want to be in charge here, but no one else was stepping up, and without me and Tom, this entire group would've imploded. We would've run out of food the day we crashed. We would've died from the cold. We would've been attacked by animals." He shakes his head. "It's through God's grace and guidance that we've made it this long."

"Yeah, you're a regular saint, aren't you?" I snap.

Aiden puts his hand on my shoulder. "Go easy, huh? We're all scared. Turning on each other right now isn't going to help anything."

I sigh and nod. Resolving to keep my mouth shut, I pick up my pace. The sooner we get out of this jungle and off this path, the better.

The three of us fall silent, but it doesn't last long when the path comes to an end. Jason stops and holds up his hand. "We're back at the beach."

"What?" I move around him to take a look. Sure enough, the beach is within my line of sight. But it's not the same stretch of beach we've called home the past few days. There's no wreckage, no fire. No signs of life.

Aiden peeks over my shoulder. "Okay, now what?"

I shrug and study the landscape. "I don't see a dock anywhere. Do you think we're close to where it should be?"

"We haven't walked far enough to be anywhere close to the dock. I think this path just looped us around to a different section of the beach," Jason says. "Maybe we should walk back to where we started, see if things have calmed down."

"You can't be serious. What if they're still there? Even if they're not, I don't want to see all that death." I shudder and hug myself.

"I agree," Aiden says. "We need to keep moving. Like you said, Jason, we need to find the dock."

"Right. So, do we keep walking through the jungle, or do we risk walking along the beach?"

My eyebrows lift, and I'm sure there's shock written all over my face. I look to Aiden for some idea as to what we should do.

"I say we walk along the tree edge," Aiden says. "Exactly like Tom said. This way, we have the cover of the jungle if we need it, but we won't get lost."

Jason nods and smiles. "Yes, that's good. We'll do that." He steps off the path and onto the beach, tilting his head to the sun and basking in it like he's on vacation or something.

What little breeze there is shifts, and a sense of dread fills me. I don't know why, but suddenly, I can't shake the fear taking root in my stomach. I grab Aiden's arm, stopping him before he can leave the confines of the jungle.

"What? What's wrong?" he asks, his face a mask of concern.

I shrug. "I don't know, but something doesn't feel right."

"Something doesn't feel right?" He repeats my words back to me as if he doesn't fully understand them. "What do you mean?"

I let out a frustrated sigh. "If I could explain, I would. But I can't. I don't know why, but I have a really bad feeling, and I don't think we should leave the jungle."

"Did you hear something or see someone?" Aiden twists around to look for signs of anything out of the ordinary. "Are there more of the inhabitants here?"

"No." I shake my head. "I mean, I don't think so. I haven't—"

"HELP!" The sounds of someone's screams silence me. Aiden races out of the jungle and toward the shouts.

"Aiden! No!" I follow, mostly because I want to make sure he's safe, but it's sheer terror that's propelling me.

One of the survivors from the crash—Penelope—comes running down the beach. "Someone help me! He's going to get me!"

One of the natives is chasing her. Jason and Aiden stop cold and stare in disbelief. I do the same. The native is tall, well over six and a half feet. He's grotesquely muscular with wild, bug-like eyes and long, straw-like greasy hair. His lips are grossly large, and his teeth stick out. For all purposes, he looks human, but he's also not.

"Help me!" She looks right at us, pleading for us to save her. We're all frozen in place, watching in horror as the scene plays out before us.

"We have to help her," Aiden says.

"How?" Jason asks.

"No!" Penelope trips and falls. She lies there for a second, unmoving. "No!" She kicks her feet and tries to scramble away as the native approaches her. He gives the evilest smile I've ever seen and steps toward her.

My heart races. "We have to do something before he gets to her." Panic laces my voice, and my hands shake.

"Chances are there's more than one of him. We get involved, we'll all get killed," Jason says.

"Doing something is better than standing here watching that poor girl die." I clench my teeth. "I don't want that on my conscience. I don't want to walk around with all of that guilt." I point at my chest to emphasize my point. But I don't say I already have a mountain of guilt weighing me down. We should have told them what we knew; we should have warned them. I told Tom they needed to know, and he didn't listen. And now all but a handful of the crash survivors are dead. Murdered in cold blood because we didn't warn them.

"Neither do I," Aiden says. His face is pale, and I guess he's thinking about his cousin.

"What good are three of us going to do against an unknown number of them?" Jason asks.

I reach down and grab the arrow from his hand. "We have this!"

"If you two distract him, I can sneak around from behind," Aiden says. He gently takes the arrow from my hand, and I don't argue. "It will give us the element of surprise long enough to get Penelope to safety."

"And what about you?" I ask.

"Don't worry about me. I'll be fine."

I don't believe him, but I nod, knowing we're running out of time. Aiden steps back into the jungle while Jason and I walk onto the beach toward Penelope. My heart's in my throat, and blood rushes to my head, making it throb.

The native turns our way and lets out a guttural cry before chanting, *"Guuawwhachaa! Guuawwhachaa! Guuawwhachaa!"*

I glance over at Jason, who's ghost white. "What is he saying? Is that even a known language?"

He shrugs. "That's the same thing I heard them saying before. I have no idea what any of it means, but I'm afraid he's calling for back-up."

I swallow hard.

The native is still approaching Penelope as she's scrambling to get away. I reach her first and grab her under the arms, pulling her back. She finally manages to get to her feet, and she clings to me like a life preserver.

Jason continues his forward ascent toward the native. He puts his hands up as if to show he's not a threat, but it doesn't make a difference. The native screeches in his unknown language and raises his bow. Jason stops. "Hey, easy there, fella. We don't want to hurt you."

From the corner of my eye, I see Aiden tiptoeing down the beach. He's attempting to sneak around behind the native. My gaze darts back to Jason, who's trying to keep the native focused on him. I hold my breath. I really want to close my eyes, but I'm too afraid if I do, something even worse will happen.

The native tugs on his long, muddy beard. It doesn't look like it's been washed in months. Or years. Now that I'm closer, I can see the scars running the length of his face, like he'd lost one too many knife fights.

"Guuawwhachaa!" The native roars and rushes at Jason.

I scream, but it's cut off when Aiden jumps on the native's back. The native bucks and thrashes, but Aiden holds on. Jason plants his fist into the native's stomach, causing him to double over. Aiden hops off and kicks the back of his knee. The native flinches but doesn't fall. He spins around to attack Aiden. His massive arm swings out and smacks Aiden across the side of the face. Aiden falls to the ground.

"No!" I shout. I make a move to go after him, to offer some sort of help, but Penelope clings to me, making it impossible for me to move. I stare at Aiden's body, praying for him to get up. After what seems like an eternity, he does. I blow out a breath.

"Hey! Over here!" Jason shouts. The native spins around, giving Aiden time to get back to his feet. The arrow he'd been carrying is lying several feet away, knocked from his hand during the fight.

The native smiles. "Boogharaa! Boogharaa!"

I pry Penelope from me and run toward the arrow. "Aiden!" When he looks at me, I toss him the arrow. He catches it and runs at the native. But he's not fast enough. The native slips past Aiden and charges toward me.

"Emily! Run!" Jason hollers.

I do, but the native is so fast. He grabs a handful of my hair and yanks so hard, tears spring to my eyes. He slams me against the ground. My body thrashes at the sudden, intense pain, and tears spring to my eyes. Stars and bright lights flash in front of me before my eyes close of their own volition.

A loud "oomph" echoes around me, and then I hear Jason shout, "Now!"

I open my eyes just enough to see Aiden ram the arrow straight into the native's neck. Blood squirts everywhere, and I roll to my side and cover my face. Tears spill down my cheeks, and I sob.

CHAPTER 29

Aiden

THE NATIVE SLUMPS TO THE ground, dead. But not before he covers me with his blood. I look down at myself, my eyes wide, and my stomach lurching. I clutch my mid-section and double over.

Oh, dear God. I just killed someone. I begin to dry heave. I must be dreaming! I draw several deep breaths through my mouth, but that makes the heaving worse. My throat is raw, and my stomach feels like it's on fire. I overhear Jason comforting Penelope, asking if she's okay. I clench fistfuls of my hair and squeeze my eyes shut. My head spins like a never ending Ferris wheel. What is wrong with me? Why did I kill that person? He's still a human being, regardless of what he did to us and our group, regardless of what he became out here.

Dear God, please forgive me. I didn't mean to kill him. I'm so sorry.

I straighten abruptly, which makes my vertigo worse, but I ignore it. "Emily!" I glance down and see her curled up in the fetal position, shaking. I crouch down next to her. "Emily? Hey, are you okay?" I roll her over and onto my lap, cradling her against me.

She sobs. "Thank you."

"What?"

Emily pulls away and looks up at me. "He was going to kill me."

My breath catches, and a lump lodges in my throat. "I killed him instead," I deadpan.

She takes my face into her hands. "Listen to me, Aiden. It was me or him. What you just did was necessary. If you didn't kill him, he would have killed all of us. You did what you had to do."

I nod as tears pool in my eyes, blurring my vision. I hug Emily to me, taking comfort in her embrace.

She trails her fingers along the nape of my neck, holding me just as tightly as I'm holding her. "You saved all of us, Aiden. Focus on that," she whispers. Her breath is warm against my sweaty skin.

"I know."

"Look!" Penelope jumps to her feet and, and a second later, she slumps to the ground. Two arrows protrude from her back.

"No!" Emily shrieks, the word mangled from her hysteria.

I yank her to her feet. "We have to go. Now!" Adrenaline fuels my every movement.

She stands then stumbles. I grip her tightly, praying she has the strength to run. "Emily, c'mon." I attempt to drag her from the beach, but she's not moving.

"Jason," she shouts. "We can't leave without him."

"Jason?" I holler. No answer. God, please don't let him be dead. He was here just a moment ago. "Jason!" I yell louder.

But for all our yelling, Jason doesn't appear. A native does, though. My heart stops. I shove Emily and scream, "Run!"

She takes off, and I follow. The native is on my heels, and I expect to feel the sharp stab of an arrow piercing my back. Each step has my heart thundering and my chest aching with harsh breaths. I really don't think I'm going to be able to outrun him. *God, please protect me and Emily.*

"Faster," I say to Emily. Then, to my left is a blur of skin and dark hair followed by a guttural howl. Jason bursts from behind a tree and tackles the native. They hit the ground with a sickening thud. I stop and watch in horror as Jason wrestles with the native. Before I can do or say anything, the native has Jason pinned on the ground.

"Get out of here," Jason shouts at me and Emily. "Run. Now!"

But I'm paralyzed with fear. I need to help him, but I don't know what to do. And my entire body is shaking—I'm not sure I have the strength to do anything. Then, the native grabs a homemade knife from somewhere behind him and jams it into Jason's chest.

My stomach lurches. Emily screams and doesn't stop.

The native glances up at us, and my stomach drops. I jerk on Emily's hand. "We need to get back to the building. It's the only safe place."

We run so hard and fast that neither of us can speak even if we wanted to. My heart is thundering in my chest. My mind keeps replaying the image of Jason saving us.

"There!" Emily gasps as we enter the clearing where the building sits.

"Get to the bunker," I say, guiding her ahead of me. I glance over my shoulder, but I don't see any sight of the native. Is he still chasing us?

We rush toward the building. Brenda is standing near the front steps, rifle aimed at us. I grab the back of Emily's shirt, and we both come to a sudden stop. I raise my hands to show her I'm not a threat.

Then, she lifts the rifle and shoots. I cringe and squeeze my eyes shut. When I don't drop dead, I slowly open my eyes and turn around. The native who was chasing us, the one who killed Jason, now lies face down on the ground. Dead.

"Is there anyone else with you?" Brenda asks.

"No," Emily says out of breath. "Those people killed everyone."

Brenda's eyes widen, and she glances over our heads. "C'mon, get inside." She motions toward the door with the barrel of her rifle.

Emily steps forward, and I keep my gaze on Brenda. She's not planning to shoot us in the back, is she? "Is Tom or Marjorie here?" I ask.

"No." She shakes her head. "They're at the airstrip."

"Alone?" I ask, incredulous. "What if they're attacked like we were?" As much as I don't want to think it, the thought screams through my mind—the only reason Emily and I made it out alive is because the natives had so many other people to kill; we were able to sneak away unnoticed among the chaos.

"Tom's armed. He'll be okay," Brenda says. "Now, get inside before another one of them comes looking for you two." She motions the rifle toward the door then steps aside so we can enter.

I step forward, then reach my hand out for Emily. But she hesitates, her eyes narrowed. Please don't let her say anything to upset Brenda. "Emily?" I say.

"Watch out," Emily screams and then shoves me through the doorway.

I barely manage to sit up before I see two natives storming out of the tree line. My eyes widen.

"Inside. Now." Brenda pushes Emily inside then slams the door shut. Emily quickly locks the door.

I scramble to my feet and rush to the front window. Brenda stands outside, the boom of her rifle echoing as she shoots at the natives. One drops, but the other continues forward. I hold my breath, praying she'll be okay.

"We have to get down to the bunker." Emily tugs on my arm, but I don't move. "Aiden. We have to go."

"We can't just leave her." And I can't believe Emily even suggested that. "Not when she's out there fighting to save us."

I turn my attention back to the window. The second native drops to the ground. Brenda doesn't lower her rifle, but she looks around. I race to the door, unlock it, and swing it open. "Get inside," I say to Brenda.

Slowly, she backs up toward the door, rifle still at the ready. When she reaches the steps, she lowers her weapon and turns around. I move out of the doorway, but before she can step over the threshold, she lurches forward, blood dripping from the corner of her mouth. And then she drops to the ground, an arrow sticking out the back of her neck.

Emily shrieks, covering her face with her hands. "No. No." She shakes her head violently and repeats the word no until it blends together as an incoherent wail.

"GO!" I shout, shoving Emily toward the kitchen. I snatch the rifle from Brenda's dead body and follow Emily through the kitchen and down the dark corridor to the bunker.

***

"They left without us," Emily says for what feels like the billionth time.

"They didn't leave without us." But the more I say that, the less sure I am of it. We've been sitting in the bunker for over five hours. Listening. Waiting. Worrying.

"They probably went back to the beach, saw all the dead bodies, assumed we were dead, too, and then left." Emily paces the length of the living room, her body a ball of tension. If her back and shoulders gets any straighter, I'm afraid they'll crack.

Footsteps sound overhead. I jump up from the couch. A sudden spike of adrenaline makes my heart race. The door to the bunker groans open, sending a sliver of light down the steps. I move to stand in front of Emily and snatch the rifle from the floor. I raise it, but my hands are shaking so badly, I can't hold it steady.

Emily grips the back of my shirt, and I can feel her body trembling behind me. I blow out a breath. "I have a gun, and I'm not afraid to shoot you," I call out, hoping whoever it is will reconsider.

"Don't shoot, Aiden. It's us," Marjorie says.

Relief floods me, and I drop the rifle. A moment later, Marjorie and then Tom appear in the bunker. Emily barrels past me and throws her arms around Marjorie. "You made it." Then she hugs Tom. "You didn't leave us here."

Tom hugs her back. "Of course I didn't leave you."

I smile, relief and happiness mixing in my heart.

"How did you get here?" Emily asks Tom. "Brenda told us you were at the airstrip."

"We were," Marjorie says. "Then we were attacked, so we left."

"The plane?" I ask.

Tom shakes his head. "Didn't show up."

"What about the communication tower?" I ask.

"Empty," Tom answers.

Emily whimpers.

There's a massive knot forming in the pit of my stomach. "Wait, so that means we're stuck here? For good? We're never getting off this island?" Hysteria sets in, and I can't breathe.

"Aiden." Emily reaches for me, but I jerk away.

"No. This is crazy. There has to be a way off this island. There has to be." I pace. Each step ratchets my fear. "Brenda must have had contact with the outside world. We need to search this bunker. There has to be something here that we can use to send for help."

"I don't know. I asked her those exact same questions, and she said she doesn't have a way to contact anyone," Tom says.

"You don't really believe that, do you?" Emily's voice is hollow.

"No, but…" Tom sighs. "It's not like we can demand answers from her now."

"She was standing in front of the building when we got here." Emily hugs herself. I want to comfort her, but I'm in no position to do so when I'm on the verge of a nervous breakdown. "We were being chased, and she saved our lives." A sob escapes, and I close my eyes, desperately wanting to block out the reality of our situation.

"What about everyone else?" Marjorie asks softly, but by the tone of her voice, I'm guessing she already knows the answer.

"Dead," I say, opening my eyes. "It was a total massacre."

"Jason sacrificed himself," Emily whispers.

Marjorie gasps. "God help us."

"Well, we're safe for the time being, so let's—" Tom begins.

"Safe?" I laugh bitterly. "On an island with human freaks who want to kill us and a government who won't rescue us? And the only person who knows what is going on is dead! What're we going to do?"

"All right, calm down." Tom holds his hands up in a show of surrender. "I'm sure there's something in Brenda's files that will help us figure all of this out."

All the hope and adrenaline leaves my body at the same time, and I can barely hold myself up. I lean against the wall and wipe the sweat from my forehead. "We're not ever getting rescued, are we?"

The room spins, and I can't get my bearings. I collapse to the floor, and the last thing I hear is Emily calling my name.

Sweet Emily. I promised her we'd be safe, that we would get off this island, that everything would be okay. I lied to her. I failed her like I failed Eddie. My eyelids flutter, and then the world goes silent.

CHAPTER 30

Emily

I DROP TO MY KNEES beside Aiden and put his head in my lap. "Aiden?" I brush his hair away from his forehead. "Aiden, wake up. Please wake up." He's out cold, and he's not so much as fluttering his eyelashes. "Tom." I look up through tear-filled eyes. "Help him."

Tom scoops Aiden up into his arms like he weighs nothing and lays him on the couch. "Marjorie, get a cold cloth from the kitchen." He turns to me. "He's been through a lot, Emily, and I know you're worried, but you need to give me some space here."

Nodding, I move to sit in the chair. And then I watch as Tom and Marjorie check Aiden over and try to wake him up.

This entire time, he's been the calm one, always telling me things were going to be okay, praying faithfully for rescue and safety. He had saved my life, and all I can do in return is sit here. It doesn't seem like enough.

God, if You're listening, please let Aiden be okay. I can't do this without him, and I promise if You don't take him for me, I'll be the best daughter ever. I'll stop drinking and partying. I'll go to church and be nicer to people. I sniffle and wipe tears with the back of my hand. I'll do anything to make sure he's okay. Anything.

A small groan escapes Aiden, and his eyelids flutter. I bolt out of the chair. *Wake up. Please wake up.* Another groan, and then he sits up. I choke back a sob. He's okay!

"Easy there, kiddo," Tom says. "Here." He takes the bottle of water Marjorie holds. "Take small sips."

"Thank you," Aiden says, his voice raspy.

"How do you feel?" Tom asks. "Are you dizzy? Seeing spots?"

Aiden shakes his head. "Just embarrassed."

Marjorie chuckles.

With Tom's concerned guidance, Aiden stands. He doesn't wobble or otherwise show any signs of something more serious that passing out. Aiden approaches me. "Sorry I scared you." He offers a tentative smile.

I hug him, burying my face against his neck. "I'm just glad you're okay." I lead Aiden back to the couch, worried he's not doing as great as he says, and we sit. "So, now what?" I ask.

"I know our situation isn't what any of us expected, but we're alive," Tom says.

I nod as tears stream down my cheeks. The severity of his words crash down on me. We're really stuck here. Forever. I'll never see my parents or my brother or my friends ever again. I go from silent tears to shoulder-shaking sobs. Aiden will never see his parents again, either. The two other people in this room are now my entire world.

"But it's going to be okay. I'll go through all of Brenda's research and see if I can make sense of it. In the meantime, we stay put, all right?"

"Yeah, okay." I hiccup.

Marjorie nods. "I'll take stock of what we have for food and other supplies."

"We need to make sure no one can get down here," Aiden says. "If we're going to hide out while you go through Brenda's stuff, we need to make sure it's safe."

Tom nods. "I'll fortify the door first, then we'll go through the bunker."

Aiden stands. "I'll help."

I lean back and close my eyes, but sleep is out of my reach. I know I should get up and help, but bone weary exhaustion keeps me rooted in place.

I have no idea what's going to happen to any of us, or how we'll survive on the limited supplies in this bunker, but I know, together, we'll survive. After all, God is with us.

CHAPTER 31

Emily

AS I WAIT FOR AIDEN to make his next move on the checkerboard, I can't help but study him. I'm doing that a lot lately. He still hasn't healed emotionally and mentally from what he did—killing that native—and the fate of the rest of the crash survivors. I worry about him, but then again, it's only been thirty-two days.

Tom has been tirelessly weeding through Brenda's research. He barely sleeps, and he eats even less. He's miserable and snaps at anyone who dares question him—which only confirms my worst fear: he hasn't found anything to help us get home.

"Your move," Aiden says, snapping me from my thoughts.

I move one of my pieces and then nod at him to go. Marjorie is in the kitchen, cleaning. She's been doing that a lot lately. Maybe it helps her cope with our situation. She's taken on the role of mom, and I'm grateful for that. It makes being stuck in this bunker a little easier.

"Emily?"

I blink. "Sorry. What did you say?"

Aiden laughs. "You okay?"

"Yeah. I'm just bored. I miss the sunshine." I sigh.

He reaches over and takes my hand. "I'm sure Tom is getting closer to finding something that will help."

I force a smile. I wish I believed that, but it's been more than a month, and he's not any closer to having answers than he was when we first locked ourselves down here.

"Lunch is almost ready. You two hungry?" Marjorie calls from the kitchen.

"Starving," Aiden answers. He begins to pack up our game, and I help. He was winning anyway.

A moment later, Tom ambles out from what used to be Brenda's room. He hasn't shaved in days, and his eyes are bloodshot from lack of sleep. There's a paper clutched in his right hand. "I think I found something."

I turn to stare at him, and the bunker falls silent. We wait for him to explain, but before he can, there's a loud banging on the bunker door. I whip around, eyes wide. Aiden steps protectively in front of me. Marjorie drops a glass and it shatters. She gasps.

Tom grabs a rifle and approaches the bunker stairs. I slip my hand into Aiden's, fear coursing through me. For thirty-two days, it's been silence. Just the four of us living here like some weirdly matched family.

Whoever is up there attempts to yank the door open, but it doesn't budge. There's another loud bang followed by, "Brenda? Open up. It's me."

Tom glances over his shoulder at the three of us as if to ask, "Who is me?"

Shock washes over me, quickly followed by hope. "Is that the contact Brenda mentioned?" I whisper.

Tom shrugs. Then he hands the rifle to Aiden. "I'm going to open the door. If anything happens to me, shoot first, ask questions later. Understand?"

Aiden nods and takes the rifle.

Fear steals my voice, and I stand frozen, watching as Tom climbs the stairs and Aiden points the rifle. Even after everything I've seen and been through, I will never get used to this. After what feels like an eternity, Tom opens the bunker door, but he's so far up, it's hard to hear what he's saying.

Then, he descends the steps. A man is right behind him. Tom takes the rifle from Aiden and while he doesn't point it at the stranger, he doesn't put it down, either.

"Who're you?" Aiden asks.

"I could ask you the same thing," the man replies.

"Sit," Tom orders the man. "What's your name?"

"Dean." The man sits. "Who are you? And why is Brenda dead?"

"If you know she's dead, why did you call her name a few minutes ago?" I ask. Suspicion bubbles up inside of me.

"She sent me a communication the day before my last scheduled supply drop. Said there was an issue on the island and to wait for another communication. I haven't heard from her in weeks, so I flew out here to check on her." Dean rubs his hands over his face, then pins Tom with a glare. "Now, who are you people, and why is Brenda dead?"

Tom dives into a lengthy explanation of who we all are, how we ended up on this island, what happened to the rest of the plane crash survivors and Brenda, and how we've been stuck here, looking for a way home.

When Tom finally stops speaking, Aiden says, "I'm sorry about Brenda. We tried to help her. We really did."

Dean nods but remains silent. I shift closer to Aiden, trying—and failing—to hold back the hope building in my chest. This man flew here, which means he can fly us home.

"Brenda was my godmother," Dean finally says. "I tried to convince her to leave this place, to just forget all about it, but she wouldn't. She insisted she needed to help save the world." He snorts and shakes his head. "I knew this island would be the death of her."

Suddenly, Brenda's refusal to reach out to her contact and her lack of information about him in this bunker makes sense. She was protecting him.

"For what it's worth," Marjorie moves from the kitchen, "Brenda helped us when we needed it the most. She was a good woman." Marjorie smiles warmly at Dean.

"In her last communication to me, she said she witnessed something that renewed her faith in humanity." Dean stood and rubbed his hands on his jeans. "I don't know what you four did to make her feel that way, but it's been the one thing she's spent her life searching for."

"We looked out for each other," Tom said. "We were willing to sacrifice ourselves to make sure we were safe. We would have done the same for her."

"Thank you." Dean smiled. Then he looked at each of us in turn, his expression turning somber. "This island is nothing but a death trap. There's no reason for anyone to be here any longer."

"Does this mean…" I can barely contain my excitement. "Are you taking us home?"

Dean nods.

I let out a squeal and throw my arms around Aiden, hugging him so tight he can barely breathe. "We're going home," I cry.

Pulling back, Aiden finds my lips and gives me a quick kiss. "Our prayers have been answered."

I smile. God is good, and I will never doubt Him again.

ABOUT THE AUTHOR

David Jemal, having graduating college with a major he created in finance and culture, jumped into the world of sales and thus began crisscrossing across North America. While he's traveling, he's busy drafting the many stories taking up residence in his mind. David lives with his wife and family in Brooklyn, New York.

ABOUT THE AUTHOR

Kara Leigh Miller combines her knowledge and prior editing experience with a passion for the written word and a love for all things young adult. She currently lives in Michigan with her husband, four kids, four pit bulls, and six cats. When she's not busy writing fun, faith-filled young adult novels, she's spending time with her family or exhausting herself at the gym.

Find her anytime at: www.karaleighmillerauthor.com.
She sporadically blogs at: www.karaleighmiller.blogspot.com.
For the most accurate, up-to-date information,
sign up for her newsletter: http://eepurl.com/bn1wyD

THE
RUNAWAY
GIRL

By

Debbie Ioanna

ISBN-13: 978-1537755533
ISBN-10: 1537755536

CONTENTS

ACKNOWLEDGMENTS

I would like to mention my 'London Wife' Laura who inspired me to get this published after holding on to the story for many years. Also to my partner Ricky who has always been there to support me. I don't know where I would be without these two wonderful people.

Introduction

It's time for some changes. I have had enough. It's becoming beyond ridiculous. Even my mum can't see what is going on and it's taking place in her own house between her only beloved child and her husband of two minutes. He is a nasty, horrible man but as far as my mum is concerned the sun shines out of his backside and I am a moody teenager.

Here's a little bit about me. Most people call me Shelly, but if I don't like you then you call me Michelle. I'm at the grand old 'rebellious age' of sixteen. I manage to act my age at times. I have the advantage of looking older so the weekends can be fun with the girls. We'll go in to town or go to the cinema. You could say I have a pretty good social life. The weekends are never dull. I have a good amount of friends and I will always be out with them at the weekend causing trouble in Bradford, or maybe even a trek to Halifax or Leeds.

I live with my mum and step-dad. My mum and *real* dad divorced many years ago. I don't know why they separated. Being young, I wasn't told everything but I know it wasn't for good reasons. I think I was only eight at the time.

My hair is dark brown, naturally wavy so hair straighteners are a must. I have been blessed, unlike most of my friends, with avoiding the cursed teen acne.

I have just finished my GCSE exams. I don't know my results yet and, to be honest, I don't really care because I have no idea what I want to do when I grow up, for real. I was thinking about staying on in sixth form but I hate my school. I've been there for five years and I want a change. I might apply to college depending on my results, or get a job so I could afford to move out of this place.

I have a good relationship with my mum. Well I did, until he came along. My step-dad is full of fake charms. I don't know what my mum sees in him. When she's around, he treats me like an angel, always complimenting me, always making great conversations with me and being civil. He acts like a real father who most kids would kill for, making my mum happy and my friends jealous. However, as soon as my mum leaves the house, he's always snapping at me, even when he isn't angry. For example, my mum went down to the shops for a few bits and he told me to make him a cup of tea or he would take away all my savings. I had saved £35 from my pocket money and I wasn't about to lose it for some measly cup of tea. If he wasn't six foot tall and built like a lumberjack I'd try smack him myself. So anyway I made this cup of tea but he still took my money. He said it had too much sugar and it was too strong. I don't understand how it can be both sweet and strong at the same time but he took my money anyway. That just proves he talks bullshit half the time. He just walked into my room and took my money without telling me. I didn't realise until later on when I went into my room. It was Friday night and I was about to meet the girls to go to *Nando's*. I went in my room, opened my little purple piggy bank and it was empty, apart for some coppers. My mum was home so I couldn't start shouting and accusing him, he would have already spent it on booze or gambling.

Now I think about it, it seems like my relationship with my mum is fading. I don't know whether that is down to Steve or just general aging mother/teenage daughter circumstances. We hardly ever see each other anymore. She stays back at work now because she thinks I will be ok left with Steve (the step dad from hell). She's turned in to a proper career woman now; working from nine till nine. While she's out she thinks Steve will feed me, help me with my homework and send me to bed on time. What she doesn't know is that I make both of our teas, clean up after my cooking, I do my homework in my room instead of at the kitchen table where I would have room to do it and get sent to my room before I am meant to. He also tends to get drunk often and shouts at me for no apparent reason. He just finds some stupid reason to argue with me. I'm getting better at arguing back now. I'm more cocky and sarcastic. As a result, I've been grounded for two weeks. All I did was get home half an hour after my curfew. He didn't believe that I had missed the bus. He just wants me out of the way so he can have my mum all to himself. He's trying to piss me off that much that I end up moving out as soon as I can. As if I would give in to him.

Chapter 1

"MICHELLE," Steve yelled. He was drunk, yet again. "Get down here now; I want a word with you!"

Here it comes. I hate it when he's had too much to drink. He always gets drunk on his days off from work, which has been a lot more frequent lately now I think about it. It's the summer holidays for me so I've had to sit with him all day. He treats me like his personal slave more than usual. He knows my mum won't be back for another few hours so he will be making the most of it.

"What do you want now?" I asked.

"Don't give me that attitude," he began. I could smell the beer on his breath from four feet away from him. He couldn't quite focus on me at first and I'm sure I spotted some drool on his chin. "I'm out of beers. Go get me some more."

"No," I said, quite blatantly.

"Do you really want to say no to me?" he asked me, holding on to his black belt with an evil glare in his eye, like he'd even have the nerve to try anything that would leave a mark on me. "Go get me some more beers now!" as he pointed his arm to the door he knocked off an empty can without even noticing. It was like something out of a comedy show but without the laughs.

I think he was trying to say that unless I buy him some beers out of my money, he would beat me to death with his fake leather belt. He always makes these slight threats me but never does anything drastic. He wouldn't dare. He's all mouth.

"I can't…" I began.

"WHY?" he yelled. "Do you really want to mess with me child?"

"Well, firstly you took all my money, or are you still going to argue that it just 'vanished' from my room?"

"We've been through this you little…" I cut him off.

"And secondly, I'm not old enough to buy alcohol. The shop owner knows I am only sixteen so he won't serve me."

"You call that an excuse?"

"Well it sounds good enough to me," I said in my sarcastic way.

"Don't play games with me. You go out drinking every weekend so don't even say you don't look old enough."

"There's a bit of a difference. I tend to dress up when I'm going out in order to make myself look older. I'm not going to dress up so you can sit here all night drinking your way further in to my psychological problems!"

"Get out of my sight, you filthy little tart," he yelled "Go on. GET OUT!"

I gladly walked out. I'm guessing that gave you a clear understanding of what I was on about. He's awful to me. Verbal abuse I can handle but what if he does start to abuse me? Not only physically but sexually too? You do hear of these stories. No, he wouldn't dare. He hasn't got the nerve to do anything like that. He might look scary but he hasn't hurt me yet. If he even lays a finger on me then I'm going straight to the police. Unless he does manage to kill me, then I might have a hard time trying to report it. He wouldn't have the guts to try anything.

"Hey sweetie," my mum said as she entered my room later that night. "Did Steve give you food poisoning; you're awfully quiet and quite pale?"

"How could Steve give me food poisoning when he doesn't even cook?" I began. I wanted to get the message through to my mum that he doesn't treat me like she wants him to. "He was too hammered to even try to make anything for me or even help me to write my CV like he told you he would. He even had the nerve to ask me to go to the shop with *my* money to buy him some beers. Is he really a good husband if he's trying to get his step daughter to buy alcohol?"

"He did seem a bit drunk." She wasn't paying attention to me at all when I said 'my money' and 'buy him alcohol'! "He passed out on the couch not long after I got home, but I'm not surprised."

"Why?" I asked. She's going to stick up for him. I know it. She always takes his side. She agreed that my money must have vanished from my room so why should I be surprised.

"I wasn't supposed to say anything but," she began, "his father had another heart attack last night. He may be a bit snappy but so would you if a member of your family nearly died."

"The way he behaves, you'd think someone in his family 'nearly' died every bloody day."

"What's that supposed to mean?" she said, she looked confused and quite taken back by my comment.

"You're so blind!" I said out loud. So loud, that Steve could probably hear me while floating in the intoxicated land of Carling.

"Excuse me?"

"You don't even notice what's going on."

"Why what's going on?" she asks. "And lower your voice; I don't want you to wake Steve."

"Oh we wouldn't want that now would we? He's not the fantastic husband you think he is. For years now I've had to put up with it."

"Put up with what? Do you not like him?"

She's quick isn't she?

"Oh no, why would you even think that?" I said, again sarcastically.

"It's your dad. You don't like us being apart and you don't want me with anyone else. I know what you're trying to do and it won't work. We're divorced and both remarried. We just didn't love each other like we did when we first married. Plus, we didn't end it on good terms so were not really talking to each other and..."

"It's not like I'm trying to get you back together. You've been apart for most of my life. I'm used to it. It's just..."

"You need some time alone with Steve, just to get to know him better. You two never really got the time to bond with each other. It was rushed for you."

What is she on about, 'Time alone with Steve'?

She has got to be kidding. That's the last thing on my mind. I'd rather play Doctors and Nurses with Hannibal Lecter and Freddie Kruger than spend more *quality* time with him.

"Well," she began, "you'll have all next week with him won't you?"

My heart stopped. I had completely forgotten. Mum would not be here next week. She's going on a course. Why did she have to be so hyped up with her new business plans? How could I get out of it?

"Oh," I began trying to lie, "Mum, I forgot, I'm staying at dad's next week. We just arranged it today."

"No you're not. He's in Portugal and still will be next week so unless you're catching a plane out there, you're staying here."

"Mum please, don't make me stay alone with him. Why can't I go stay with Grandma?"

"You can't stay there! Aunty Lynne and your cousins are living there for the next few weeks while their house is being redecorated. No, you're staying here and that's final." She stood up to leave the room. "And don't try hiding at Chrissie or Lou's house. I'll be ringing every night and you had better be at home. Ok?"

"Ok," I said.

"Shell, I mean it. You and Steve need this. I don't want you hating him because he tries really hard with you. He wants you to see him in a fatherly way. Promise me you will try."

"Fine, I promise." But no way is he replacing my dad.

Well it's settled. Unless I run away I have to stay here. Run away? No. I would not run away. Things couldn't possibly be that bad. If I just stay out of his way then I won't annoy him for any ridiculous reason he makes up. It's the summer holidays so I'm sure I would be able to find some way to keep busy and out of his way.

I wish my dad was here. I love him so much, and I miss him too. He's on his honeymoon. He's been in Portugal for almost a month now. I wish he would come home so I could stay with him. He would understand my problems with Steve. I've been stupid to not tell him before. I think I was just always worried that it would cause more arguments and upset between him and my mum and, being a child, it was always upsetting to see them not getting along. The thing is, if I opened up and told my dad now then he will know that I've been lying to him.

It'd be best to just keep my mouth shut. For now.

Chapter 2

"Right then," my mum said on the morning when she was setting off to Birmingham for the course. "You be good," she kissed my cheek, "and you…" she said hugging Steve, "take care of her, and tomorrow, remember to take her shopping for a new coat. She's grown out of the one she has now and she'll need a smart jacket if she's going to be going for interviews for a summer job so make sure she hands some CVs in some shops. Now she's off for two months she could use the money. Oh and treat her to lunch. Maybe go to a restaurant or something. I think it will be a good chance for you two to bond a little bit."

"OK I'll book something special for us both later. Maybe we could try that new Chinese Buffet in town. How about it Shelly?" he said, sounding far too enthusiastic for my liking. I didn't have high hopes for anything to happen or for us to even make it to town.

Anyway, how dare he call me Shelly? I never gave him permission to do so. It's Michelle to him. I nodded but didn't look him in the eye.

"See you next week darling. I love you and will miss you so much," he said as she walked out the door. She kissed him once again on the cheek then smiled and walked down the driveway to her car. I ran to her giving her another hug.

"Mum, can't I come with you?" I whispered in her ear. "I'll be good, I promise. You won't even notice me. I'll stay out of your way the whole time."

"Don't start this again Shell please, I don't have time now. Steve will look after you. I think this will be really good for you both and it will mean so much to me." Emotional blackmail. She looked at her watch. "I have to dash. I don't want to catch the rush hour. Bye."

She drove away blowing yet another kiss to Steve. Sickening.

"Are you coming in? Or would you like me to lock you out for the day? You can stay out all week if you want, doesn't bother me in the slightest." Well that took all of about ten seconds, record time for his split personality syndrome. He had the look of power on his face. I walked in slowly, dragging my feet, staring him in the eye.

I walk into the room and it suddenly hits me that she's gone. It's just the two of us. I was instructed by mum to not hide at a friend's house for the whole week. I had to stay in with him. She had given me ten pounds to treat myself to something in town. I am really dreading tomorrow. I can stay in my room tonight, but to go to town with him! Be alone with him in charge! Do what he says! This week is going to be hell. My life is rubbish. I can't wait to move out.

"SHELL," he banged on my door the next morning, "Get up or I'm going to town on my own and spending the money on something for me. Come on I am not waiting all day."

Here is the day I have been dreading all night. I do not want to spend all day with him. No one will ever understand how much I want to get out of this. I was invited out with some friends but was forced to say "no". I just went straight to bed last night. I cooked him his tea and made him drinks like he told me to and went straight upstairs. If I was upstairs then I could avoid being shouted at. I took some food up with me so I didn't need to go downstairs for any reason.

"Get your money out," he said as the bus pulled up to the bus stop. "You're paying for me too by the way because I'm already paying for your coat."

"No you're not. Mum is," I replied but he didn't seem to care.

I ended up paying for him. I was too tired and couldn't be bothered to argue. The less I argued then the less I would want to throw myself under a bus.

When we get to town, I have a hard time trying to walk at his speed. He suddenly sees the bookies.

"Here's £20, go get your coat and I'll meet you at home later."

He disappeared. I thought he had no money? I didn't care though. At least I can do what I want now. Hang on a minute. This isn't a £20 note. It's a fiver. That big, old, fat bastard! I hate him. I could really kill him sometimes. He makes me want to scream, I want to punch him! I can't go in the bookies because I'm underage. The owner is a friend of my uncles so he knows I'm sixteen. What an absolute bastard he is. A nasty, horrible bully of a man.

My phone rings.

"Hello?" I answered, frustrated.

"Hi Shell? It's mum. Are you ok?"

"Hi mum, yeah I'm ok?"

"You sound annoyed."

"No, I'm fine."

"Where's Steve?"

"He's…busy at the moment." I don't know why I was protecting him. I didn't want mum to worry I suppose. Not like she'd believe me anyway. Or take my side for that matter. I feel like I could tell her that I was watching him receive a lap dance and she still wouldn't believe me.

"Oh well, I'll tell you the good news," she began, "I'll just be here for four days. I thought it was meant to be a week but two of the lecturers couldn't make it so their presentation has been delayed for a month or so. So I will see you in four maybe five days."

"Oh brilliant. That's really good! Cool, ok I'll see you then." Suddenly I had perked up.

Wow so I don't have to put up with that great ape all week. I felt like celebrating. I find a small café and buy a hot chocolate and a bun. I was so happy.

After about half an hour my phone rings again. I had wandered in to one of the pound shops and was pondering over the sweets and biscuits.

"Hello?" I say in a cheery kind of way, not even checking who was actually calling me.

"It's me," said this gruff voice. It was Steve. He was drunk, already. It didn't take long. He's such a lightweight. "I just wanted to tell you that you're making your own tea tonight and for the rest of the week." I expected him to make me do that anyway. "You can also do all the house work and don't bother spending that money you have. I want it. I need to put some bets on. If you weren't living with us then I wouldn't need to..." he breaks to have another swig of whatever he was drinking. "I would be rich if you weren't around. I could buy your mother whatever she wanted. But I can't. You have ruined my life and all my plans. If you weren't with us I might be happy and so would your mother. I hate you. You're an inconvenience to us both. I wouldn't care if you died! Go walk in front of a bus on your way home." And with that he hung up.

My eyes filled with water, after everything, how can he still upset me like this? I felt like throwing my phone through the window. I was suddenly filled with hatred and anger. I wanted to march over to the pub, walk up to him and... oh I don't know what I would do. All I know is I don't ever want to see him again. He's hurt me more now than he ever had before.

That was the last straw. He was going to pay. There was only one thing to do.

Chapter 3

"Where you going love?" asked the bus driver as I got on. He was skinny with a bald head. I could see the bones in his cheeks move as he smiled at me. He had a tooth missing which I thought was gross. Mum had always taken me to the dentist every six months to make sure my teeth would be healthy when I'm older. I never liked it and avoided it if I could but I think I'll definitely go now, just to avoid losing teeth!

"Half fare to Queensbury please. Thanks."

"How old are you love?" he looked at me with suspicion. He had a queer voice.

"I've forgotten my pass." I gave him a smile and hoped he would sympathise. They don't usually, these bus drivers, but I was hoping my tear stained cheeks would help.

"Hmm well ok then, here ya go love."

I sat on a seat near the front. I could not believe what I was about to do. I was going to get revenge on Steve. I was going to get him into the most trouble a man could get in to. I was going to make my mum see him for what he really was. I was going to make him want me at home for the first time ever since he moved in. I was going to run away!

As I sat on the bus, I wondered where I should go. I didn't want to go anywhere local. What about London? London isn't a bad place. I've only been there once. My dad took me there for a weekend. London is huge; no one would think to look for me there. Even if they did, they wouldn't be able to find me. I wouldn't be gone for long; just a week or so. Just long enough for Steve to worry. It might even be a fun break, London is amazing! There's so much to do and see, it'd be a blast.

I get home in a panic. I can feel my heart pounding hard against my ribs. Should I do this? Yes, Steve needs to learn his lesson. Think of when my mum gets home and realises that her loving husband has driven away her only child. It wouldn't be so bad anyway, I would be back soon.

Ok, so I have this fiver and some random change, and there's £30 of Steve's upstairs... which I suspect is mine he took from my room, and I think my mum has some money around so all together I have £55. That will be ok, won't it? I don't know. I've never had to fend for myself before. I'll get a loaf of bread from downstairs, a bottle of water, and some biscuits and get them packed away in my bag. I'll need a sleeping bag too.

I find one shoved under my bed and soon have it rolled up and in my bag. Whilst making my way down the stairs I was skipping steps and felt like I was flying. Clearly too excited at my big venture. I leave my bags by the door and head to the kitchen to grab the bread and other bits. In my bag they go and out the door I go!

"Good afternoon Michelle," said my elderly neighbour as I walk out the door. I can never remember her name so I refer to her as Mrs Next Door. "Where are you going with that huge bag and sleeping bag?" she spoke with a very polite and posh voice. She reminded me of Dot Cotton from *Eastenders*; very well spoken but a rough voice which has been plagued by years of smoking.

"Err...I'm staying at my grandmas in Leeds. I'm just going to get the bus now."

"Where is your step-father, Steve? He's meant to be taking care of you isn't he, for the week? Whilst your Mother is away?" she is so nosy.

I felt like saying, "No, it's only a few days now. My mum rang up earlier and said it's for four days. Steve doesn't know though. He'd rather stay in a pub and spend my money on booze," but I didn't want her to pry into any more of my business. So I just said, "He was meant to be looking after me but his dad had another heart attack the other day so he's looking after him and I'm going to my Nan's."

This is obviously a bit more believable and considering she probably already knows about Steve's father's heart attack, it's no wonder she happily continues to smoke on her cigarette in her doorway asking no more questions.

The bus pulls up just as I make it to the stop. It's a big old fat guy driving. Not fashionable to wear a shirt with ketchup down the front, or even professional.

"Where to luv?" he asked, with a horrid grumpy voice. It was a different man this time. The total opposite of the guy I had before. He was chubby with nice teeth but too much fat on his face to see the cheek bones. He looked impatient. Nice to know our bus drivers are very enthusiastic about their job.

"To the interchange please."

"Do you want a return? It's cheaper if you're coming back," he asked me.

"No, just a one way please."

I choose a seat at the back so no one I know has a chance of walking past me and noticing me. I had my back to the rest of the bus. I thought about going upstairs but people will see me as I get up there. I cannot be recognised. I want no clues to my whereabouts. Mum will be glad to know that Steve was having the time of his life spending all their money in a rotten, smelly old pub while I was at home trying to find the sleeping bag so I would have something to sleep in on the streets. Funny how he claims to have no money yet there is always money for booze...

I finally get to the interchange and make my way up the escalator to the train station. How much is it to London? Where's the timetable? Oh my god. Sixty five quid. Sixty five bloody quid. It's a train for God's sake, not a private limo. What am I going to do now? I'm not going home no way. Not now. It was too late for that. Maybe I could rob a bank. Or why don't I just ring the Queen? And ask her for a few bob maybe that would be better. Come on Michelle THINK.

"Shelly? Is that you?"

Oh damn. Its Mrs Next door again. What is she doing here? And how did she get here before me? She probably rode in on her broom. In fact, I bet she followed me. Spying on me.

"Hi Mrs... Hanson." Her name finally comes to me.

"I thought you were going on the bus to your

Grandma's? What's happened? Why do you need a train?" she looked down on me. Snobby cow.

I suddenly had a good idea.

"Oh did I say bus? I was meant to say train. She lives in err... in err... Liverpool. Not Leeds. I got confused. And as luck would have it I haven't got enough fair to get there." Very bad manners approaching. "You wouldn't have a tenner on you would you?"

She gives me an awkward look. "Yes," she says, "here." She reaches in to her purse and takes out a crisp, new £10 note.

"Oh thank you so much. You are a lifesaver. I'll pay you back as soon as possible. In fact, if you ask Steve later on, he can pay you."

"Are you sure everything is alright Michelle? Do you want me to call your Mother? I can if you like dear; I do have a mobile telephone now."

"No please it's fine, she is in and out of meetings anyway so she won't be able to talk. Steve will be able to explain later on when you see him." I couldn't help but wonder what on earth he would say... or imagine the look on his face.

"Ok Michelle, if you say so," she reaches in to her bag and takes out a pen and small bit of paper and starts to write something down. "Take my mobile telephone number and call me if you need me for anything, OK?"

"Thank you Mrs Hanson," I take the piece of paper, "I will do, thank you."

She finally walks off looking very suspicious but I don't care because I'm going to London.

"Yes flower, how may I help you?" asked the woman behind the ticket counter. My dad used to call me 'Flower'.

"Err yes, can I have a one way ticket to London please?" I asked. I was afraid in case she called security on me or something, how often do people my age with a northern accent ask for a one way ticket to London?

"Yes you can, where about in London do you want to go?"

How many train stations can one city have?

"Erm, the main one…" To be fair, Bradford has 2 train stations so I shouldn't be surprised that London will have a couple too.

"Kings Cross?" The lady asked, looking slightly concerned but also that she didn't really care where I was going.

"That's the one," I said, "I can never remember the name of it!" I was starting to blush, please don't let her become suspicious.

"Right that will be £65 please. Thank you, and here is your ticket, changes in Leeds. Train leaves in ten minutes. You might want to hurry, platform three."

I thank the lady, grab my bags and make a dash for the platform. Once I'm on a train I try to put my bag on the rack above me but it proves to be a little difficult, that damned sleeping bag. Luckily a nice middle aged man in a suit helps me. He must be heading to London, you don't see many men around here in suits like that. Maybe he works with Alan Sugar?

Chapter 4

The train from Leeds to London was already on the platform when I arrived. It didn't take long for it to set off on its merry way down south. I'm always hearing of a better life down there now I've had time to think about it. I may only be sixteen but you never know what might happen. I won't be there forever anyway. Just for a week or so. I just want my mum to realise that me and Steve hate each other and I am not living there while he's there, so she is going to have to make a choice. Maybe I'll like it in London and stay forever, my mum could come visit me when I'm settled, and the girls. My Grandma could come down and we could go sight-seeing together.

There are some proper weirdos on this train. There's a snobby fat woman staring at me with a look of disgust. I don't know what her problem is. She's having a cappuccino. She's got some of it around her mouth. Oh no I'm mistaken, that's an actual moustache she's got. She reminds me of Steve's mum. His mum is skinny though. So skinny she looks like an old witch. Like mother like son.

Ok, next weird person to criticize. I didn't have to

look far. It must be her husband. I won't bother. It's too easy.

I wonder how long till we get there. I then start to wonder about a lot of things; Where am I going to go when I get off the train? Am I going to sleep in the station, by a road or in an alley? Dare I sleep out in the open? Where else could be safe? There could be so many weirdoes out at night, on the prowl for young teenage girls to rape or murder. I didn't think this through properly. I was beginning to get scared.

I buy a cup of tea and a bun with some left over change in my purse. I wonder where we are now. I can see a lot of fields out the window. That doesn't help me at all.

A couple of hours later I have another look around my carriage. I see a little girl hugging her daddy. It reminds me of my dad. I miss him. I wish I was on my way to his house instead of London. I love the stories he used to tell me and if he were here now he could take me home and make me that gorgeous hot chocolate with marshmallows and cream and tell me stories till I fell asleep. Ok don't cry Shelly, don't cry. You're heading towards a better life now. A life where there's no one stealing your money for booze or treating you like shit and not caring whether you got murdered or turned to prostitution for some spare cash, as long as he got a share of it. From now on, my money stays my money. Oh my God. Money. I spent all my money on this ticket. Why didn't I get a return? At least then I would have some guarantee of getting home. Oh god. I am on a train going hundreds of miles from home and I have no money and nowhere to spend the night. What am I going to do?!

Chapter 5

"Good Afternoon ladies and gentleman and thank you for travelling with us today," a voice started over the speakers waking me up from my nap. "We will shortly be arriving at London's King Cross Station where this service will terminate. Please make sure you take all your belongings from the train and have your tickets ready for inspection. Once again, thank you for travelling with us today."

I look around and notice everyone is grabbing their bags and suitcases and coats. Within minutes we had pulled in to the station and the doors were opening. I grab my bag and make my way to leave the train. I had just dreamt that my dad was telling me a story. I was five years old again; just the right size to fit on his knee so he could hug me and hold me close. He was reading this story from a book. The pictures however were not matching the story he was telling me. The story was about a cat, but the pictures were from a family album. They were of my mum and dad when they were still married and when they loved each other. I wasn't in them.

The station is big and full people, all of them seem

in a rush to get somewhere. Wherever you walk, you manage to bump into someone, or they bump in to you. No one apologises. There are many guards checking tickets.

"'Ere miss," said one of the security guards, noticing I was stood and staring at my surroundings, not very incognito Shell. "Should you be on your own round here? It's not safe you know. How old are you?"

"Erm… I'm sixteen." The way I said it made me sound like I was lying. He'd startled me though, I really was in a world of my own for a moment.

"Sixteen eh?" he said looking at me "Well I do apologise for scarin' you. Its jus' we do get a lot of young runaways comin' down 'ere ya know. Its jus' routine to ask. Can I check your ticket please?"

"Ok," I said, like I was going to tell him that I'd just run away from home! Silly man. I was going to ask if he could tell me exactly where I was but I didn't want to give the game away. I just show him my ticket and follow the crowd outside.

My phone rings. It's my beloved step father, six hours later. I run to a quiet corner and answer.

"Hello?" I say

"Shelly where the HELL are you?" he screams.

"Why? Do you miss me?"

"Listen, you get home right now. Mrs Hanson has just come round to say you borrowed £10 from her and there's all sorts of money missing from upstairs. When I get my hands on you there will be hell to pay. You just come home now!"

"No, I am not coming home." I check to make sure the guard can't hear my conversation. "I am gone for good so you can explain to mum when she gets back that you drove her only daughter to suicide. Oh I can just see it now, headlines 'Girl, 16, found dead with suicide note blaming stepfather.'"

"You just listen to me young lady. Come home right now before your mum comes back on Friday."

"Actually mum rang and said she would be back in four days. Have fun looking for me." I hang up the phone. He hates it when I hang up the phone on him when he isn't finished.

At least I know he's worrying. Not about me though, about how my mum will kill him. My poor mum. She will be so heartbroken.

Well, I can't worry about that now. I have to figure out where I am sleeping tonight. Now, how do I get into the town? It can't be much bigger than Bradford, can it?

I walk out the door, around the corner, across the road, around another corner until all I can see is streets and corners and shops and more roads. I don't want to be in the middle of London where there will be a lot of people to see me. I need to get a bus somewhere. But where and with what? I have no money. I have 45p. It'll cost more than that surely. Oh look, there's one of those buses that you just hop onto the back of. Maybe if I get on and not pay I might get away with it. Even if they asked me for some money, I don't have any to give them, so what can they do? Arrest me for being a quid or two short?

I hop on. There's some people staring at me like they know what I'm going to do, but I don't care. It's none of their business.

I jump off when we get to a place that looks safe and quiet. There are some small alleys and not a person in sight. It should be ok for tonight. I make my way behind a big dumpster. It's damp and doesn't smell particularly nice but it's quite warm. I set up my bed for the night. I have a slice of my bread, and then wonder how I'm planning on surviving. Maybe in the morning I could beg for the money to get back home. It will take ages to raise enough money. But I'll have to try. If I don't get enough money I might have to hitchhike home. I'll call that plan B. It wouldn't be the best option.

I don't want to go home though. I want Steve to ring me, actually crying for me to come home, not shouting at me and demanding me to go home. I won't go though. I'll wait until mum rings me telling me that she's divorcing Steve. Then I'll go home, if I find the money!

*

I opened my eyes and I wasn't in my nice, cosy room in my warm bed. I was next to a cold and smelly dumpster with a rat staring me in the eye. I've never been scared by rodents of any kind, but this one startled me. It looked like it was on steroids. I kicked it away. I looked at my watch and it was half past eight. I get up and rummage around for my bread. I'm pretty hungry now. I haven't eaten anything proper since yesterday lunch time. Where is it? All I can see is an empty packet... oh no. It's not happened. It's not true. I swear and curse out loud. Those rats have scavenged my bread and my biscuits. I sit and begin to cry, I realise that my great idea isn't so great. I cry until I hear a voice. I see a face looking at me.

"Hello," said a woman. "Are you ok?"

"No," I completely break down. "I've run away from home and I have no food or money to buy food, and I don't know what to do. It was a mistake to come here." I'm crying very hard by this point. I knew it was a stranger I was telling all this to but I didn't care. It could have been a police woman and I wouldn't have cared. I wanted to go home. It was a stupid idea to do this. I don't know how I thought I was going to change in my life.

"Aww, well come with me and I'll buy you a cuppa. Come on. I've got to be somewhere in a bit." I look at the woman. She seems friendly. She wasn't a police woman. She looked like a business woman, and she wanted to help.

I stand up, wondering whether I should go with this woman, but I was thirsty, and by this point desperate. So I get my things together and walk with her.

We arrive at a café called "Bill's Diner". I thought it was kind of cheesy and dodgy but I wasn't about to ask questions. I didn't want to push my luck. I was desperate for a drink, and maybe she could help me.

She orders two cups of tea and we sit in a corner.

"What's your name?" she asked me.

"Michelle."

"So, Michelle, what's your story?" she asks me. She asked me in a way that made me think that she had talked to many runaways. Maybe she's a councillor or something. So I tell her my story. About my mum and the problems I have with Steve. She tells me that I'm not the first girl to run away because of reasons like that.

"Listen Shelly, I'm not here to pry into your business. I won't help you if you don't want me to but I help young runaway girls to live like they should.

Not putting up with family problems or begging on the streets. I own a block of flats, well bedsits really. It's not much but it's the cheapest place around here. For the first week it's free but you have to pay after that. Its only £40 a week. If you can't find a job after a week then I can help you there too. Here's my card. It's got the address on. I have to dash. Here's some money. Buy yourself something to eat and then make your way to the flats at about eleven o'clock. See you later Michelle." And then she was gone. I drank my tea, and then the rest of hers. I then take the money and order two sandwiches. I eat one and put the other in my bag.

"Eya, Miss," said the waiter. I guessed he was Bill. "I couldn't help over hearin'. Do you know who that woman was?"

"No, I don't think she gave me a name."

"Well, that's Rebecca Jones. I wouldn't get too attached to her if I was you."

"Why?" I asked.

"Just don't get attached to her, ok?" He must have seen the look of confusion on my face. "If I was you, I'd stay away. She's trouble. You don't want to get into her line of business."

"What line of business is that?"

"Just do yourself a favour, and go home."

Ok Bill I'll just fly home shall I? Trouble or not, she is offering me free accommodation for a week. What's the worst that could happen?

Chapter 6

Later in the morning I was still confused. When I finished, I looked at the clock. It was half past ten. Should I take the man's advice and stay away from her, or go find the place? I didn't want to spend another night with the rats. Also, she said the first week was free... I only wanted to stay here for a week anyway. I could always try figure a way to earn some money to get home and by then I won't owe any rent! I grab my stuff and leave. I look at the card. How bad could it be? What's the address? 12 Burnsten Drive.

"Excuse me," I ask someone. "Can you help me find 12 Burnsten Drive?"

"Yeah," says a young man with a grin on his face. I don't understand why he grinned. Maybe he knows someone there. "It's right down there," he said while checking me out. Creep. What's his problem?

He points down a small road. I make my way down there. I see a building. It doesn't look like it gets a lot of money. There's a boarded up window. Broken glass bottles outside. Doesn't look very homey. Well it looks better than the dumpster.

I get the feeling that I should turn back when I

hear "Michelle, you came!" I look around and I see Rebecca with a big grin on her face.

She grabs my bag and leads me inside. She goes behind a small counter and gets a key. She then leads me up some small narrow stairs and unlocks a door. When she puts the light on I am surprised by what I see. From the outside it looks old and poor. But this room looked different. It had a made bed. Drawers and cupboards, a window, curtains and it looked clean. There was even a TV in the corner. It wasn't a big room but it looked cosy. I couldn't believe I could live here rent free for a week. The room was bigger than mine at home.

"I know it's not much but it has to be better than that small alley. If you go through that door there you have your own bathroom. It's only a toilet, a sink and a small bath. Just take today to get used to it. Maybe clean it up a bit. Move furniture to how you want it. I'll be up later to check on you. Are you going to be ok?" she looks me in the eye.

"Yes, thank you. I don't know what to say."

"Well, if you need anything my mobile number is on the card. There's a pay phone outside. I might be up in about four hours. See you then."

She then walks out and locks me in. Why did she lock me in? It must be a mistake. I didn't really care at that point. I was grateful that she wanted to help me. She didn't have to, but she did. After I walked round my new room, I unpacked my stuff and went to the bathroom. I filled the bath with hot water and got in, soaked for about half an hour and got out. I found a towel in a small cupboard and dried myself and put on a clean t-shirt and the jeans I had on. I didn't bring any spare trousers. I lie on the bed and shut my eyes. I soon fall asleep and dream that my mum and I are sat at home. We're both watching television when mum turns to me and says, "Shell, come home," and with that she disappears. I hear myself calling "Mum". I wake up when I hear the door unlock. I sit up and wipe my eyes. Rebecca walks in with a drink and some toast, bacon and eggs.

"Here you are darling. Get this down you. Are you ok? Oh it's ok darling. You'll get used to it. I know it's not much." There was a knock at the door. "Oh that'll be Annie. Come in love."

A girl walks in. She looked about eighteen. She was tall, thin and had caramel coloured skin. Her hair was brown and looked like it had been curled professionally but it was all natural. It was gorgeous, she was gorgeous.

"Michelle, this is Annie. I sent her up to keep you company for a few minutes. I thought you could get to know someone so you'd have a friend. If I'm ever not in then call Annie. She can help you to settle in. I'd better go. Have a good chat you two." She then turns to Annie. "Do you have my money? It's no good shaking your head girl." She glances over at me and then back at Annie. "I want it first thing in the morning. Don't be long, you're working soon." She then walks out the door.

Annie looks at me and smiles. "So, how do you like your room? I'm just next door so if you need me just bang on the wall."

"Thanks," I manage to say to this stranger.

"So, where did you come from? What's your story?" she looked at me like she knew that I was hiding something. Like she knew what I was going through.

"What do you mean? Why would I have a story?"

"Listen Michelle, you're young and you're pretty. Pretty girls don't come down to London for any reason with no money, especially all the way from Yorkshire. Why do you think I'm here? I came here two years ago because of my step dad. He always…" she stopped as there was a door knocking. It wasn't my door. It was hers next door. She looked at her watch. "Oh Christ, listen Michelle, I have to go. Just do me a favour tonight and think about what you are doing. What you are giving up. I don't want you to turn out like the rest of us. Go home, do you hear me? Leave as soon as you can."

The door suddenly opened. It was Rebecca. "Annie! What the hell are you doing? Get next door NOW!" she was furious.

Annie took one more glance at me before leaving. Rebecca turned to me. "Are you ok dear?" she asked me.

"Yeah, I'm fine. Where's Annie going?"

She smiled and said to me in a very serious voice, "Never you mind that. Keep yourself busy for a bit. Watch TV or something and I'll see you in the morning."

I was too tired to think. I was too tired to do anything. The bed looked so comfy. As I was slowly falling asleep, I was disturbed by music coming from next door. It was pretty loud and kept me awake for a while. I didn't want to sleep anyway. All I wanted to do was think about what I was giving up. My mum would be home in a couple of days. I'll bet Steve will make up that I'm sleeping at a friend's house or something. All I need is that phone call from my mum to tell me that she's left him. I want her to leave him so we can go back to being happy. Go back to renting girly movies every Friday night and her packing my bag ready for when my dad came for me on Saturday morning. Then when I returned every Sunday afternoon she would have a Sunday meal prepared. Those days were the best. Everything was so simple. Steve and I never used to see each other because he stayed at the house when I was at my dad's. Mum used to give me a lift to school but when Steve moved in he insisted that I started to walk so I would 'stay fit'. It was only so he could spend time with her on a morning and so I would get pneumonia because it was pissing down with rain. Why did he have to come into our lives? Why couldn't things go back to how they were? Why did she choose him? Why didn't she see what he was doing to me? Why wasn't she taking more notice of me? I found myself crying and suddenly realised I was blaming my mum for all this. Why was I blaming her? She hasn't done anything. Or has she? She's the one who always took his side. Why choose her husband over her only child? The last time I saw her I tried to tell her how I felt. I had never shouted at her like that before but she didn't care. She stuck up for him again. Doesn't she love me anymore?

I can't think about this right now. I just want to sleep. What time is it? I look at my watch and its only quarter passed eight. The music next door suddenly stopped and a door opened and shut. I heard heavy footsteps walking away down the hallway. That wasn't Annie or Rebecca, surely.

I get up and walk out to her door. I knock on the

door but there is no answer.

"Michelle? What are you doing?" I turn round to see Rebecca talking to me.

"Erm… I was just seeing… if Annie was ok."

"Yes, she's fine. You'll see her in the morning. Go back to your room. Do you want anything? Would you like to use the phone? Ring your mum? She'll be home now wont she? She'd want to know that you were safe."

"No, I don't want to talk to her. She's not home for a few days anyway. Goodnight Rebecca. Thanks for everything."

With everything that Rebecca had done for me, I didn't want to irritate her, she could kick me out just as quick as she invited me in. I just strolled back to my room and got into my bed. I pick up my mobile but I have no signal. So I can't text my mum or a friend or anyone. I put the TV on. It's not a perfect signal but I can watch the news at least. I wonder how long it is until mum reports I'm missing, and then I'm on the news.

I then turn off the TV and lay down. I don't bother getting changed. I close my eyes and hope that I will soon fall asleep.

Chapter 7

I jump as I wake up in my old bedroom room. I hear screaming downstairs. I run downstairs. There's my mum. She's in tears with blood coming from her head. She's lying on the floor, motionless. Steve then walks in holding a baseball bat. Neither of them sees me. I am invisible to them. "Who do you love? Me? Or that brat of yours?" he yelled. "Steve please," she cries, "Steve please, don't!" she screamed. He ignores her and with his bat he strikes her head several times and all I can do is scream. I cannot move. I cannot help her. I cannot answer her cries. He then turns to me. "Look what your clever scheme did. Glad you ran away now?" he then runs towards me with the bat. I scream and scream till my throat hurts…

I wake up hot, with sweat on my face. "Mum," I said to myself. "Mum I'm sorry!" I burst into a flood of tears. I look at the clock and it's half five. There's no way I can go back to sleep now. I get up and make my way to the bathroom. I look in the mirror. I have bags under my eyes and my face is sticky from all the crying. I wash my face then brush my teeth. I get myself some clean clothes on and pack my things. By the time I'm done its eight o'clock. I can't stay here and leave my mum with him. That wasn't just a dream. It was a warning. I have to get out of here!

I hear someone walking down the hall. They stop at my door and come in. "Shelly dear are you awake? Oh, there you are. What time did you wake up?"

"I... err... I couldn't sleep. Things on my mind. Bad dreams."

"You going somewhere dear?" she saw the packed bags.

"Erm well I was thinking about maybe going home."

"Don't let a silly dream put you off! Most girls have bad dreams after their first night. Completely normal, now cut this nonsense and unpack again. You can't get home anyway. You have no money do you? Unless you were planning to walk?"

"But I..."

"No I don't want to hear it. Come on, unpack and I shall bring your breakfast up."

When she leaves I wait a second then go to the door to check the coast is clear. What's this? It's locked! She locked the door! Why did she lock the door? She was making me nervous. She didn't want me to leave and wouldn't let me talk to Annie.

I didn't unpack my things. I was going to leave when I had the opportunity.

She came back soon enough with a cup of tea and two slices of toast for me.

"Right then," she said when I finished, "we need to start with finding a job. You could go out and find a job in a little shop, or you could earn your money the same as all the other girls living here. And when you get enough, you can move out and do whatever you want! Or you could stay and earn more if you enjoy your work."

"Erm, Rebecca, I want to go home. I talked to Annie and she was telling me that I should go…"

"Annie?" she looked a bit taken back that Annie had told me to go. "She told you to go?" she stood up. "What did she say?"

I could see that I was getting Annie into trouble.

"Erm, she… she said that I should think about what I want… so I thought about my life and realised that my place is at home."

"Don't be ridiculous! I mean… obviously now you think that, but don't you want to be more independent? Learn how to live life on your own away from all your troubles? The people who caused your troubles are long gone now. Besides, how are you going to get the money? It will be about… £60 for a ticket home wont it?"

"I suppose, yeah you're right. I need to get used to things don't I? Maybe I could get a job and maybe stay here for a while."

"Yes, that's more like it. Now get washed and get ready. I'm taking you shopping. You won't have brought many clothes with you will you? I will give you an hour while I run round the apartments. Some of the girls owe me rent. I'll be back soon."

She had gone. I decided to stay. My mum always says I make drastic decisions so I should probably stick this out for a while. Maybe this would be a good experience for me. Living on my own, being independent. Learning the values of life. I wouldn't have to go to college; I could just work and live off my money. Doing whatever I wanted without Steve ruining it for me. I had started to doubt Rebecca but here she was offering to help me. Yeah, this is what I needed. I will stay.

Chapter 8

I go get myself sorted out and soon enough Rebecca returns.

"All ready?" she asks, "Ok then, let's go!"

We go outside and she unlocks the doors to a dark blue *Renault Megane*. She drives us to the local town. We park up in a small car park and walk to the shops. The first shop we entered was *Topshop*. I had been in this shop back home. I bought most of my clothes from here, when I had money. She starts to look at trousers and then on to skirts. I had never worn skirts before because Steve said I looked like a prostitute. I suppose it didn't matter what he said now. He wasn't here to judge me.

"How about these?" she pulled one out. It was black, quite nice. Looked like something you would wear for going on a night out. It looked like it would come just above my knee. "This one's nice. You would look very grown up in this. What size are you?"

"I'm a ten, sometimes a twelve."

"Hmm well you can try both sizes on. C'mon let's look at tops. Do you like this one?"

She pulled a top from off the rack. I had to admit,

it was very nice. It was red, sleeveless like a tube top. It showed a lot of cleavage. It had creamy pink slashes down the front. Very classy. It had to be expensive. And it was. £35 just for that.

"Size twelve you say?" she took the top and made her way to lingerie. She picked up a few thongs and told me to go into the changing room and try everything on.

It all seemed a bit odd. I thought she was buying me casual clothes. Maybe she was trying to smarten me up so I could get a job like she said. Yes, that's what she was doing. I tried on the clothes and I fitted into the size twelve skirts so I chose them. She kept bringing more clothes in. Skirts and tops of all types.

She paid for my clothes and we went into the next shop. It was a shoe shop called "Mysties". It looked quite expensive. We went to look at the boots. She chose some black leather knee high boots. They were really nice but £50.

"No not these," I said, "they're too expensive."

"Michelle, you're in London. Everything is expensive here. What size shoe are you?"

I tried on boots, strapless sandals, everything. After shopping she took me to an Italian bistro and we both had a bowl of lasagne. We talked for almost an hour. She was great. She told me that she was a runaway when she was only fifteen. I asked if she regretted it but she didn't. Things worked out for her and now she owns her own block of flats and a business. How good is that?

*

When we got back I went in my room carrying eight heavy bags. Rebecca must have spent around

£400 on me. I couldn't believe it. I never had this much money spent on me in one day. I would obviously pay her back as soon as I was earning some money. My mum used to buy me anything I wanted until Steve decided I was getting too spoilt. Rebecca told me to put my clothes away and then go out exploring the neighbourhood. She had given me £10 to buy something to eat. She said she had some business to attend to and new potential clients to meet. I set off walking and came across a small café. I went in and ordered a cup of tea. I had put on my new boots with some new jeans and my new jacket. Rebecca bought me all these today, including a necklace, some sexy stocking from *Ann Summers* and some makeup. I got myself all dressed up and thought I would have a better chance of getting a job if I looked smart.

"Hey," I heard a voice. I looked round and saw a lad. He looked about eighteen. He had dark hair and was gorgeous. I thought he was a waiter at first. "Can I sit here?"

"Yes of course," I said.

"Thanks. I'm Tony."

"I'm Michelle."

"Hey, you're not from around here are you?"

"No, I'm from Bradford. I moved here a couple of days ago."

"I thought so with that accent, who did you move with?" he asked. "Your family?"

"No I came down on my own."

"How come? How old are you?"

"I'm sixteen," I said.

"Sixteen? And you came down here all on your own? You're braver than me. I'm twenty and I'm still scared to roam around these streets," he began. "So do you know your way around yet?"

"No not yet. I have a bad sense of direction," I laughed. "I daren't walk too far on my own."

"Do you want me to show you around sometime?" he asked. He was too gorgeous to say no to.

"Ok, yeah I would. Sounds like fun, I could do with getting to know the area. I will be here for a while."

"Ok I'll call you then. Do you have a mobile?" he asked.

"Yes I do. But where I am doesn't have a very good signal."

"That doesn't matter. I might be able to catch you sometime."

We exchanged numbers and he left after a few minutes. He was on his break from work. He works at HMV and told me he gets loads of freebies so he could be a handy friend!

I made my way back at about five o'clock and while walking to my room I bumped into Annie.

"Hey, Annie!"

"Hi Michelle."

"Oh you can call me Shell."

"Well, Shell, you look happy."

"I've had a good day. You know Rebecca? She spent so much money on me today! Can you believe it?"

"She did what?" her smile dropped and a kind of frightened look appeared on her face, or was it jealousy? "Did she say how she wanted paying back?"

"She didn't really tell me to pay her back. I can get a job and pay her from that though." I got worried. "Will she want paying back straight away?"

"Erm, look, forget it. Did you find a job while in town?"

"No, I think I said something about a job while in *New Look* but she told me not to worry about getting a job. She said she would sort me out with something. Maybe in a couple of days she said so who knows?"

Annie looked kind of angry. Not like she was jealous of me because I had all that money spent on me, it was like she was angry at Rebecca for some reason. But I didn't know why.

"Don't let her spend any money on you. She'll demand it back in the worst way possible. That's why I'm stuck here. She did the same to me when I first came here."

There was shouting from downstairs. It was Rebecca. "What do you mean you don't have my money?" she was shouting at Julie, another girl staying here.

"Come in here." She pulled me in her room. "Have you figured out what this place is yet?"

"It's just some apartments for runaway girls isn't it?"

"No, it's a business, Rebecca's business. You're a very attractive girl. You're sixteen so you have that whole innocent look about you. You look like you could have men drooling over you. When she found you on the street, if you weren't that pretty or were fat then she wouldn't have helped you."

"Why not?" I asked.

"You wouldn't have been any good for her. Shell,

this is no holiday hotel. It's like what you would call a brothel."

My heart stopped. A brothel? No, it wasn't true.

"Shell, are you ok? Look, I would lend you the money to pay her back but it won't only be that money she demands. She will eventually want rent as well. We all have to pay £40 a week and then the majority of what we earn. You're ok for this week but she will want something next week."

"If I don't get a job, how do I get the money?" I think I knew the answer before I asked it but I didn't want to guess. I wanted to know the truth.

"Rebecca has been in this business a long time. She used to just work on the streets till she got enough money to sort out this place. She found powerful men to support her for money in exchange for…" she didn't want to finish what she was going to tell me. But I wanted to know.

"Tell me, what did she have to do?"

"Sleep with them."

"And what will I have to do to earn money?" I didn't want to hear this. I don't think I was prepared.

"You would have to do the same as the rest of us. Sleep with men."

I sat down on her bed.

"It's not like a back alley place with drug addicts coming in for sex whilst they're high. They are mostly rich men who will pay up to £100 for a night, and they might offer you more for… extras but you don't have to accept. A lot of them are Rebecca's 'investors' who can be very demanding."

"Can't I just leave now? Pack my things and go?"

"And go where? You have no money. I'd give you some but I don't have enough for a ticket back to Yorkshire."

"You mean I have to do this? I can't call the police?"

"No you can't do that! Do you realise what that would do to us? None of us have any money and if you do that then you would be sending over a dozen moneyless girls to the streets! Half of them in here *do* spend their money on drugs so they don't even have a bit saved. Please don't call the police."

"So I have to do this?" I had begun to cry. "She can't do this! Why would she do this to us? I'm only sixteen, I'm a virgin, this is wrong!" I was getting hysterical.

"Shelly, please calm down, if she hears you then she will come up!"

"Calm down? How can I calm down after what you just told me?"

"Is something wrong?" Rebecca was standing in the doorway.

"No, we're ok. Everything's fine." Annie said.

"Annie dear I have been so kind to you. I wouldn't expect you of all people to lie to me. I heard your little conversation. Thanks for filling her in, you saved me the job. Michelle, are you ready to work? You start tomorrow night."

"What?" I said in disgust. "You can't do that!"

"Oh yes I can. You owe me money Michelle. And I intend on getting it back. Annie will help you get ready tomorrow. You can wear your new clothes." She said it as if it was a good thing. "I'll see you both tomorrow." She left the room.

I sat down, and cried as Annie put her arm around me.

Chapter 9

"Shelly, are you finished?" Annie asked me. I had been in the shower and was just sat in my towel.

"Yeah I'm done. Come in." In three hours my first customer would be here. I don't want to do it. I'm a virgin! I can't lose it like this. Apparently, Rebecca told this guy that I was a virgin so that's why he picked me out of everyone, and he apparently offered a very good price. There must be something attractive about it. I can't imagine what.

"Hi, are you ok?" she asked as she walked in. "Ah Shelly honey, please stop crying. If Rebecca sees you like this there'll be trouble."

"I don't care. She can do what she wants. I'm not sleeping with a strange guy. What's his story? Wife left him, he can't get any girlfriends so he goes around paying for sex 'cause he can't get any, is that it?"

"Wow, got it in one. Don't forget he's rich, and supports many of the girls here," Rebecca walked in. "So you'd better do a good job. He knows you're a virgin so he won't expect you to do much, he likes that you'll be a bit shy."

She strolled into the bathroom holding some clothes.

"Come on Annie, I told you I want her ready in two hours. I want her wearing these clothes. Dry her hair and get it straightened. Put makeup on her. Not a lot though, I want her to maintain the young and innocent look. C'mon, hurry up. I'll be back in exactly two hours."

She left the room and I looked at the clothes. I suddenly knew why Steve didn't want me wearing skirts that small. They're what prostitutes wear. And knee high boots. And that tube top. I was going to look like a prostitute. I was going to be a prostitute. There is no way I can possibly return home after this.

Within the two hours I was ready. I had straightened hair, shaved legs, and shaved other parts to look 'sexier'. I couldn't believe I was letting myself go through this. What had I got myself into? Coming here was just to get back at Steve! Not ruin my life. I had a few minutes until Rebecca would be back up. Maybe I could run for it. Just leave my things and go for it. I walk to the door when I hear footsteps walking towards it. My heart in pumping so fast I want to be sick. This is it, I thought. This is how I ruin my life. I feel myself wanting to cry again just as Rebecca walks through the door.

"Well," she begins, "Aren't we looking sexy? Mr Bracknell will be here shortly so I thought you would like a drink. It's only orange juice with a shot of vodka, I thought you might need something strong." She then gave me a look of compassion, like she could actually sympathise with my situation. "Everything will be alright Shelly. Sorry to be a bitch about this but we all need money round here. I am a nice person, honestly."

I drink it quickly, wishing it was all vodka. I didn't normally drink much alcohol but I feel like I could drink anything right now.

"Very good." She looked at me strangely. It was like she was expecting something to happen. "How are you feeling now?"

She spiked my drink with something. I know it.

"What did you put in it?" I demanded.

"Nothing," she lied. "Ok maybe I put a little something in it. All the new girls need something on their first night. You might be feeling a bit dizzy soon so I suggest you stay sat down to avoid falling over."

"What was it?" I asked again.

She turned round to look at me. "Just something to relax you. Just so you can't run away. Like I said, we all need money around here."

Then she was gone. I heard her lock my door. I stood up. I must have stood up too fast because now I have a head rush. I feel really dizzy. I need to sit down. I turn round to the bed but I think it's spinning. Everything is spinning. I manage to collapse on the bed. I want to fall asleep but I'm scared to shut my eyes in case I don't wake up. Or unless I do wake up and find a man in my room, or on me. I should be ok if I shut my eyes for a second. Just rest them for a few minutes. I hear muttering outside. My door opens. I don't feel strong enough to lift my head. I manage to look round and see a man stood by my bed. I can't focus on his face, but he's a big man. Even if I wasn't drugged, I wouldn't be able to run away from this guy.

I can feel his eyes on me. He moved to lay down next to me and put his hand on my face. I try to move but my body is paralysed. His hand is slowly moving from my face to my chest. He touches and gropes my chest and his hands move further down my body touching places that have never been touched by anyone else before. I hear the sound of his zip as he begins to remove his pants.

"Just relax," the sound of his deep voice makes me jump. "It won't hurt for long."

Chapter 10

Is it morning? It still seems dark. I can hardly open my eyes. I don't want to in case he's still here. It seems quiet. He must have gone. When I do look around I see a condom wrapper on the side table, plus some money. I pick it up and count £100. It did seem like quite a lot, till I remembered it is all going to Rebecca. What time is it? I look for my watch. Its half past eight. I manage to get up out of bed. I'm naked, and in pain, everything feels so sore. I find a big old t-shirt of mine and put it on. All my clothes had been thrown on the floor. I didn't remember him taking them off. I must have passed out from that drink. I look at myself in the mirror. There were red marks on my thighs and chest. I look through my drawers and find something to wear. There were some clean knickers so I grabbed them too and walk steadily into the bathroom. I was still pretty dizzy. I walk up to the mirror to look at myself again. I look like a mess. Bags under my eyes, smudged make up, hair all messed up. I go to the toilet and it stings. Does it sting because it was my first time? Or was he rough? I wish I knew, but on the other hand, I'd rather I forgot all about it.

After two hours I had showered and sorted myself out. I knew Rebecca would be in here soon, demanding money. And I was right.

"Michelle, are you up?" I walk out of the bathroom. "Ah, there you are. And I see you have my money!"

"Yeah I do. I suppose you want it all then?"

"No, you'll need some money. Otherwise how would you eat? I cannot provide you with money for food everyday Michelle, I'm not the servant around here. I won't take any rent from you this time. I'll wait until you have paid your debt. I'll just take £80 every time until you have paid me £400 and then you can just pay rent plus a percentage like everyone else."

I pass her the £80 and she eventually leaves. I owe her money so, unless I get a decent job, I shouldn't have to do it again. But if I don't get a job, who knows when I have to do it again? Oh, well. I have £20 to myself. I might as well make the most of it. I could save for a ticket home. But if I'm asked how I got the money for a ticket home, what will I say? No, I can't go home now. Steve went mad when he thought I was sleeping with my last boyfriend. What's he going to say about this? I feel so filthy and embarrassed... I can't go home. Not now.

I take a few minutes to think about last night. It hasn't dawned on me that it actually happened. I take a look in the mirror. I can't believe that this was my first time. I wanted my first time to be with a boyfriend that I love and trust. Not with a forty year old man. I start to cry, and I don't try to stop myself. I cry and let it all out. I cry about meeting Rebecca. I cry about actually trusting her and letting her buy me things. Why did I have to come here?

"Hey, Annie," I called through her door, "Annie you there?"

"Hey, are you ok?" she asked with a look of concern. "How did last night go? Or do you not want to talk about it?"

"I'd rather forget it. I can't actually remember anything. Rebecca spiked my drink."

"Oh, yeah she does that with the new girls. So what's up?"

"Do you have some change by any chance? I want to ring my mum and let her know I'm safe."

"Oh yes of course." She reaches in to her pocket, "Here that should be enough."

"Thanks so much. I'll see you later on."

I make my way downstairs and outside to the nearest phone box. I put in the change and dial my mum's mobile.

"Hello?" Steve answers. "Hello? Who is this?"

I wait a bit before I reply.

"Hi, it's me. Is err, is my mum there?"

"Now why do you want to talk to her?"

"I want to let her know I'm safe. I don't want her to worry about me. Is she there?"

"Now you see I don't want you to talk to her. Why should I do you a favour? She's out anyway. You'll have to try again later." And then he hangs up on me.

He'll tell mum I rang won't he? What if he doesn't? What if he answers all the house calls and all her mobile calls? What if I never get through to my mum, and she never knows I'm safe? She must be going crazy, wondering where I am. If only I could talk to her.

My mobile rings. I beg that it's my mum.

"Hello?"

"Hi, is that Michelle?" a boy's voice asks.

"It is. Who's this please?" I ask.

"It's Tony. Remember me?"

"Oh yeah I remember."

"Erm, is this a bad time? You seem a bit pissed off about something."

"No, sorry I'm just tired. I'm fine."

"Oh, ok good. Erm, are you busy today?" he asks.

"No, I'm free all day. Why?"

"Well, I'm working right now but I take my break in half an hour. I was wondering if you wanted to meet up. The place we were at the other day."

"Erm, yeah sure. Half an hour you say?"

"Yeah, if you want to that is."

"Yeah sure. I'll see you there then. Bye."

"See you."

I immediately run back inside and sort myself out. I brush my hair and put some make up on. Not a lot of makeup, just a bit. I look in the mirror and I look ok. I don't know if I'm in the mood to go out. I can't cry forever though. Maybe it will cheer me up.

I make my way down to the café and see him sat at the same table. I was a few minutes late.

"Hey, I'm sorry I'm late," I say.

"Oh no it's fine; I've only just walked in myself. Do you want a cup of tea?"

"Yeah please."

"Ok, I'll be back in a few minutes."

He walks casually over to the counter and orders

two teas. I couldn't help but stare at his bum. It looked gorgeous.

He returns with two drinks and some sachets of sugar. He was wearing his work uniform. I saw he had a badge with his name on. It didn't say 'Tony' it said 'Anthony'. He did look incredibly cute today. I didn't try to flirt though. I just wanted a friend. I need one today.

"I wasn't sure whether you took sugar or not, so I brought a few."

"How many do you have?" I ask.

"Erm, four!" he laughs.

"Four?" I laugh too. "Isn't it too sweet with four?"

"No, it's just right. Anyway, there's never enough sugar in a sachet."

We talk for about an hour. He has to rush back to work though because he stayed twenty minutes longer than he should have. I hope he didn't get in trouble. We were talking about possible jobs for me. I like the idea of working in a clothes shop. He said he would let me know if he sees any available jobs while in town. It was full at HMV.

Meeting with Tony really cheered me up. I managed to forget all about the night before. I finish my drink and make my way back home. Home? Yes, I suppose this is home now. Just until I feel it's time to go to my real home. I might try ringing mum again. I'll try her mobile.

It rings and rings and rings until finally: "Hello?" it was my mum's voice.

I wonder whether I should speak, what should I say?

"Michelle honey, is that you?"

I can feel my eyes filling with water.

"Shelly," she hesitates at first. "If this is you I just want to let you know, I love you so much. I know it's been hard here with Steven, I realise it now and I should have paid more attention to you but I was too obsessed with work and I suppose I focussed on my marriage but that's because I didn't want to waste it again." Should I say something? "You can come home whenever you want, I don't want to put you under any pressure to do anything you don't want to. Please Shelly, look after yourself. If you need money then please give me your address and I'll send you some. I won't come looking for you I just want to know you are safe." I shouldn't ask for money, she'll worry about me even more then. "Shelly, you need to know that… I love you." She was crying. It all got too much for the both of us.

"I love you too mum." And then I hang up.

Chapter 11

"Shell? What's the matter?" Annie walked in my room. I stayed quiet.

"I've just spoke to my mum."

"Oh yeah?" she asked in a positive way, "What did she say?"

"She told me she's not going to force me to come home and that she loves me."

"Well that's good. What did you say?"

"Nothing. I said nothing." I stood up. "I've been trying to ring my mum but couldn't always get through. Now that I had the chance to, I didn't say anything. I could've told her that I'm safe, that I'm happy even though I'm not, and I could have told her that I love her too but I didn't. I DIDN'T!" I kicked at my door.

"Shelly calm down, calm down its going to be ok." She puts her arms around me. What an emotional day this has been.

"What do you want to do? Do you want to go home?"

I don't know. Do I?

*

I had to think about that. Do I want to go home? Do I want to live with him again? Do I want his bullying comments and insults? Do I want to be his servant again? Yeah, when I return things could be ok to begin with, but how long until I'm in the house alone with him, doing all his crap for him? How long till I'm back to square one? Mum doesn't understand what it was like with him. She was just saying that so I was reassured that going home would be a good idea. What will happen if I stayed here? I would get a fulltime job in a shop somewhere, I would get a lot of money a week, I could pay rent and what I owe to Rebecca and then have some money to spend on myself. I wouldn't have to sleep with any dirty old men, I could stay here. Even if I did have to sleep with men, it's only sex. It's not going to kill me is it? All my friends are having sex and they enjoy it. Why can't I enjoy it? I still owe Rebecca £320 but as soon as that's paid I will have to pay rent and plus extra but it could be worse, I could still be sleeping with the rats, or under the same roof as Steve.

Chapter 12

"So where's this lad taking you?" Annie asked me. I had been in London for just under two weeks now and was feeling a bit more settled. I'd had a few customers by then. It wasn't getting any easier. All I could think about was getting myself out of debt and finding a way to move out and move on.

"He's taking me out for a meal. I don't know where. He asked me if I liked Italian so we're probably going to a bistro."

"Does he know?"

"Know what? Know where he's taking me? I hope so," I laughed.

"No you fool. I mean does he know, you know, about this place. Have you told him yet?"

"No not yet. I don't want to."

"It's probably best he knows now. If he falls for you and then finds out it will make it a lot worse."

I knew she was right. I didn't want to lose him. I really liked him. We had talked on the phone and we get on so well. I have to tell him tonight. I'll try get on to the conversation, somehow.

"Oh, and also, Rebecca doesn't allow us to have boyfriends. So anything that happens between you two will have to stay secret."

Shit, now I have to tell him.

"So, do you like Italian then?" Tony asked me as we pulled up to 'Luigi's'.

"I love Italian," I said. "My dad used to cook it all the time when I stayed at his."

We were shown to our Italian laid table by a very English waiter. I would have preferred an Italian waiter. It would have made this place more authentic.

"So, your parents are separated then I take it?" he asked me as we picked up our menus.

"Yeah, it happened a long time ago."

"My mum is remarried too,' he started. 'She can be a bitch but Jack, my step dad, he's cool."

"What about your real dad?" I asked.

"He was a dick head. I hate the man."

"Why do you hate him so much?" I didn't want to pry.

"He mistreated my mum and me. So what are you having?"

I could tell he didn't want to talk about it. I could understand. I wasn't really in the mood to talk about Steve. We can avoid the dad/step-dad conversation for now.

We talked for a whole hour. We talked about what we did in school, what we want to achieve in life and what films we could go see next week. There was only one thing left to talk about. I didn't know how to bring it up.

"So Michelle, there's something I've been wanting

to ask you. You're sixteen years old, why would you come to London on your own?"

"I had a fall out with my step dad. He's a dick head too."

"So you came to London all on your own? How are you supporting yourself? Do you have any money saved? If you don't mind me asking."

"Well, my first night here I was in an alley but this woman is letting me stay at her bed and breakfast if I do some work for her. She's a very nice woman."

"What's this work then?" he knows.

"Err, just random house work she needs doing. You know like…" he cut me off.

"Shell, I know what you're doing. It happens all the time. Especially in a town like this one. Young girls run away, they have no money. What else can they do?" He looked deep in to my eye. "Do you do it?"

"What would you think of me?"

"I wouldn't think any less of you. I pretty much know you for who you are. So, do you?"

"Yes, but I'm really not proud of it," I began, trying to defend myself. "I hate it. When I think of those dirty old men on top of me, doing what they do, I feel like I can't go home. Everyone would be so ashamed of me. I want to be sick, and now I'm trapped and I have no escape."

"You're not trapped. You'll have me, always. Shell," he reached for my hand, "I really like you. I'm not going to turn my back on you."

"Really?" I asked. "I didn't think you'd take it like this."

"Why not?" he asked.

"I thought you would be ashamed to be here with me."

"Shell, this is London. Even worse, it's a bloody dodgy part of London. Half the girls around the area are working girls. I've grown up with quite a few of them. All they needed was a friend. A male friend so they knew that not all men are dirty and rotten. I know them for who they are. You don't have to feel awkward with me knowing. You're not a monster. You're you, and I like you. Just promise to call me if there is any trouble and I will be straight there to help you." He squeezed my hand tight.

"Thank you. You don't seem dirty or rotten so I like you too." He smiled at me and I smiled back.

"Now come on. Wipe those tears and let's order another bottle of this over priced wine!"

Chapter 13

"Are you ready?" Rebecca asks me two nights after my date with Tony. It was time to do it again.

"Ready as I'll ever be."

"Good, well this man is another important man. He supports maybe five or six girls in here. So, if he asks you to do something, then do it. Ok?"

I was going to ask "like what?" but she'd already left my room. I'd have to do stuff? Like what? Make him a cup of tea, bring him a biscuit, what?

There was a knock at my door. I answer it and see a man standing there. He looked wealthy. He had gelled back black hair, a goatee, and a black suit. He looked quite charming. He pulled some money out of his pocket. I guessed there was about £100 there.

"Can I come in?" he asked in a charmingly deep voice with a bit of a Russian twang to it.

"Yes, sorry, please come in."

He put the money on the table next to my bed. He then pulled what looked like a flask out of his jacket pocket.

"Want some?" he asked.

"What is it?"

"Whisky."

"No thanks." I didn't want to be rude, but I hated whisky.

"Suit yourself." He took a large drink of it and then removed his jacket and sat on my bed. "So what do you know about me?"

"Rebecca told me that you were important to a lot of the girls here and that you might ask me to do extra stuff."

"That's right. You'll be paid for that extra stuff of course. I brought with me a lot of money that could be quite helpful to someone like you." He pulled another £100 out of his pocket. "You do what I ask, you get this extra money. You don't do what I ask, I walk straight out taking this money and that money on there and no one in this building sees me again. That will mean half a dozen girls wanting you dead."

"Ok." I was beginning to wish I was drugged up again. It would be a lot easier. "What do you want me to do?" I didn't want him to answer that. I wanted it to just be sex and then it's over. What will I have to do?

The smile that had disappeared from my face suddenly reappeared on his. I just realised that, if this was going to be my choice, then this was going to be my way of life for a long time.

Chapter 14

The girls have invited me out round the town. I've never been clubbing with the girls before so it should be a good experience. It was going to be me, Claire, Tanya and some other girls but I can't remember their names. Annie couldn't come. She's not been feeling well today so she's in bed. I think a few of the girls were hoping to get some private business so they could keep all the money without Rebecca knowing. I didn't want to. I was glad of the night off.

"We're going in to Tokyo's first. Come on ladies!" Tanya shouted. She grabbed my arm. "You ok Shelly? You look nervous."

"No, I'm ok. Not been out round town since, you know, before I came here."

"It's going to be ok. We're going to show you the time of your life," she laughed. "It's your night off anyway so cheer up girl!"

When we walked into the club we didn't need to show any ID. We were practically wearing our ID. With the amount of cleavage we were wearing between us we could jump queues. The bouncers were regular visitors to our flats after a long night's work. The girls headed straight to the toilets so I followed. I didn't need to go but I didn't want to be left stood on my own.

"Right, where are they?" a girl asked. I think her name was Chantelle.

"What you looking for?" I asked, thinking she needed a tampon or something.

"Aha! These." She held out a small bag with some small white pills in.

"What are they?"

"What are these?" she giggled. "Oh kid, you need to get out more. It's ecstasy."

"You lot take ecstasy?" I asked, kind of shocked.

"I swear by it," a ginger girl said. "If you survive working where we do without taking drugs at least once, well then you need a fucking medal." She took one of them and put it in her mouth.

"Why don't you try one?" Chantelle asked. "Just for fun?"

"I don't know." I didn't want to be a drug addict. I've read stories about the effects of ex and it didn't sound too appealing.

One by one the other girls took a pill each. There was just me who hadn't taken one, and only one pill left. Should I take it? I wouldn't have to do it again. If I overdosed on ex I would probably die but I don't think just one could cause too much damage.

"Do you want it?" Chantelle asked, as the girls watched me. "If you don't like it then you don't ever have to take it again. One night won't kill you will it?"

"What the hell," I said. I was getting a buzz already and I hadn't even taken it yet. Chantelle took the pill out of the bag and gave it to me. I held it for a second. It was smaller than a birth control pill, and looks to have a clover imprinted in to the front of it. It's too small to be sure. I put the pill in my mouth and swallowed it pretty easily.

"How do you feel?" the ginger girl asked.

"Ok at the moment. How long till it kicks in?"

"Not long now babe. It'll just hit you when it wants to."

"Does alcohol affect it?"

The girls laughed insanely. "Let's find out!"

We left the toilets and went straight to the bar. As soon as I walked out I can feel it kicking in. The music seemed to have more of a beat and was making my head pound. I feel funny. My mouth is all dry. I need some water.

"You ok Shell?" Tanya asked.

"Yeah, I just need a drink, my mouth is dry."

"What do you want? I'll get it."

"Can I have some water?" I asked.

"Water? Water won't help it to kick in. The girls are going to do shots but you can have a vodka and orange if you want."

"Yeah, whatever. I just need a drink."

She came back with a drink for me. I downed it in one but wanted another. My mouth was so dry.

I saw Chantelle and the girls heading to the dance floor. Maybe a dance would make me feel better. I walked down and we found a space to dance. My head started spinning. Suddenly, a big smile appeared on my face and out of nowhere I just started to laugh. I was laughing at the people around me, I was laughing at the music and I was laughing at myself. I was uncontrollably dancing. It was so much fun. I can't believe I never tried this before. Everything felt great, the feel of my clothes was so soft, my hair like silk, the beat of the music pounding through my body, the air like a cool breeze on a hot day, I loved it all and didn't want it to end.

The dancing continued long into the night, including endless drinking and getting off with random guys whose faces I cannot even remember. They could have been pensioners for all I knew. At around half past three we trekked home. We were still hyper but the clubs were getting empty.

"Night!" we all said to each other.

When I sat down in my dark, quiet room, I could hear a ringing sound in my ears. It didn't seem to stop. I was sobering up by this point and the ex was wearing off. Suddenly something wasn't right. I stood up and then ran as quick as I could to the toilet to be sick.

*

I wasn't a pretty sight the next morning. I had passed out on the bathroom floor with sick still in my mouth and all over my clothes. I had fallen asleep in it so my hair was all crusty. Just to make myself feel even more attractive, I threw up again. The bathroom was a mess. I was a mess. My head was banging. I couldn't remember much from the night before. I just turned the shower on and got in with my clothes on. I didn't want to touch any of the sick so I just dropped my clothed off in the bath. I'd probably just throw them away later. I didn't know where to begin with cleaning my bathroom. I could probably just get an old towel and use it as mop.

I had a headache and was sick all day. I didn't manage to eat anything until Annie came round with some sandwiches for me. It was nice, and I was grateful. She was so mad with me though for taking the pill. "You don't know what could have happened to you!" she shouted in to my pounding head. After she went I threw my sandwich back up. If you ever want to make yourself puke for a whole day, then ex is the thing for you. Otherwise, never again for me.

Chapter 15

I think people are starting to recognise me in the streets. I think even a blind person can tell who we are. It's a small village where I'm living so people can easily recognise us girls. The elderly women stare at us with disgust. The elderly men however stare at us with dirty, desperate eyes. Mothers whisper to their children as I walk by. They're told to stay away from our "sort". My only escape from this torture is being with Tony. When I am on my own people stare at me like I am trouble and dirty. When I am with Tony, no one takes a second glance and I can be free. People think we are a couple. Even Rebecca gets suspicious when she sees us. She doesn't let us have boyfriends because it complicates things, people get jealous and a lot of trouble starts.

Last week however I was on my own and people saw me. On this particular night it was six men in their twenties enjoying a night out. Annie and I were out for a quiet drink so we could talk about life and how depressing it can be doing what we do. We were in one of those moods where we thought our days were just repeating themselves and our situation was never going to improve, basically feeling sorry for ourselves. Tonight there would be no drugs. Annie made me promise to never do it again. She was mad with the girls for letting me have an ecstasy pill. She went through the same thing when she first came here. She saw how the girls were spending their money on drugs and she didn't want to go down the same road so she convinced me that it was the wrong way to go. I myself was in no hurry to take any pills or drugs again.

She went to the bar to get some more drinks. It was busy so she was ordering two drinks each at a time. The bar was so crowded. I stayed at the table so no one stole our seats. That was when the first man approached me.

"Hey there," he began. "Can I sit down?" he didn't seem so bad, but I was not in the mood for men tonight. It was my night off. Also, it wouldn't have been very pleasant...

"Sorry, this seat is taken."

He went away like I hoped. I looked for Annie. She was nowhere near being served. Not long after the man walked away, two different men approached the table.

"How much?" the one on the left asked.

"Excuse me?" I asked.

"How much for the both of us?" they laughed. They were both very drunk. They were just being dickheads.

"I'm sorry, I'm not in to that kind of stuff, excuse me." I grabbed my bag hoping to get away from them to find Annie, but they both sat either side of me trapping me in.

"Come on girl, give us a good night." He leant in to me. "It's my birthday, how about a freebie?"

"Listen mister you need to get yourself away from me. I am not who you think I am."

"Oh yeah?" one of them said. "I think our friend Matt would disagree."

"Matt!" shouted the other guy. "Matt, get over here."

Matt and his three other friends walked over. I recognised Matt, but I didn't want any trouble. He was a customer of mine about two weeks ago. He was a bit of a loser. He actually dressed up in a nice suit and tie the night he came to me but was really nervous and didn't seem to know what he was doing.

"Matt, is this or is this not the girl who you shagged the other week?" the guy sitting next to me asked.

"Yes," he replied, looking ashamed and embarrassed. "It is."

"Now why would you lie to us?" he asked turning his attention back to me. "We're trying to make a business deal with you."

"I'm not interested in your business deal," I said. "Excuse me." I tried to get up but the guy on the left of me pulled me down on to his knee and held on to me.

"Oh, come on babe," he said. "You know you want to."

"Get off me," I shouted. I couldn't see Annie anymore. I don't know where she went.

"Oh get a feel of this, lads." By now he had managed to keep one hand holding me down and another groping me. He tried to put his hand up my skirt.

"Get off me!" I shouted. No one around us could hear me. My shouts were drowned out by the music.

Eventually, I was saved.

Three bouncers came over and dragged the men off me. Annie grabbed my hand and pulled me away as the bouncers threw the other men out. They weren't soft with them either. They literally grabbed them under their arms and because the bouncers were so big they managed to pick the men up and throw them out. It's handy having bouncers as friends. Or should I say its handy having bouncers as regulars.

"Are you ok?" Annie asked me.

"I don't know." I was really shaken by the ordeal. I couldn't believe it had happened. I don't know if I was ok or not. I needed Tony. I can't run to his every time something happens though. Obviously this wouldn't be the only time I would get attacked.

"Come on, let's go." We spent the rest of the evening in Bill's Diner. We never went in to a club again for a very long time. Bill let us stay in there for an hour after closing so we could get some peace and quiet. He didn't mind us being there. He knew the kind of problems we faced in our line of business. After all, he did warn me about it on my first morning here.

Chapter 16

The weeks in London turned into months, and the months eventually turned in to seven whole months of dirty men, deceitful Rebecca and fun loving gorgeous Tony. Things have got a lot better here. I have a bank account now with around £1,200 in it. I'm good at saving my money. I work up to five, maybe six times a week. Some overtime (and some undeclared work so Rebecca need not see a penny of it).

I'm surprised at how much money I have managed to save, most of the girls here blow their money straight away and will probably be stuck here forever. I don't want to be here much longer, I don't want to go home though. I'm going to wait until I have a lot more so I can afford to get my own place, I would need a lot more though to live in London. Anywhere away from here will be great though. It's not so easy though. This is the only work I can get while living here. Rebecca won't let me work anywhere else unless I move out. I've applied for places to work but when I give them my address and telephone number so they can contact me, they suddenly say, "Oh, well err don't call us, we'll call you." They obviously knew what I worked as by the name of my address and didn't want a prostitute working for them. Narrow minded gits.

To be honest I feel like I have really settled in here. Obviously I don't look forward to the evening work, but it usually only lasts an hour or two. Some men stay over but most of them leave straight away. Depending on whether they're new to it. Some of the men aren't that bad if I'm honest, I've gotten to know a few. Mark for example, he is a lovely man. He comes here about once a month and asks for me every time. He's quite good looking if I'm honest but he does have issues with women and relationships. He is divorced, no children. His wife cheated on him a lot so now he devotes his life to his work and comes to see me when he can. On the other hand there are men like Charles Davidson ll. He is partnered in a very big law firm (which I cannot disclose for reasons which would get me in to lots of trouble!) but he isn't as nice and sensitive as Mark. Charles has a really old fashioned moustache, grey hair, and when he walks in to my room he starts to breathe heavily and lick his lips whilst staring at me. I particularly don't look forward to his visits.

Things are ok with my mum. I finally got the courage to talk to her. We talk often, behind Steve's back of course. I told her that I work in a shop somewhere. When she heard how much money I was making she was so happy for me. She actually said she was proud of me. I could never tell her the truth. It would break her heart. She has my address so she can send me any post that comes to the house. I gave her the address only because she promised never to come down here. I have a lot of birthday cards piled on my drawers waiting to be opened tomorrow. I wasn't expecting anything from anyone here. Annie says she is coming round later. Then after that, Tony is taking me out for my tea. I can't see him tomorrow because he is visiting his step brother in Scarborough for the day. He's my best friend. It didn't work with us seeing each other because of my job, but we got on so well that we stayed friends. We tell each other everything. I was so worried about telling him where I worked. I thought he'd call me a slut or something but he's stood by me all this time and he takes care of me when things get bad. I got a new customer once, and he was drunk when he got here and he smacked me for no reason at all. I just ran out and went straight down to Tony's and stayed there for the night. Rebecca wasn't even angry at me. If I was still a new girl then she wouldn't have cared, but because she knows she can trust me she stood by me, plus she gets a lot of money from me. She's ok now, Rebecca. I pay her when she wants paying and I'm popular with the men so she's always treating me decently just so I stay, for her sake obviously. We manage to have a laugh together and she comes clubbing with the girls and me on a weekend. The girls say that she favours me. It might sound selfish of me but I didn't care what the rest of the girls thought about me, most of them are high on smack most of the time anyway. They might be jealous but as long as I can live here and not have Rebecca as a threat to me then so be it. Unlucky for them.

"Hey Shell, how you doing?" Annie walked in. "I can't stay for long; I'm working in an hour and I need to get ready. I've just brought you a card and a present for tomorrow."

"Oh thanks Annie," I gave her a big hug, "you

shouldn't have really."

"Oh it's ok. Open it now," she demanded.

I open the present and I see this gorgeous blue top. It was silky and very sexy.

"Oh, wow it's beautiful!"

"You think so?"

"Yeah, I love it. Thank you so much."

"I thought maybe you could wear it tonight. You know, for lover boy!"

"He's not my 'lover boy'. He's my friend and he's taking me out for dinner."

"And his parents happen to be joining you?"

"Well, we've been friends for a while and I haven't met them yet have I?"

"You talk about him all the time. He's always round here, or you're at his flat or out somewhere. I think you love him."

"I do not love him. Well, not like that anyway. He's… a big part of my life."

"Hmm, well anyway, hope you have fun tonight with lover boy," she laughs. "I'll see you later Shell."

"Bye."

I try my top on and it fits perfectly. It matches my knee length skirt and boots. I straighten my hair and put on some make up and walk outside. He was picking me up in his car and we were meeting his parents at the restaurant.

His blue *Ford Focus* pulls up and he gets out and looks at me.

"Wow, you look gorgeous!" he says.

"Oh thanks," I say, with a big smile on my face. I felt excited to be going out somewhere with him. We had been out places before but never for a meal to a posh restaurant like this. I felt really grown up in my attire.

"No really you do." He looks into my eyes. I look into his and step towards him. He puts his hands on my waist and leans in to kiss me. It was so unexpected, but it was perfect. He then steps away and says, "Happy Birthday." I smile at him. I wasn't expecting a kiss like that, maybe a kiss on the cheek, but not a passionate snog! It made me blush.

It took about fifteen minutes to get to the restaurant. While on the way up I couldn't help thinking about that kiss. I just couldn't stop thinking about it. We'd kissed before but it had never been that good. I mean, I kiss men all the time with what I do but they're just empty kisses. Did it mean something? I didn't even notice that we had parked up outside the restaurant.

"We're meeting my parents inside. I think that's their car over there," he said, pointing across the car park. "Yes, they're here already. You ready?"

"Yep, let's go."

As we were walking up to the door, I grab his hand and pull him towards me and kiss him again. We were kissing for about a minute before we were interrupted by the door man telling us we were blocking the entrance. While walking towards the table he was holding my hand. It seemed so perfect. It was like he was my boyfriend and I was being introduced to his parents.

"This is my mum, Libby, and my step-dad, Jack. Mum, Jack, this is Michelle."

"Nice to meet you," his step-dad said, shaking my

hand. He was a jolly looking man with a great smile. He seemed really nice.

I went to shake his mum's hand but she didn't shake mine. She only repeated what Jack said, but with less enthusiasm. She didn't have the 'nice' look that Jack did. She had thick dark eyebrows which gave her an evil kind of look, like a witch.

I'm guessing that they knew what I did for a living. His mum was obviously ashamed to be having dinner with me. She barely spoke to me all night. Jack, on the other hand, didn't stop talking to me all night. I knew he was trying to make an effort seeing as his wife was being a first class stubborn bitch.

"So where are you from Michelle? Tony tells me you are from up north."

"Yeah I'm from Yorkshire," I said.

"Ah yes, we're going up there tomorrow, Scarborough. Is that near where you come from?"

"No, that's in North Yorkshire. I'm from Bradford, in the West."

"Oh yes. I don't think we've been there. Might have driven through it a few times I think but never actually walked round Bradford."

"It's an ok place but it's not great. It can be quite bad in the town. It's not always a nice place to be, depending where you go of course."

"Yes, too many prostitutes around for my liking," Libby finally said, not looking at me.

"Yes, well, Michelle is hoping to get a new place here and move out of those flats," Tony said, trying to change the subject. "Didn't you want a flat somewhere in the middle of London?"

"Oh yes?" Jack said looking at me. "I own some of the buildings around London. I could help you if you like? Are you looking for a bigger place?"

"No, I only want a small place. It will only be me living there. But I might go back home and get a place nearer to my mum's house. I haven't seen her in a long time. Thank you though; I'm still only thinking about it. It's not really definite yet."

"I think *home* is the best place to go."

"Libby!" Jack said.

"Go home and stay away from my son!" snapped Libby. She was only whispering when speaking but in an aggressive way. She obviously didn't want any attention bringing to the situation. "I don't want your sort to be consorting with my son, playing with his mind and making him fall in love with you." She stood up. "You will only break his heart in the end."

"Excuse me?" I said, quite taken back by what she had to say. Did she really just say those words to me?

"Mum! What are you doing?"

"Libby, sit down right now," Jack finally said. She looked him in the eye.

"I'll meet you at the car Jack." Then she walked out.

"I am so sorry Michelle. I'd better go after her. It was very nice meeting you." He shook my hand and then left.

Chapter 17

The journey back to my place was long and silent. Tony didn't talk. I think he was too embarrassed and pissed off about what his mum had said. I didn't really feel like talking either. I knew what people thought about me but I've never been confronted by anyone like that before. Did Tony think that? Is that why it didn't work out us seeing each other a few months back? After that night I didn't feel like continuing with the 'game'. I just wanted to go home. I have never felt this much like a dirty whore in my life. Most people I come across usually keep their opinions to themselves.

"Here we are then," Tony said as we pulled up outside.

"Do you want to come in for a bit?" I asked him.

"I don't know, I really have to go, I'm up early tomorrow and its ten o'clock now."

"Please? Just for a little while."

I don't know why I was inviting him in. I wasn't in the mood for talking, and I don't think he was either.

"Ok, just for a bit though."

I guess I just wanted the company for a while. I

was hoping Rebecca wasn't in. She might think he was a customer and demand some money from me in the morning. We walk inside the flats, up the stairs and into my room. We stood for a minute until he finally spoke.

"I am so sorry about my mum. She promised she'd be civil and keep her mouth shut but she's so uptight she really pisses me off sometimes. She speaks when she shouldn't, she always gives her opinion when it's not wanted, she always has to be right, even with Jack, she makes all the decisions, I really don't know how he puts up with it I really don't. Sometimes I just think that…"

I kissed him.

"What was that for?" he asked me.

"I don't know. I just felt like it."

"Fair enough," he said. He looked in to my eyes and we both leaned in.

Then he kissed me.

We kissed for ages. It was the best and most passionate kiss you could ever imagine. He placed his hands on my waist and they slowly went up my body and deep into my hair. First, I had my hands on his waist too, but I moved them round the back and down his body, and then back round to his chest. I began to unbutton his shirt and he started to unzip my skirt. I felt my skirt fall as I threw his shirt to the floor. Then he pulled my new top up and over my head. When it was off, his hands moved to my chest, and his lips soon joined, kissing me all around my neck getting lower and lower. We moved closer to the bed and soon enough, I found myself lying down with him on top of me. I unzipped his trousers. Soon, we were both in our underwear, till he took my bra off, and then my tiny G-string. I took his shorts off and we were both naked, touching each other. We both knew what was going to happen, and what we wanted to happen.

"Are you sure about this?" he asked me.

"Yes I am," I replied.

Chapter 18

We slept together. In the many months I have done this as an occupation, I have never enjoyed it as much as I did last night. It was passionate. It was perfect. I had my very first orgasm from a man! Afterward, we both fell asleep in each other's arms. This is how sex should be, not something to be paid for. When I awoke in the morning, I was alone in my bed. I heard the toilet flush and the tap run. I got up and put my dressing gown on. When he came out of the bathroom, he didn't look me in the eye. He was dressed and it looked like he was about to go.

"Good morning you." He didn't look at me. "Are you ok?" I asked him.

"Yeah, yeah I'm fine. Listen, I'm sorry about last night. It shouldn't have happened."

"What do you mean?" I asked him.

"Well, this is your job so last night probably meant nothing to you. How could it? The only difference was I wasn't intending to pay you but I did sleep with you so here's some money. I don't know how much you normally accept and I don't have that much but here take this."

He puts £50 in my hand.

"I don't want this."

He wouldn't accept it back. He made his way towards the door.

"Yes you do. It's what you work for. I slept with you, it wouldn't be right if I didn't pay you. Why should I be any different? Happy Birthday." Bang. He slammed the door as he left my room.

Where did all that come from? Why was he so angry? And why was he angry at me? Last night was about me and him, not his money. I didn't want his money. I wasn't even thinking about what I did for a living. I just wanted him. I wanted to sleep with him. All I thought about was me and him and us two being together in the most passionate way possible. I love him. Oh my god, I love him! Why didn't I realise this before?

I threw the money on to the top of my drawers and ran out my room and down the stairs to catch up with him. I ran outside but he was already driving away in his car. I waved at him to come back but he didn't see me. When I got back to my room, I looked at the clock and it was half past seven. I saw the money on my drawers and then there was a knock at my door. I threw the money in my top drawer in case it was Rebecca.

"Come in," I said.

"Are you ok?" Annie said as she walked in my door. My eyes were filled with tears. "Oh, sweetie, come here. I heard everything. You did nothing wrong, ok? You did nothing wrong. It's just, it's probably hard for him because this is your job, he will have felt like another customer and he doesn't want to be a customer, he wants to be with you. Ok? He loves you. Do you love him?"

"Yeah I do," I said, "I love him. I always have. Last night was the best night of my life."

"Call him. Shell you need to call him. Tell him you love him. Let him know you don't want to lose him. I need to go, I need to avoid Rebecca today, this guy I had last night didn't pay and just ran out afterwards but she won't believe me. Get a shower, think about what you want, and then call him."

When she went, I did what she said. I took a shower; I sorted myself out and worked up the courage to call him.

I called him from my mobile. It just kept ringing and ringing. It finally reached his voicemail, so I left a message: "Hi Tony, it's me. Listen, I don't think last night was a mistake. I thought it was great and it was the best night of my life. I know you might find that hard to believe but it's true. I don't want your money, you can have it back. I think I'm going to go home. I'm tired of doing what I do. I need a couple of days to sort things out but I don't plan to be here this time next week. I love you." I began to cry. "I love you so much, and I'll miss you."

*

Later on that day, I went to find Rebecca.

"Rebecca?" I called as I knocked on her office door. "Can I come in?"

"Yes, yes come in dear." She looked like she was in a good mood. She was just reading through some papers. "Are you ok? You look upset."

"Rebecca I'm sorry, but I have to leave this place."

"You have to leave? Why?" She put down what

she was reading and stood up. She seemed quite shocked that I had to leave.

"Things aren't going so well for me at the moment. I don't want to be doing this for the rest of my life. It's too late to go back to school but I want to start a fresh. Get a job somewhere back home and take it from there. I might even be able to go to college. I'm seventeen, I have my whole life ahead of me and I miss my family. I hope you can understand." My lip had started quivering.

"Well, I wasn't expecting that over my breakfast this morning. Err, I am disappointed that you want to leave but I can't keep you forever," she hesitated, "I have had a few girls wanting to go home when they get to your age if they have managed to not get addicted to drugs. They realise they have better lives at home so, ok. What can I say exactly? Your next rent is due in four days. I would rather you didn't go back though. I like having you around. If you ever change your mind, you are more than welcome to come back, please remember that, just in case things don't work out at home you will always have a place here."

"Really?" I was shocked that she was so easy going with all of this.

"Shelly I am not the Wicked Witch of London. Yes, I was strict to begin with but it's the only way to get the new girls motivated. I can't have them all timid and shy can I? Now go on, I'm sure you have things to sort out and I'm in the middle of a crisis at the moment. One of the new girls got upset and pushed away a regular and he's not happy. He sent a rather rude email to me this morning and I can't lose his business."

"Ok then, I'll see you later then. Thank you for understanding. I don't want to cause any inconvenience. Bye."

"Oh Shell?"

"Yeah?"

"Happy Birthday!" She handed me a card.

Chapter 19

Soon after my conversation with Rebecca, I went to get a ticket sorted straight away. I decided not to tell my mum I was coming home. I thought it would be a great surprise if I just turned up on the doorstep. And also I wanted to see the look on Steve's face when he saw me walk through the door, unexpectedly. He'd be so happy he would actually cry. My mum will probably cry, especially since I haven't seen her in so long. The last time she saw me I was a little girl. Things have sure changed.

"How can I help you?" asked the ticket woman, sitting behind a computer.

"I'm going up to Bradford in a couple of days, can I get a ticket now or do I get it on the day?"

"You can get it and pay for it now if you like."

"Ok can I do that then?"

"Of course you can. What day do you want to travel and will it be a one way travel or return?" she browsed through her computer.

"Wednesday, please, and it will be one way."

"What time?"

"What times are there trains leaving?"

"There's one in the morning at nine, then one at twelve and the last one is at six."

"I'll go at twelve then." I will have time to say my goodbyes to the girls then.

"Ok, that's £70 please."

I hand her the money and she printed out a ticket.

"Thank you," I said.

"Have a safe journey."

When I got back to my room I thought it best to sort through of all my clothes and decide what I was keeping and what I was throwing away. I have a lot more clothes than I did when I first came. To say I started out with one pair of jeans and a couple of tops, I've come a long way. I need a new suitcase. I threw my other bag away. I didn't think I would need it again. And also it had marks where the rats had sneaked in to steal my food. I don't want a large suitcase, just one big enough to fit dozens and dozens of clothes, shoes and bags! I'll have to go out and buy one. There's a bag shop in the village, they'll have one there. How much money do I have left in my purse? £70. I think that will be enough for one suitcase.

When I get to the shop, I see a big selection of suitcases and bags of all kind. Big ones, small ones, red ones and blue ones. It's not a small shop, but it is a bit cramped. I find a few suitcases that are the perfect size for me. There's one with a handle and wheels, that one looks quite handy. The rest are ones that you carry. I think I'll be better off with one with wheels. I won't be able to carry all of my things, they'll be too heavy. I settle for the black one. Its £15. Quite light too, so I will have no problem carrying that back up the street.

I pay for it and the man who served me kept eying me up. He knew where I lived and what I did. I think he was one of my customers a few months back. He did look a bit familiar. He was beginning to freak me out so I left before he could make me any offers.

When I eventually get back to my room, I put it on my bed and open it up. I open my top drawer and begin to empty it into the suitcase. I could be here a while!

Chapter 20

The night before I leave for Bradford, Annie and a couple of the girls come into my room with four bottles of wine.

"I can't believe you're leaving. You have way more courage than me. I'd be too scared to go back home," said Tanya.

"I could probably go home, when my drunk, wife beating bastard of a dad keels over and dies painfully," Claire said.

"I'm going to miss you all. I've given each of you my number and address so you can call me or visit whenever you want."

"I don't think we'll be able to visit you, but we will definitely call you. Or write to you. We'll never forget you," Annie reassured me.

We each had a bottle of wine to drink and finished them after a few hours. We were all drunk and very giddy. We were talking about the men we've had to sleep with. We were comparing who'd had the best, who'd had the worst, who'd had the fittest, who'd had the ugliest and all daft things like that. Comparing sizes was the funniest. It was fun. We spent an hour laughing at Tanya's story about the man who couldn't actually get it up for two hours.

I would never forget these girls. Especially Annie, she's been there for me when I needed someone to talk to. We used to go shopping together, which is why I have so many clothes. She is a fashion Goddess. She knows where all the best sales and bargains are.

They all left at midnight. I wouldn't see Tanya or Claire in the morning because they have places to be so we said our goodbyes then. Annie was coming with me to the station. She wanted to see me off because she said I'd have, "No one to wave to from the train!" She was messing, but she did want to see me off. So, we didn't say a massive goodbye at the door. She had to help Claire carry Tanya to her room because she couldn't walk! Tanya had also brought a bottle of vodka and was downing it a lot of the night.

When they went, I looked round my room. It looked empty. I didn't have a lot on display, just a few photos of mine and Annie's day in London. There were some of us outside Buckingham Palace, Big Ben and some of us on the London Eye. That was such a good day. They were all in my suitcase now. I set my alarm for nine o'clock. I didn't even have anything planned to say for when I turned up on my mum's doorstep. I didn't tell her I was coming home. I wanted it to be a surprise.

When I finally got in bed, I couldn't sleep. All I could think about was Tony. Would I ever see him again? Would I ever talk to him again? I might text him; tell him I'm going home tomorrow. Maybe he'll turn up at the station, telling me to stay with him. I doubt he will. He didn't even reply to the voice mail I left him.

When I awoke the next morning, the sun was shining on my face. Rebecca brought up some breakfast for me. She couldn't stay long but wished me the best of luck with my mum and told me that she would miss me. I thanked her for getting me off the street even though it wasn't the best option to go for. She called me and Annie a taxi.

"I can't believe this will be the last time I'll see you," Annie said to me as we walked on the station platform.

"It won't be the last time. I'll come visit you or you could maybe get a weekend off and come up to Yorkshire."

"I hope so. I like the sound of going up to Yorkshire. All those fields and farms. I've never been to a farm. Maybe we could go?" I nodded and she hugged me. "Call me when you get there. I want to know how it went with your mum."

"I will, I promise." I gave her one final hug while a lad who worked on the train took my suitcase.

"You'll 'ave to come aboard miss, the train sets off in five minutes."

Annie and I had one last hug just before I climbed onto the train. I walked past a lot of people who I had never seen before. I found a seat next to the window so I could wave to Annie. No sooner had I sat down did the train begin to move. I looked out at Annie and saw she had a tear in her eye. It soon set me off. I waved until she was out of site. An elderly woman sat opposite me offered me a tissue.

"Thanks," I managed to say.

I wave until Annie is out of site.

"Are you not going to see her for a while?" asked this woman.

"No, I'll see her again." But when? Annie wouldn't be able to afford a return ticket to Bradford. And I don't think she would be able to afford the time off either. I really hope I get to see her again. Other than Tony, she was my best friend.

Chapter 21

I stood at the gate and stared at the house. I didn't want to go in. Not just yet. I was hoping that my mum would glance out of the window, notice me standing there and then rush out to me and give me the biggest hug, but I don't think anyone was in. The car wasn't in the drive. I searched through my handbag and found my old key. I was hoping Steve hadn't changed the locks. Knowing him he would've changed them the day after I left. Surprisingly he hadn't and I was able to walk through the door and into the hallway. I was expecting him to have converted my room into an office. I won't know until I go in though.

"Hello?" I called, hoping Steve wouldn't be the one replying to me. "Mum?" I called. There was still no reply.

I left my suitcase by the door and wandered around the house but couldn't find anyone. I grabbed my suitcase and made my way up to my room. It took me a while to actually step into my room after opening the door. I stared inside for a minute. It looked completely different. It wasn't an office. It was my room. All my things were still there and in the same place, but it looked different somehow but I don't know what has changed. The last time I was in this room I was a naive little girl. It was tidy for once. All my dirty washing was washed and in a clean pile on my bed, my curtains were open, my bed was made and there were no plates or cups on my desk. I placed my suitcase in the doorway and walked round my room. I looked at the posters on my walls of Henry Cavill. I was obsessed with him. Tony had taken me to see the new Superman film to feed my obsession with him. It worked out for both of us as he had loved Superman since he was young.

I then walked over to the photos on my shelves. There were loads of me and my friends. I hadn't spoken to them in a long time. They sent me loads of letters via my mum but I never replied. I never knew what to say to them. They all asked me the same questions over and over again. "Where are you? When are you coming home? Can we come visit?" I wasn't sure when I would be coming home and no they couldn't visit because I didn't want them to know I was living and working in a brothel.

After I finished unpacking I made my way back downstairs. There was hardly any food in the house. Only a few slices of bread and a little strawberry jam. Just enough for a sandwich. I made myself some dinner and a cup of tea. I decided to give Annie a call to let her know I was home safely.

"Hello?"

"Hey Annie, its Shell!"

"Hey Sweetie! How'd it go with your mum?" she asked.

"It didn't," I began. "No one's home except me.

It's almost seven and I have no idea where she is."

"She'll be home. This could give you time to prepare what you're going to say."

"Yeah true. What am I going to say?" I asked hoping for an answer.

"I really don't know. I think in a situation like this it's a kind of momentary thing. You don't know what's going to happen till it happens. But that doesn't mean you can't prepare for it. You could tidy things up a bit. Maybe then you'd be able to think of something."

"Yeah I guess. Everything is tidy though. It's so weird being back here. My room looks bigger than when I left it."

"It'll take time for you to settle in again. Like when you first arrived here things were strange. When your mum gets back it could be awkward for a bit but things will be back to how they used to be in no time."

"I hope so. I'm not taking any shit off Steve this time. He can just go to hell."

"Good for you. You faced worse creatures than him when you were here. Anyway babe I have to go."

"Ok Ann, I'll ring or maybe text you later."

"OK, make sure you do. I don't want you forgetting about me."

"I won't forget you, ever. I'll talk to you later."

I didn't want her to go. I wanted to chat. I never liked being on my own; especially in this house. I used to be afraid that Steve would pop up from somewhere and beat me to shit. I suppose I have nothing to worry about though. I'm seventeen now, I can look after myself. I have looked after myself for over half a year and nothing is going to get in the way of it. I've changed a lot since I was last here.

It was soon approaching ten o'clock. Mum should be home soon. She never stays out this late. Even when she's gone out for a meal with Steve she was always back by nine. I'll go check the calendar. Wherever she is it would certainly be written on there.

I couldn't believe what I had just read. I had to read it five times to be sure. They're both in Majorca and aren't due back for four more days. No wonder there wasn't any food in the house. I couldn't believe I was going to be here on my own till then. I'll have to go shopping in the morning and buy some food otherwise I won't have anything to eat. I could buy some extra food for when they return get back. We could have a kind of celebration. I could invite Dad and my friends and then it would be a party. I was too tired to plan things right now, though I wanted to. I had got myself excited about the idea. I locked the front door and made my way up the stairs and into my strange looking room. I found some clean pyjamas in my drawer and decided to watch one of my old favourite movies; 'Never Been Kissed'.

When I got into bed I began to think of Tony. I wondered what he was doing. Was he thinking of me? No, course he wasn't. He hated me the last time he saw me. He thought I'd taken advantage of him. Used my occupation to get him into bed, but I didn't. I love him, and I want to be with him. I wonder what he thought when he heard my message. I guess I'll never know.

Chapter 22

I awoke the next morning with a strange smile on my face. I was in my bed, in my room and in my house. The only thing missing was my mum, but that would be sorted in three days. I look round my room. The sun was shining through my yellow blind so everything had a yellow tint to it. Everything seemed so familiar and somewhat comforting.

I decided to go for a shower, get dressed and then go into town. I need some sophisticated clothes. Not clothes that say, "Men slept with me for money!" I also need some food, for me and for the party.

I walk to the bus stop. I'm wearing my beige knee length skirt and my black halter neck top. I was also wearing my black knee length boots. I hope I don't bump into anyone I knew. I looked like a slapper, a classy one but a slapper none the less. The only thing keeping me concealed was a small black jacket, but even that was a fitted blazer. Men were driving past in cars shouting rude remarks and beeping their horns. I don't know who they thought they were. It's not like I'm going to shag them just because they shout things.

The bus driver gives me a strange look as I walk on. He managed to stare at me as I walked away too. I could feel his dirty eyes on my body. I can't wait to buy some trousers.

I walk into *Dorothy Perkins* first. I need to buy some decent clothes and get out of these things. I find a section of jeans and other trousers. I buy three pairs. A black pair of combats, a pair of jeans and some black trousers for job interviews or special occasions. Along with them, I buy three vest tops; red, pink and black. I decide to treat myself to a new denim jacket too. I also buy some trainers and some casual shoes. Altogether in *Dorothy Perkins*, *Topshop* and *New Look* I have spent nearly £200! Only a slight dip in to my savings…

When I had finished clothes shopping I sneaked in to some café loos and changed into my jeans and pink top. I bought myself a drink and a sandwich. I sat in the corner, hoping not to be seen by anyone I knew.

After that I popped into Tesco and bought some typical party-buffet food; bread, ham, tuna, mayonnaise and cheese. I'm sure I could combine all that together and make a few dozen sandwiches. All I need to buy now is some crisps, drinks, puddings and other food to last till next week when Steve and my mum go shopping. I wonder if I can get away with buying some wine. I might just pop to the off-licence later on. The wine might add to the tremendous weight of the shopping.

Getting on the bus was another story. I had five bags full of clothes and food and on top of that I had to scramble through my bag to find my return ticket. I put all my bags in the space provided and sat at the front so I could guard them. I didn't trust people. After living in London you can't just abandon your bags somewhere and not expect other people to leave them alone and not go through them.

While on the bus, a familiar face got on. She was an elderly woman with a look of permanent envy on her face. Who was she? Suddenly it dawned on me; as soon as she spoke I knew exactly who it was.

"Shelly?" Cried Mrs Next Door. "Is that really you?"

"Yep," I smiled, "it's me." She sat next to me. I didn't mind. I was actually happy to see her.

"Oh it's so good to see you. Your mum said you went to live with some family down in London. I didn't even know you had any family in London."

"Yeah well I needed to get away. Steve was driving me insane. I just went down there, did my own thing, earned some money while at it and decided to come back home. I missed everyone too much."

"I got quite worried. Your mum told me where you were and assured me that everything was ok, but about a couple of weeks after you left, your dad turned up on your doorstep demanding to see Steve. He was shouting and causing a scene. I think the house on the other side of you was going to call the police because of all the noise he was making. Does he know you're home yet?"

"No, not yet. I'm going to sort things out when I get home and ring him. Erm, what are you doing on Saturday?"

"Nothing I don't think. Why?" she asks.

"Well," I begin, "my mum doesn't know I've come back and I want to surprise her. I didn't know she was on holiday you see. So I want to have a small gathering. People I haven't seen in such a long time. So, do you want to come?"

"Oh Shell I'd love to come. What time will it be? Oh wait we need to get off, this is our stop. Here I'll help you with these."

"Oh, thanks." She takes some of my bags and we struggle off the bus. She puts the bags in front of my gate.

"So what time will it be on Saturday?" she asks while putting the bags down.

"Erm, I think they will be due back about four so if you want to come round for about three? Is that ok?"

"Yes, yes that will be just fine. I tell you what, I'll come over at lunch time and help you get food sorted. That way when people turn up, you can talk to them and you won't have to worry about a thing. How about that?"

"Err, yeah, if you wouldn't mind actually. There'll be a lot to do though."

"It will be a pleasure. I'll see you on Saturday then."

"Yeah, bye." I never realised how nice she was. Was she always this caring? Maybe she was and I was just too blind to see it.

Chapter 23

It was approaching six o'clock. I had put all the food away, put my new clothes away and thrown away some of the clothes I had from London. I didn't want to look at them again. Some of them were suitable for casual wear and maybe parties or nights out, but others had bad memories behind them. Some I would rather forget.

I rang Annie and told her about the party and what time it was. It was a shame she couldn't come. After ringing Annie and a few other people there was just one more call to make. I was so nervous about making this call, but I had to do it.

"Hello?" said a deep and familiar voice.

"Dad?"

There was a long silence. Why wasn't he saying anything?

"Dad? Are you there?" I asked.

"Err, yes, yes I'm here," he said, sounding shocked. "Shell? Is that really you?" His voice was beginning to break.

"Yes, it's me."

"Wh... where are you?" he stuttered. He never stutters. I guess he was really surprised. I don't blame him.

"I'm at home. I came back yesterday."

"Are Steve and your mum back yet?" I guess he knew they were away.

"No, not till Saturday."

"So you're home alone then? Well why don't you come here?" I felt so sorry for him. It was wrong of me not to call. "I can sort your bedroom out and I'll come pick you up tonight, no now. I'll get my keys and get you now." He was speaking very fast and in a way seemed nervously giddy.

"Dad calm down. I can't go stay there. I want to be on my own here for a bit. You know, get readjusted to things here. But you can come over on Saturday. Mum is back off her holiday and she doesn't know I'm back so I want to surprise her with a party for when she gets back. Everyone could be here and then I would be sat in the room when she walks in."

"I'll come over there then," he said. "Tomorrow first thing I'll come over."

"No dad please, I need to settle in here. I've had a long week and I really need some peace. I hope you don't mind."

"I missed you Shell. You should have come straight here, instead of London."

"I wanted to, but you were on your never ending honeymoon when everything was going on."

"Where did you go? I know you were in London, but where did you stay? Who did you stay with?"

"Erm, I stayed with a friend. I knew her from school, she moved down there a year ago." I didn't want to lie. I wanted to tell the truth. The whole truth, but I couldn't. I wanted to tell him about Rebecca, about the men, about why they gave me so much money for an hour's work, but I couldn't.

"Huh, which friend?" he asked with a tone interest.

"You don't know her, she's called Annie."

"Can I ask you something Shell?"

"Erm, yeah sure." I was scared of what he was going to ask.

"Why did you run away?"

"I needed to get away. You know what things were like here with Steve, I couldn't bare it and…"

"Steve? It was him who drove you away? That son of a… I swear the next time I see him I'm gonna…"

"Dad please don't. It will be so over whelming for mum I don't want anything to upset her. Kick his arse after the party."

"Are you really home Shell? Or am I dreaming this call?"

"I'm home dad, I promise."

We both laugh and get onto reminiscing about when I used to go stay at his house. He reminded me about all the times I used to cry before I had to go home when I was younger. I told him that I used to love his stories he used to tell me so before I hung up, he told me an old favourite, a story that I loved when I was ten. I made him tell me it every time I saw him. After I hung up, I cried.

Chapter 24

Saturday morning was eventful. Mrs Next Door came round to help me get things ready. Then, three hours before anyone was due, six of my best mates came round! Mrs Next Door said she would sort things out and told us to go upstairs to talk and catch up. It was fantastic. There was Sam, Leah, Chrissie, Janey, Elli and Lou.

As soon as we got into my room, we all stood quiet. They were looking at me and I was looking at them. Then, like we counted down to it in our heads, we all screamed and jumped into a great big group hug! I hadn't seen them in such a long time. These were my girls! They had changed so much. They were all taller, they were all gorgeous and they all had blonde, red or black dye in their hair.

"Look at you with the makeup on!" Chrissie said. "You never used to wear makeup! What changed there?"

"Well, people in London are so sophisticated so you have to fit in don't you?" I said.

"Did you see anyone famous?" Trust Elli to ask that. She was a celebrity fanatic.

"Erm, yeah I bumped into the Queen in New Look! She was buying some French knickers. She wanted to spice things up with Phillip," I laughed. The others laughed too. "Yes Elli I did, erm, a couple of times I saw cars from Buckingham Palace go past but I never saw who was in them. Oh, I got a glance of Geri Halliwell too."

"Wow," said Elli, "where was Geri when you saw her?"

"She was walking out of a café with a friend. I was walking in and didn't realise it was her till I heard someone tell me that was who I had knocked with my bag." The girls laughed. "I didn't even say sorry, I was in too much of a rush."

"Why didn't you call us?" asked Lou. Everyone stopped laughing and looked at me. Lou had been sat quiet since they arrived. Out of all these girls, she was my best friend. We were a group, but always paired off for certain things. I could tell that she was upset. "Just one of us at least. You didn't have to call us all. Just one."

"I'm sorry. I needed to get away on my own. It's got nothing to do with any of you I just had to be completely on my own. And I don't want to talk about it tonight. I want to have fun with you, my girls."

After half an hour of chatting about London and all the places I went and all the things I saw, the girls made their way downstairs. When I got changed into my black trousers and the top that Annie bought me, I too made my way downstairs to join the others. Some other friends had arrived. The girls put music on and put food out and I greeted people as they came in. My grandma was already crying when she came in. Mrs Next Door and I escorted her into the room. I was stood at the doorway of the room and I heard a familiar voice behind me.

"Hello Flower."

"DAD!" I ran to my dad and jumped in his arms. He hugged me so hard I could hardly breathe, but I didn't care. I just wanted him to hug me. We were hugging for ages. Just to make up for missed hugs.

When we finally let go of each other he says, "Wow, look at you. You're all grown up! Not my little girl anymore. You remember Jane, my wife." A timid blonde approached us.

"Yeah course I do," I never liked Jane but seeing as though I'm 'all grown up' I say, "Hi Jane how are you?"

"I'm ok, how was your journey back up here?" she asked. I think she was nervous about talking to me. She was just trying to make conversation. We hadn't really talked before. I always tried to avoid it.

"It was ok yeah. How was the honeymoon?" I asked her. Dad had gone to talk to my Grandma and to try and calm her down. She still hadn't stopped crying.

"Oh it was brilliant. I've never had a holiday like it."

"Oh that's good, that's really good," not knowing what to say now, I wanted to go. The door bell rang. "Oh, I'd better go get that." Saved by the bell.

It was some more friends from school, Jessie, Mark, Stacy and Jason. We hugged and laughed and then they all joined the girls and the others in the room.

"Their car has just pulled up," Mrs Next Door shouted. "They're here! Everyone by the door. Shell, go sit in the living room. Girls if you sit with her that would be brilliant." You'd think she used to be a party planner! "Ok everyone quiet."

I heard the door open. "Hi!" everyone said together.

"What the hell is going on?" I heard my mum say.

"What's everyone doing here?" the king of happiness shouted. "How the hell did you all get in here?"

"Peter?" my mum said looking at my dad, "What's going on?"

"Go in the room and see for yourself. Not you Steve, you stay here."

"You're stopping me entering my own house? Who do you think you are?" he answered back.

"I'm a father. That's who I am."

"What the hell could be in here that I want to see?" she walks into the room. "Leah, Janey, what are you girls doing here?" She finally looked at me. "Sh... Shell? Is that really you?"

"It's me," I said, standing up.

"Oh my God I can't believe you're back." I went to hug her before she passed out, and so she knew I was really there and she wasn't imagining it. "You're really here," she cried, making me start. "I can't believe you came home. This is the best thing that's ever happened." She pulled away again to look at me. "Look at you. You look gorgeous. I can hardly recognise you."

"I'm glad I'm back. I came back the other day. I didn't know you were away though."

"Let me through, this is my house let me through." Steve barged into the room. He looked at me. "Oh, you're home. When err, when did you get back?" He was trying to act happy that I had returned.

"A few days ago," Lou called out. She knows what I used to go through with him. I told her everything about him. "You weren't gutted when she went but you're gutted now she's back."

He stood silent. He looked at all the people who were staring at him. He wanted to say something but I don't think he wanted to make a scene. He saw how happy my mum was and I don't think he wanted to ruin it, my mum on the other hand seemed oblivious to the sudden change of tension in the room. "I'll go unpack then shall I? I might go for a sleep too. I'm a bit tired." He walked upstairs. I was surprised for a while that my mum didn't go up to stop him. I guess she wanted to stay with me.

Chrissie put the music back on.

It was a great night. By nine o'clock and after a few glasses of wine, Grandma managed to calm down and even started to have a dance with Mark and Jason. I was telling Lou about Annie and how she looked after me when I got to London. My mum came up to me and put her arm around me.

"Shell dear, you have a visitor. I don't know who he is; I've never seen him before."

'He'? I thought. Who's 'he'? When I went into the hall I saw who 'he' was.

"Tony?" I couldn't believe it. "How did you know… what are you doing here?" I was so happy but since things weren't so great with us, I tried to hide it.

"Annie called me. Can we go somewhere to talk?" he asked, knowing my mum was eavesdropping on us.

"Yeah, come in to the kitchen." I lead him down the hall.

"So what're you doing here then? How did you find out where I live?" I asked.

"Annie called me and gave me your address. She told me you were gone and that if I ever wanted to see you again, I'd have to come see you in person. I was worried I was going to lose contact with you. I just needed some time to think. We need to talk about what happened."

"Ok, well, I meant what I said. I didn't regret it, and I didn't want your money. It's in my bag. I can go get it if..."

"Just leave it. I don't need the money. I need to tell you something."

"What? What's wrong?" I asked.

"Well, after Annie called, I started to think, and I realised that... I love you. I love you Shell. I don't want to live without you. We've had such good times together. It's been the most fun I've ever had. You've been there for me, you've listened. I could tell you stuff I would never tell anyone else. Like about my dad and how he used to hit me? You told me all about your step dad, Steve is it? We could relate to each other's feelings and emotions and I think that's perfect. And about that night, it was perfect. I just thought it was too perfect and I couldn't sleep that night thinking why it happened. I know you're not a spiteful person so you wouldn't do that for my money. It was great and I'm sorry. I want you to forgive me, but I understand if you don't want to."

"Of course I forgive you. I love you too." Then we kissed. We kissed then hugged but were interrupted by a very drunk old woman.

"Shell, Shell my dear." She stumbled in.

"Hi Grandma, are you ok?" She had been drinking sherry all night.

"I have come to say goodbye," she slurred. "Your son... my dad... no, that's wrong."

"You mean my dad?" I corrected her, trying not to laugh.

"Yes, my dad is telling me I need to sleep," I laughed as she nearly fell again. "My taxi is waiting for me." She either hugged me or fell on me at that point. "I'm so glad you're back."

I walked her to the door and then my mum took over by taking her to the taxi. I grabbed Tony's hand and lead him into the room to meet everyone.

"Everyone," I said aloud, "everyone, this is Tony. Tony this is everyone."

"Hi," he said, looking around everyone.

"Hi," my dad said, approaching him. "I'm Peter, Shell's dad."

"I've heard a lot about you. I'm Shell's boyfriend." He looked at me and smiled. I smiled back. I was so happy. This was the best night. Nothing could ruin it. Not long after an interview with my dad, Tony was talking to Mrs Next Door. He knew not to say anything about what I used to do. His mum made a bad enough scene and he didn't want anyone else to do that. He went with the story that I lived with an old school friend and worked in a clothes shop. He seemed to have trouble understanding her broad Yorkshire accent.

"How're you doing?" Lou asked me.

"Really good. This has been a great night. Thanks so much for coming." I went to hug her. Tony came over.

"It's been a pleasure meeting you too," Lou said to Tony, shaking his hand.

"Yeah you too," he said to her.

"What a great day this has been," my mum said as she walked over. "This has been the best welcome home present. Will you be staying here tonight Tony?"

"Err, I didn't actually think of that," he said, laughing nervously, "Would it be ok?"

"Of course it would. I'm sure Steve wouldn't mind at all." She looked to the hallway. "Talk of the devil."

He walked in the room, not looking at me or my dad. He looked at the people in the room. Not many people noticed him. A lot of people had left now. It was getting late. Then nothing could have prepared me for what was about to happen.

"Tony?" Steve said.

"Dad?"

Chapter 25

'Dad'? I thought. What did he mean 'Dad'? Surely this wasn't his dad. His dad had an affair with another woman about nine years ago. She was married too, apparently. A number of years later they got married and Tony hasn't seen him since then.

"What are you doing here?" Steve asked Tony.

"What's going on?" I asked them both.

"Shell," Tony said, with a look of disgust on his face, "this is my dad." He didn't take his eyes off Steve.

"You haven't answered my question boy, what are you doing here?" He was looking him straight in the eye. He didn't seem angry that Tony was here but he didn't seem too pleased either. People were beginning to pay attention to what was going on.

"I'm here with Michelle."

"Steve," my mum finally said, "you didn't tell me you had a son."

"Sandra," he looked at everyone and quietly said, "we'll discuss this later when everyone's gone." He walked out and into the kitchen. My mum followed. I turned to Tony.

"Are you ok?" I asked him.

"Shell darling," my dad said, "we're going to go now." Referring to him and Jane. "We'll ring you sometime this week and maybe take you out for lunch somewhere ok?"

"Ok dad I'll see you later. I love you."

After that, many more people went. Lou and Chrissie were the last to leave. When everyone had gone, I found Tony sat alone on the stairs.

"Hey."

"Hey," he replied. "What time is it?" he asked.

"Half past eleven. You want to go to bed? You look tired."

"Yeah, I might do."

The kitchen door opened. Steve came out, followed by my mum. It was pretty obvious that she had persuaded him to come out and try to sort things out.

"Can we talk?" he said to Tony.

"I don't know. I'm quite tired." He stared at the floor. "I've had a long day."

"I think we need to talk." He took a deep breath. "If you are going to be with Michelle and you're going to be here then we can't have a brick wall between us. We need to sort things out."

"What if I don't want to sort things out? What if I was glad when you left? What if I wished I would never see you again and for nearly a long time that almost came true." He stood up and faced Steve. "Did you not tell her about this?" he said, pointing to my mum. My mum just stared at the floor. "Did you not tell her about me and your parenting techniques?

About how you used to drink when babysitting me and how you used to beat me? I was four when you first smacked me, I was five when you made me watch you beat my mum and then lock me in my room." He began to shout. "You threw me down the stairs because I was playing with my toys on the landing! What kind of a father does that? You were no father to me. I hate you. I hope I never have to look at you again." He turned round and walked up the stairs.

"He's lying. No way did I used to beat him," he said, laughing nervously. "He used to lie as a child. He was what you call a problem child. I'm used to it. It seems like he still needs to grow up." When my mum eventually looked up she had a look of suspicion on her face. She looked quite scared too. We looked at each other and I think she was thinking the same as me. "I tried, that's all I can do. Michelle, you're better without him." He was acting like he had won the battle.

"Shut up," I said. I followed Tony up the stairs. He was pacing around my room. I didn't know what to do.

"That man, he pisses me off so much."

"I know. I am so sorry. I didn't know."

"I know you didn't. I'm sorry Shell," he stopped pacing the room and he put his arms around me. "I know you didn't know. How could you? He changed his last name for God's sake. Is your mum ok?"

"I don't think so. She seems to have been off with him all night. She wouldn't normally have let him just go upstairs and leave us like that. She would have at least gone up to see him every now and then. I don't think they're ok. I don't think they've been ok for a while, something didn't feel right between them, and I think me coming back has made things worse."

"She seemed quiet when he was around. Is she normally like that?"

"No, when he used to get annoyed she used to be the one saying 'oh get over it Steve'. Not in an angry or serious kind of way but, she didn't even say anything to him while we were there. I think there's something going on. And I don't like it."

"Surely he's not… you know… being violent with her too."

"I don't know. I don't want to make a big thing about it until we know for sure. It's too late now but I could maybe get mum on her own for a few hours. Maybe take her out to lunch. She'd tell me if something like that was going on."

"Well I'm going back down to London soon to sort things out so you could talk to her then. Maybe she'd feel better if Steve was relaxed about me not being here." He sat on my bed. "We'll talk about this in the morning when we can think straight. I don't know about you but I am knackered."

"I'm exhausted," I said as he kissed me. "Want to go to bed?"

"Hmm, might do." He kissed me on the lips and put his hand on my chest. I pulled away.

"I thought you were tired."

"I'm not that tired."

Chapter 26

Tony has been back in London for two weeks now. We have spoken every night and are texting each other all day long. I have to wait until Steve goes to bed till I can ring him. He'll get annoyed if he knew I talk to his son whom he despises. Most of the time we are planning on how I can ask my mum what's going on with Steve but so far it is proving to be quite difficult. I know there's something wrong with her because once I even said, "So what was going on with you and Steve when I was away?"

She replied, "Oh, the usual, went out, did normal stuff like we used to. Do you want a drink?"

I noticed that she was drinking at least two glasses of wine a day. Some days it was four and once she got through two bottles. When she goes to bed, she's not tired, she's drunk. She doesn't work anymore. Steve wanted her to stay at home so she left the best job she had ever had just because he said to.

How can I say something about all this to her when she goes to get a glass of wine every time I try? Enough was enough. I was going to take her somewhere she couldn't drink. Somewhere she has no access to a bottle of wine, Budweiser or even Gin. I was going to get to the bottom of this. I'm going to talk to her before Tony gets here tonight.

"How about going out for lunch today?"

"That sounds great. Where do you have in mind?"

"Err, what about that place in Leeds we were going to go to, but never did?" I couldn't remember what it was called. All I knew is that it was in Leeds and we never went when we said we would. It was a café, no access to alcohol.

"I went with your Nan a few months back. It's not so great. Overpriced, and very poor for your money."

"Oh." That was out of the window then. Where could we go? There has to be somewhere. We could go to the White Rose shopping centre and I could talk to her in the car on the way there or on the way back. She can do some shopping and get all relaxed and happy and then she would have no reason not to tell me anything. "Why don't we go shopping then?"

"Ok, that sounds good," she said in a cheerful kind of way. "Where do you have in mind?"

"What about White Rose?" I suggested. "I've not been there in so long. Or the Trafford Centre?"

"Yeah, ok, I need some things anyway. When do you want to go?"

"What about now?" The sooner we went the better really.

"Ok, I'll go get my coat."

"Hello?" the door slammed. Steve was home. Why was he home? He's not meant to be home for another five hours. "Is no one going to answer me?"

"Yes," my mum said. She jumped when he

slammed the door. "We're in here."

"What are you doing home?" I asked him.

"What do you mean what am I doing home? This is my home. I'm not exactly going to run away am I?"

"What's that meant to mean?" he ignored me. "We're off out. We're going shopping."

"Are you?" he looked at my mum.

"Well, we were going to, but it wasn't definite. I could stay here if you like?"

"Well, I am home. It would be nice to have some company here with me," he looked at her in a threatening way.

"Ok, I'll stay," she said at once. "Would anyone like a drink?"

"What you having?" I asked her. She looked at me as if to say 'let me have a drink'.

"Err, I'm going to put the kettle on. Do you want a drink Shell?" I nodded. "Darling, do you want a coffee?" She went off to make the drinks. I couldn't believe she just gave up on me like that. All because of him.

"So, Shell. What are you planning on doing with your life now that you're back?"

"What do you mean?" I asked.

"Well, are you going to be working? You can't go back to school, you threw that opportunity away. So you'll have to get a job. And, now we're on the subject, I want you paying board money. I don't want you thinking this is a free lodging for the homeless."

"Ok, how much do you want a week?"

He looked surprised that I wasn't going to argue about it.

"Excuse me?"

"How much do you want?" I repeated.

"How about £25 every week?"

"Ok."

"You mean you actually have money?" he seemed extremely surprised. I think he wanted me to have no money whatsoever so he could force me to get a crap job. What he didn't know is that I had enough money for board for the next year in advance.

"I shall pay you £25 every week. Well, I'll pay it to my mum because it is her house after all isn't it? I will have a word with my mum soon and I'll sort it out. Ok?"

"Ok. You know you could just give it to me. I live here too and I pay the bills."

"You're right I could, but mum pays the mortgage, and she buys the food. So really it will be better going to her." There was no way I was going to give my money to him.

"Just out of curiosity, where did you get your money from?"

"By working, obviously."

"So, you just got a job, just like that? Where were you living?"

"With a friend I used to go to school with. She moved to London a few years ago."

"How did you find out where this girl lived?"

"What do you mean?"

"You got on a train to London and just walked around until you found this girl?"

"You ever heard of mobile phones? Apparently people can text each other. Maybe I texted her when I was on the train and she met me at the station?"

I know he didn't believe my sarcasm. He never believed me. Even when I was telling the truth, he always accused me of lying. He always got his way too.

Later that day, when I was in my room watching a film, I hear the phone ring. I hear Steve talking and shouting but it wasn't clear enough to understand what was being said. He sounded really agitated. I had just been texting Tony. He was meant to be coming down today and staying for a few days, but his mum and dad had had a major argument so he needed to stay with them for a few more days to sort things out. I got the idea he was keeping something from me. I didn't make anything of it. I was missing him too much so I didn't want to begin an argument. He had run out of credit too so I would have to ring him later.

Almost half an hour later, Steve was still shouting. I don't think he's even on the phone anymore. I'd better go see what he's doing. It does not sound good.

"Did she tell you?" I heard Steve shout at my mum as I was walking down the stairs. "I'll bet she told you everything? You two are as bad as each other, keeping things from me. You think I didn't know about you making calls and sending letters?" When I get into the room, my mum is crying on the floor. She was on her knees, shielding her face from Steve, just like my dream I had when I was in London for the first time.

"What the hell is going on?" I yell. "Mum? Mum, what's happening? What did he do to you?"

"Don't dare talk to her," he shouted to my mum.

"Don't give her orders!" I shouted back to him.

"You filthy little bitch. I don't know how you dare show your face around here." Steve had suddenly turned on me. "Having a party too, to welcome you back from your little trip." He looked at my mum. "I don't want you anywhere near her you understand me? Well?" she didn't reply.

"Could someone please tell me what is going on?" I asked.

"I've just had a phone call, from my ex wife, Libby." The bitch, I know she hates me but why stick her nose into my business. Why couldn't she keep out of this? What did she say? "She is Tony's mother." I know who she is. "She told me all about London, and your 'job'." Oh shit. "Care to say anything? Or do *you* want to tell me?" he said looking at my mum, "my honest little wife?"

"She doesn't know anything. Just leave her alone."

"Oh, do you want to confess then? Do you want to tell your mother or shall I?"

"Tell me what?" she looked at me with tears in her eyes. There was blood coming from her mouth. "Shell, what is it?" I had to save her, but I couldn't bring myself to admit to it.

I hate him, and I hate that bitch. Why did she have to call? I was home now, what harm was I causing her? What harm did I ever cause her?

"Your daughter," he began, "didn't have a job in a shop like she told you." I could have got on my knees and begged him not to say anything. "She slept with men for her money." My mum cried more and more. "The dirty little slapper got paid to have sex, she was a filthy little whore!" he shouted. He walked away from my mum and walked towards me.

He pushed me into the wall.

"Leave me alone!" I demanded, but he wouldn't. He just kept pushing and pushing. No matter what I did or said, it had no effect. I had fallen on to the floor. He kicked me and stamped me in the leg several times. I was in absolute agony. He pulled me up and smacked me in the face. I could feel the warmth of blood as it ran down my cheek. I couldn't move. When I realised what was happening, I realised that I was being dragged up the stairs by my hair. I struggled and tried to stand up, but my leg was hurting too much. There was so much blood in my mouth. He eventually pulled me up and threw me into my room.

"If you ever set foot outside this room," he said in a quiet and scary voice, "I'll kill your mother. You understand me?" he slammed my door shut and I laid there crying.

I felt completely paralysed. I could hear my mum screaming as he struck her again and again. I wanted to help her but I would have been completely useless.

So, this is me not taking any shit from him, eh? Good one Shell.

Chapter 27

Things went on like that for a while. Most nights I heard my mum screaming in pain. She cried so loud I wished someone outside would hear her. I couldn't go down to help her because he would get me too, as selfish as it sounded. If my mum wouldn't do anything about it then she was more stupid than I thought. I was losing all respect for her for marrying him and letting him hurt me like that. I was hoping my dad would come round to save us but Steve had rung him telling him that he was taking us on holiday as a surprise, so naturally, he didn't come round. My leg was badly swollen and bruised so I could hardly walk on it. When the swelling on my face went down, I was able to see clearly so I could hop down the stairs to see my mum. Steve didn't care that I was downstairs, as long as he was at work and didn't know about it. I tried to persuade my mum to call the police or even my dad, but she wouldn't. She just kept drinking and drinking until she was in no state to do anything, not even feed herself. I could see her wasting away in that blood stained chair. Sometimes I used to feed her soup just before she passed out or threw up. That was the only time she could eat. She couldn't eat when she was sober because all she did then was cry and sleep. Every day she had new bruises and cuts. It was the same routine all day for a week. Steve left at nine so I went downstairs. He came back at five so I went back up at half four. If I was to sneak food up with me, I had to hide it somewhere he wouldn't look. He regularly came in to inspect. He occasionally brought me bread and water thinking that was all I had all day. Once, he saw the unwashed soup bowl and came upstairs. He knew I had helped my mum. He knew I had gone downstairs. My eye was swollen for three days after that. It's only just going down now. I wanted to ring Tony, but Steve had taken my phone. He unplugged the house phone and smashed it too so we couldn't call anyone. The doors were always locked and Steve had taken our keys. The only hope was my mums' mobile, but she couldn't remember where she had left it. She was really starting to piss me off.

"Why don't you just walk out and leave that bastard husband of yours?" I shouted. I didn't care that she was crying, or drunk.

"Oh, yeah I'll walk out! You just call him and ask him to give me my keys back."

"You don't fight back! All you do all day is drink and drink and drink. You're letting him win. Why don't you just smash him over the head with the damn thing rather than drink from it?"

"He doesn't mean to do it. It's your fault." What the hell was she saying? My fault?

"And what is it I am meant to have done?"

"I don't know." She looked weak and pathetic. She didn't know what she was saying. "Will you go into the kitchen and get me a bottle of wine Shell dear?"

"Yeah course." I walked into the kitchen, got the bottle, walked back into the room. "Here's your bottle." I threw it into the wall. Glass and wine went everywhere. My mum looked at me in horror.

"What the hell is your problem?" she cried. That was her last bottle.

"My problem? Yes, I have the problem, because I'm the one drinking from dawn till dusk."

"You have no idea. I need that drink, it keeps me going."

"No, the only thing that keeps you going is Steve's pathetic little apologies at night. The worst part is; you're gullible enough to believe them."

The door slammed. Steve was home. Shit, I was still downstairs. He walked into the room. He looked straight at me.

"Shell, you're downstairs."

"No shit," I said. I didn't care anymore. He could kill me for all I cared.

"I don't think it's a good time to get sarcastic with me is it?" He walked right up to me.

"Do I look like I care? Really do I?" He was getting frustrated with me. I wasn't cowering like my mum, I was standing tall.

There it was. Smack! Right in my face. I fell to the floor.

"Why all this glass?" he asked. "Was this you?" He picked up a piece of glass and put in right in front of my mum's face. "Did you get drunk again? What have I told you about drinking?"

Smack. Steve fell into the wall. I had found an

empty wine bottle and smashed it round the back of his head. I grabbed my mum and we made our way to the door. She was too weak to run so I had to drag her there, which was made even more difficult because my leg was still badly bruised. As I struggled to open the door, I heard Steve stumble as he stood up. I looked round to see him stood two feet behind me. He still had the glass in his hand. He looked at my mum. He kicks her in the stomach. That was it. I jump on him. It was all happening so fast that I couldn't believe that what I only see on television was happening in my own house. No one can stand to see their mum being treated like this, like an animal. Someone has to stop it, and that someone was me. As I jumped on his back, I felt a pain in my neck. A kind of thick, warm liquid pours down my neck. I look at Steve and he is staring at me in horror. I suddenly fall to the ground. I feel paralysed. I can hear noises. Loud, banging noises. Someone lifts me up. It's dark.

"Hold on Shell. Hold on."

Chapter 28

Everything was a blur. Nothing around me seemed to make sense. All I could see was white walls, white sheets and white dresses floating by. What had happened to me? Where was I?

"Shell?" I looked to my left. I saw Tony sat there. He looked absolutely exhausted. Like he had been there for days with no food or sleep. I tried to say his name, but my mouth was so dry that I could barely open it.

"What?" he asks. "What do you want? Water?"

I mutter something that sounds like 'yes'. He pours me a glass and helps me to drink it. That was much better. I tried to sit up, but felt an unbearable pain in my neck.

"No, lay down. Don't try get up."

I put a hand to my neck. I can feel something strangling me. It's a bandage.

"Why do I have this here?" I managed to say. "What happened?"

"I don't know what was happening but you had a deep slash in your neck. The police found my dad's prints on a piece of glass with your blood on and need to ask you what happened."

"How did they know this had happened? We couldn't ring anyone. Steve unplugged the phones and took my mobile."

"Well, after trying to ring you for almost two weeks and not being able to get through, I was getting really worried. My mum said if I left the house to go see you then she would ring your parents and tell them all about London. I didn't know she had taken your number from my phone. Anyway, I quickly packed some things and got on the first train I could. When I got here, I was talking to that lady who lives next door to you. She was stood staring at your house. She said she could hear screaming from inside. I knew immediately that my mum had rung so I ran to the door and heard banging and shouts and screams like someone was in serious pain. Your neighbour had already called the police. They pulled up with two cars and an ambulance as I bashed the door open and found you on the floor. I held you in my arms as they ran and arrested my dad."

"What did you say to your mum when you found out she rung?"

"Well, I told her what happened, and that it was *my* dad that did it, she suddenly felt extremely guilty, and I told her to fuck herself. I don't ever want to see her or talk to her ever again." He held my hand. "Obviously I have to go down to sort my things out but I hate her so much. I'm moving out as soon as I can. My step-dad is even considering moving out. She doesn't know yet though."

"Where's my mum?"

"She's in some kind of medical centre in Leeds. She

has admitted to being an alcoholic and has been told by doctors that she suffers from severe depression, the clinic is meant to help her overcome it." I couldn't believe it but was relieved she was getting help. "She's recovering though. She doesn't have that much damage to her. Just a few bruises. Enough to send my dad down for a long time. The police need an interview from you as soon as possible though."

"Ah, awake at last." A nurse had suddenly appeared at my side. She was a bit of a plump, and was carrying a clipboard. "How are we feeling?"

"My neck is a bit sore. Can I sit up?" the light above my head was blinding.

"Yes, yes of course. Let me put my hand under your head. Could you just help me please?" Tony held my hand and put his other hand under my back. "Here we go, one, two and three."

That hurt so much. My neck was not only sore, it was aching. I think my back was bruised too.

"Why does my leg hurt so much?" I couldn't move it. I think there was a big pot on it or something.

"Well, when we examined you, we saw that it was recovering from having severe internal bruising. A bone had been chipped too. We think that in your struggle, something snapped it. And now it's broken."

"Great," I said, "what I always wanted." She wasn't offended by my sarcasm, I didn't mean for it to sound like it was aimed at her.

"Ok, I'll be back later to check on you. I think the police could be coming in later to ask you some questions. Do you want me to ring anyone?"

"Yes, my dad needs to know."

"I called him," Tony said. "He's been sat here with

me for the last couple of days. He went home this morning to sort himself out. He should be back soon."

"Ok, that's sorted. Anyone else?"

"No, not yet."

"Ok, I'll see you about tea time then."

She waddled away with her clipboard. She didn't even use it while she was here so I didn't see the point in bringing it. Not long after, a doctor turned up. He injected me with some morphine.

Tony had been staying with Mrs Next Door. I told him to get my key off her and stay at mine. I know my mum wouldn't mind. She thought he was great. He and Mrs Next Door had both been in to clean things up. Apparently there was my blood all over the hall way, the living room and my room.

When my dad came later on he brought me some chocolate! *Dairy Milk* chocolate, the best. I love my dad. He gave me a hug but had to be careful in case my neck started to bleed. He was upset that he let it happen. I told him there was no way he could have known.

He had been to visit my mum. She should be out in a week. The doctors said she had made a massive improvement. She hasn't had a drink since she got admitted and has started to put weight back on. They just need to observe her for another week to check she's eating well and responding well to the medication. Again, just like me.

The police came round later. They wanted to know the events of that night. I told them everything. Apparently Steve had come up with some pathetic story that the police did not believe at all. He said that my mum and I were the ones beating him up, even though there was no scratch on him, just the bump on his head from me with the bottle. They said they had everything they needed to send him down for a long time. He could be charged with attempted murder. I hope I never see him again.

*

"You have a phone call," the nurse said to me one morning. She put me in my wheel chair and steered me to the reception.

"Hello?" I said as I picked up the phone.

"Hi Shell."

"Hi dad."

"Steve's been to court."

"And?" This was it. "What's happened?" He was seen as innocent, I know it.

"Six years at the least they think. More than I expected but at least you and your mum will be safe. It's not final yet though. It could be another month till the final sentencing. He's asked to be released but they won't allow it. He'll be locked up until sentencing. He's definitely going to be put away though." He was as relieved as I was. "I visited your mum today."

"How's she doing? Is she ok?"

"She is doing fine. She's off her medication now. She can't wait to go home tomorrow. I'm going to go for her and then pick you up."

"Nice one. I can't wait to get home. They're taking me in to physio-therapy tonight to see how I can handle crutches. If I'm ok with them then I can finally get out of this wheel chair. I think it's fun having someone wheel you round all day. I love being awkward," I laughed.

"I think you'd better try your hardest with the crutches then."

"Oi!" I said.

We couldn't talk for too long. The physio-therapy nurse wanted me down to practice with crutches as soon as possible. She wants me to be able to walk up and down my ward with them. I didn't like this nurse. She was more sarcastic and cocky than me. It just wasn't acceptable.

Chapter 29

I was absolutely fine with the crutches. It was a shame really. I wanted to stay in the wheel chair. I found it difficult going up and down stairs at first with the crutches, but that was where Tony came in. Mum, dad and Tony arrived in the afternoon to pick me up. When mum and I saw each other, we gave each other such a big hug. We hadn't seen each other since it all happened. I think we were both relieved that we were both ok and that we would never see Steve again, or for a very long time. She just kept apologising for letting this happen. I told her I didn't care anymore and I was glad to have her back. It was all over and I finally had things how they used to be.

The stitches in my neck had finally been taken out, though it was still a bit sore. I had to wrap myself up in cling film when I went in the shower. The doctors said it was best to have a bath and have someone assist me when I washed my hair.

My leg was still potted up too. That was annoying. I needed to stretch my knee so bad. I had rung Annie while I was in the hospital. She cried when I told her what had happened that day. I assured her that everything was ok and she promised to come and visit in the summer time.

Tony presented me with some flowers at the hospital. They were gorgeous. A dozen long stem red roses. When I got into the car I saw my mum had some from him too.

The house was all nice and tidy when we got back. My mum was pleased to see that Tony kept it so clean and was amazed that he and my dad had managed to get the blood stains off the walls, although one wall might need repainting. He had been staying at our house while we were away. He kept it clean and even replaced the living room carpet. The blood was not going to come out of it apparently. My mum thought Tony was great. That was when she said it.

"Tony, I really appreciate everything you have done for me and Shelly so, I would be thrilled if you moved in with us. There's no point coming back and forth or staying in a hotel. I'm sure Shell wouldn't mind."

We were over the moon. Dad stayed for lunch but then had to go. He was taking Jane away for a few days. He had hardly spent any time with her with what had been going on. Jane completely understood though. She had even been to keep my mum company on one occasion.

My mum was grateful for what my dad and Tony had done for us. She thought that letting Tony move in was the least she could do. I was also glad that she and my dad were getting on so well. I know they're not going to get back together ever, but I'm glad they are finally civil with each other.

Mum told me all about how she met Steve, and

she admitted that she was the one he was having an affair with. Obviously, she was having an affair too. That's why she and my dad broke up.

Tony hasn't spoken to his mum. I don't think he ever will. He went home; packed all his clothes, personal belongings and whatever else he wanted to keep. One of his friends owns a van so he helped Tony pack and drove him back up.

Almost a month after Tony officially moved in, my leg was fixed and it was Summer. Mum had been seeing this man from work a few times and mine and Tony's relationship was as strong as ever. Annie managed to come up for a week. It was great seeing her.

Steve got his sentence. Ten years, seven at the least. Tony's mum even turned up for the sentencing. We all had a celebration afterwards. Tony's mum wasn't invited to that. In a way we do owe her, but she did nearly get us killed.

Printed in Germany
by Amazon Distribution
GmbH, Leipzig